FORGED *in the* FIRE

FORGED
in the
FIRE

NEW YORK TIMES BESTSELLING AUTHOR
A.L. JACKSON

Entangled Publishing, LLC
644 Shrewsbury Commons Ave., STE 181
Shrewsbury, PA 17361
rights@entangledpublishing.com

Amara is an imprint of Entangled Publishing, LLC.
Visit our website at www.entangledpublishing.com.

Cover and edge design by LJ Anderson
Cover images by Ismael/gettyimages
Edge images by Okea/gettyimages, dulancristian/gettyimages
Interior original illustrations by Kait Bethune
Edited by SS Stylistic Editing
Interior design by Toni Kerr

ISBN 978-1-68281-660-8

Manufactured in the United States of America

First Edition June 2026

10 9 8 7 6 5 4 3 2 1

ALSO BY A.L. JACKSON

Crimson Crows

Forged in the Fire

Moonlit Ridge

From Here to Eternity
Under an Endless Moon
At the Edge of Surrender
Beyond the Blue Horizon
On the Brink of Bliss

Redemption Hills

Give Me a Reason
Say It's Forever
Never Look Back
Promise Me Always

Forged in the Fire is a sexy, stand-alone dark romance set in a fictional MC world where you'll experience intense drama, mystery, and a breathtaking romance with a HEA. However, the story includes elements that might not be suitable for all readers including profanity, violence, guns, blood, elements of motorcycle club lifestyle, death, loss, reference to a sexual assault, references to drug use, the use of alcohol and smoking, and many graphic sexual scenes. Readers who may be sensitive to these elements, please take note.

1

Silas

It was a little before five when I stepped out from an open bay at Torque & Talon Autobody Shop, wiping my hands on an oil-stained rag.

My guts in fuckin' knots as I let my attention travel over the gravel drive that led onto the property.

I squinted against the sunlight pouring from above. A thick, stagnant heat saturated the summer air and slicked my skin in sweat.

Or maybe it was just the irritation boiling inside me that made me feel like I was getting burned alive.

Trevan was already out there, leaning against the white exterior wall and sipping from a bottle of beer.

His own anxiety rolled from his burly frame as he eyed me from the side.

"You think this is a good idea?" he finally asked, hard voice cutting through the tension, verbalizing the same damned thing I'd been asking myself all day.

A heavy sigh pilfered from between my lips as I looked in his direction.

Dude was pure beast.

Dark brown hair and even darker eyes. A mountain of muscle that was covered in ink and oozing the type of ferocity required of my second in command.

He was also my oldest friend. With me from childhood. I trusted him more than anyone else.

I scoffed at my own expense. "Afraid it might be one of the biggest mistakes I've ever made."

Inviting more danger onto our property than we were already facing.

We'd packed our shit and left Moonlit Ridge to get my sister farther away from the bullshit I'd gotten us mixed in there, and we'd come here to Crimson Creek, a small town in Southern Oregon.

But it seemed no matter where I went, peril loved to hunt me down.

He took another swig of his beer, dark eyes narrowed back at me. "Then why are you making it?"

He was the only one with balls big enough to question me. More than that? He was the only one who'd earned the right to do it.

"He was intrinsic in saving my sister. I owe him the favor."

Trevan chuckled a disbelieving sound. "Thought that favor was leaving him alive? Not that the bastard won't end up dead, anyway."

Air heaved from my lungs, and I sank back against the wall next to him as I dove frustrated fingers through my hair. "Have to believe there is some kind of good in him since he came to me and offered the information."

"Or did he know he was a dead man otherwise?"

Uncertainty bound up my insides.

I considered myself a damned good judge of character. You didn't live long with a life like mine if you weren't.

But there was something about Dereck Webber that I couldn't put my finger on.

Instinct told me he couldn't fully be trusted.

"Don't know. But the one thing I do know is that his sister is innocent of the whole thing."

Trevan's brows raised like he was questioning that, too. "You sure about that?"

"As far as I know, she doesn't know a thing."

Was clueless as to what her brother was really involved in.

"Only thing that matters is that this arrangement gets us what we need," I insisted. "He'd never dish if he didn't think he was getting something out of it."

Incredulity heaved out of Trevan. "There are other ways to get information out of someone."

"Can't take the chance that he would remain tight-lipped before Phoenix killed him."

Phoenix was the club's sergeant at arms.

Amused agreement huffed from Trevan before he shook his head. "You're breaking every fuckin' one of your own rules, man. You know that, right?"

I scrubbed a palm over my face. "Yup."

It didn't matter, though. With one thought of my baby sister, Elena, I knew what I had to do.

Dereck Webber might have been a low-life scumbag piece of shit, but when he'd had the barrel of my gun shoved down his throat, his one concern had been his sister.

To me, that counted for something.

"As long as you don't mind when I tell you 'I told you so'," Trevan goaded around another gulp of his beer.

"As long as you don't mind when I kick your ass when you do it," I tossed back.

"Would like to see you try."

Fucker tried to hide his grin before he sobered. "Seriously, though. I get it. Just worried it's gonna bring us trouble, and God knows we already have plenty of that."

Nah, trouble wasn't anything new to us.

Being a part of a brutal MC tended to do that to you, and you could be sure the Crimson Crows were no strangers to strife and turmoil.

Funny that motorcycle club acted as a front for what we really did. The minor crimes we let fly flagrant used as a distraction from the monsters we became under the shadows of the night.

But it was my one big fuckup that brought us here, and I'd do anything I had to in order to rectify it.

"We'll handle it if it comes to that," I told him. "We always do."

I let my attention skate over our new compound.

It was ten acres surrounded by twelve-foot walls. Tucked at the edge of the woods on the outskirts of Crimson Creek, my motorcycle club was named after my hometown. A town I'd left at sixteen and had just returned to.

Drawn here, I guess.

By the history. The loss. The ghosts that remained.

The front building housed our main legal gig.

An autobody shop.

The skill was something I learned when I was nothing but a kid.

A semblance of peace found when I took the mangled and broken and made it whole again.

Figured it was a paradoxical sort of thing. A balance to the destruction I caused.

Forging metal into something beautiful while my hands were stained crimson red.

Make no mistake, I wore that truth as proudly as I wore the Crimson Crows patch on my back, but I craved the respite, too. When, for a few moments, the weight I carried didn't feel like it would crush me.

Our clubhouse was on the left side of the property, tucked out of sight from the everyday patrons, though plenty had come gawking, thinking they were going to sneak a peek at the violent MC that had rolled into town.

Yeah, we'd come with a reputation.

Hidden deep in the massive trees in the deepest recesses of our land were two houses. One was reserved for my second in command, Trevan, and the other for my family.

My guts tangled and coiled.

In the end? They were the only thing that truly mattered. They were the reason I did everything.

The sound of a high-pitched engine carried on the rustle of the trees, a car screaming a path down the two-lane road.

My twisted guts coiled up tighter, and I gritted my teeth as I watched the yellow sedan come into view, a blazing blip of color blinking through the forest.

"Here we go," Trevan rumbled under his breath.

The car slowed to make the left onto the gravel drive, and it came through the large gate that sat wide open as if everyone were welcome when it was half my crew's job to make sure the ones who didn't belong here never got through.

Gravel crunched beneath the turning of the tires as the Honda came to a stop in front of me and Trevan.

A flurry of energy radiated from it.

Chaos.

Rage.

Confusion.

I could taste each one of them the same as I could taste the clean, fresh woods on my tongue as I inhaled a steeling breath.

A brunette was in the passenger seat, shifted toward the driver, shouting something that I couldn't quite make out.

Then she threw open the door and jumped from her seat, slamming the door shut behind her.

She looked like autumn riding in on a hurricane.

Long locks of hair threaded with strands the color of harvest leaves blowing around her. Golds and reds and browns, the shade of freshly whittled bark on a tree.

Eyes the same tumbled hue, though they glowed the brightest flames.

Not to mention a body that could incite a fucking riot.

All legs and tits and curves.

She sent me a glare that could decimate an entire village right before she spat, "You."

This woman was a wildfire.

And standing there, maybe I somehow knew she was going to burn the whole place down.

2

Brinley

THREE HOURS EARLIER

"You can't be serious." I chased behind my younger brother as he stormed down the hall and into my room.

"I'm very fucking serious," he grunted as he ducked into my closet and pulled my suitcase from the back and tossed it onto my bed.

With a huff, I stopped in the doorway and crossed my arms over my chest. "Well, I'm not doing whatever this nonsense is you're asking me to do."

I was no stranger to cleaning up Dereck's messes. They tended to be careless and bountiful.

But this one?

Not a chance.

"Told you I owe this guy a favor, and he called it in," he said like that answered every single one of my questions. The most he'd given me was a grunt of the man's name.

Dereck unzipped the suitcase, flung it open, then turned his back on me as he clomped over to my dresser.

He might have been trying to act casual, but I knew him better than anyone, which meant I knew he was lying.

"A favor?" I challenged, disbelief in my voice.

"Yup," he grunted back as he snatched a giant pile of shirts from a drawer then turned and dumped them into the suitcase with total disregard for what I was supposed to pair them with.

As if that was my biggest problem with all of this.

"I have a job, Dereck. I can't just leave."

"You're going to have to put in for vacation or sick time."

Was he serious?

Worry threaded with the anger. "What, do you owe him money or something?"

Irritation billowed up. It was the typical culprit. Dereck getting himself in deep at every turn.

Drinking.

Betting.

Losing jobs left and right.

I shifted away from him, scratching at the furrows creasing my brow as I tried to gather myself.

To stop the anger and fear from bursting free.

It was my job to take care of Dereck.

It'd always been.

Unfortunately, that task was often more painful than I wanted it to be.

Annoying at times and excruciating at others.

But underneath it all, he was a good guy.

I inhaled a steadying breath, then exhaled as I began to speak. "Listen, we'll figure it out. Whatever you owe him, I'll get it handled."

How, I wasn't sure.

But we always managed.

Dereck shook his head, his shaggy brown hair hanging limply in his face, his jaw going taut as he shoved a few more things into the suitcase. "The only way to handle this one is to do what I say."

It was right then that I noticed his tall, lean body appeared frailer than it normally did. The bags under his eyes darker and deeper.

Dread twisted my stomach.

"Is this guy...?" Bile rolled up my throat as worry took over, and I moved from the doorway to his side. My hand was soft as I set it on his forearm. "Is this guy threatening you or something?"

It wouldn't be the first time Dereck got himself in *that* kind of trouble, and my insides quaked with the memory.

I gritted my teeth against the vision and forced myself to focus on what was going on right then.

Yeah, he made mistakes.

But he was human.

Made up of blood and flesh and soul.

And he was my brother. The one thing I had.

I would never allow any harm to come to him.

Dereck huffed out a gush of air, seeming to contemplate, then he whirled fully toward me and grabbed me by the outside of the arms.

He gripped on tight as he angled closer.

"Please, just do what I'm asking you, Brinley. Just this once. Then I promise you that this is going to end. I'm going to get myself together and you won't have to worry about taking care of me anymore."

He squeezed a little tighter when he rushed, "I am going to fix this. So please, do this one thing for me."

My throat thickened as fear crawled through my being. "What are you fixing, Dere?"

For a moment, I swore that his golden eyes that were the same color as mine flared with guilt.

Then they went cold and flat.

"Just repaying a debt," he said like it was no big deal as he turned away, moved to my closet, and hauled off a row of dresses.

While sickness curdled my stomach.

"You're paying a debt with me." The words were thin. Not a question.

"Do you remember what happened last time?" I heaved it out. Apparently, the skeleton I normally kept locked at the back of my closet, the thing that hovered in the air but we never talked about, had been given an escape route with Dereck dragging out my things.

With his back to me, he froze. Hair lifting at his nape. "It's nothing like that, Brinley. Nothing."

Guilt oozed out with it, then he seemed to shake it off and grumbled, "Whatever you might want to have over the next couple of weeks, I suggest you get it packed."

• • •

Was I a doormat?

A pushover?

Nothing but a dumpster?

You know, just go ahead and pile all your trash on top of me.

Because here I was, sitting in the passenger seat of my brother's car as we traveled through the desolate forest. Winding higher and higher up a mountain.

A blur of trees blinked by as we sat in uncomfortable silence.

My bags packed in the trunk and my heart beating a manic rhythm out ahead of me.

I couldn't believe I was doing this. That I let Dereck talk me into this without him giving me any real details.

It only made it worse that he was a bottled stir of anxiety, continually glancing in the rearview mirror like we were running away from something rather than heading toward something terrible.

But no matter how hard I shook him, he just wouldn't crack. Refusing to offer anything else during the two-hour trip we'd taken.

"If you'd just tell me what's going on..." I finally released into the suffocating tension.

"Would you just leave it, Brinley?" The words stabbed the air like little daggers.

I let go of a sound of disbelief. "You got me wound up in something that I don't understand, involved in paying back a debt that I don't know the cost of, and you want me to just leave it?"

He glanced over at me.

It was the first time I really saw what he was feeling.

Fear.

Blatant and etched on every one of his features.

So distinct it nearly pinned me to the side of the door.

"I need you to trust me. Just this once," he forced out.

Trust him?

God. He'd broken my trust so many times that I wondered if he understood what earning it meant.

He knew what it cost me.

The wounds that had been gouged and gashed into my being.

I shoved it all back down where it belonged, refusing the flashes of memories that wanted to inundate my mind, then I shifted forward in my seat when we suddenly broke out of the woods.

A town was sprawled out below. Nestled in a little valley up high on the mountain.

The single two-lane road ran right through the middle of it.

We passed by a sign that read:

NOW ENTERING CRIMSON CREEK
EST 1832

It was a lovely little town with quaint buildings painted soft white with colorful accents. Some roofs were spired, others flat or pitched.

A mishmash of shapes and sizes and styles.

The sidewalks were brick and had these gorgeous planters with flowering shrubs situated in front of the shops and restaurants.

It looked like a place I'd love to visit if it didn't feel like I was being marched to my execution.

Dereck drove directly through then made a left at the end of the main drag onto another two-lane road that wound up a hill.

On either side of us were family neighborhoods with small homes sheltered in the trees.

About a mile farther, the road curved to the right and the houses gave way to industrial buildings.

A cement business and a scrap yard.

A roofing company and a two-story building with what looked like commercial offices.

My brother's agitation amplified as what appeared to be a freshly painted sign came into view.

TORQUE & TALON AUTOBODY SHOP

He slowed and took the left turn into the lot, easing his car through a big iron gate that sat wide open. The entire place was surrounded by these massive walls that made it feel like we were entering some kind of fortress.

There were a few automobiles sprinkled about the edges of the lot, and an enormous metal building sat in front of us. It had a lobby door on the right and four bays to work on cars on the left.

But it was the men leaning against the wall that sent my stomach toppling to my feet.

Two giants slung casually against the wall like they were simply waiting on their prey to slink right on by so they could reach out and nab it.

Both wearing coveralls that were unzipped and rolled down to the waist. White tees that had seen far better days underneath.

The thin fabric stretched over their muscled frames, and tattoos covered every inch of exposed flesh.

There was just something about the look that sent my attention racing. Calculating as Dereck came to a stop in front of them.

Motorcycles.

There was a row of them on the left side of the building.

All glinting metal and dark leather and bad intentions.

It didn't take a whole lot to add it up.

Rage boiled to the surface.

I whirled toward Dereck, and I let the disgust pour from my mouth. "Bikers? Are you freaking kidding me, Dereck? Great. Just freaking great. I don't know what the hell you've gotten yourself into, but this is—"

"They're good guys, Brinley," Dereck gritted, cutting me off, his knuckles white as he clamped down on the steering wheel.

"Oh, I'm sure they're law-abiding, upstanding citizens."

Panicked terror flickered inside me. Rather than succumb to it, I let the anger flood it. Gasoline tossed on a live wire.

"If you think for one second I'm gonna allow myself to get passed around like some kind of meat, then you have another thing coming. Because I can assure you that's not going to happen."

"I already told you, no one will touch you here." It was close to a growl.

"You're damn right they won't."

Incited by the fury, I tossed open the door and jumped out.

I ran smack into a wall of heat, basically giving myself whiplash as I slammed into the intensity.

A stark intensity slammed into me and kicked my heart into overdrive.

The offender?

The guy on the left who had pushed from the wall.

He had that *type* of energy.

Casually cool but far too keen.

Laid-back but oozing a ferocity that warned you'd do well not to mess with him.

In a flash, I knew he was king.

"You."

Crap. Had I just seethed that out loud? It probably wasn't the best move.

But damn it, he needed to know I wasn't about to go along with whatever he was up to.

Wasn't about to stand for however he was planning on manipulating my brother. However he was going to use me against him.

Or maybe his only intention was to use me to punish him.

Not gonna happen, buddy.

"Me?" He basically mouthed it, like he was confused by the accusation.

"Yes, you." I let the words drop like stones.

The man beside him, who was this hulking heap of muscle, chuckled as he lifted a beer bottle and drained the golden fluid, wryness flitting through every grooved line of his features as he mumbled, "Told you so."

The *king* only smirked like the two of them were sharing an inside joke.

I wanted to smack the amusement right off his ridiculously handsome face.

And when I said ridiculous, I actually meant terrifying.

Warm brown hair that was shorter on the sides and longer on top whipped around his razor-sharp cheekbones.

It sat at odds with a plush mouth that was clearly created to whisper the most decadent of lies.

His nose straight and his jaw chiseled.

He looked like Heaven and Hades had a baby, but the wickedness won out.

I heard Dereck's door creak open then close softly.

The man shifted his attention to him for the barest moment.

In it, I saw a thousand things flash through his expression.

Hatred.

Disgust.

Fear.

The last one I didn't get because I was certain this man was accustomed to everyone bowing at his feet.

He took a step forward, and I swore the ground trembled below, the muscles of his arms flexing and bowing over the black, shadowy designs that covered every exposed inch of skin as he clenched his hands into fists.

It drew attention to a crow in full flight with a skull hanging from its talons that he had tattooed on the back of his left hand.

I tried to conceal the shiver that rolled through me as I took him in.

I didn't want to let him see me shrink.

But it was hard to hide when there was no mistaking his big body was nothing but a weapon. Not quite bulky but rippling with the type of strength that looked like it could strike you from a mile away.

A flash of lightning.

"Brinley," Dereck all but choked. "This is Silas Mercer. He's the one

I told you about. The one you're going to be staying with for a little while."

Silas's hazel eyes glowed, and another one of those smirks lit at the edge of his wickedly sexy mouth. "I'd say it's a pleasure to meet you, gorgeous, but I'm pretty sure the sentiment would not be returned."

3

Silas

"I'll show you to your room." I didn't look back at her as I started across the property in the direction of the clubhouse.

Since apparently she thought she had to pack her entire fucking closet, I had a suitcase in each hand and a giant duffel bag slung across my body.

Boots pounding the dirt while I did my best to keep my shit together when every single thing about this situation had me riding a crumbling edge.

Nerves frayed and guard so fucking high I couldn't see over the top of it.

Could feel her gaze whipping between me and her scumbag brother's retreating car, irritation and befuddlement stirring her into a ball of disorder as he peeled out onto the road.

Dude tucking tail when I'd strode up to him like I was gonna give him one of those affable man hug/claps on the back thingies, only instead, I'd leaned down to his ear and rumbled, "Get the fuck off my property before you don't have the ability to do so."

Coward had her bags out of the trunk and was shoving his car into reverse in ten seconds flat.

She was still wavering there, anger billowing off her in waves, before she finally gave a little shriek of frustration and scrambled to catch up to me.

A wildfire enclosing fast.

"What, do you expect me to just follow you wherever you tell me to go?" she huffed at my back.

"That's exactly what I expect you to do," I grunted, barely glancing her way.

A fall of honey-strung brown hair whipped around her stunning face, red and gold strands lighting up beneath the sunlight that slanted through the air as the sun began to descend to the west.

Rays of it struck along the ferocious slash of her cheeks. Her pink, full lips glinted like blades as she curled her mouth in dissatisfaction.

No woman should be that beautiful.

Or that pissed off.

It pushed me one more inch closer to that edge.

"Well, my brother might have caved to whatever *debt* he owes you that you called in, but I'll have you know, my loyalties do not belong to you. I'm not about to fall for however you manipulated him into bending to your will."

Is that what she thought? That I manipulated her brother?

That fucking little weasel.

I tried to ignore her, but she just kept right up behind me. "If you think I'm going to concede to whatever sick, twisted games you're playing, you picked the wrong girl."

My nostrils flared as her words impaled me in the back.

And did she stop firing them?

No.

Not this one.

"I'm not afraid of you," she spat.

Her suitcases hit the ground with a thud, and I whirled on her so fast she jarred back like she'd slammed into a brick wall.

She might as well have with the way every muscle in my body had gone rigid and hard.

The air between us simmered and shook, and it took everything I had not to fist my hands in her tight white tee.

Her tits pushed up over the top. That riot of a body burning with hate.

I leaned in her direction, trying to shield myself from her scent that suddenly invaded my senses.

This intoxicating mixture of almonds and apples, all encased in a sweet cream I had the sudden urge to dip my fingers into.

"You sure about that?"

Those harvest eyes went wide. A swirl of browns and reds and golds whirling with exactly what she said she didn't feel.

Fear.

Though it was nearly obliterated in the hatred that blazed within it.

Wildfire.

"Very," she tossed back.

Air puffed from my nose, and I cocked my head to the side. "Let's get something straight, *Brinley*."

I said her name like it was a curse, my words coming out slow and sure.

"You can think whatever you want about me, but while you're here, on my property, you operate under my rules."

She crossed her arms over her chest. "Because you're the king, I presume?"

She shot a glance in the direction of the row of bikes lined against the left side of the shop like she was offering up some sort of evidence of my guilt.

She wouldn't be wrong.

"President," I corrected.

"Right," she said with enough vitriol to supply electricity to the compound for an entire week. "And what exactly does the *president* plan to do with me?"

My imagination took it upon itself to catalogue all the plans I really wanted to make.

Pushing her up against the wall of the shop and fucking her out in the open sounded like a really good place to start, knowing she'd be chanting my name rather than the virulence she was spewing.

Or maybe just stuffing her smart mouth full of my cock would do the trick.

It didn't really seem to have a preference of the location. Either would do.

But that was not gonna fucking happen.

I already warned my entire crew that she was abso-fucking-lutely off-limits.

I needed to remember that command for myself.

"You're going to be a good girl and do what I say."

Spite narrowed those eyes, and I knew there was zero chance of that.

But hey, a man could try.

"And how long am I supposed to stay your prisoner?"

My brows shot for the sky. "My prisoner?"

"That's what this is, isn't it?"

Maybe it was best she thought so. Maybe I should inject her full of fear.

Warn her of the things that would happen to her if she didn't obey.

Instead, I snatched up her bags and mumbled, "Think whatever you want to," as I turned on my heel and returned to storming a path across the area between the shop and the clubhouse.

Through the massive white oaks that stood proud over most of the property, the two-story building came into view.

The square, block structure hedged within the dense, leaf-laden branches.

It basically looked like a bar out front, two swinging doors leading into the fray normally going down within the walls.

A slew of motorcycles were parked facing it, and heavy music poured from the walls. No doubt, my crew had already kicked the unwinding at the end of the day into gear.

They'd be getting messy by six and devolving into complete debauchery by ten.

Which was why I angled around the side of the building toward the staircase at the back, hoping to keep Brinley out of the thick of it the best that I could.

I glanced back at her to make sure she was keeping up.

She glared at me with that prideful head held high, a pro as she strode along in these black patent leather heels that were sky-fucking-high.

Red-painted toes peeping out.

Black pants hugging every delicious curve, that delectable body making her plain white tee appear designer.

God.

Just what I needed.

A stunner strutting around on my property.

I rounded to the back of the building. The volume of the music faded to a dull throb on this side, and I started up the set of wooden stairs.

She hesitated at the bottom.

"You'd better hurry up so I can show you to your cell." I injected as much sarcasm into it as I could.

I could feel the huff of her breath, then those heels began to click against the slats as she hurried to catch up.

With her breathing down my neck, I dropped one of her suitcases and punched the code into the pad next to the door.

"85641. Don't forget it," I said as the lock beeped and automatically disengaged. "Only my vice president and sergeant at arms have this code."

I held the door open for her.

She scowled at me as she passed. "Is that supposed to make me feel better? Like I'm supposed to trust them?"

I pushed through the doorway and had her pinned to the interior hallway wall in a flash.

That sweet apple pie scent nearly bowled me over.

I angled in close, my voice a low scrape. "I would think that would be preferential to trusting your brother."

Harvest eyes widened.

Wild and confused, and her mouth popped open like she was looking for the appropriate retort.

I didn't wait around for it. I grabbed her bags and stalked to the first door on the left. I shoved it open and tossed her things inside.

I felt her hovering at the doorway, peering in, that gaze burning up my back.

"This is your room while you're here. It's off-limits to anyone but you."

Had to at least give her that assurance.

She blinked. Confused again as she wandered into the space.

Elena'd had a field day when she learned about our *guest*. Descending on the square box in a furor of pink and confetti.

There was a new pink comforter on the full bed on the left wall, pink towels in the attached bathroom.

She had stocked the little bookshelf next to the door full of every kind of girly book you could imagine. Romances and self-help and what I was pretty sure were makeup manuals.

And on the desk, she'd left a handwritten note that said 'Welcome' like she was greeting a guest at the Ritz.

Bewildered, Brinley took a hardback, staring down at it as she edged deeper into the room, her attention snagging on the message Elena had left her.

I forced out, "I'll have someone bring you dinner up here tonight so you can get settled. Breakfast is served downstairs at seven, then you're due at the autobody shop at eight."

I pulled the last one out of my ass right at that moment.

I'd asked Cash Cunningham, Sovereign Sanctum's hacker over

in Moonlit Ridge, for every detail he could get on Brinley Webber. I remembered seeing that she worked as a bookkeeper in an accountant's office, and I knew to survive this, I was going to need to keep the woman busy.

A frown knitted her brow.

Fuck me.

It shouldn't be so damned appealing.

"The autobody shop?"

"Heard you were good with numbers. You're going to be working in the office."

That frown reached for the sky. "Are you serious? You have me staying here to work off my brother's debt in your office?" Her voice was full of suspicion.

Yeah, it sounded like bullshit to me, too.

Her eyes narrowed as she shook her head. "This whole situation is truly messed up. I don't know what you're holding over my brother, but I've got some money saved up. You just need to take me back to my apartment, and I'll get you whatever he owes."

There was a hint of desperation that tinged her words. Worry and dread for her brother. Her care bleeding out.

My stomach twisted, sure that she really had no fucking clue the kind of danger she was in.

"You aren't going anywhere, Brinley." The words left me like barbs. Scraping my raw throat.

Anger rushed in to take her worry's place. "You can't keep me here. I'll leave, and if you try to follow me, I'll go to the police. You know this is extortion…or…or kidnapping."

I had the urge to tell her what her brother was in, but it had been agreed upon that it was best if she wasn't in the know.

Sometimes it was safest in the darkness.

I dumped her duffel onto the floor, and I took one step toward her, then another, until I was standing in her flames.

She was fucking tall, but I still towered over her.

She kept that fierce chin tilted up toward me, though I could feel her trembling all the way down to the bones.

"You want to run to the cops? Go for it. See what happens. But if you want to see to it that your brother makes it out of this with his head still attached to his shoulders, you'll do exactly what I say."

Each word flew out of me like a bullet.

A pure, blatant threat.

My voice hardened further. "You won't stray from the boundaries of this compound without my approval and an escort. You'll eat when you're told and sleep when you're told, and you're going to show up at the shop at eight-fucking-o'clock in the morning like the good girl you are."

Was pretty sure that *good girl* wanted to spit in my face.

Just to drive home the point, I lifted my hand and ran the tip of my index finger down the side of her neck.

Shock parted her mouth, and she stood frozen minus the shaking that wracked her body.

Outrage and something else blistered from her being.

Forcing a smirk, I said, "Paying off your brother's debt at the autobody shop is a whole lot better than paying it off with *this body*, don't you think?"

Dick move, yeah.

But I needed this woman afraid of me. For her to grasp what was riding on this without her truly knowing a thing.

I didn't give her time to answer before I turned on my heel and strode to the door, holding onto the knob as I turned to look back at her.

"I'll see you at eight tomorrow morning."

I snapped the door shut one second before the book she'd been holding crashed against the wood.

"Fucking wildfire," I grumbled as I shoved out the main door and into the approaching twilight.

4

Brinley

My heart beat violently in my chest, a thunderclap of blood thumping so hard I thought I could taste it on my tongue as I tried to keep my footsteps quiet.

Breaths shallow and jutted as I slipped along the outside of the building in the dark of night.

Trying to convince myself that the lightheadedness I was experiencing was due to the adrenaline and not the fact that I was shaking in my literal boots from fear.

But I promised myself a long time ago I wouldn't allow the fear to hold me back.

Okay, fine. This wasn't exactly correlated to the promise I had made to myself. It wasn't like I'd sworn to go looking after trouble for the sake of proving that I hadn't been broken.

But I couldn't stay put for a second longer.

I tried, but by nine o'clock, I was crawling the walls and feeling like I was going to come out of my skin.

Locked in that room that looked like a girl's dream retreat, complete with little designer shampoos and soaps in the bathroom.

Someone seriously had to be playing mind games with me.

That and the sounds of the clubhouse reverberating through the floorboards and the hatred for a man I had just met seemed to drive me to madness.

That's what this had to be.

Madness.

The fact that I was here.

Held in some sort of weird hostage situation where I had the code to enter my cell and was sentenced to work in a freaking autobody shop.

I didn't buy it.

I didn't buy any of it.

Not Dereck's lame explanation or the bizarre threats Silas Mercer had made.

There was just something about them that made me think he was bluffing.

Or…hiding something.

Lying about something I couldn't clearly see.

Either way, I couldn't sit idle. Not when my texts to Dereck had remained unanswered after two hours.

Me: *I need to know what's really going on here.*

Me: *Should I be afraid of this guy?*

Me: *Am I a prisoner?*

Me: *Please, Dereck. This whole thing is freaking me out.*

Me: *Just tell me this. Are you in danger?*

He'd seen them. I knew he had. I'd seen those little bubbles dancing on and off for about five minutes before they'd been completely silenced.

I loved my brother, but God, he could be such a coward. Always hiding when he got himself into hot water. Allowing me to step in front of his accusers.

Throwing him lifeline after lifeline.

And yes, my therapist had encouraged me to recognize that I was one hundred percent enabling it, but time and again, I always seemed to be right back doing the same thing.

I guess I'd reached my tipping point.

Because this?

After what I'd been through?

What he was asking of me was too much, and I was going to get to the bottom of what the hell was happening.

I wasn't going to be some pathetic wilting flower who bent to the will of a psychopath.

I kept creeping along the edge of the building. The Docs I'd ditched my heels for were quiet on the soft earth, not that my footsteps could have been heard over the blare of music coming from within the clubhouse, anyway.

But still…

I kept low as I crouched at the corner and peered out into the shadows in front of the club.

The number of motorcycles must have tripled since I'd followed Silas up to my room a few hours earlier.

Bikers mingled about. Sitting at picnic tables or standing around the bonfire that raged in the clearing.

Laughter and voices rolled as they drank beers and probably bragged about their latest kill.

Half the men wore jeans and black leather vests with a morbid emblem on the back.

A gathering of three crows sitting on a headstone with blood dripping from their talons. Another prancing on the grave.

Crimson Crows was stitched in red and arched over the scene.

It was no shocker that a group of crows was called a murder.

For these guys, it was undoubtedly fitting.

My stomach tightened, and a little of that fear flashed up my spine.

This was seriously fucked up.

Fiction that I shouldn't be living. The type of fiction it seemed only Dereck could drag me into.

I glanced around, trying to decide on my next move. Discern exactly what I hoped to achieve by slinking around here, having no idea what I was even looking for.

Shrill laughter rang from a woman who was being tossed over a man's shoulder, the brute carrying her away as he pawed at her ass.

I nearly rolled my eyes.

How cliché.

Is this how they really lived? At least from where I was standing, no one was having sex right out in the open.

I started to edge around the corner when my skin prickled in awareness.

A shivery sensation flying across my flesh and lifting the hairs at the nape of my neck.

That was only a second before I felt the actual breath panted against the same spot.

Terror gripped me, and panic streaked through my veins. My mind spun through every self-defense move I had ever learned.

Only before I could ram my elbow into the offender's gut, that elbow was encased by a hot, heavy hand, held firm as I was yanked back against a wall of stony muscle.

Fire burned at the contact point, and the air was ripped from my lungs, hurled into the shadows where we were concealed beneath the trees.

The low voice that had tormented me all night rumbled in my ear, "Thought I told you to be a good girl?"

Each word was a blade. A shallow carving against my flesh.

I inhaled a shattered breath. Too bad I was sucking the scent of him down into my heaving lungs.

He smelled like cherries drenched in whiskey.

It was a horribly delicious combination.

"You never told me I couldn't leave my room." I snarled it through clenched teeth, my back bowed as I tried to peel my body away from the gravity of his.

"No, I didn't, but that doesn't mean I don't know you're up to no good." He cinched down tighter on my elbow, and my heart hammered at my chest.

Fear and something else there was no way I was feeling careened through my senses.

"Let me go." I yanked my arm, the words coming out a whole lot more like a plea rather than the vicious demand I was going for.

I expected it to be a fight.

To have to wrestle out of his hold.

But the second I said it, his hand was gone.

It sent me lurching forward, and I barely caught myself before I fell to my knees.

I whirled back in his direction.

I shouldn't have.

I should have remained facing away.

Or better yet, I should have remained locked in the confines of that room upstairs.

I definitely should not have been standing so close to Silas Mercer right then.

Half concealed in the shadows created by the branches of the trees, though silvered moonlight dabbled down through the leaves to illuminate his face.

The man was all sharp angles. Like one of those animations where his jaw and cheeks were drawn with a single, slashed stroke. So defined you could take a ruler to it, and it wouldn't go out of line.

Brow just as severe.

Too violently beautiful to be real.

Wearing dark jeans and a black shirt, the sinewy muscle that outlined his deadly frame carved in the same severe striations.

But where things got dicey were with his eyes and lips.

That was where the harsh, flat planes came alive.

Expressive and roiling.

Teeth clamped down on his plush bottom lip and the flecks of green in his hazel eyes glowing like he was a beast.

Hunted.

That's what I'd been.

I bet he knew the second I sneaked out of that room.

His head canted to the side. "Is that what you are, Brinley? Up to no good?"

I searched for the missing oxygen, forcing myself to get it together. I was not about to let this man see me flustered.

I searched around for a good excuse.

"I was looking for something to drink."

"And a full refrigerator wasn't enough for you?"

Right.

There was that mini fridge in the closet. You know, stocked full of every drink imaginable. The selection was far better than the last hotel I stayed at.

They should win a medal for being such good hostage hosts.

I tipped up my chin. "I wanted ice."

A slow, wicked smile crept to Silas's obscenely handsome face, and he took a measured step forward.

I gulped but held my ground. Keeping my eyes pinned on him as he came to cover me in his shadow.

Energy crackled. Zapped and zipped across my skin.

He was so freaking tall it meant my head was tipped all the way back, and he leaned down even closer.

"You want to know what I think?" The words were gravel.

No, I probably did not want access to this guy's mind. Instead of telling him so, I narrowed my eyes at him. He seemed to take it as an invitation and dipped in even closer.

Heat rippled from his ink-covered flesh, and his lips were so close that I could feel their movement against mine when he spoke.

"I think you're looking for something else."

My pulse scattered, and somehow, I managed to grit out, "And what am I looking for?"

Silas's big hand was suddenly on the back of my neck, holding me up since the man had me nearly bent in two.

"Trouble." His eyes blazed, and I realized they were more green than anything else. "Think you're lookin' for trouble, Brinley, and I don't think you have the first clue the kind of trouble you're already in."

Confusion pinched the corners of my eyes, and a ball of dread filled the entire cavity of my chest.

There was something different laced in his voice. His gaze flitting all over my face like he was searching for my understanding. Like he was trying to get me to hear something he couldn't say.

He straightened then, pulling me upright and leaving me disoriented, my knees weak as he shoved his hands into his pockets and backed away.

Then his tone turned cold again. "There's plenty enough of it to go around for each of us. I'd suggest you don't make it worse."

He turned on his heel and strode back through the trees.

I guess the man was completely right about me looking for trouble.

Because I staggered along behind him.

Dipping behind the trunks of giant oaks as I went like he didn't fully know I was there.

Ridiculous, but I couldn't stop.

That gravity beckoning me forward.

Or maybe I just had a grim sense of curiosity.

He finally broke out of the trees ahead of me where there was a dirt road.

I stalled out because standing there waiting on him was a young woman who was probably a few years younger than me, though I could be wrong since I couldn't make her out very well in the distance.

But what there was no mistaking was the small child who was holding her hand.

A child who bobbed his knees then went running toward Silas.

Silas swooped him up and hooked him onto his hip, and the man tipped his laughter toward the star-strewn canopy above before they casually turned and strolled down the lane.

While I stood there gaping, wondering who the actual fuck this guy was.

5

Silas

The next morning, I slowly eased down the steps from the second floor of my house to the chaos happening below.

Exhaustion had me wanting to crawl directly back into my bed, which seemed like some kind of oxymoron considering my bed hadn't brought any reprieve.

Only thing I'd done was toss in it all night.

Guts tied up with the *mistake* that I had made. Thoughts hooked on a woman who I'd stashed across the property, thinking her presence wouldn't have a whole lot of effect on me.

Fat fucking chance.

I should have known things had taken a sharp turn south when I nearly panicked when the notification blipped on my phone that she'd slinked out of her room. Should have known I was traversing treacherous ground when I'd diverged course and made a beeline toward the clubhouse.

Figuring I'd cut her off at the pass if she thought she was going to run because that bullshit wasn't gonna fly on my watch.

Only I found her sneaking along the edge of the building like some kind of cat burglar five seconds from falling into a trap.

Thinking she was all kinds of sly and stealthy when she was precisely five point two seconds from stumbling into debauchery.

And if she wasn't careful, that *debauchery* was gonna be me.

A peal of laughter reverberated the walls of the house, and I blew out a sigh and forced myself to keep moving.

We'd only been living here three months. The house was large, fitting for all of us. Nice but nothing fancy. The entire thing was painted cream with white molding, except for a few walls that had floral wallpaper.

A bit old lady, but hell, I figured it suited the situation just fine.

I hit the bottom landing and hooked a right through the archway that led into the kitchen.

My eyes took in the scene.

On the far-left side of the room, beyond the long counter that separated the space into two sections, my grandmother stood at the stove, and my sister was chopping something at the counter next to her.

Their laughter rolled as they bantered and teased.

On this side of the counter was a small circular table tucked into the right corner of the room.

Large enough to seat us all but small enough that when we gathered, it was cramped.

My gaze kept traveling, right to the kid who was buckled in his highchair next to the table.

"*Siwas*, you wake up?" Kai scrunched up his adorable button nose when he saw me standing at the squared entryway. The kid holding an orange slice without the rind on it in both hands, smashing it to smithereens.

Juice dribbled down his dimpled chin.

My chest tightened at the sight. Wasn't sure how looking at a single person could cause so much terror and joy.

Golden brown hair a smidge lighter than mine and eyes the same hazel as the rest of ours.

Bare, chubby feet hung out from under the highchair tray, his face full of the type of happiness I was terrified could ever fully reach fruition.

Rage burned in my guts while the loyalty glowed bright.

I was going to see to it that he did reach it. I was going to see that this threat was crushed. See to it that he didn't have to live through the same type of torment the rest of us had.

Unfortunately, the way I normally *crushed* didn't seem that prudent of an idea, though there was a part of me that thought it might be for the better.

Part of me thinking it would be worth shredding my last bit of humanity.

"I sure did," I told him, my words twisted into something soft.

He beamed, his little mouth curled into a precious smile as he stretched out his arm, the orange slice offered in his hand. "You bite?"

A rough chuckle scraped out, and I moved over to him so I could ruffle my fingers through his soft hair. Trying to keep my cool when looking at him tended to send me over the edge. “Thank you for the offer, buddy, but that slice is for you.”

“I’ll take it,” Elena teased as she popped her butt onto the counter on the far side of the kitchen.

“No way, no *Wena*.” Giggling, Kai snatched it against his chest.

“Hey. I thought I was your favorite?” Elena drew out like she was completely offended.

She had her hair that was so dark it was nearly black up in a ponytail, and she still wore these ridiculous pink pajamas that read *Knockout* across the top in silver sequins.

Knew it wasn’t an exaggeration considering the way all the assholes around here took her in when they didn’t think I was watching, which only made me five thousand times more protective of her.

She was lucky I hadn’t exchanged all her clothes for burlap sacks.

But I guess I’d already stolen enough from her, so I tried to give her at least a modicum of autonomy for herself.

I didn’t know how it was possible that my baby sister was alive and whole and filled with this zest for life that should have been stubbed out long ago.

Not after the bullshit she’d been through.

Kai’s head whipped back and forth. “No way. *Siwas* is my *favit*.”

“What?” Elena cried, peeking over at me with playful eyes.

Our grandmother chuckled low as she flipped eggs in a skillet, her craggy voice joining the conversation.

“Now, what have I told you all? There are no favorites. We just love one another for each different, special thing about us.”

“Sounds like the perfect way for you to hide the fact that I’m actually your favorite.”

At the sudden gravelly words coming from behind, I glanced over my shoulder to find Brody shuffling through the archway. Wearing no shirt. New tats exposed on his chest.

His dark brown hair stuck up in every direction, except for where it was mashed down on one side. The bags under his eyes were so heavy that it looked like he had to have come crawling back to the house at sunrise.

Knowing my younger brother, that’s exactly the way it’d gone down.

Meems, which I’d started calling our grandmother when I was learning to speak, tsked and waved a spatula at him. "You know better than that. I love you all equally." Staunch affection rolled out of her as she turned back to the eggs she was frying. "But you can be sure what I'm not *loving* right now is you looking like you spent the night tussling around in a dumpster."

"Oh, I'm sure he spent the night tussling around with something." Elena wagged her brows.

Brody only grinned a cheshire grin.

I was going to need to have a talk with him about that.

I'd all but forbade him not to run with this life, but he'd insisted on trying to patch in, and I was worried he was taking the challenge too far.

We might have lived outside of rules and boundaries, but I still demanded structure.

"Too handsome for his own good, I tell you that," Meems muttered.

Rounding the counter, he ambled up behind our grandmother and pecked a kiss to her cheek. "See, you do love me."

"Always," she gushed. "Now grab me some milk so I can finish up this gravy."

"Yes, ma'am," he said, tossing me a knowing smirk as he turned and moved toward the refrigerator.

"Now, is someone going to put me out of my misery and tell me about the guest we have on the property?" Swiveling a fraction, Meems looked directly at me when she asked it.

That was all it took for my stomach to fist.

Last thing I needed were reminders of that stunning face.

"Oh my God, Meems. She's soooo pretty." Elena groaned it toward the ceiling. "Wait until you see her."

My eyes narrowed. "And when did you see her?"

Elena had been instructed to leave Brinley Webber alone. Knowing Elena, she'd have her upstairs in her room braiding her hair or some shit, and she needed to know Brinley was not her fucking friend.

After what happened to Elena a few months back, you'd think she'd be more cautious. Realize she couldn't be stepping out and inviting people in.

My sister was far too fucking trusting.

Innocent.

And my enemies were all too willing to take advantage of that.

A blade of guilt stabbed into my spirit.

I never should have let it happen, and now…

"Um, how do you think I saw her? Did you think I was just going to stay in my room?" She widened her hazel eyes like I was dense.

Of course not. It wasn't like she ever listened to what I said.

"But don't worry. I made sure I was set up in prime position to get a peek at her without drawing attention to myself when you showed her to her room. Out of sight like you told me."

She gave me a sass-filled look that declared my rules were ridiculous. Then she arched an accusing brow. "She didn't seem to like you all that much."

Brody laughed as he set the milk onto the counter next to Meems. "What sane woman does? Why all these passarounds try to catch Silas's eye, I'll never know."

"Now, none of that," Meems scolded. "We've got little ears in the house."

I glanced at Kai who was sweetly oblivious, back to sucking at another orange slice that had been set on his tray.

"Want you all to keep your distance from her," I warned as I strode around the counter, heading for the coffee pot. "Know you want to make her feel welcome, Elena, but this isn't playtime."

"You don't need to talk to me like I'm five, Silas," she spouted back. "I know it's not playtime, but I don't see anything wrong with her feeling like she isn't alone while she's here. You could at least be nice to her."

"There's no need for her to like me," I grumbled as I filled a travel mug full of dark brew.

Steam billowed out from the top, and I took a sip of the hot liquid, that first hit soothing my senses.

I turned to my family.

Gaze pointed. "My only concern is her safety, same as the rest of yours. I expect you to respect that."

"So you plan on keeping her in a box the way you do me?" It was a straight accusation from Elena.

Frustration huffed from my lungs. "I don't keep you in a box."

"Twelve-foot-high walls in a perfect square around ten acres." Elena lifted her hands like she was juggling an equation. "Seems to me the property is quite literally a box."

I sighed, not in the mood to argue with her. "What I plan on is you keeping your distance from her. I don't need this situation any messier than it already is. Have enough on my plate without having to worry about what she's up to, or what you're up to, for that matter."

Hated that it looked like hurt that bunched up Elena's brow, but fuck, she had no idea the burden that was sitting on my shoulders.

My head barely above water.

Meems must have picked up on my agitation because she shuffled over to me.

Our grandmother was nearing eighty. Plump and her head barely coming up to my chest.

She might have looked frail, her gait hobbled a bit, her back slouched with her age, but she was the strongest woman I'd ever known.

She was the one who'd stepped in and cared for us when there was no one left to do it.

The one who remained at my side even after I made a choice she begged me not to make.

She set her hand on my cheek, her hazel eyes peering into mine like she was searching for someone she used to know.

"You don't have to carry it all, Silas. I'm right here."

She glanced at my brother and sister, who were staring back at us, before she returned her attention to me.

"We're all right here. And we're always going to be. I know you think everything falls on you, but it doesn't. And we do respect you. We respect who you are and all that you've done for this family. But if that girl is here and doesn't know anything like you said, then she's probably scared and feeling alone, and she's going to need support. It's not right to treat her like a prisoner."

Brinley Webber scared? Not even close.

My stomach clutched around the thought. Something about it didn't sit right. Not when it was clear what had been in her voice when she demanded that I release her last night.

Terror.

Terror hidden behind black, viscid rage.

"She's not going to be alone," I forced out around the lump in my throat. "She's going to be working at the shop."

Elena fucking clapped, giddy as hell. "Best news ever! Guess I'm going to have to take a jaunt over there today and formally introduce myself."

I started to tell her not a chance in hell but clipped off with a grunt of surrender when Meems sent me a warning glare.

I took a swig of my blazing hot coffee. Burning the fuck out of my tongue.

Yup.

This was a mistake.

A terrible fucking mistake.

6

Silas

What in God's name was she wearing?

I stood in the doorway that led from the shop into the dingy lobby and office area.

Three plastic chairs sat to my right under the windows that overlooked the customer parking lot.

A high counter cut the room in two and acted as reception, and two desks were situated behind it, elbowed together in an L shape. One directly under the counter and another against the far wall in front of me.

A row of old-style filing cabinets decorated the wall to my left.

Ancient calendars and fliers still tacked to it from the previous owners who'd vacated the property four years ago.

The woman was there, bent over the desk that was directly in my line of sight.

Her ass wagging in the air like a ripe piece of fruit as she punched at the keys of a dated computer, the pert, perfect globes barely covered by the satiny light blue material of her dress's skirt that brushed up high on her thighs.

Wearing sky-high heels again. This time colored nude. Bare legs for fucking miles.

My dick jumped.

Fuck me. This was a disaster.

"Are you kidding me?" she grumbled under her breath. "Am I really supposed to do something with this pile of crap? Freaking bikers, thinking they can actually run a business."

Wow. She clearly thought highly of me.

"I don't see the problem here." It bled from me like irony. "We bikers like to make sure our offices are stocked with the latest state-of-the-art equipment."

At the sound of my voice, Brinley gasped and whirled around.

Her hand flew to her chest.

Shock gripping her striking features before it gave way to wrathful displeasure.

Those harvest eyes were wide as they traveled over me where I leaned against the jamb before they narrowed in hostility. "I don't appreciate you sneaking up on me like that."

"Huh?" Scratching at my temple with a single finger, I said it like I was perplexed. "And here I thought sneaking was your specialty?"

She inhaled a shaky breath and straightened herself out.

Only thing it did was draw my attention to her front side.

That fucking satin skirt short as hell. Baby blue and hemmed in beige lace. The top two buttons of her blouse were undone, giving just a peek of cleavage underneath.

Untamed brown and gold curls framed her face.

Motherfucking wildfire.

She lifted her chin. "If I'm going to be staying here, then I need to be comfortable moving around. I don't want to feel like I'm trapped."

"Fair."

Second I said it, I wished I could take it back. But maybe Meems was right. Maybe I needed to budge a little.

Surprise jolted her back. "Are you serious?"

Before she got too comfortable, I cocked my head. I made sure the warning clipped off on a threat. "As long as you keep your nose out of where it doesn't belong."

"And where is that?" she challenged.

Pretty much everywhere, but she didn't need to know that.

"If it seems like a place you shouldn't tread, then don't go there. You're a smart girl."

I didn't even try to keep the mocking edge out of my words.

She couldn't gain access to the places I didn't want her, anyway, so it really didn't matter all that much. But I didn't like the thought of her wandering around the property by herself, either.

Yeah, the guys knew the score.

She was not to be fucking touched.

It didn't stop an army of ants from marching across my flesh at the thought.

Brinley sent me a scowl. "Super clear. Thanks. About as clear as whatever the hell I'm supposed to be doing around here."

She waved a flustered hand at the pile of junk behind her.

"We haven't been here that long, and we're still getting set up." I pushed from the doorway and took a couple of steps into the lobby.

I was instantly hit with that scent.

Almonds and apples dipped in sweet cream.

Did she light a damned candle?

"So, this isn't how you always operate?" It was loaded with sarcasm.

Didn't know what the hell I was doing, but I kept moving toward her. Boots thudding against the ground in time with her panted breaths.

I stopped an inch from her.

Eclipsing her in my shadow.

Her ass hit the edge of the desk as she backed away, and I kept angling for her, pinning her to the wood.

Her heavy breaths pelted the front of my neck, and a wisp of her hair brushed across my cheek.

Every line of her body had gone both pliant and rigid. Everything gathering to a shivery pinpoint as she waited for what I was going to do.

I edged even closer, my movements slow as I reached around her and flicked on the button for the computer.

The motor whirred to life as I edged back a fraction, though I remained close enough to whisper in her ear, dragging out each word like a blade, "Even us *bikers* know how to run businesses, *Brinley*."

Then I pushed back, leaving her panting where she was splayed out on the desk.

Disconcertment flitted all over her face.

Then she shot back to her feet.

A tall, raging fire.

"You're an asshole, do you know that?" she hissed.

My chuckle was raw. "Tell me something I don't know."

Wild curls thrashed around her as she slowly stole in my direction.

Clearly, she wasn't about to back down.

Hips swaying from side to side as she approached.

A frisson of energy swelled in the room.

She cocked her head. "You want me to tell you something that you don't know? How about this?"

She reached out with her pointer finger and jabbed me hard in the middle of the chest. "I am not a toy, and I'm not here to entertain you or play your games. If working in this shithole fulfills my brother's debt, then so be it."

She kept jabbing the sharp tip of her fingernail in the same spot, driving home her point. "But I will not allow you to mess with me. Not you or any one of these assholes around here. Do you understand me?"

I snatched her by the wrist.

A motherfucking flame licked up my arm.

Ferocity whirled through her eyes as she glared up at me.

I mashed my teeth together, and something very stupid deep inside my chest tightened in a way it shouldn't.

"I think I like you, Brinley Webber."

It might have come out a taunt, but I was the motherfucking fool who meant it.

Huffing, she ripped her arm out of my hold. "Screw you, Silas Mercer."

Distrust and hate blazed out of her as she took three steps back.

"And for the record, it's pretty gross, you getting that close to me, when you have a kid and a wife or a girlfriend or old lady or whatever the hell you call her. But I guess that's just another way *bikers* operate."

A kid and a girlfriend?

I couldn't help the smirk that climbed to the edge of my mouth, because her words were pure disgust peppered with a little of something else.

"Ah, the things we discover when we're sneaking around," I goaded.

Of course I was aware she was stumbling along behind me through the woods when I walked away from her last night.

There was no escaping the heat of those eyes.

I realized then the assumption she made.

I didn't correct her.

Instead, I crossed my arms over my chest and canted my head to the side. "You jealous?"

A fluster of revulsion and loathing flashed through her face, but I felt the rest of it, too.

Attraction.

Whatever that wired, swarming energy was that she emitted.

I figured it had to be just as dangerous as the rest of her.

"You wish," she tossed out.

It might as well have been a lasso. One where she got me right around the neck.

Because I was stalking forward again. Coming within a foot of her. My stupid hand reaching out so I could trace a single finger down the side of her face.

I was nearly overcome with the need to dip all the way in. Hands itching to sink into her flesh.

What I really needed to do was grow a fucking conscience and step away.

But I was inhaling it. The curious desire that wafted off her skin and filled my nostrils with that sweetness.

Almonds and apples.

A confectionery drug that would poison us both.

And still I was muttering, "Wondering which one of us is really doing all the wishing."

Brinley's mouth parted on a wheezed exhale. Those wild curls kissing her pink, overheated cheeks.

Clearly, I was a masochist.

A glutton for punishment because there was no stopping myself from brushing the pad of my thumb across her plump, pink lips.

Only thing it seemed to do was hasten the stirring of her storm.

Woman looking like a hurricane in November.

"Wildfire," I murmured.

The main entrance door swinging open tore our attention that way.

A plain, local guy waltzed through.

Brinley reeled back like she'd been released from a trap.

Maybe that's exactly what I was.

A trap.

Trying to touch on something that I knew better than touching.

I knew better.

I fucking knew better.

The dude stumbled once he noticed us standing there. No question he knew he was stepping into a field of landmines.

The tension was stretched so tight between me and Brinley it probably felt like he was inhaling bricks.

At the sight of me, his eyes widened. Natural instinct kicking in and slowing him with a caution flag.

I knew in one single second that this guy wasn't a threat.

Always a good start to the day when I didn't have to murder someone before eight.

I looked back at Brinley with a smirk. "Looks like you have your first customer. I'll let you get to it."

Then I swiveled around and got the hell out of there before I made any more mistakes.

Because with Brinley Webber? I was afraid they might just prove fatal.

• • •

Me: *Did you pinpoint anything?*

Cash: *Still digging.*

I blew out a rigid sigh as I read Cash's response on our secure thread.

One he'd set up for us several years ago when we'd started assisting one another.

Dread clamored around inside me, inciting me into pacing what felt like a six-foot-deep trench into the ground on the far side of the autobody shop.

If I wasn't careful, the fucking strain was going to bury me.

Me: *Need this taken care of.*

Cash Cunningham was the best in the business. That was if your business was hacking into sleazebags' lives and ridding them of everything they held near and dear.

And what these bastards held near and dear to their hearts tended to run the lines of guns and drugs and trafficking of every sort.

Their millions made on others' agony and pain.

Cash and his crew, Sovereign Sanctum, focused on the abused. Helping women and children in horrible domestic situations get free and setting them up with new lives.

My crew?

We specialized in wiping out the organized.

Expunging the filthy underworld that stained society.

Cash's crew and mine turned to each other when we needed the help.

Right then, I was in dire need of it.

For years, I'd been hunting for a way to extinguish Kent Ellison. The motherfucker who'd stolen everything from me.

I'd been so close until Kent had somehow managed to get to my sister, thinking he was getting me under his thumb by doing so.

Little did he know, he'd incited a war.

Now, everything was riding on this plan.

Cash: *I know, man. But you know this situation is delicate. It's going to take perfect planning.*

I could feel his empathy. The dude had been the broodiest fucker I'd known until the only woman who could break through his wounds had made her way back to him.

Daisy and her three kids softening his hard, impenetrable heart.

Honestly, I'd do anything for the guy just because he'd do anything for me.

But what had me truly indebted to him? He was the one who'd physically gotten Elena out.

He'd gone in during the dead of night and rescued her.

Me: *I know. But now that Dereck's sister is here, it feels like a race against the clock.*

I paced in the other direction, boots clomping across the dirt, hesitating before I tapped out another text, trying to put a finger on exactly what I was feeling.

Stomach unsettled and my mind spinning.

Me: *Don't trust him, man.*

Cash: *No. I don't, either, but we're still going to need to use the information he's providing.*

It was the deal.

Protection for Dereck's sister and the gift of his pathetic life for the exact locations of Kent Ellison's operations.

And it all had to come down on one specific night.

Me: *I know.*

Me: *But if he betrays us?*

Cash: *I'm working overtime to verify everything he says. He was true with the intel he gave on Elena. Right down to the second.*

Cash: *You can be sure I will do everything I can to validate whatever he gives.*

Me: *And how sure are you that you can do that?*

It took all of a second for a text to blip through.

Cash: *You questioning my skill?*

I could feel the humor he injected into it.

Me: *Never. Just…*

Cash: *I know, Silas. I get it. And I promise we're doing everything we can on our end.*

Me: *How long?*

Cash: *I'd plan for two to three weeks. Seems he's getting buzz about a big shipment around then. We'll have to piece everything else together around it.*

Air blustered from my nose, and I scrubbed a hand over my face, forcing myself not to send back a message that said that was unacceptable.

I had to be patient.

If you rushed into jobs, things got flubbed and the wrong people got dead.

And the only ones I planned on putting in the ground were the ones who deserved to be there.

Me: *Okay.*

Cash: *Good. And how is the girl?*

How was the girl?

Infuriating.

Gorgeous.

A giant pain in my ass.

Me: *Clueless. Thinks she's working off a debt for her scumbag brother. A feisty thing, though.*

Cash: *Keep it that way.*

I glanced up like I might be able to see her through two layers of block wall.

I figured I could feel her, though. That burn knew no boundaries.

Me: *I will.*

Cash: *I'll keep you posted as details come in. For now, get your men ready.*

Me: *You can be sure they will be.*

I started to trudge back in the direction of the clubhouse, needing to go over a couple of issues with Colby, one of our enforcers, when my phone vibrated in my hand again.

I expected it to be Cash bidding farewell, so I stalled out in my tracks when I saw who it was from.

PJ.

It wasn't like I was going to save the piece of shit's contact as *Dear Ol' Dad*.

PJ: *You have a lot of fucking nerve.*

Me: *And you apparently have a death wish.*

I sent it with enough spite that I'd be surprised if it didn't strike him down at the knees.

PJ: *Big talk for a small-time criminal.*

Was he kidding me? Like he hadn't spent his entire pathetic existence scamming his way through life. One hand conning some unsuspecting target and the other swinging blows at his family.

That was if he wasn't completely destroying the good.

Me: *What do you want?*

PJ: *You know what I want.*

Me: *And you know there's not one fucking chance I'm giving him back to you.*

My teeth ground as I sent it, the oath I made slashing through my consciousness with the same depth as a five-inch blade.

PJ: *Then you're gonna pay for him.*

Scumbag was always the same. Wondering how he was going to benefit from every situation. How he'd spin it so it landed in his favor. Like that little boy was a bartering chip.

Me: *You can fuck off to whatever hole you crawled out of because you aren't getting anything from me.*

PJ: *We'll see about that.*

Me: *Try it, old man, and find out just how serious I am.*

Because I might have been weak then.

Unable to stop it.

But I would never allow him to hurt the innocent again.

7

Silas

SEVEN YEARS OLD

"Come on, Silas, baby! Knock it out of the park."

With the bat cocked over his shoulder, he peeked in the direction of the voice and caught sight of his momma at the fence. Her face was pressed to the metal and her fingers were curled into the chain links.

Her smile was as big as the sun.

At least that's what it felt like, the way his whole chest felt fuzzy and warm.

He barely tweaked a smile and focused on the pitcher at the mound.

The boy threw it, kind of wobbly and off to the side, but Silas swung for it, anyway.

It cracked when it made contact. Vibrating up his arms as surprise took him over. He watched it hit the ground just past the pitcher and go rolling toward the outfield.

"Run, baby, run!" his momma shouted, the same as his coach, and Silas jumped into action. Pumping his legs just as fast as they would take him, running for first base.

He stomped on it, and his momma yelled, "Keep going!"

He turned and headed for second, his breaths hard pants.

He didn't know if he was going to make it because a kid on the other team finally snatched the ball from the ground and cocked it over his shoulder to throw it to second.

Instead of it going sailing, he fumbled and dropped it.

Silas knew all the rules, and he touched his toe on second then kept right on going. Running like the wind, the sun on his face, his mother's voice in his ear.

She had the prettiest one. Always singing loudly in the car and in the house.

"All the way home!" She was jumping at the fence then, smiling so wide as he rounded third and pushed with all his might to make it.

He couldn't wait to make her proud the way she always told him he did, his chest puffed out as he pounded his feet across the dirt.

The other team was shouting, too, and he was pretty sure someone was coming up on his tail.

He tried to run even faster. His heart went pound, pound, pound as he felt someone getting closer.

The base was super close, but he could hear the footsteps right behind him.

He dove his feet for the base like his coach taught him to do since he wasn't on the baby team anymore.

He slid, the side of his body scraping across the rough dirt as he stretched out his toes, reaching for home plate.

He touched it.

Cheers and shouts rose all around him.

He made it.

"Home run, baby!" his momma called, and his chest was puffing out again as he climbed to his feet, his grin as big as his momma's as the rest of his team cheered the winning point.

He ran for his mom when she stepped around the fence. "Did you see it?"

"I sure did. You hit that ball so far, I thought it was going to go into outer space."

Silas beamed. "I'm as fast as Flash!"

With a light laugh, she brushed her fingers through his hair. "I bet you are. How about we go for ice cream to celebrate?"

"Because I did so good?"

She tapped his nose. "No, because you tried really hard."

"I know, I know, we just always gotta try our best even if it doesn't feel like we're the best."

At least, that's what she always told him.

"That's right. We try hard and we love harder. Because we've got love inside." She touched his chest.

He got that gooey feeling, then he started running out ahead of her, laughing as he looked back. "Bet you can't catch up to me even if you try your best."

She laughed and tried to chase after him, but her stomach was giant because he was getting a little sister, so her best was super slow.

It didn't seem to make her upset, though.

But his stomach was sinking to the ground when he made it across the field to the parking lot because his daddy was pulling into the spot next to his momma's, and he looked real mad the way he always did.

8

Brinley

"That stupid, arrogant, assface, piece of—" I clipped off the slew of profanities I was gritting through my teeth when the front door of the office swept open.

Great.

Another customer. Just what I needed when I'd had zero clue how to answer the questions of the first guy who came in.

But I guess I was really good at faking my way through.

Pinning an artificial smile to my face, I pushed to standing from where I'd been sitting in front of that dinosaur computer pretending like I was actually going to accomplish something using it.

Then my teeth were actually snapping shut when I saw who came through the door.

Nerves scattered through me on a gust of apprehension.

It was the woman and tiny boy from last night.

The toddler's hand was in hers, and she was smiling this dazzling, sweet smile, like she'd expected walking through the office door was going to be the highlight of her day.

I itched on my heels.

Maybe it was gawk at the prisoner day.

Only warmth was oozing out of the young woman as she stepped inside, her voice riddled with anticipation. "Oh my gosh, you have to be Brinley."

Gulping, I struggled to keep that smile pinned to my face. "Yep, that's me."

"When I heard you were coming here, I couldn't wait to meet you."

I wondered what she'd think if she knew the way Silas had had me pressed against that desk two hours ago.

Because it'd felt…scandalous. Like we'd been two seconds from something splintering between us and igniting into what it absolutely could not.

Or maybe I'd only been projecting, imagining that he was feeling the same insanity I was feeling whenever the man got within a hundred-yard radius of me.

A fool wondering what it would be like if he slipped his hand under my skirt.

Which that right there was the most outrageous, implausible part of it all.

The fact that I would even think it. Allowing even a moment's entertainment of something that normally sent me into a spiral.

And he just had to be the man I was having those preposterous flashes of fantasies about. Not really afraid of him but afraid of the way he made me feel.

It made me sick.

I knew what this was, though.

It was the clashing of strain and trauma. The memories up against whatever bullshit Dereck had gotten himself into.

That was it and nothing more, and I wasn't about to allow myself to fall prey to my own weaknesses and insecurities.

It had nothing to do with the fact that Silas Mercer was regrettably the hottest man I'd ever seen and had this lure about him that kept creeping into my thoughts and whispering across my flesh.

A shiver raced again. I stomped it down into nonexistence where it belonged.

Get your shit together, Brinley.

This guy was married or taken or what the hell ever.

I mean, she was standing right in front of me.

She had that fresh-face look. Rich, dark brown hair with matching freckles sprinkled across her cheeks.

Adorable.

Obviously sweet.

Bristling with some kind of unfound excitement.

I returned a smile that I hoped matched hers. I was lucky that poor little boy didn't burst into tears because I was pretty sure the only thing I looked was deranged.

But he was grinning too, dancing back and forth on his little feet as he clung to the woman's hand, a blue blanket that looked like he dragged it everywhere with him hooked in his elbow.

Okay.

Woman felt like a stretch.

She was young.

Twenty-one to twenty-three, tops.

More evidence against Silas Mercer's lackluster character.

What a skeeze.

She had to be ten years younger than him.

"I'm Elena." Her shoulders hitched to her ears when she said it. "We almost came over first thing this morning when Silas said you started at eight, but I figured I needed to give you a little time to get settled before we descended on you."

Get settled?

There wasn't going to be any 'getting settled' into this place.

Surviving or escaping were clearly the only options.

Escaping sounded like a really good plan right then.

"And this is our favorite little Kai." Adoration gushing from her, she gestured at the little boy.

He raised his tiny, chubby hand that clutched a toy motorcycle and vroomed it through the air.

"Kai *mowercycle*!"

His little voice was garbled as he showed off what clearly was a prized possession.

I looked around, wondering how exactly I was supposed to be handling this.

I felt like I was being attacked by sweetness.

Kind of like death by chocolate but a little less enjoyable.

Or maybe the whole problem was them walking through the door was the first bit of comfort I felt since I came to this place.

"Hi, Kai. I'm Brinley," I whispered.

"Hi, *Bwinwey.* I got a *mowercycle. Vroooom.*"

He flew it through the air.

Bwinwey.

God, was it possible a child could steal your heart in a beat? Because crap, this kid was adorable.

"That's an awesome motorcycle," I forced out.

"You *likes* it?" He beamed like I'd just paid him the greatest compliment. His soft brown hair curling around his ears and wisping down his neck.

Cheeks chubby and pink.

"I do."

"I is one," he told me with a bob of his head.

He'd come clad in black jeans and a white tee and Converse on his feet. He had a fake tattoo of a heart that was beginning to peel on the back of his hand.

Hands down, he was the cutest little rebel ever. Hopefully his father's bad behavior didn't rub off on him.

"Almost two," Elena clarified. "And I am twenty-two."

With a slight laugh, she shimmied her shoulders, sending her ponytail swishing.

Elena was clad in a pink tank, high-waisted jeans, and sandals.

Definitely not dressed like the few women I'd seen hanging out around the bonfire last night.

She dipped down and scooped up Kai.

"You probably didn't actually want to know that." Self-deprecation rolled out of her as she inched closer to the high counter that separated us. "But just in case you see me sipping on a beer, I didn't want you to run over and snatch it away from me like some of these punks like to do!"

She raised the last portion like the handful of men working in the bays attached to the office would overhear.

"I swear to God, they treat me like I'm ten," she mumbled under her breath.

She leaned against the countertop, a tease all over her face. "Or maybe you did want to know because friends know these things about each other, right?"

It sounded almost hopeful.

My head spun. I was having a heck of a time trying to keep up with what in the world was happening.

"Um, yeah, I guess they do."

Silence wafted around us before her brows lifted to her hairline in a prodding question.

Wait, what?

Is that what she was suggesting?

That we were supposed to be friends? And if so, then clearly I was supposed to reciprocate.

"I'm twenty-six." I choked out the words.

I was surprised she didn't fist pump the air with the way she grinned. "I feel like that's perfect. I mean, there are a lot of women roaming around here, but I don't think they really like me."

Okay, I thought it was impossible not to *like* her, and I hated Silas Mercer even more for it.

I bet he treated her terribly.

I bet he lied and manwhored and complained and left her waiting for him at night.

That was if he didn't treat her *really, really* badly, as if all of that wasn't horrible enough.

Rage blistered through my insides at the thought.

If he did, I'd take her with me when I left. I'd figure out a way to get her and that adorable little boy out of here to someplace safe.

Maybe I'd take this whole freaking place down when I went.

Set it on fire.

"And how in the world could someone not like you?" I couldn't help but give her the truth.

"Right?" She tossed her head back with a tinkling laugh, then she was back to looking at me with a cheeky smile.

"And maybe they don't *not* like me. I think maybe they're just leery of me or something? You know, because of my position?"

She whispered that part like it was a secret.

Right.

Her position.

Being with Silas, their president. I was suddenly burning with a thousand *friendly* questions.

Like how long had they been together and how on God's green earth did she put up with his pompous ass?

But I didn't let any of them go, and her smile was softening as she peered at me. "What do you think of your room? I know it's small and everything, but I wanted to make sure it was cute and comfortable."

Surprise jetted free. "You're the one who decorated my room?"

She shrugged a self-conscious shoulder. "I hope you like pink. It's my favorite, obviously."

"What kind of weirdo doesn't like pink?"

I had to admit I was feeling a whole lot better about that pink knowing where it came from. Thankful that room wasn't some sort of strange kinky torture chamber.

"Right?" She giggled, swaying Kai before a bit of shyness ridged her demeanor. "I knew I was going to like you."

I felt a gush of emotion roll out of her.

Not loneliness.

Something similar but different.

Isolation, I thought. Like maybe she was trapped.

Another rush of worry blustered beneath the surface of my skin.

Concerned about how she'd ended up here.

I had no idea who these men were or what they were like, but I'm sure they were capable of deplorable acts.

She snuggled Kai closer, and her voice dropped in gentle emphasis. "And I want you to know if you need anything at all, you can come to me. I know Silas probably told you to keep away from me, being the grumpy boss that he is, but as far as I'm concerned, he doesn't get to control everything."

Confusion bound with the dread I felt for her.

She glanced toward the door that separated the office from the shop that had a small window in it before she returned her gaze back to me.

"I mean, I know he only worries with everything going on and he wants to protect everyone, but sometimes what we really need are people there to support us. Not just the muscle."

Lightness filled the roll of her eyes.

I blinked, trying to make sense of her. Of this place.

Did she know I was little more than a prisoner?

Forced to come here to pay off a debt for my brother?

Was she okay with this?

I leaned toward her, and my words left me on a cautious whisper. "Does your husband always boss you around?"

Maybe she'd confide in me what was really going on here.

Confusion bunched up her brow. "My husband?"

Okay, not married.

"Silas. Your boyfriend or husband or...whatever you call him."

That confusion took a quick turn when she cackled with amusement, snorting and laughing and spluttering all over the place. "Oh, God. Eww. Gross."

She wretched like she was going to vomit before more giggles followed. It made Kai giggle, too.

What the hell?

"You think I'm with Silas?"

I held onto the edge of the counter, trying to keep my footing.

I peeked over at the small window in the door, and I could barely see where Silas was bent over a car, facing away.

Only I would be so reprehensible as to notice how his coveralls fit snug on that dangerous body.

I looked back at her, my tongue stroking nervously over my dried lips. "You aren't?"

More giggles. "No. God, no. Silas is my brother."

"My *brover.*" Kai smacked himself in the chest with his toy motorcycle.

And I was just then realizing that her eyes were pretty much the exact same shade as Silas's. Hazel. Predominantly sage green and rimmed in brown.

Humiliation rushed in.

God, that's what assumptions got you, didn't they?

"Oh," I wheezed. Flustered and totally embarrassed.

Then I was thinking what a bastard Silas really was, not having the decency to correct me when I'd pressed him on it earlier.

I bet the sadist loved feeding on people's discomfort.

Elena let go of a laugh, though she was watching me with a sly look in her eye. "Why do you look so relieved?"

"Um, because that man is far too old for you."

And a raging asshole, but I bet she already knew that.

Conspiratorially, she leaned forward. "And as far as the word on the street goes, and by that, I mean in the clubhouse, crazy hot and really good in the sack."

There was a full razzing to her words.

It was my turn to curl up my nose and say, "Eww and gross and never in my life."

Old wounds suddenly groaned from within.

Never in my life.

She didn't seem to notice my sudden discomfort.

I was an old pro at burying it.

She laughed outright. "Probably for the best. He's not the snuggling type."

Yeah. Me, neither.

She let a puff of air filter from her nose as her gaze wandered to the window on the door. Her demeanor shifted a fraction. "Not many of them are. These guys blaze through women like it's their job."

Sincerity filled her expression when she looked back. "But under it all, they're good guys, Brinley. I want you to know that. I want you to know you're safe here."

Something deep and resonating flooded from her voice.

Still, I had to suppress an incredulous laugh.

Safe?

Safe was the last thing I felt.

"I go *mowercycle*?" Kai pointed a little finger toward the shop, angling himself that way like it would get him there faster.

My chest tightened as questions pummeled me again. "And Kai? He's…yours?"

I was almost knocked off my feet by the swell of protectiveness that suddenly poured from her. A torrent of it. She held the baby a little closer as she pressed a kiss to the side of his head, breathing him in.

Something passed through her features that I couldn't read. "He's my heart, but not my son."

Silas's son, then.

I heaved a breath, wary of the limbo of questions that whirled through my mind.

"Well, I'd better get Kai out there before he stages a revolt. Motorcycles are serious business for him." Elena laughed a light sound as she bounced the small child.

She started to back away, and I could see her contemplating before she rushed, "There's a party at the clubhouse tonight. Well, there's usually always a party at the clubhouse, but tonight, there's a special one. It's Trevan's birthday, so I get to go."

Excitement lit up her expression. "You should come."

"I think your brother might have something to say about that."

Her voice turned playful. "He doesn't get to make all the rules, remember?"

She paused at the door, looking back at me, softness in her gaze. "I'm really glad you're here, Brinley."

She said it like I'd found my way home and this wasn't some sort of cruel and unjust penalty I was paying.

A penalty I didn't even understand.

A bit of the anger flared, but I somehow managed to smile without it being a grimace.

Because I meant what I originally said.

It was impossible not to like her.

"Thank you for that."

She gave me a deep nod before she tossed open the door. The sound of tools and voices poured in like a wave from beyond, before the din returned to a dull drone when the door drifted closed behind her.

Maybe Silas had hit the nail on the head.

Maybe I really was looking for trouble.

Because I couldn't do anything but edge out from behind the counter.

Couldn't do anything but peer like a creeper through the window, hooked on the action as he rose from where he'd been leaned over a car's engine and strode toward Elena and Kai.

Kai waved both hands, whipping that motorcycle around with a thrill.

Silas took him.

Swung him up in the air, his affect easy, but his body still rippling with menace and intimidation as he moved to where a bunch of motorcycles were situated in the far bay.

He swung onto one, taking Kai with him and settling the child so he was straddling the seat.

Kai's little arms stretched out to grip onto the middle portion of the handlebars since they weren't even close to being long enough to make it to the grips.

My chest squeezed. Squeezed in a way that I couldn't fathom.

I couldn't stop staring. Watching as joy filled Kai's cherub face, and I thought it was sheer protection that took over Silas's as he dipped down and pressed a tender kiss to the little boy's head.

A surge of unequivocal loyalty ruptured out.

Beneath it was violence. The clear evidence of what would happen if anyone tried to hurt the child.

I tremored in the magnitude of it, nearly blown back when Silas lifted his penetrating gaze and laid it on me.

Green, roiling flames.

Harshness slashed into the savage angles of his face.

He kept staring at me. His nostrils flared, and I swore there was some kind of hidden message in it.

The muted sound of Elena's laughter broke the bubble, and I stumbled back because I refused to be the fool who got lost in the trap.

9

Brinley

I'd never taken myself for a masochist, but here I was.

Slipping out from what might as well have been a cell and edging down the exterior steps like a thief in the approaching night.

Wearing heeled boots and tight jeans and the sexiest blouse I owned tucked into the waist.

The shirt plunging at the neckline and slinking all over my upper body.

Last night I was sneaking. Tonight, I was strutting.

I decided I wasn't about to let Silas Mercer back me into a corner. Wasn't about to allow him to leave me submissive and afraid.

On top of that, the freaking dry as hell ham and cheese sandwich that had been delivered to my room didn't compare to the mouthwatering scent of barbecue wafting up from below.

Twilight wisped through the cover of the trees, and voices and laughter carried on the gentle breeze.

The air was tinged with a faint coolness that clashed with the sweat that slicked my skin.

I inhaled it.

Shakily before I curled my hands into fists and moved through the thick toward the commotion happening at the front of the clubhouse.

Sitting around shy wasn't going to win me any answers.

I still hadn't heard from Dereck, even after I sent him fifteen demanding texts throughout the day.

Telling him I was worried.

That I needed to know what was happening.

That he was the only thing I could think about.

And what did I get in return?

Silence.

I was so going to kick his ass once I got out of this.

Even though I'd put on a chunky heel, my boots still sunk into the soft ground below as I trudged around the side of the building.

I had planned to storm out there with my head held high, only I stumbled at the periphery.

Looking out on the scene.

The party was in full swing.

There were way more people out there tonight.

A slew of motorcycles sat beneath the trees on the far side of the clearing, making what amounted to a semi-circle around the front.

As if all that leather and glinting metal could act as a barricade from the rest of the world.

In the middle, another bonfire roared, though this one was three times the size it'd been yesterday.

Sparks licked up from the flames and kissed the gauzy night that filtered in from above.

Bikers were everywhere.

Wearing their cuts with that gruesome emblem on the back.

Women who clearly strutted far better than I did roamed through the throng, and the men didn't hesitate to reach out and snag them as they waltzed by.

They didn't seem to mind so much since giggles erupted as the bikers pawed at their bodies.

Honestly, I couldn't tell who was hunting who.

No wonder Silas didn't normally let Elena mingle with his pack.

I had half a mind to drag her out of there myself, except she was near the fire, sipping from a beer with that exuberance radiating from her.

Like she was maybe having the most fun she'd ever had.

Wearing jean shorts, a white top, and matching sneakers.

Looking so out of place it was almost comical.

She stood next to the same brute of a man who'd been in front of the autobody shop when I arrived yesterday afternoon.

His massive arms were crossed over his chest, and I could almost see the aggression oozing from his pores as he kept watch over her.

Clearly on guard duty.

One point Silas.

At least he wasn't throwing his little sister to the wolves.

Sucking it all down, I lifted my chin and forced myself to move out into the fray.

My heart thundered in my chest. Anxiety woven in every walloping beat.

I'd almost convinced myself to turn around because it would be a whole lot safer to serve out my sentence hidden behind the fortitude of the walls of my room when Elena suddenly glanced in my direction.

Glee lit her face.

"Brinley! You came! I was about to storm up to your room and drag you out here." She widened her arms in welcome.

The guy next to her swiveled my way as I approached.

A glower took to his brow, and his dark gaze drifted down me like I was a blight.

Clearly, he wasn't as excited to see me as Elena.

I searched around inside myself for a good excuse for coming down here. "How was I supposed to resist the smell of that barbecue?"

She hiked a coy shoulder. "Why do you think I had Silas send up a boring, bland sandwich?"

"Diabolical." I couldn't help but grin.

"I told you I have my ways around here."

"Where's Kai?" Was it weird that I felt a little panic that he was nowhere in sight? But I couldn't imagine Elena would leave him with someone who wouldn't fully look out for him.

"With Meems."

My brows lifted. "Meems?"

"Our grandmother."

"Grandmother?" I didn't know why it came out so uncertain.

Elena lowered her voice as she glanced around. "We don't bring Kai to the clubhouse at night."

She must have seen the spate of questions roll through my mind because she added, "We all live in a house on the backside of the property."

"Silas, too?" It came out a demand.

Her brow arched. "Are you interested in where my brother sleeps at night?"

I curled my nose. It seemed the appropriate reaction.

She laughed again, then my attention was suddenly stolen by a surging energy that came from across the clearing.

Hot spikes of animosity that arrowed through the night.

Someplace inside me wanted to cower.

Instead, I lifted my chin in a challenge to meet the ferocity staring back.

I guess I shouldn't have because the force of it nearly blew me back ten feet.

I could hardly make him out where he stood on the opposite side of the bonfire in the shadows.

Just the crude outline of an intimidating, overbearing silhouette.

It didn't matter. I could still feel the cruel wickedness blazing from the green flames of his eyes.

I sent him my best scowl.

I didn't know if he could see it since I couldn't actually make out his expression, but I knew there was no humor ridging his arrogant demeanor tonight.

It was all power.

The president standing there in all his twisted, fucked up glory.

The *King* in full play.

Elena looped her arm through mine, jerking my attention from the thousand-ton magnet lurking on the far side of the lot.

"Come and meet the birthday boy." She pulled me toward the guy she'd been standing beside.

Like he was a cinnamon roll and not some murderous beast.

"Brinley, meet Trevan. Crimson Crows's vice president and Silas's best friend and basically a giant pain in my ass."

Her voice rolled with the tease.

Trevan grunted, though there was no missing the softness as he looked at her.

"That's because you're a giant pain in mine, having to keep after you." His voice was a low rumble of affection.

She rolled her pretty eyes and released me so she could lean her shoulder into his side. "You know you love me."

I wondered if I was the only one who noticed the way he minimally leaned into her and his hands twitched.

Like he wanted to touch her but couldn't.

She lingered for a second like she was begging him to, but when he refrained, something came over her face before she popped off him and grabbed me by the hand.

"So, tell me you're hungry because you are in for a treat."

In theory, I shouldn't be able to eat a bite with the way my stomach was in knots of apprehension, but that barbecue and I were so going to go down.

Apparently, I was a stress eater. "Starving," I told her.

"Then let's get that belly fed." Her grin suddenly turned to a frown. "You do look a little peaked. Did Silas work you too hard today?"

I almost choked over a laugh.

If she was referring to Silas leaving me to wander through a mile-high pile of unpaid invoices and bills discarded in random stacks on the desk, a fool who decided she was actually going to sort through the total mess, then yes.

It wasn't like I could just sit there idle all day, anyway.

I had to do something with my hands or those hands would have ended up around Silas's throat.

The few times he'd wandered by the office door, the asshole had never even glanced my way.

As if he had zero care that I was there.

I didn't know why that pissed me off even more, but it did.

Elena began to haul me toward the main entrance of the clubhouse, which was two swinging doors with the Crimson Crows emblem stamped on the front.

I wasn't surprised that I could feel that brute of a man tromping along behind us, though he was hanging back in the distance.

You'd think he'd be given a break from guard duty on his birthday. The most problematic part was it appeared that maybe he didn't want one.

Elena pushed through to the chaos on the other side.

Heavy metal music blared, and while there were a ton of people outside, it seemed the main gathering was in there.

It was a full biker bar. A private one, clearly, but lacking no amenities.

High-top tables were situated up front, three pool tables running down the middle, and couches were hidden in the shadows along the right wall.

Toward the back on the left was an L-shaped bar, probably ten or so stools running each length, and to the back right was a stage elevated by two feet with a dance floor below it.

A haze of smoke curled through the dim lights, making the people scattered everywhere appear like figments of vapor.

A few dancing. Some tossing back shots while others were drinking straight from the bottle.

Laughing.

Shouting.

"Is everyone here a part of Crimson Crows?" I basically shouted it so Elena could hear above the raucous din.

It wasn't like I knew much about biker life.

It'd always been a bit of fiction to me. Something fanciful and romanticized.

Full disclosure, what was going down in there was far from *romantic.*

People groping each other in the darkened corners, one woman propped on a table while a biker kissed up between her thighs.

Elena gave a slight shake of her head. "Normally only family is allowed, but not tonight."

Family.

She considered these brutes family.

She shrugged a little. "But the guys wanted to give Trevan a real bash, so they basically did a word-of-mouth invitation. A ton of old friends came from the last town where we lived, so I recognize most."

A tiny frown tugged between her eyes. "But I think there are a bunch of people from Crimson Creek here, too. Probably out looking for a little taste of the wild side."

"Is that what this really is? Wild?" I was pressing her.

But I needed to know.

I needed to know what the hell they were involved in and just how my brother had gotten himself entangled in it.

Air puffed from her nose as she continued to wind us through the mob.

Then she leaned close. "It's a different lifestyle, Brinley, and at times it can be wild."

She hesitated, peeking around like she was worried she was going to get caught dishing a betrayal, before she whispered, "Dangerous."

Then she rushed, "But what they do is really important."

Confusion smacked through me at her words. "What they do?"

How could living this type of life be *important*?

I was thinking more like a scourge.

Surprised guilt seemed to make her stumble a step, and her eyes widened in regret.

No question, she'd let something slip that she wasn't supposed to.

"What does that mean?"

She pasted the first fake smile I'd seen her wear onto her face. "It's nothing."

Shucking it off like she didn't have my brain swirling with questions, she pulled out ahead of me, dragging me along.

"Come on. If you think Lulu's chicken smelled good, wait until you taste it."

She angled us through a doorway and into another room.

It was like walking into another realm. The lights were brighter in there, and a few people were sitting at the three picnic tables that ran against the right wall.

On the left was a long buffet table.

The room basically a mess hall.

The delicious barbecue Elena was referring to was piled high on heated silver platters, and every side dish you could imagine was set out as offerings.

Trevan didn't follow us.

I could only imagine he was leaning against the other side of the wall, standing like a sentry with his arms crossed over his chest.

An older woman was at the buffet, dumping a bowl of ribs slathered in sauce into one of the chafing dishes.

Her gray hair was twisted into a bun, and she wore a Crimson Crows T-shirt.

Tell me these guys didn't actually have a fan club and merch.

"Lulu, look who I have!" Elena ushered me forward.

The woman's eyes widened in appraisal before settling into welcome. "Well, if it isn't our most anticipated guest."

Guest?

That was a stretch.

"It's about time you came down here and gave me a visit. And after I made my special French toast this morning just for you."

There was no anger to it. Just a casual, easy warmth.

Uh, yeah, I'd skipped out on the breakfast Silas had mentioned last night since I would have gagged had I put anything in my mouth.

I shifted uncomfortably on my feet. "Oh, well, I'm sorry. I...wasn't very hungry this morning."

Her mouth stretched into a knowing grin. "Don't you worry, honey. It's a lot to take in."

Wrinkles weathered her face, like tracks of harrowed memories.

Honestly, she looked like she'd been dragged to hell and back.

Worn down by years and tragedies.

If I had to bet on it, I'd guess she was probably in her early fifties, ten years younger than she appeared.

Elena snatched my hand and swung it between us. "Isn't she sooo freaking pretty, Lulu? I told you."

"Stunnin'," Lulu drawled.

I shook my head as I looked at Elena. "You're ridiculous. Have you looked in the mirror?"

Elena beamed like she'd never received a compliment before. "Really?"

Lulu chuckled. "Sweet girl, you're gorgeous. No one tells you since they know they'll get their jugular ripped out by your brother if they do."

Frustration filled the roll of Elena's eyes. "He's so overbearing sometimes, I want to scream."

"Well, you know why he is the way he is," Lulu said softly. "After everything, I think you're lucky he lets you out of the house at all."

My attention volleyed between them. Trying to catch up. To understand the flash of what looked like terror rip through Elena's expression.

Then she sighed and looked away as she mumbled, "I know."

When she looked back, she was all bright smiles again. "Okay, Brinley is starving, and you know that will never do around here. We must feed her."

"She's come to the right place." Lulu hobbled back to the buffet table, showing off a significant limp in her left leg.

While I stood there with the walls spinning around me.

Unsure of what was going on. I hadn't expected anyone to extend any welcome, and these two had to be the most genuine people I'd ever met.

But I needed to remember what brought me here. Remember the man who was out haunting the periphery of the fire.

Lulu started making me a plate, scooping up giant spoonfuls of potato salad and buttered corn and cole slaw.

I moved to her side. "I can do that."

"Oh no. It's what I do around here, unless you don't like something?"

I shifted in discomfort.

Was she here paying off a debt, too? Was she stuck working for this jerk?

I didn't like it. Not one bit.

I gulped down the ire. "Everything looks amazing."

Elena curled an arm through Lulu's and set her head on the outside of her shoulder. "It's how she loves us. Through her food."

Oh.

Okay. Fine.

Not what I was thinking.

"Believe me, between her and Meems," Elena continued, "you're going to be well fed while you're here. You may never want to leave."

Yeah, that was not going to happen.

Lulu passed me the plate, then she insisted on making one for Elena, too.

"Thank you," I murmured.

Flustered.

So out of sorts I didn't know what to make of anything.

I followed Elena over to a table and sat down.

It felt like a moment's reprieve.

A breath so I could try to figure out what I was really doing down here.

I scanned, gaze skating over the faces of the few who were in the mess hall.

A couple of super young bikers who were scarfing down their meals, and an older guy sitting a couple of chairs down from them.

Elena chattered beside me. I had no doubt she was keeping to safe topics, clearly confining herself to the parameters that she'd been given since she'd let herself slip earlier.

Going on like this was some sort of resort rather than a pit of depravity.

Then the air suddenly shifted.

A bolt of energy staking through the atmosphere.

A blast of that intensity there was no chance I could miss.

Her voice faded away as my attention snapped up to peer through the long open sections of the wall that ran above the buffet.

Sections that didn't contain any glass, I assumed so food could easily be passed through.

Beyond them was what looked to be a hall of some sort.

A group of men were walking by, only their faces and shoulders exposed.

Trevan and three other men I didn't know the names of, but one who I'd seen out in the autobody shop earlier today.

They were jostling and messing with each other. Laughter rolling.

But it was the one striding out ahead of them that sent a cold dread slipping through my veins.

A slick of fear and interest and fiery hate.

Power oozed from his tattooed flesh, and I swore it was obscenity that was scored on his stealthy body.

Every slashed angle of him as sharp as a blade.

For one fleeting second, his face turned in my direction.

I didn't even know what the hell was written in it.

I figured he was just conjuring up ideas of exactly how he was going to torture me.

Elena didn't seem to notice as they strode by as she told me about some new boots she'd ordered last night.

Each volatile man blipping by like a meteor set on a path of destruction.

This was it.

My opportunity.

I needed to know what they were up to.

"Um...where is the restroom?" I basically cut her off, and her head rocked back in surprise.

"Oh." She glanced around before she gestured toward a door at the far-right side of the windows and buffet. "It's right down that hall, first door on the right."

She started to climb from the bench. "I'll go with you."

I popped to my feet faster than I should have, attempting to school the shaky anticipation that ripped through me. I pushed out a hand to stop her. "Oh no, that's fine. Finish your dinner. I'll be right back."

Concern curved her brow. "Are you sure?"

"Yep. I'm all good. I figure I'm going to need to learn my way around here if I'm going to be staying, right?"

I wondered if she could decipher the guilt in my laugh.

Without waiting for her to change her mind, I beelined toward the door, putting on a show that I really needed to pee.

Sucking for breath as I curled my hand around the doorknob, my pulse thundering and thumping as I pulled it open to the dimly-lit hall on the other side.

The second I stepped into the darkened, dingy corridor, the air seemed to become nonexistent.

Stagnant and stale.

I might as well have been taking a bath in the stench of the corruption.

Music echoed from the left, beyond another swinging door that must lead back into the bar area.

A hall that was so long that I couldn't see its end beyond the gloom that swallowed it to my right.

It appeared all the rooms were likely linked by the long hall.

My blood sloshed and careened.

I glanced back once more to make sure no one was around before I began to edge down the long corridor.

Sweat slicked my skin, just waiting on one of these assholes to reach out and grab me.

But no one was there.

With my breaths heaving, I crept down the passageway.

I noted the door to the bathroom that Elena had indicated. I bypassed it and kept on moving.

The quiet click of my heels that I tried to subdue made my heart beat even faster as I was drawn deeper into the murky shadows like one of those first to go in a slasher film.

And maybe I was making every horrible decision that I could.

Just begging to get myself chopped into pieces and fed to the pigs.

But this was *my* life.

My *brother's* life.

I wasn't going to sit like a *good girl* and get complacent.

Silas Mercer did not know who he was dealing with.

I made it to another door on the right, and I pressed my ear to the wood.

Moaning.

Okay.

Not what I was looking for.

I kept moving, my heart beating so loud I might as well have been shouting that I was coming.

Another door.

No sound.

Another and another until I made it to the very end.

Here, there were double doors.

The heavy wood extended the entire expanse and reached up to touch the ceiling.

Massive and foreboding.

That emblem was carved right in the middle.

The crows on the gravestone and the one celebrating on the grave.

Crimson Crows arched over the top of the scene, the words stretched across both doors.

My chest tightened to the point of pain, and the fear that crawled up my spine nearly had me retreating.

But the low tenor that barely seeped through the wood had me creeping all the way forward.

I pressed my ear to it. Frustration bubbled up when I was barely able to make out what was being said.

"You think he's getting ready to betray us? Set us up?"

Half the words were garbled, so I wasn't sure I was getting the full extent of the conversation.

A frown slashed into my brow.

Rocks in my throat, I pressed my ear closer, desperate to hear the exchange.

An unintelligible mumble then a, "…sure."

A different voice. "…already dead."

What?

What were they saying?

Dereck?

Is that who they were talking about?

Alarm clamored through my senses, and I might as well have become one with the wood with the way I was trying to get through it when there was the intonation of a voice that I couldn't make out at all.

Crap.

Crap. Crap. Crap.

"…the girl?"

"…kill…handle it."

A cold dread slithered beneath the surface of my skin.

Kill.

Panic shot through me faster than a bullet.

I had to get out of there.

Warn Dereck and protect myself.

Stop whatever was about to happen because whatever it was, I was sure it was bad.

I certainly didn't mean for my elbow to smack against the door when I whirled away, but it made agonizing contact against the wood.

Pain streaked up my arm and nearly dropped me to my knees.

But the real problem was the bang of the impact reverberated as loud as a clash of cymbals in the echoey corridor.

No question, they heard because the voices clipped off.

And I was running.

Running down the hall as fast as my boots could carry me.

Breaths raking from my lungs as I fled.

The walls blurred around me as I pushed myself as fast as I could go.

Whizzing by the doors, then the long window that overlooked the mess hall where Elena likely still remained.

Did she know? Did she know who these people really were? Did she know what they planned to do?

I wasn't about to wait around for an answer.

Finally, the swinging door at the opposite end of the hall came into view, and I put my hands out, busting through it without slowing.

Because I could feel explosive energy behind me. A gathering of severity that blistered through the air.

Without looking back, I flew out into the bar.

The lights were low and the music was loud and people were everywhere.

So many bikers in every direction that it made me dizzy.

The air clogged with viscous, sticky fog.

I weaved through, sidestepping as much as I could to remain out of their reach, my eyes narrowed on one thing.

Escape.

I made it to the main swinging doors, and I burst out into the tacky night.

For one beat, I froze at the horde of bikers at the fire, wondering if they could smell my terror, before I shot into action, cutting right, hoping to duck into the cover of the forest on that side.

Praying I could make it to the property line. My mind calculated, wondering how the hell I'd make it over a twelve-foot wall, but people did miraculous things when their lives depended on it.

I would fight it out, but there were far too many of these assholes to take them down.

I would have to run.

Or maybe hide.

Whatever it was, I simply knew I had to get away.

Only there were footsteps behind me.

Heavy and hard.

The cool air coerced into brutality.

I ran beneath the trees.

Branches swishing and smacking against my flesh.

"Brinley!" The cruel, coarse voice curled around me, so harsh it could almost act as chains.

My heart thumped so frantically I couldn't see as I raced through the underbrush in the darkness.

Only I could make out something in the distance.

Oh my God.

Up ahead, there was a fence.

A legit chain-link fence in the wall's place where the forest was its thickest, one I doubted many new existed.

I could make it.

I had to.

I pushed myself as hard as I could go.

Boots pounding below me.

The fence three feet away.

Only one second before I made it, two massive arms curled around me.

A scream tore out of my lungs as I was getting tackled to the ground.

10

Silas

This was the last thing I needed after a really bad day.

Chasing down a wildfire that blazed through the woods. Her energy torching every damned thing.

She was fuckin' fast in those heeled boots. Still, it didn't take me all that long to catch up to her.

My crew had cast me concerned glances when I'd come crashing out the main doors thirty seconds after her, no doubt wondering if they should jump in and help as she took a frantic jaunt into the woods.

I sent them all glares.

Stay the fuck where you are.

Told them she was off-limits, and I meant that in every regard.

No one was taking her down but me.

Wasn't sure if I was going to take some sort of sick pleasure in it or if I absolutely abhorred it.

What I did know was I couldn't stomach what was roiling from her volatile spirit.

The absolute fear that poured out of her.

Masked by that ferocious fight that she was.

"Brinley!" I gritted behind her.

I didn't think she even heard my voice.

Not when she was in all-out panic mode.

Fuck.

What had she overheard that had sent her running like this?

The little sneak sniffing around outside the club's Church door. No doubt, eavesdropping on the meeting I'd been having with my highest in command. My brothers. The men I trusted above anyone else.

Brinley cut through the woods, her breaths these haggard pants that jutted into the cool night air.

Distraught, she ran, hands out as she batted at the brush and branches that fought to keep her back.

She suddenly heaved some kind of relief, and I immediately knew what she was angling for.

The twelve-foot chain-link fence that lined this section of the property.

A section I'd been meaning to get replaced by the solid wall the rest of the perimeter was surrounded in.

Just my fucking luck that I hadn't thought it a priority.

"Brinley!" I hollered again, voice the low sling of a command that she didn't heed.

I couldn't tell if she planned on scaling that fence or plowing right through it, but either way, I knew she was going to hurt herself trying to get beyond it.

Which was why I increased my speed.

Erasing the distance in three pounding steps before I reached out and wrapped my arms around her waist.

No question, it was the only way to stop her.

The momentum sent us toppling to the forest floor.

A scream tore out of her.

Nah, it wasn't out of pain.

It was an eruption of hate.

Spite and animosity injected with a high dose of terror as she thrashed below me.

Her chest to the ground as I laid across her.

"No!" she cried. "You can't do this. I won't let you."

"Where the fuck do you think you're going?" I growled in her ear.

She only shrieked in some kind of rabid venom as she continued to fight against me.

That perfect fucking ass hugged in those jeans I figured she must have picked to drive me out of my ever-lovin' mind bucked against my cock as she battled to get free.

I gritted my teeth, refusing the burn that ignited at the feel of her, my own breaths shallow as I grappled to grip her by the wrists.

I finally got hold of them, and I pinned them on either side of her head.

Woman staked face down on the ground below me.

"You asshole!" she seethed.

All that autumn hair was bunched in my face, and her delicious skin was slicked in a sheen of sweat.

The scent coming off her made me lightheaded.

Almonds, apples, and cream.

Sweet fucking poison.

Delirium-inducing.

That's what I had to be.

Delirious.

Way she had me so spun up I didn't know if I wanted to punish her or please her.

My weight pinned her down, and I angled closer to her ear, words coming low and rough. "Yeah. And you're a little sneak. Told you that you weren't doing anything but looking for trouble."

Brinley gasped and spluttered like I was the one who wasn't respecting the boundaries.

And one thing I demanded around here was respect.

I pressed her fists harder to the ground, letting the words slice through the disorder. "Told you what I expected of you. That while you're here, you follow my rules. Told you that you weren't to leave this property without my knowledge and an escort."

I dipped in even closer, the warning cleaving like a blade. "Running included."

The woman was a rage. So fucking hot it was a wonder I didn't light up in flames.

"Fuck you, *King*." She spat it as she thrashed.

A clear disparage to my position in the club.

I pressed myself harder against her.

I was inundated by an onslaught of lust.

I wondered if she felt it.

If she could sense it because a frenzy suddenly took her over, and she wheezed, "Let me go."

It was there again.

The same terror that had riddled her when I'd had hold of her last night.

Hidden below the fury that incinerated the air.

It stirred my own rage. The kind that made me want to go on a rampage and find the exact culprit of the feral potency she possessed.

"You gonna run?"

"No."

The second she said it, I surged back onto my knees, releasing her.

In that same second, she was on her feet and hurtling toward the fence.

Motherfucker.

Here we went again.

I jumped to mine, catching up to her the second those little hands were fisting in the metal to propel herself up.

I grabbed her and yanked her down.

In a flash, I had her spun around, and I took her hands and pinned them to the fence above her head.

Heat blistered in the space between us.

A fine line between loathing and desire.

Autumn eyes flashed. Sparking gold flames.

"Wildfire," I gritted through clenched teeth. "You want to play with me? Test me?"

Brinley lifted that chin.

Fuck, she was stunning.

Every gorgeous angle of her face carved in fiery desperation.

"I won't let you do this. I won't."

"And what exactly is it you think I'm going to do?"

My stomach soured when I asked it. Wishing I could sift around in her pretty little brain and discover what she was thinking and exactly what she'd overheard.

What would she think if she uncovered what her cum stain brother had her in?

Doubted she'd go running the way she was trying to do if she had even a dash of the details.

Her throat rolled and her chest heaved as something that looked a whole lot like vulnerability rushed up to the surface before that rage was swallowing it again.

I was fully aware that I was asking for all kinds of trouble of my own, but when she didn't say anything, there was nothing I could do but lean in closer.

It was on the bare flecks remaining of my conscience to make her understand.

Probably didn't need my lips grazing up her flushed cheek as I inclined toward her ear, but I couldn't resist that, either.

"You go over that fence, you get dead."

Figured the warning would hit her like blunt force trauma. That she'd realize what was at stake here.

What I didn't expect was her sudden assault.

Brinley whipped up her knee and hit me full in the junk.

Pain blacked out my sight.

"Motherfuck." It was a straight howl, and there was nothing I could do but double over in agony.

And there went that wildfire, scrambling up the side of the fence again.

That time when I ripped her down, I flung her around, cinched her hands tight to her sides, and wedged my knee between her thighs.

Fully caging her in.

A gasp ripped out of her, and Brinley arched.

And fuck, I was assailed with every atrocious thing I wanted to do to her.

Dip my dirty fingers into the fire that she was. Let her burn me up.

Urges of it hit me from all sides.

A sneak fucking attack.

It was obscene the way I wanted to peel her out of those jeans and show her exactly who was *King.*

Except she was suddenly pleading, "I don't know what it is my brother owes you or what he did, but I'll figure out how to repay you. Please, just… don't hurt him. I know he's an idiot, but I'll fix it."

My mind spun through her turbulent words.

There was no missing what she was leaving out crashing through her impetuous gaze.

She thought I was going to hurt her.

I might be the destroyer, but not in the way she was imagining.

My hands tightened around her wrists as I drew them up between us, and I gave her a good tug so she was plastered against me.

Autumn eyes went wide and wild.

Mouth parted on the remnants of the plea she'd released.

"If I wanted either of you dead, you'd already be that way." The words were gravel.

Horrified surprise had her boots digging into the ground in an attempt to scramble away.

No question, she saw it plain. She knew right then and there exactly what I was capable of.

I didn't release her. I only hauled her closer.

That tight body seared into mine.

I dipped in, inhaling a mouthful of hot apple pie.

Then I was gritting, "I'm not going to hurt you."

Unfortunately, the jury was still out on her brother.

There was a chance I was going to have to put that scum in the ground.

Phoenix was already planning it.

I pressed on, "Believe me when I tell you that you're much safer on this side of that fence."

We were lucky the disgusted disbelief that gusted from her didn't vaporize the trees.

"And why would I trust you?" Brinley fumed it in the direction of my face.

My hands were so tight around her wrists they might as well have been shackles as I drew her knuckles up to my lips.

I whispered against them, hoping she'd fucking get the severity of what I was saying. "Because I'm the only thing you've got."

Then I released her, dropping her hands like they were bricks.

Necessary considering if I kept touching her, whatever insanity I was feeling would crush me.

Hoping to fuck I got through to her, I turned on my heel and forced myself back through the woods, storming in the direction of the clubhouse.

Feeling the heat of that gaze once again scoring into my back.

Wondering when it would be that wildfire finally consumed me.

11

Brinley

Sleepless nights: 2

Brinley: 0

All thanks to that, I stood in front of the crappy little coffee maker that sat on a table under the far window of the office, praying to the coffee gods for their life-sustaining nectar.

Probably appearing like a rabid squirrel with the way my attention kept skittishly darting in every direction while I waited impatiently for each precious, percolated drop to fill my cup.

It wasn't like I could show my face in the mess hall this morning.

I could only imagine what these people thought of me.

Could only imagine what they were whispering under their breaths.

That I was weak.

Pathetic.

An easy freaking target considering I'd come skulking back through the trees with my tail tucked between my legs.

And seriously, in what kind of alternate universe would I have thought biker gossip would one day be something I'd be concerned about?

Fuck you very much, Dereck, for getting me into this.

Whatever it was.

And whatever it was, I knew it was very, very bad.

That was what really had kept me tossing last night.

The fact that I had felt it like steel bands woven in Silas's words, though not quite as loud as I felt it howling from his grip.

My being here wasn't about me paying off some debt.

Dereck had us in deep.

The biggest problem was I had no details.

I was completely in the dark.

How was I supposed to get us out of it if I didn't know what we were pitted against?

One thing I knew for sure was Silas had the answers. I knew down to my soul that whatever they'd been meeting about last night involved Dereck.

Involved me.

A tremor rolled down my spine.

What I wouldn't give to shun everything Silas had said.

The warnings that had dripped from his cruel, arrogant mouth.

But I knew he meant it.

Knew he was uttering nothing but the truth.

And because of it, I was subject to his reign.

God, that pissed me off, too.

It'd been clear as day when the text had come through last night. I'd rushed to get it, thinking it was Dereck, only it was from an unknown number.

Unknown: *You made the right choice, going back to your room. Would not have made me happy if I had to drag you back onto my property.*

Unknown: *Didn't love getting kneed in the balls, either, so let's make sure that doesn't happen again, yeah?*

Me: *How did you get my number?*

Unknown: *I know a whole lot more than you think.*

When I didn't respond in a few minutes, another text had blipped through.

Unknown: *If you need me, use this number, and don't make me have to chase after you again. Are we clear?*

Me: *Loud and clear.*

I'd sent it with a sneer.

God, I despised him and his crooked crown and the fact that he held my well-being over my head.

The truth that he was the only thing I had.

I'd quickly saved his contact as *King*.

The cup finally filled, and I brought it to my lips.

I breathed out in relief as the steaming liquid hit my tongue, then every molecule in my body was tightening and expanding when I felt the squall of energy rise behind me.

A flashflood of it when he swung open the door.

It wasn't necessary to turn around to know it was him.

The man had his own special brand of volatility.

That casual arrogance that infiltrated the space, though there'd been nothing casual about it last night.

I could feel him take a step inside from the shop. Felt him lean against the wall.

Hell, I could almost see him crossing those violent arms over his broad chest.

And I was the sheep who wanted to see.

Slowly, I turned around, holding onto that mug like it might be a lifeline when the undertow of the man threatened to sweep me away.

Silas Mercer was in the exact position I'd imagined.

Dressed in jeans and motorcycle boots and a freaking Henley.

Brown hair damp.

But that fresh out of the shower look didn't do anything to soften his sharp edges.

His cheeks and eyes were blades.

Brow slashed and severe.

Too violently beautiful to be real.

I'd worked really hard not to lie to myself, and honestly, I could stare at him all day and not get tired of doing it.

Then the jerk had to go and open his mouth.

"I see you're being a good girl this morning."

I bristled. Hackles rising in defense.

I really hoped my chin didn't quiver when I lifted it. "It seems I'm stuck here for a while, doesn't it?"

God, I really disliked the way it made it sound like I was surrendering. But it wasn't like I had a whole lot of choices.

From where he leaned against the wall, Silas let his gaze wander over me.

Slowly.

Casually.

Like the bastard had earned the right.

Hazel orbs flicking down and lifting chills on my skin as they went.

Flashing with something that I felt like a rugged caress dragging over my flesh.

The sensation was so overwhelming that I wasn't sure if I detested it or yearned to feel more of it.

This foreign feeling that bubbled in my belly and scattered through me like the flapping of hummingbird wings.

It'd been there last night, too, when he'd pretty much been manhandling me.

Though then it'd been distorted.

Mangled by the fear and charged by the adrenaline that had pumped through my veins.

Now, it was just disorienting.

"The fuck are you wearin'?" The gruff words scraped through the air.

A frown slashed deep, and I looked down to take in my attire.

The lacy white dress that hit me mid-thigh, cinched at the waist with a black belt and flowy in the skirt, my favorite peep-toe black heels on my feet.

"What, am I not dressed appropriately for you? I figured if I was working in your office representing your fine, upstanding company, I'd better look good doing it."

I added as much spite to it as I could conjure.

So maybe there was a valid reason I was here, but that didn't mean I trusted this guy, and it wasn't like he was offering any answers.

And Silas was dangerous. Up to no good. Involved in foul, nefarious things.

Hands down.

Signed and sealed.

Hell, that shit could be notarized.

Perilous in a way that Dereck should have stayed far away from.

But my brother had always had a sick fascination with villains.

Silas pushed from the wall and came my way.

His stride long yet somehow slowed. Stalking his prey with no covertness to it.

He stopped right in front of me, and I steeled myself as he leaned in close and rumbled in my ear, "I think what you're trying to do is do me in."

Every word was serrated, and the breath I inhaled was sharp. The only thing it did was drag that horribly delicious scent into my aching lungs.

Cherries drenched in whiskey.

I wondered if he'd been hitting the bottle at eight in the morning.

"Do you in? I'm pretty sure it's me who's at the disadvantage."

"I guess it's only fair then." He said it like we were even.

A shock of disbelief puffed out of me. "There's nothing fair about this. You bossing me around and not telling me why you're doing it."

"You haven't come close to seeing me bossy, Brinley."

I scoffed, and a vat of indignation filled my voice. "You tossing me around last night wasn't you being bossy?"

Silas somehow managed to angle closer. So close his chest hit my mug that I had clutched between us.

"Not even close."

Air hefted free. "Is that what you want? Me afraid of you? Well, I'm not."

It was a blatant lie. There was no question this man could tear me to shreds, and he would take great pleasure in doing it.

I didn't want to wonder how many kills he had notched on his belt, but right then, it was the other *notches* I was irresponsibly speculating about.

A fool who was wondering if he'd wandered back to that party last night and snatched up one of the willing women after he'd left me panting and confused.

My underwear soaked and my ego bruised.

I hated him for that, too.

Hated that he wielded this stupid power over me. Power I would be nothing but an idiot to submit to him.

I didn't know if I wanted to flinch or lean into it when he lifted his hand and lightly fluttered his fingertips down the angle of my cheek.

The only thing I knew was my heart careened.

Battering hard and fast.

One brush of his hand, and he shifted everything into overdrive.

His sage eyes deepened a shade darker as they narrowed. "You should be afraid, Brinley. But not of me."

I gulped around the razors in my throat. "Tell me what the hell is going on."

Contemplation filled his gaze, and for a beat, his voice softened in regret. "Can't let you in on that."

Anger surged. Ire and disbelief.

This was such bullshit.

"All these secrets are driving me crazy."

"Some things are better left unknown."

Was he serious?

"At least be man enough to give me something. Am I here to fulfill my brother's debt?"

I couldn't even try to pinpoint exactly what it was that flashed through his expression, there were so many emotions that came all at once.

Repulsion and distaste and deep-seated fury.

And concern, maybe?

Or maybe I was just grasping at straws. Praying my captor wasn't as vile as he appeared to be, the ridiculous urges he'd ignited in me warping my common sense.

Silas's head barely shook, and the words ground from between his lips. "No, Brinley, this isn't about money or debt. You're here so I can protect you from the very fucking stupid decisions your brother has made."

So many accusations were woven into that one sentence that I couldn't make sense of them all.

The clear statement that Silas was making.

That my brother was bad to the core.

My chest tightened, and I heaved, "You're a liar."

He tipped his head in challenge. "Am I?"

I didn't want to believe it. Didn't want to accept what he was implying.

No, I didn't have a whole lot to go on.

But it was enough to know after Silas's actions last night and what he was saying this morning, plus the way Dereck had been acting, that things were much worse than I'd even imagined.

And believe me, my imagination was morbid.

Morbid because I'd seen to the depths of perversion.

I gulped, trying to suppress the way those terrors had carved the deepest scars.

It hurt knowing Dereck had been responsible for those, too.

God, I was so tired of it. Tired of him dragging me around like a rag doll.

Disregarded.

Always his last concern when he'd always been my number one.

My oath to take care of him more than just a fleeting promise. It was my last connection. An act of my love and eternal loyalty.

And there that concern was again, ballooning up in me and pushing out every other thought.

"Is he going to be okay?"

Something passed through Silas's features. Something deep as he lifted his hand again, that time to brush the pad of his thumb along the edge of my mouth.

My stomach tightened, disgusted that I liked it so much.

"Look at you." His voice had gone grumbly. Too soft for my own good. "Confined here without knowing why and the one thing you're worried about is him."

"He's my brother. The only thing I have." I probably shouldn't admit it, but maybe this guy needed to understand what was on the line.

My entire heart.

His nod was slow. "I get it, but I'm going to need you to be fighting for yourself."

"Fighting is about the only thing I know. But it makes it difficult when I don't know who's supposed to be the enemy."

Every unforgiving edge of his body sharpened. "You're safe with me."

"Am I?"

Because nothing had ever felt so perilous as right then.

The quivering of my belly and the shivering of my soul.

He ran his knuckles under my chin. "Want to do a thousand different things to you, Brinley Webber, but hurting you isn't one of them."

The desire that bubbled up inside me was so distinct there was no mistaking it any longer.

And that was probably the most dangerous part of all.

"I thought you told me that I didn't have to pay off my brother's debt with my body?" I snarled it, looking for restraint, for a way to toss back up a wall, knowing I was teetering on a crumbling ledge.

Standing at the edge of a canyon to get a better look. But I wasn't about to be too reckless to realize I was about to fall to my death.

A wicked smile took to his terrifyingly beautiful face. "There's no debt to repay, remember?"

My fight or flight kicked in.

So rather than pummeling him in the chest with my fists like I had half a mind to do, I ducked away, winding myself from his trap, shaking myself off as I stared at him from three feet away.

"Then I guess this ridiculous job is no longer necessary."

He angled back casually. Cruel satisfaction climbed to his face as he tucked his tattooed hands into his pockets.

"Nah. Seems like a fitting way for you to earn your keep. You are kind of a handful."

Swiveling his menacing body around, he strolled back for the door that led to the shop like he hadn't just suggested what he had.

Like he didn't have my traitorous body coiled up in knots. Knots that both terrified and exhilarated me.

An infuriating smirk on his face as he glanced back from over his shoulder. "That's your cue to get back to work."

What. A. Dick.

Turning away, he dragged open the door.

It took everything I had not to hurl my mug at the back of his arrogant head.

Instead, I catapulted a shrieked, "I hate you!" at his back.

He paused to glance at me once more. "That's good, Little Wildfire. Think it would be best if we kept it that way."

12

Silas

Ten Years Old

The only lights in the living room were from the gold flames dancing in the fireplace and the twinkling Christmas lights on the tree.

That's the way Silas's momma liked it.

Cozy.

He felt that way right then. His stomach full of a mug of hot chocolate and marshmallows, his momma singing with her pretty voice as she put the last ornaments on the tree.

He sat on the couch with a big book on his lap, and his sister Elena was on her knees at his side, babbling and pointing at the pictures as he read. "I see Santa! Santa come?"

"Santa's definitely gonna come," he told her, excitement blustering up in his stomach the same way as the snow blustered outside.

He and his sister were both dressed in their pajamas. Elena's a full body pink suit that had feet and zipped all the way from bottom to top, and his had long pants and a long-sleeved shirt with baseballs all over it.

Their baby brother was already asleep in his crib.

"But we gotta be extra good so we don't get on the naughty list."

Silas figured it was his job to help his momma teach her about all the important things in life.

The tiniest giggles rolled out of Elena, her chubby cheeks denting with her dimples that looked like the same ones their momma had. "I not naughty."

Their momma danced over to them with her big smile.

Their momma softly poked Elena's belly. "Are you sure my little Lena-

Lou isn't on the naughty list?"

She shook her head like crazy, her messy brown hair whipping around her face. "I am good, Momma!"

Silas grinned, warmth covering him whole.

"You are such a good girl, aren't you, my angel?" their mother cooed before she turned that cooing on him. "And my big, strong Silas who is turning into such a good man."

She set her palm on his cheek.

That's what he wanted to be.

Good.

Sometimes he got into trouble at school because he talked a lot, but his momma told him that didn't make him bad.

"Mom," he drew out, fighting the red on his cheeks.

"What? I'm just stating the truth, and my baby is getting so big and kind and thoughtful that sometimes it makes my heart ache because I'm so proud of him."

His chest stretched full.

"Because we've got love inside," he told her.

Her laugh was a tinkle. "And he's smart, too."

"Only because you told me it five million times." He shook his head with a roll of his eyes like he was annoyed.

Chuckling, she ran her fingers through his hair. "Just because I always want you to remember. No matter what."

She knelt in front of him and set her hand on his chest. "Because we have to remember to always love with everything we have, even when it scares us."

"I will," he promised.

Her smile was soft. "It's your heart."

Silas noticed that her attention darted to the big clock over the fireplace again. She'd done it the whole night when she didn't think he was watching, the hours ticking by and his dad's plate still sitting on the table.

He'd been home a lot lately, and it was better when he was because then his momma didn't seem so upset, and the worst thing in Silas's life was when his momma got sad.

He could see that sadness clouding at the very edges of her eyes, making tiny wrinkles, even though she forced it back.

"All right, you two. It's time for bed."

"I not tired." Elena always said that and then fell asleep in five seconds flat. But Silas really wasn't tired. He wanted to stay up and keep his momma company so she wasn't alone.

But when she told him to get up and brush his teeth, he did, helping his little sister, too. Telling her to open wide as she stood on her tippy toes on the stool next to him as he helped her brush her tiny teeth.

She gurgled and giggled and grinned, and he helped her wipe her mouth when they finished, then took her hand and led her to her crib that sat in the corner across from his bed.

Their momma swept Elena up, peppered her face with kisses, then tucked her under her covers.

He'd already crawled into his bed when she turned around, her smile so soft as she looked at him. She knelt at his side, ran her hands through his hair the way she always did, murmured, "My big helper. Thank you."

"I can do everything you need, Mom."

"I know you can, but you're supposed to have fun too." It sounded like a tease mixed up with something bad.

He almost rolled his eyes. He always had a lot of fun, and he had a ton of Little League games and practices. Besides, his momma always made everything a game, even if it was work.

"You don't gotta worry, Mom."

"I always worry about you."

"How come?"

She played with his bangs. "Because it's natural to worry about someone when we love them so much."

He guessed he worried about her, too.

Worried so much when a long time later the front door came banging open.

He could almost hear the shift in the mood.

That sadness he was talking about curling through the air.

So quiet but it still blared in his ears.

He heard his momma's voice break. "You promised."

His daddy scoffed. "You gonna start nagging me the second I walk through the door?"

"You're drunk."

The voices swam down the hall from the kitchen.

"Well, aren't you sharp. You want an award?"

"I want a husband who doesn't tell me lies."

Mean laughter floated all around.

Silas's stomach felt sick.

"Guess you picked the wrong guy, then."

"I guess I did." His momma sounded like she was giving up on something important.

A loud crack echoed against the walls, and his momma quietly cried out. Silas was on his feet and racing to the end of the hall, halting in the doorway to the kitchen.

His dad stood over his mom, who was on her knees, holding her face, and the sickness in Silas's stomach crawled up his throat.

His heart pounded so fast. So fast. Like it didn't know how to stay behind his ribs and was going to bust all the way out. The way it did whenever his dad got home and was mad like this.

"You want to talk to me like that again?"

His dad's clothes were dirty. His hair was sticking up and he smelled disgusting. It made Silas want to throw up.

His momma lifted her face to him. It was streaked with tears.

Something hot and ugly curled inside Silas. Like fiery ropes that twisted through his guts and made him want to do bad things.

His momma slowly rose to her feet, her shoulders sagging but her chin tipped up. "I know you spent that money. I saw the bank account. It's gone, isn't it? The deposit and first and last month's rent for the new house?"

His dad scuffed a garbled sound. "Don't you worry about that."

A huff of disappointment shot from her. "Don't worry about it? Worrying about it is all I do. I'm the only one who worries about anything. About whether the kids have food or a roof over their heads. You clearly don't care."

"Always dramatic. Beggin' for a fight."

She choked a strangled sound. "So this is my fault?"

"If you weren't such a greedy bitch, things would be just fine."

"Just go. Leave the way you always do. But this time, don't come back. I'll figure this out on my own." Her voice was too soft, and he was worried his dad wouldn't know she meant it.

But Silas was sure that she did.

He could feel it like a thunderbolt in his chest.

Like one of those storms that sometimes shook the walls and made it feel like the whole house would come tumbling down.

Fear and something else careened through him when his dad suddenly grabbed his momma by the hair. She yelped when he yanked it back. "You really think you're gonna get rid of me? You ain't ever gonna be rid of me. Think it's time you learned that lesson."

He started to drag her by the hair, and all the ugly burned through Silas like he'd burst into a fire. He screeched as he went running toward his dad, his arms outstretched, and he pushed into his side with all his might.

"Let her go!" he screamed, and he hit and banged his fists against his side.

His momma gasped a horrified sound, trying to curl her voice into a demand, but it sounded more like she was begging. "Silas, go back to bed."

But he couldn't move.

He was too mad. He knew he wasn't supposed to hate, but he hated him. He hated him so bad that he wished he was dead.

So he told him.

"I wish you were dead."

His dad laughed as he smacked him across the side of the head, the strike knocking him onto his butt.

He blinked, fighting the tears from the clattering of pain that rocked through him. He wasn't a baby and he was gonna prove it.

"PJ!" his momma shouted, and his dad released the hold he had on her hair, making her stumble forward.

Silas didn't even care that his dad turned and towered over him like a beast, putting all his attention on him.

Just as long as he forgot about his momma.

His dad leaned over him, and Silas wanted to throw up again. Something thick like poison coming off his breath.

"Ah, just like your dad, aren't you? Mean little fucker."

Silas wanted to scream. Or maybe spit in his face. Tell him to take it back.

"I'm not like you."

His dad chuckled a sound that rolled through Silas like he was giving him a punishment. "Look in the mirror, kid. You're me, through and through. My blood is strong. Might as well accept it. You're always gonna be who you are."

He patted Silas on the cheek with a big meaty palm. Hard enough to make his head rattle.

His momma surged to his dad's side, and she tugged at his arm. "Come on, honey, don't worry about him. I was just mad you were late for dinner. Let me make it up to you."

Her whole body shook out of control as she led him away, urging him to sit at the little table in the corner. "Here, let me warm this up for you."

She took the plate and turned around. She fumbled and stared at Silas for one long beat.

And he knew right then he'd never forget the sad look on her face.

13

Silas

I gritted my teeth as I strained at the wrench with all my might, the bolt refusing to give as I worked at the old beat-up Ford that had been brought in for restoration.

"Motherfucking piece of shit." I grumbled it beneath my breath as I fought for a cool that had evaporated like steamy mist. All thanks to one fiery brunette who had proven fatal to my sanity.

The bay doors were rolled open, and sticky, late-afternoon heat saturated the air.

Sweat slicking down my neck and back.

But it was the fire inside that was about to consume me after another illicit interaction with Brinley this morning. Unable to fucking help myself.

Irritation bubbled in my guts as I put all my energy into getting the rusted bolt loose, my insides a stir of mayhem that promised I was one minute from snapping.

I leaned my full weight into it.

The wrench slipped off the bolt.

Of course it did.

And, of course, it sent my knuckles bashing into the undercarriage of the car.

"Ah, fuck!" I shouted as I dropped the wrench. Metal clattered to the cement floor, and I grabbed my wrist and flapped my injured hand all over the place.

Dancing around like an idiot as I swore a hundred curses under my breath.

All of them directed at myself.

It was my fault, asking for this. Inviting more trouble than I already had onto my property.

Forty-eight hours and I'd already allowed myself to get fucked in the head by the woman in the office who had somehow managed to wedge herself right under my skin.

She might as well have taken a blade to it and carved me open wide.

My guts in fuckin' knots and my mind devolving into the indecency I kept threatening her with.

Couldn't believe I let those words fall from my mouth.

All but confessing every depraved way I wanted to tear her apart when she was the last woman on earth I could get dirty with.

Hate sex was my favorite, which I rarely had the privilege of, considering the patch bunnies were all too eager to get on their knees or on top of my dick.

Every single one of them had the unfortunate delusion that one day it was going to land them the coveted spot on the back of my bike.

It was never going to happen, but it didn't stop them from trying.

I didn't fault them for it.

Didn't judge them for it.

We all had our needs and desires.

But I also never led them to believe there would be a different result.

"Someone is awful surly today." Trevan drew it out with that low amusement that told me he thought he had me pegged from where he stood beneath a late-model BMW that was hoisted on a lift.

Problem was, the asshole always did.

"Just fucking peachy," I rumbled, giving another shake to my hand, fisting it once to make sure nothing was broken.

He laughed, pushing on like I'd responded in the affirmative. "Wouldn't have anything to do with the fiery brunette who's been glaring daggers at you through the window the whole day, would it?"

"She's never even crossed my mind."

What bullshit.

She was the only thing I could think about. Wondering exactly how I was supposed to keep her safe when she had hazard stamped all over her.

Far too eager to put her nose where it didn't belong.

Knew she wasn't about to settle for the vague warnings I'd given her, and I figured it was no less than a miracle that she hadn't tried to escape again in the middle of the night.

"Well, she sure crossed mine." Dice rocked his hips. Kid cracking up like he thought the shit was funny.

Dice was a prospect who wasn't older than eighteen. Trevan had found him begging for a dime on the streets and had dragged him back here to give him a chance at becoming one of us.

He was kind of clueless and a whole lot reckless, but he had goodness woven in there somewhere, too.

Still, I was grating low, "You want to die today?" as I strolled for the wall of tools, deciding I was going to have to cut off the bolt. "Already warned you she is off-limits. Looking at her included."

I should take my own damned advice considering every time I glanced her way, a bolt of lightning shot straight to my dick.

Phoenix, my sergeant at arms, stood and wiped his hands on a rag. My enforcer was a wall of muscle. Even in the light of day, covered in gloom and shade. Black hair and eyes that were somehow a fraction darker.

A canvas of tattoos covered his light skin.

A demon who wasn't so much in disguise.

"Told you this whole thing was a mistake," he said, the back of his left hand flashing the tattoo with the crow in full flight, a skull dangling from its talons.

Every patched-in Crow had the same one. A permanent badge of the oath they had made.

At the accusation, unease skimmed the already tense air.

Phoenix voted no on bringing Brinley here. Had warned it was bound to make things uglier than they already were.

Complicate the complex.

Sure after everything went down, we were going to have to bring Dereck to his end and the lines would get skewed.

Protectiveness swilled through my senses. A whirring of foreboding and dry heat.

"She's getting us closer to where we need to be." I rumbled it like a warning.

He scoffed and raked his teeth over his bottom lip. "Seems like she's nothing but a distraction to me."

It was his own warning.

"A distraction she is. Pretty sure every damned jaw dropped to the ground when she came waltzing up to the bonfire last night." Wasn't sure why Trevan found it in himself to stir the pot.

Possession fisted my chest.

Fuck.

I did not like the feeling.

Trevan grinned at me, all teeth. “Mainly, you.”

“Ah, someone finally caught Prez’s eye.” Dice was rocking his hips again, the little punk.

“She’s off-limits, and I fuckin’ mean it. And that extends to every single one of us.” The growl bisected the suffocating air.

“What she is, is collateral.” Phoenix stamped it like a reminder.

I loved the guy, but I wanted to drive a chisel through his eye. Problem was, the fucker would probably like it.

The door to the shop suddenly whipped open.

And there she was in that motherfucking dress.

The lace kissed up high on her toned thighs, all that leg bare, emphasized by those mile-high heels.

Wild curls accentuated the venom on her face.

She crossed her arms over her chest and the only thing the action did was draw attention to her tits.

This riot of a woman standing there glowering at me like I was responsible for the conflict she was in.

“Since you told me I need an escort wherever I go, I need a ride into town to pick up a few things.” Her voice was throaty and sultry and honed to a point meant to cut right through me.

All too eager, Dice let the metal grinder he was holding clatter to the worktop. “At your service, ma’am.”

“Not a fucking chance.” Didn’t mean for it to whip out like a snarl, but there it was.

Trevan chuckled as he turned back to his bike, mumbling, “That’s what I thought.”

A grunt of disapproval rolled out of Phoenix.

“Oh yeah.” Dice rocked his hips again.

Doubted the kid would try it if he knew what I was really about.

“You want your ass permanently kicked from the property, keep it up,” I warned.

The exuberance on his face melted into humiliation. “Sorry, Prez. Just messing around.”

"This shit isn't a joke. Now get back to work. All of you."

I turned my attention to Brinley who looked like maybe she was second-guessing her request with the animosity that clogged the atmosphere.

No question about it when I angled my head in the direction of my bike that rested like a vicious chariot in front of the far bay. "Let's go."

Shock blustered out of Trevan.

Yeah, it blustered out of me, too.

What the fuck was I thinking?

I shot him daggers.

I didn't need any more of his bullshit. Not when I was clearly spiraling.

Brinley huffed out in disbelief and gestured at herself. "Do I look like I'm dressed to ride on a motorcycle?"

Yeah.

She definitely did.

That and my cock.

I angled my head. "You want a ride or not?"

Agitation bristled around her.

A hurricane gathering strength.

Then she basically stomped one of those heels and seethed, "Fine."

I peeled myself out of my coveralls then slung into my cut.

I rarely went out without wearing it. Every asshole in this town needed to know who I was and what I represented, though they never got the full inside of what that meant.

I strode for my bike.

Brinley hesitated in the doorway before she finally came scrambling to catch up.

Far too talented on those heels.

"Where are we going?" I asked, tossing a look over my shoulder.

Shouldn't have since the sight of her nearly made me stumble.

"The store." The roll of her eyes was so exaggerated it was a wonder they didn't get stuck in the back of her head.

"What, you didn't have everything you needed packed in those bags?"

"Since no one had the decency to tell me how long I was going to be here, I wasn't sure exactly what I was going to need." She was all sass and fire.

I casually strolled toward my bike while blood surged through my veins. "Seemed to me you brought enough for five weeks."

She'd already pulled three outfits out of those bags that were enough to bring me to my knees. What more could she need?

"Oh, I forgot my vibrator." It was a blatant taunt, and I whirled on her, getting smacked in the face by that lust-inducing scent.

What I would give to dive in and take a long, gulping drink.

A fucking masochist, I inclined her way, voice a low scrape near her ear. "You say the word, and you don't need one."

She floundered for one beat before she edged back and hitched a saucy grin. "Good idea. That Phoenix guy is pretty cute."

Possession prowled around in my chest.

And did she call Phoenix cute?

Dude looked like the reaper.

"Not gonna happen." The words were nothing but splinters and shards.

She strode forward and brushed her fingers over my chest, murmuring what amounted to a threat. "That's right. Not with anyone."

She kept moving for my bike.

Her ass swayed back and forth in that skirt.

Leaving a trail of fire in her wake.

Air hefted from my lungs, and I forced myself to move, catching up to her and moving to my Harley.

I looked down at the matte-black metal that was basically my throne.

The helm from where I ruled.

I never allowed anyone to ride on it with me, save for the couple of times it'd been necessary for Elena to hop on and, of course, I'd taken Kai out for a spin or two since the kid was obsessed with motorcycles. Never going more than five miles an hour around the property.

Other than that?

Never.

It sent all the wrong messages, and the last thing I needed was that kind of drama in my life.

Trevan warned I was breaking every one of my rules by bringing Brinley here.

I figured what the hell was another.

14

Brinley

My stomach took a tumble down a cliff.

I was playing with fire. I knew I was.

But after the way Silas had me last night and then again this morning? I needed to regain control. Let this smug bastard know that he didn't get to toy with me.

Up my game and in a big way. No question, since after he'd put on that stupid cut, my brain had nearly short-circuited.

Blitzed out by a lightning strike.

Bad boys were so not my thing.

Not at all.

I mean, that was if I ever actually went on a date.

I'd dealt with enough lowlifes thanks to Dereck that I knew precisely who to stay far the hell away from.

And the man who swung onto his motorcycle? He was nothing but a poster child for bad decisions.

Tattooed fingers curled around the handlebars.

Worn boots stretched out as he balanced the calamitous metal, the promise of anarchy and destruction billowing off him in waves.

Macabre faces rose up from Silas's neckline, the tattoos covering his throat, and the sleeves of that Henley were pushed up his forearms, showing off the black feathers that covered his lower arms.

He had the same tattoo on the back of his hand as the rest of the Crows I'd seen.

A crow sitting atop a skull.

Beneath his were the words, *The Verdict is Death.*

I didn't know who that judgement was being delivered to. Him or the poor souls who got in his way.

Rays of sunlight slashed down to emphasize the severe edges of his harsh, unforgiving face.

His brow was knitted in something I couldn't read as he stared at me.

I itched on my feet.

Crap.

Was I really going to do this?

"You gonna stand there all day, or are we going to go? I've got things to do."

"If I'm putting you out, you could just have someone else take me."

Hazel eyes narrowed to darts, and his hands flexed tighter around the handlebars. "I don't want you leaving this property without me."

I huffed. "I already told you I wasn't going to run."

"And I already told you that you're safe with me, and I'm going to make sure of it." Each word was stone.

Still, I was pretty sure I heard genuine worry woven with them.

My stomach fisted.

Did he care? Did he care at all what was going on here?

He hooked the heel of his boot to the kick starter, and he supported himself with the other foot as he rose up high.

Then he slammed it down and pulled back on the throttle.

The engine roared to life as he revved it.

So loud and heavy that I felt a pulse of power ricochet through my body.

A little breath heaved from my lungs.

He looked like mayhem and greed and lethal decadence.

He revved the throttle again while he glared at me.

It was a clear command.

I gulped down the reservations that told me I could do without the trip to the store and forced myself to take action on this perilous endeavor.

I needed to see for myself that I was actually allowed off the property. I needed reassurance this place really wasn't a cell, and I was only there for my own good.

But I was pretty sure nothing *good* could come of this when Silas stretched out his hand so he could help me onto the back of his bike.

The power I felt a moment ago clapped through me like a sonic boom when he took my hand as I swung over.

My skirt rode up high on my thighs, and I did my best to keep from brushing against any part of Silas.

We did not want a repeat of last night.

"You're going to need to get a whole lot closer and hold on tight." He shouted it above the rumbling of his bike.

I hesitated before I scooched forward and wrapped myself around his back.

Flames sparked at every contact point.

Shock gushed out of me on a breath, and I started to scramble back.

His big mitt landing on my upper thigh stopped me in my tracks.

Tattooed fingers sank into my bare flesh to keep me steady or maybe just to keep me from running.

His grip both softened and deepened as he shifted enough so I could see the defined profile of his jaw. His ridiculously plump lips moving with his promise.

"Have you, and I told you I wouldn't let anything happen to you. Need you to stick close, Brinley."

I could barely hear him, yet somehow, I understood every word.

I knew he wasn't only referring to holding on tight while he had me on the back of his bike.

A shuddered exhalation escaped from my lungs, and I surrendered.

Shimmying my butt forward until I was completely plastered against him.

My arms tight around his waist and my chin hooked on his shoulder.

My thighs wrapped around the outside of his hips.

That strange sensation between us whipped so fiercely I could hear it in my ears.

It was a buzz that both incited and calmed.

Every muscle in his body was rigid.

Hard and packed.

And I knew when he kicked the stand and swiveled the bike around and started us in the direction of the gate that I should be terrified.

I guess that I hated myself a little bit that I wasn't.

15

Silas

Late afternoon light spilled from the vast blue sky, blinking down through the leaves of the trees that grew so high against the road that they nearly touched overhead.

Beneath it, it felt like we might be traveling a passageway of peace.

The roar of the engine and the vibration of my Harley rolling through me like comfort.

A familiar caress for a hardened man.

All except for the fact that Brinley's hot body was tucked tight against mine.

The woman had her arms locked around my waist and her shallow breaths were panted on the side of my cheek.

Scent of her all around.

Lulling me into a calm that I hadn't felt in a long, long time.

I knew better than to fall into the false security of it, though.

In my world, you didn't get complacent. When you did, you ended up in a shallow grave somewhere deep in the forest. Nothing to show for your life but the bones pirated by the scavengers that sniffed out your decaying flesh.

Besides, this wasn't a joy ride.

This was business.

Duty.

I had something significant to protect, and I wasn't about to botch this job by getting stupid.

I kept the throttle steady as we rode by the industrial buildings near the property before Deer Creek Lane curved left and the road gave way to the family neighborhoods that hugged each side of the road.

My bike rising and dipping over the humps.

Brinley's arms cinched tighter when we hit the height of each one, and I could only imagine her belly was plunging and soaring.

Both exhilarated and afraid.

I could feel each emotion radiate from her.

This ferocious woman with the faintest traces of vulnerability hidden right below the surface.

I slowed as we came to the T and made the right onto Crimson Creek Blvd, the main drag that cut through the small town.

Crimson Creek wasn't big.

But it was quaint.

Cozy.

Tucked in the deepest part of the forest about two hours from the southern Oregon border.

I still wasn't sure what'd possessed me to return here. This place haunted by ghosts and written in horrors. Memories so thick and chilling, each driven into my brain like an icepick.

Her voice still lingered on the breeze. At one with the trees as they swished overhead.

It's your heart.

It was a simple statement and had seemed so simple then. Before that promise had become defiled by hate.

Most of Crimson Creek was spread out. Roads turning off and winding you down into the different neighborhoods. A cool restaurant, a motel, and some shops on the river.

But there was a congested area right in the middle built up with buildings and streets.

Most of them old but revamped.

It had a bit of an eclectic vibe. A ton of art galleries and quirky shops.

Before we made it to the center of it, I made a right at Crimson Creek's only stoplight that led to the section of town that was less touristy.

A hardware store, some medical and professional offices, a couple of banks, a grocery store.

I slowed even more and slid into the lane to make a left into the drugstore.

My bike chugged low as it carried us through the parking lot and to an empty spot at the front, and I angled the metal around so I could use my feet to back us in.

My attention swept left and right to ensure nothing was amiss. To ensure I wasn't recklessly hauling her out and making her a target.

Apparently, the only thing *amiss* was me.

I wondered if the residents here remembered me. If they knew exactly who we were and what had happened all those years ago. If our family had become gossip and speculation.

A faded headline that had come back to repeat itself. Nothing but a *Dateline* exposé.

Because every damned eye in the parking lot swung toward us.

Taking note of my presence.

Wary and unsure.

Whatever they remembered, the one thing they were certain of was that I'd brought trouble to their town.

Sticky fear slipping down their spines.

Didn't really relish injecting it, but it was necessary.

My position commanded respect, and as much as they might like to think they were condemning me, I could still feel the most fundamental part of them bowing to me.

Killing the engine, I grabbed Brinley's hand.

"Hop off."

"I'm not sure I can walk after that." Her breath was raspy and low and fuck, one sentence out of her mouth could trip a circuit in my brain.

I chuckled low. "That was four miles, not a cross-country trip."

I could almost feel the roll of those harvest eyes. "I'm no biker, Silas Mercer."

"No?" I said it like I hadn't felt her shaking out of time during the whole ride.

"Not a scrap of leather in my closet."

"Well, that is a shame. Guess we'll have to rectify that."

Horrible plan.

What she'd been prancing around in was bad enough.

Stunner on my property doing exactly that.

I couldn't imagine what the sight of her clad in black lace and leather would do to me.

"I'm good, thank you." Nothing but sass, this one. "Besides, I won't be around long enough for that."

Right.

The thought of it should bring relief, not that antsy feeling rising up in me again.

I beat it back, changed the subject as I gritted my teeth. "Keep those legs away from the exhaust pipe. It's hot as fuck, and believe me when I tell you that you don't want that kind of burn."

She nodded in understanding then swung off, that skirt hiked up so high it gave me a peep of satiny white underwear.

Fuck me.

This temptress had to be doing it on purpose.

Maybe she was the demon in this whole scenario.

Pure succubus who'd been sent to distract me from the objective.

Ending the monsters who'd hurt my sister and uncountable others.

My only goal destroying their kind.

There would be no rest until they were extinct, and I still had no idea if her brother was going to come through or end up a casualty of that.

How badly would she hate me then?

I swung off and stood on my feet. "This way."

I gestured for her to go ahead of me.

Another terrible idea but one that was necessary.

I needed to be able to keep an eye in every direction of her.

Watching who was out ahead all while being a writhing, human shield from behind.

A virtual catastrophe since it meant those hips were sashaying back and forth, right in my line of sight.

Hypnotizing.

Fisting my hands, I inhaled a breath and forced my attention up where it belonged.

The double doors swished open as we approached, and the second she was inside, Brinley turned and cut through the store, heading to the cosmetics and self-care at the back.

She went directly for the hair products, scanning before she picked up a bottle to inspect its ingredients.

I peered over her shoulder.

Heat protectant and detangler.

"Are you shitting me?"

She flung half her body around, wide-eyed and innocent. "What?"

"You demanded someone take you into town so you could buy hair detangler?"

On all things holy, she might be worse than Elena. At least she hadn't beelined to the glitter section.

I figured she'd started her period or some shit, and we were on a tampon run.

"Have you seen my hair?" She said it like she was suffering a tragedy. "These curls are impossible."

She flicked one over her shoulder as evidence.

She was what was impossible.

But she didn't know.

Had no real clue that every time she stepped out of the shelter of the club, she was taking a risk.

Yeah, I warned her.

But unless you were in the thick of it?

Unless you'd seen it firsthand?

You couldn't quite fully grasp it.

Didn't mean I wasn't irritated as fuck.

"You heard of this little thing called delivery?"

Brinley huffed. "I haven't had my detangler for two mornings in a row, and I'm afraid if I go one more day, the only option left will be to cut it off."

On second thought, this was an emergency.

I had to stop myself from reaching and twining my finger around one of the wild, wayward locks.

Those curls were honestly a hot mess.

A riot of brown woven with those reds and golds.

A thousand times worse—or better, however you wanted to look at it—since she'd been on the back of my bike.

"Guess that won't do, now, will it?" My voice went low and gruff.

Severity arced between us, and something shifted in her gaze.

Confusion and flickers of need.

Did she feel it?

The attraction that buzzed across my flesh?

Funny how you always wanted the things you couldn't have.

"My mom's hair was just like this," she suddenly whispered, vulnerability slipping into the words. "I've been growing it for years."

That fierce veil dropped for a beat, and it allowed a river of sorrow to flood through.

Fuck.

I knew that kind of pain.

Knew that she was talking about her mother in the past tense.

Knew the gutting sense of missing something that you were never going to get back.

My throat felt too fucking thick, and I had no clue what was happening to me. “I bet she was beautiful.”

Brinley’s face pinched in an old sort of agony. “There was no one like her.”

“There was no one like my mother, either.” Couldn’t believe that I gave her that when I never mentioned my mother to anyone but my family, and even with them, the words were brutal.

Dispatched like tragedy and grief.

A moment was held between us. Something like understanding and camaraderie passing in the bare, shivery space.

Then she blinked frantically and turned away, rushed as she grabbed two more bottles.

“I think I’m ready.” It was a rasp of her own tragedy and grief.

I stepped back, giving her space because I was in dire need of it, too.

Had no clue what it was about her.

Why this stranger, this woman who was under my charge and my protection, had me twisted up the way she did.

She was so off-limits, touching her would be no less than a religious desecration.

The oath I made to Dereck a badge of my loyalty.

Not that the twat deserved it, but Brinley did.

But it was the oath made to my family and crew that mattered.

She was collateral.

Resource and reserve.

A down payment that her piece of shit brother would come through.

And going there would be treachery.

She moved into line, and her attention snagged on the snacks set up near the register.

Her interest piqued. All cute as her face lit up as she spied what she was looking for.

Gummy worms.

She grabbed a bag.

"Those are disgusting." I grunted it under my breath.

"You're disgusting," she shot back.

Touché.

She wasn't wrong.

Then she grabbed three packages of Peanut M&Ms and a bag of barbecue potato chips like she was stockpiling for the apocalypse.

"What? Lulu's food isn't good enough for you?"

Her glance at me was exaggerated. "Like I'm ever going to be able to show my face in front of Lulu or Elena again. I can only imagine what they thought when I went running out the door last night."

Apparently, I wasn't a quick learner because I couldn't help but edge closer.

Mouth not quite hitting the shell of her ear as I murmured, "Never be ashamed of fighting, Brinley. In this world, we do what we need to in order to survive. You were just fighting the wrong person."

Energy blasted from her.

That fine line between hate and desire tossing her into uncertainty.

Unfortunately, right then, that hate didn't seem so severe.

I hesitated then added, "Elena was worried about you this morning."

"How you have people who are so sweet related to you, I have no idea." There was no fire behind it. It almost sounded like a tease.

I grunted as Elena and Kai's faces traipsed through my mind.

Barbs of loyalty speared through my consciousness.

"At the end of it all, my family is the only thing that matters."

"The club?" she asked, her head tilting to the side.

"Sure, they're a part of that. My family. But my blood? They're the reason I'm in this life. So I can take care of them."

Fuck.

She didn't even ask me, and I was dishing dirt like I was a TMZ reporter.

So fuckin' reckless.

Brinley peered up at me. Devotion fully exposed. "Taking care of my family is the most important thing to me, too."

A tiny, self-conscious laugh rippled from her. "Though Dereck is the only one I've got left."

Unease twisted my stomach. My abhorrence of her brother clashing with the clear care she held for him.

I hated it for her.

That she got tangled in his bad decisions and she didn't even know, but I suppose that was often the way life went down. You were trapped before you realized you'd become a pawn.

We both startled when the cashier called, "Next," and my head popped up to find the customer in front of us scrambling to grab their bags, scuddling out the door like a spooked cat.

Casting wary glances behind them as they raced to safety.

No doubt, thinking I was gonna rob the place.

Brinley stepped up to the cashier.

Piled her things onto the counter.

The guy working behind it scanned the items while he clocked me from the corner of his eye.

Likely thinking it, too.

I wondered if every single one of them could taste it. The violence that dribbled from my flesh, or if it was just the exterior on which they cast their verdict.

Didn't matter either way. They had a right to be leery. They should be.

The guy rang up Brinley's items, and she went for something in her pocket, but I was already pulling out a hundred from my wallet and leaning around her to set it onto the counter.

My chest brushed her back as I did.

She exhaled a shaky sound. Then that irritation rose again. "I can pay for my own things."

"Not on my watch, you can't."

She huffed out in disbelief, though I could feel some amusement rimming it as she took her bag while the cashier counted out the change.

She glanced back at me. "Do you think buying me sweets is going to make me like you more?"

I reached around her again, accepting the change, my lips just brushing her jaw. "A man can only try, can't he?"

Was I flirting with this girl? I edged back, trying to shake whatever insane reaction she conjured in me, and started to usher her out.

A hand at the small of her back.

That touch I convinced myself was only due to the fact that I needed to stand guard over her.

Keep close.

It had nothing to do with itching to let my hands roam over every lush curve of her body.

Her ass swayed just below my hand. A stirring of dark vibrancy with each brush.

By the time we stepped outside, her breaths had gone shallow, and she inhaled something deep like the fresh air might squash the heat.

All while I forced myself to take in our surroundings.

Glittery light embossed the late afternoon air. The sun beginning its descent toward the verdant canopy of trees.

Birds flitted from branch to branch.

But in it, there wasn't a modicum of peace.

There might as well have been a viper curling up my leg with the way I sensed it.

The wickedness that rolled over me.

I was in front of Brinley in a flash, gun pulled from the holster I had hidden at my back, though I kept it low and close in hopes the few people out in the lot wouldn't notice.

A disjointed breath shot out of Brinley, and I gritted, "Stay behind me."

For the first time since I met her, she didn't have a cunning retort flying off her tongue.

She just curled one of those hands into the bottom of my cut like some kind of horrified promise.

It was the barest relief.

The smallest solace in knowing that maybe she did get that I was here to protect her and had no intention of keeping her trapped.

My attention scanned the few cars and faces.

It didn't take long to land on the figure on the far-right side of the lot up close to the road.

His bottom half was concealed where he stood near the hood of his car on the opposite side of us.

There wasn't really anything about him that should set me off.

To the normal eye, he looked like some harmless forty-year-old man.

Jeans and a casual button-down.

Dull brown hair.

Probably swinging in to grab something for his wife on his way home from the office.

But my gut told me that was all wrong.

I could almost see the waves of depravity rolling off him.

Hellsmoke and ire.

Was sure of it when his eyes met mine from over the top of his hood.

They were full of a challenge.

Maybe a warning.

That and the fact that he didn't cower when he saw me standing there clearly prepared to go on a murder spree.

Instead, he punted what amounted to a mocking grin.

Fucker ignorant enough to think he might have the upper hand.

Teeth gritted and my heart thundering, I curled my finger around the trigger when he moved.

Prepared for things to get messy.

Though the asshole just kept smirking that smug smile as he edged back to his door and slipped into the driver's seat, started the engine, and pulled from the lot.

Had half a mind to go chasing him down as the tail of his black sedan disappeared down the road.

But Brinley was gasping and shaking, and a fury I shouldn't feel suddenly scorched through my veins.

Singeing everything in its path.

Warily, I tucked my gun back into its holster, not wanting to draw more attention than we already had, gaze still flashing from side to side.

"Who was that?" Brinley wheezed.

Panic laced her shuddery voice.

Her fear saturating the air.

That enraged me, too.

"We need to get back to the compound," I gritted rather than answering.

Should have known she wasn't going to back down with that non-response.

Woman refusing to budge as I tried to tow her toward my bike.

The spikes of her heels might as well have become one with the concrete.

"I asked you a question."

I swiveled around, ducking in close to her face.

Harvest eyes went wide with surprise.

"That was exactly the reason you need to be secure behind the compound's walls until we get this sorted." The words were nothing but shards.

"Was he after me?" There she was again. Indignation pouring out of her demand.

"Don't know."

She scoffed out a sound of disbelief and frustration, her expression pinching in the same dissatisfaction.

"So, you're saying it could have been nothing?" She lowered her voice even further, her brows scrunching together with the clear accusation. "You pulled a gun on someone, and it could have been a regular ol' citizen of Crimson Creek?"

Exasperation flurried in my chest. "I said I didn't know, but I'm not willing to take the chance. Now get on my bike."

"I want to know what's happening, Silas." She might have lifted a defiant chin, but the quivering in it told me everything I needed to know.

She was terrified and trying to tap it behind all that ferocity.

"You want me to toss you over my shoulder and carry you to my bike, you just keep right on standing there," I warned.

"You wouldn't dare," she seethed.

"Try me." I growled it near her face, then I turned and started for my bike, never dropping my guard, even though it likely appeared that I didn't give two fucks.

The problem was all the fucks I was actually giving.

Way I felt like I might splinter apart as I watched for anything that might be a threat.

That wildfire at my back.

Her flames ten seconds from consuming.

She finally started to clamber up behind me.

Thank fuck.

Because I hadn't been bullshitting when I warned her I was going to toss her over my shoulder.

It was pretty much the only thing I wanted to do.

I wanted to pick her up and wrap myself around her and protect her from the monsters that loomed.

I knew they were there.

Lurking in the periphery.

I couldn't stomach it, and it was becoming clear that I'd gotten lost in the wilderness.

Five thousand miles off course.

All rationale lost.

Because the second I made it to my bike, I was turning and sweeping her into my arms.

I got a flash of that wild, surprised gaze, her lips parted in confoundment and incredulity, before I jostled her around and planted her sweet ass on the seat of my bike.

Then I swung on behind her.

Pinning her back to my chest as I reached for the handlebars.

Shock gusted from her. "What are you doing?"

My mouth dropped to her ear.

Easy since I was fully wrapped around her, my body a steel blanket covering her whole.

Heat blasted from her skin, and my guts twisted into those knots that I was pretty sure were going to squeeze the life out of me.

"Told you I wasn't going to let anything happen to you," I grumbled low. "And I'll do it by any means necessary. You want to get stubborn with me? Get rebellious? Then that means you're going to find me putting you back in your place."

Yeah, I was being a dick.

But she didn't know who she was contending with.

I hooked my heel on the kick starter and struck it.

The engine roared as I pulled back on the throttle.

Power vibrated through the metal.

"Hold onto the handlebars."

It had to be the eighth wonder of the world that she actually listened.

Adrenaline pounding, I eased us down through the lot, dread glomming up my insides as I turned my head left and right, searching for deviants hiding within the trees.

Not sure if we were being ambushed or if someone was trying to send a message.

My guts tangled in a fist.

If we'd been compromised…

I gritted my teeth and took to the street.

Going faster than I had on our way here but still trying to keep our speed controlled.

Painful when I wanted to go flying back to the compound.

The position with Brinley in front of me should have been awkward.

But no.

Leave it to her to mold perfectly into my body.

Taking my shape as if she were meant to do it.

Trembles rolled through her as I took a curve hard then barely stopped at the red light to make the left onto Crimson Creek Blvd.

The second we were on it, I pulled back on the throttle, ticking the tempo upward.

Motor roaring in our ears and the trees blurring by on the sides. Flashes of greens and browns blearing into an abstract painting.

I came up to a car in front of us, and I whipped around the left to pass, then glided back into the lane before I hit the brakes about a quarter of a mile up to make the left onto Deer Springs Lane.

The back tire skidded a bit, and I put my boot out and let it skim the pavement to keep us steady, then the bike righted as I pulled back on the throttle again.

I could feel Brinley's heart bash against her ribs.

There were always kids out playing in this area, so I forced our pace slower through the neighborhood.

I never ceased in my vigilance. Eyes darting in every direction, and every few moments, I threw a peek over my shoulder to make sure there weren't any beasts coming up on our rear.

Brinley might as well have been wearing armor with the way I was covering her. A shroud who would take a thousand bullets to protect.

I'd always known my death would likely be precipitated by trying to protect an innocent.

But there was something about this that felt different.

The lengths I would go.

Similar to what I felt when Elena had been held hostage by Kent Ellison. The outright desperation to get her to safety.

Similar to when I'd found out what was happening with Kai, and I knew I had to get him out of that place.

But this was skewed and contorted.

Like new DNA had formed inside me.

Completely foreign. Changing me in a way that I could no longer recognize myself.

We finally came up on the big curve on the right, the sporadic industrial buildings blipping by before we were taking the left through the open gate and onto my property.

The shop doors had been rolled down and locked tight for the night.

I kept moving, my Harley jostling over the gravel drive as I rounded the shop on the left.

Soon, under the cover of trees, the clubhouse came into view.

An army of motorcycles were gathered out front.

We had Church tonight, which meant every member would be in attendance.

I weaved around to the backside of the large building and came to a quick stop near the exterior staircase.

Brinley heaved strained breaths as she shoved me off.

Pushing me out of her way as she somehow managed to get off the bike with me still on it.

Climbing up onto the seat, her ass in my face, before she hopped off the side.

She didn't even slow to look back at me. The grocery bag filled with all her treats dangled at her side as she stormed up the steps.

I was right behind her, pulling out my phone and texting Brody as I went.

Me: *Bring the truck to the backside of the clubhouse. STAT.*

My heavy boots clomped against the wood as I climbed.

They might as well have been a base drum with the way it drove the intensity higher.

Brinley's obstinate spirit thrashed in the twilight.

Sparks of energy that glinted and flared.

Wild curls flying around her.

Fuck.

She was a force to contend with.

I caught up as she got to the landing, and I went to reach around her to input the code when she smacked my hand.

"I can do it myself, so you can just leave me alone," she hissed.

"Obviously you can do it, but you aren't staying here."

She whipped around. The gold in her eyes flashed.

As bright as an emergency flare.

"What? Did the heat get too much for you?" she snarled. "Was that guy too big of a contender? Are you scared of the trouble I bring, and you're kicking me out?"

Each word was a barb.

She might have been irate, but I could see what was written below the spite.

Hurt.

Like she thought I was just going to abandon her.

Leave her to fend for herself.

Had the sinking sense that was the way it had always been for her, and I was pretty sure her reaction had nothing to do with her dislike of me but was a survival instinct.

With her back to the door, I reached around her and punched in the code.

"No, you're coming to my house," I grated.

"What?" she screeched, her expression morphing in a beat.

The door blipped and gave, and I basically picked her up and set her aside so I could get through.

She was a firestorm licking at my heels.

The beat of music from below throbbed through the baseboards. A distant thud of mayhem when I was standing in the middle of the pandemonium.

Wasn't sure which of us was causing it.

Brinley or me, with her panting these jagged breaths at my backside, and me charging the few steps down the hall and into her room.

I threw open the door. Wood clattered against the interior wall, and I strode for where I knew her suitcases were stuffed under the bed.

"Are you freaking kidding me?" It was a gust of dubiety from where she stood aghast in the doorway. "I'm not staying at your house, Silas."

"It's not up for debate," I growled, pulling out the suitcases and tossing them onto the bed.

This would be a whole lot easier if she hadn't packed her entire damned closet.

"Oh, but it is, *King*." She spat the last, and I could feel her cross her arms over her chest.

A torrent of anger surged around her fear.

"I'm so tired of people thinking that they can just toss me around, keep me in the dark and tell me they're doing it for my safety, like that is enough for me to blindly go along with your bullshit. First my brother telling me where I was going, what I *had* to do, and now you. *I count.*"

Her tone was pure venom until the last two words croaked out of her.

I turned to witness her clutching both hands over her chest, and fuck, she might as well have driven a blade directly into my mangled heart.

Because I was moving.

Stalking her way.

Little did she know that she was the one with all the power.

The one who was sucking me in like she was her own orbit.

That thing about her that made her so dangerous to me glinting around her like a halo.

"You want to know what's going on, Brinley? You want to know that your brother is involved with vile, horrible people? You want to know what it felt like when they had my sister?"

Horror unhinged her jaw. "Elena?"

The fire in her drained, likely doused as the torment I felt when Elena had been Kent Ellison's prisoner gushed out of me like a ruptured dam.

Her throat bobbed as she swallowed heavily. Those eyes ablaze as they searched mine.

I pushed on, grating through the fury and hate. "You want to know that she still sometimes wakes up screaming at night? Terrified? Do you want to know how I refuse to let that happen to you?"

I was so close to her that I could feel the fine hairs lift on her arms. So close that the chills that raced across her flesh became mine.

My spirit lurched forward without my permission.

"You *count* more than you fucking know." It wheezed out. Stakes that struck into the ground like they were the one thing that could keep both of us steady.

Yeah. I was a fool to admit it. I shouldn't let on the way she had me on uneven ground.

Our noses brushed, and I was inundated with her scent.

Almonds and apples and cream.

Leave it to Brinley Webber to have the ability to turn my voice into a forlorn plea. "Please…just let me take care of you."

Confusion knitted her brow, though I could feel her softening. "I'm not weak or helpless, Silas."

"No. You're not, are you?" I breathed in what she exhaled. "But this is my job, Brinley. Taking care of people is the only thing I have. The only power I've got."

I figured if I was already giving this much away, I might as well fully lay it out.

"Need you not to fight me on this. Because in my home? That's where I protect the people I care about most."

And I wasn't about to let her out of my sight.

16

Brinley

Night seeped into the blue and pink sky, deepening it in ashen hues. But I guess the silence had seeped even deeper as we traveled farther into the property toward Silas's house.

Winding through the thicket of trees set in a dusky haze.

I sat in the front passenger seat of a pickup truck, my bags stowed in the back.

I hadn't been able to process what was happening in the time that Silas had stuffed all my belongings into my bags and had me packed.

While I'd stood there dazed.

Trying to make sense of what had happened today.

What should have been an easy trip into town to buy hair supplies and snacks had turned terrifying.

I could admit that.

When Silas had drawn that gun and told me to stay behind him, I'd been petrified.

Then I was pissed. Just freaking pissed that I was in this position. That I'd lost all control. That I was just supposed to concede to every command that Silas Mercer made since no one had done me the courtesy of telling me anything.

Then Silas had pretty much let on too much, and I'd been stunned silent while he'd flown like a maniac through my things.

Of course, the jerk had paused an extra beat while he'd tossed in my panties.

I hadn't even been able to hurl any snark at him for doing it because I'd been too caught up trying to wrap my head around what he'd implied.

Elena had been kidnapped by whoever these guys were who were apparently after me?

And...and Dereck was involved?

A toil of sickness toppled over my guts.

I attempted to blink through the nausea. To stub the visions down because I couldn't accept it.

My brother wouldn't do something so atrocious.

Would he?

Silas glanced over at me as he maneuvered the wheel from the driver's seat.

I really hated to look at him after what he said.

"Need you not to fight me on this. Because in my home? That's where I protect the people I care about most."

I knew rationally that statement didn't apply to me.

It couldn't.

He didn't even know me, and I didn't know him, and the few things I did, I sure as hell didn't like.

Well, except I kind of wasn't hating the sensation that licked up my arm and crawled to my cheeks when he stared across at me.

It felt fluttery and warm and nice.

God knew it shouldn't.

Not when that dastardly gaze was fully intrusive and breaching all boundaries of human decency and respect for privacy.

He might as well have been flaying off layers of my flesh to see what was hidden underneath.

But still, nice.

I knew it made me an outright lunatic for even thinking it, but God, I was so tired of fighting all these battles on my own.

Who could blame me that it gave me a tick of comfort to maybe have someone else in my corner?

Probably every logical person out there, but guess what, there was no logic here.

Not when I was in this mess. Treading dark, dangerous waters that were bound to drag me to their depths.

Demons laughing raucously as they pinned me down so I would drown.

I just hadn't quite put my finger on whether Silas was one of them or not.

I finally looked his way.

I knew better, and I had to barricade myself against the outright severity that blasted back.

It was truly unfair that he was so obscenely hot.

My stomach that had been in knots of dread flipped with something it shouldn't.

He arched a sharp brow. "You good?"

An incredulous laugh arrowed off my tongue. "Am I good? I just saw you pull a gun on a man who may or may not have been out to hurt me, then you fly back here like a bat out of hell and throw all my clothes into my bags, demanding that I stay at your house, and you want to know if I'm *good*?"

"Yeah." He offered it with a shrug.

Like it was just another simple hiccup in a regular day as he wound down the gravel lane through the dense thicket of trees.

I blew out a flustered sigh. "No, Silas, I'm not *good*."

Hazel eyes found me again.

A flash of fire and an assuaging of fear.

Maybe I really was in shock because the second he looked at me it was tempered.

"I'm going to see to it that you are."

"Is that a promise?" I tried to make it come out a taunt, but it was shaky.

Clearly, I was losing my touch.

A big, tattooed hand landed on my thigh, and he gave it a squeeze.

I nearly flew out of my skin.

"Yeah, Brinley. It is."

Boundaries.

Boundaries.

Boundaries.

I silently chanted it like I could erect them between us.

But did I want them?

Did I want him to stop touching me?

I shouldn't feel like this—especially with a man like him—but part of me liked it.

Wanted it.

The buzz and the burn that lit every time he came into my space.

Apparently, I was becoming as reckless as Dereck.

The woods finally broke open to a two-story house nestled in the trees.

A second, smaller one sat to the left, the two buildings separated by a few hundred yards.

The larger one was painted powder blue with white trim.

A quaint porch sat out front, decorated with four rocking chairs and a mishmash of potted flowers.

It looked like a granny's old house rather than a biker's lair.

But I supposed that lair was hidden at the end of the hall I'd gone running from last night.

Mind-jarring since that felt like a lifetime ago.

Going from the terror that Silas was set on butchering me into pieces to him bringing me to his house after he'd implied that in some way I was important to him.

As a job, I was sure.

I bet I was nothing more than a bargaining chip.

Insurance promising Dereck would fulfill whatever oath he had made to Silas.

I wouldn't be of any value to him if I were dead, and I wasn't ignorant enough not to know something else was definitely going on here.

Silas pulled the truck to a stop up near the front and one second later, the screen door blew open.

Elena came barreling out with little Kai in her arms.

Both their faces gleamed with smiles and excitement.

That crater inside my chest that normally only accommodated my dread and worry over my brother expanded in a fit.

Pressing at the vacant places.

An older woman shuffled out behind them. Short and plump with those same sage eyes threaded with blues and browns shining with something that looked a whole lot like mischief.

"And here's the welcome committee." Silas muttered it with affectionate irritation.

I chewed on my bottom lip. "I'm not so sure this is a good idea."

I mean, was I really supposed to stay here? With them?

"I thought we already discussed this?"

If he meant growling at me exactly what was going to happen, then I guess he could consider it a *discussion*.

At least he'd said 'please'.

"I still don't know what I'm doing here."

"Letting me take care of you, that's what."

I huffed in frustration, then Silas pushed toward me, leaning over the console. It made my heart take off at a sprint.

"You let go a little, and you just might find that you like it."

It was packed with innuendo, and I nearly choked on the lust that suddenly addled the air.

"It's not going to happen, *King*." How I managed to make it sound like I was disgusted by the prospect, I'd never know.

Silas chuckled a dark sound as he pulled away, taking my breath with him.

Every intimidating inch of him was written in arrogance.

The tattoos on his arms and neck seemed to crawl with the same crude appeal as his eyes watched me with right then.

"You sure about that?" The words scratched across me. Silken sandpaper.

Crappity crap, this man was dangerous.

And not in that 'he'll pull a gun in broad daylight and raze his enemies' sort of way.

It was in a 'Brinley could make very terrible, heart-decimating mistakes with him' kind of way.

I could already feel my ribs creaking under the pressure.

I needed to remember the first was just as valid. If Dereck didn't come through with whatever Silas wanted, I'd likely end up with a blade to my throat.

"Very," I tossed out like I'd rather eat a piece of gum stuck to my shoe and threw open my door, needing to get the hell out of the confined space I was sharing with him before I combusted.

By the time my heels hit the ground, Elena's voice was carrying on the wind, except she'd lowered it like some kind of bro who was prepping for a rager.

"Brinley in the house!"

An impetuous giggle erupted. Reckless beyond measure.

Apparently, when my life was at stake, I had no problem laughing. I guess sometimes the only way people survived was laughing their way through the treacherous things.

"*Bwinwey* house!" Kai waved a fist in the air, clearly trying to mimic his aunt.

That hole inside me throbbed all over again with the way he said my name.

Precious.

I tried to fight against it. Not to let my ribs expand to make extra room, but I figured that type of fight would prove fruitless.

I glanced over the hood of the truck so I could gauge Silas's reaction to seeing his son after a long day.

I'd be a liar if I said I hadn't really liked the sight of it yesterday.

Proof that he might not be all cold blood and killer.

His expression morphed.

Adoration and loyalty poured out, mixed with something that looked a whole lot like terror.

Nothing cold about it, but there was still something grim congealing the surface.

Clearing my throat, I threw my arms up like I was arriving to the party and I hadn't been dragged over here against my quickly faltering will. "That's right, Brinley in the house!"

What I was doing, I didn't know, but I'd always been a fake it till you make it kind of girl.

No use in changing that now.

"Party time, baby!" Elena shouted from the porch. "We already have dinner ready, then we can watch a movie or listen to music or shop online, or whatever you want to do. I'm about to lose my mind from boredom."

It sounded exactly like my kind of rager.

Silas shut his door. "Brinley isn't here for you to play house with, Elena. And wasn't the party enough for you last night?"

"Letting me out of my cage for two hours is hardly going to break the deep-seated boredom that has sunk into my bones."

Her droll tone promised she was on the verge of death.

Silas rolled his eyes, so casual as he strolled toward the back of his truck. "Dramatic much?"

"Bossy much?" she hollered back.

Another reckless giggle shot from me as I moved for the bed to grab my overnight bag since Silas seemed insistent on carrying my suitcases.

"What are you laughing about?" he rumbled under his breath.

"Your sister is both shy and a badass. Don't blame me for loving it."

He sighed, his voice contained so only I could hear. "The shy part is because of me. Keeping her in that cage."

"Because you're overprotective?"

I winced when I said it, quick to remember what he'd just told me.

These faceless bad guys I hadn't known existed had abducted Elena.

My spirit clenched as old visions threatened to flash, my soul sick with the idea that Elena might have been tormented the same way.

"No such thing as overprotective, Brinley." Hate ground from his mouth. "Not when you know the type of fiends that are walking this world. I've been trying to protect her since she was a little girl. Turns out, I'm not always so good at it."

"I don't believe that."

Was that true?

"Doesn't matter what you think."

It was a sudden dismissal of the subject as Silas dropped the tailgate, grabbed the duffel and slung the strap over his shoulder, then pulled out the suitcases, taking one in each hand.

"I am capable of carrying something."

"Unnecessary," was all he gave before he went clomping his way around the truck and toward the porch steps.

His strides were so long I thought I'd have to employ my old high school track skills in order to catch up.

I probably needed to rethink my shoe choices while I was here, but honestly, that was not going to happen.

The additional height gave me an extra boost of confidence.

When I towered over someone, it made me feel like they couldn't touch me.

Grievously, Silas still had me by three inches when I had them on.

I marched five feet behind him, head held high while my nerves zipped and zinged.

Firing in every direction.

Both apprehensive and kind of excited by the prospect of being here.

Elena's gaze sparked beneath the dingy light that bled down from the sconces on either side of the door.

"Why does this feel like I have a long-lost friend moving in?" She sounded a little teary-eyed when she said it.

Part of me thought I should rip off the Band-Aid and remind her that I wouldn't be staying here for that long, but something about it just felt mean.

So instead I tittered like a fool again, trying to inject some lightness into my voice as I climbed up the steps behind Silas, doing my best to avoid looking at the man's perfect ass. "Are you trying to convince me this is some sort of mountain vacation?"

"What do you mean? Any time with me is a vacation," she said, deadpan.

A chuckle rolled, then my gaze was gliding to the older woman standing to the left as she muttered, "My, my, my. It's about time you brought her around. I've been dying to get a look at this one. I'm Meems."

"Isn't she so pretty, Meems? I told you." Elena effused it at me with that gleam in her eye.

I wasn't exactly shy, but I was still ducking my head under their scrutiny.

"Oh, more than pretty, I'd say."

Silas grunted. "You two mind your manners. Brinley is our guest."

Their manners? Had the man met himself?

And guest?

Meems tsked with an arch of a drawn-in brow. "Says my ruffian. I'm surprised you haven't run her off yet."

Oh, I tried to run, all right.

And *her ruffian*?

She broadcast it like he was a cute little boy tussling in the yard rather than king of whatever organized crime racket he was heading.

He didn't answer her, only dropped in to peck a kiss to her cheek.

Who was this guy?

Then he swiveled, doing the same to Kai and making the toddler squeal, then he planted one at Elena's temple.

Never setting those bags down when he did.

This was no time for my heart to go pitter-patter.

Without saying anything else, Silas maneuvered around to open the screen door, kicking it wide so he could stride in.

Elena gave me a purely anticipatory look, her shoulders hiking to her ears and her teeth clamping down on her bottom lip to contain her thrill.

I really shouldn't feel any of it, but apparently, it was catching.

"Welcome to our home, Brinley," Meems encouraged in a soft, raspy voice. "I hope you feel safe and supported here. Loved."

"We got *wove*." Kai drawled it in his little baby babble.

A surprised, gooey breath left me.

I hadn't had love inside my house in a long, long time.

My spirit moaned. Missing it, only a faint inkling of recollection of what that'd been like.

"You need something, you come to me." Meems gave me a pointed look. "Woman to woman. These hoodlums running around here don't know their hands from their asses."

It was all a tease, and I choked over her words.

"Thank you," I managed around the rocks in my throat.

"If you all could stop badgering Brinley so I can show her to her room, that'd be great." Exasperation colored Silas's voice as he hollered from inside.

"Badgering? Hardly." Elena scoffed as she pulled back open the screen door.

It appeared maybe he wasn't *king* around here.

Then she turned to me with a grin. "After you."

"Thank you," I mumbled again, then I ducked through the door.

Yep.

Just as expected.

This place screamed Grandmacore.

Floral furniture and lace doilies and some truly uncomfortably-posed pictures on the walls.

And there it was—yarn and knitting sticks sitting on the arm of the couch.

"This way," Silas grunted as he marched up the stairs.

I hurried up behind him.

He hit the landing, gestured with his chin to the only door on the left. "Meems's room."

He turned right down the long hall that seemed to run the full length of the house on the upper floor.

He ticked his head toward the first door on the right. "Brody's room, my younger brother who is trying to patch in. For lack of better words, he's a goddamned nuisance, so just ignore him."

I gulped.

"Noted."

"Opposite him is an extra bathroom."

He kept moving. "At the very end of the hall is Elena's room."

He stopped at the two doors that sat between Brody's at the front of the hall and Elena's at the end.

"Kai's room is here on the left. Mine is this one on the right." He pushed open that door and strode in with my bags.

Blood careened through my veins.

I dashed to catch up to him, stalling out in the doorway because I was knocked senseless by the overpowering scent of him.

His presence multiplied.

I worried if I stepped through his door, I would be the one who was bathing in whiskey and cherries.

A giant bed sat against the right wall.

Drenched in black.

Shocker.

A dresser was opposite it, and there was a couch directly across from the door, tucked under a picturesque window that overlooked the front of the house.

He dumped my suitcases on the floor and jutted his chin at the door to the left side of his bed. "Bathroom and closet are through there. Use what you need."

"Oh, I don't want to take your room from you, Silas. I can sleep on the couch."

Look at me, being charitable.

He unwound the duffel's strap from his shoulder and let it drop to the massive bed.

Then he was stealing his way back to me.

Stalking, really.

That energy flashed, that tumbly thing in my stomach that I absolutely couldn't feel hurtling me straight over a cliff.

He stopped an inch away, and I inhaled a frantic breath as he leaned close to my ear.

Only that breath was gone when he muttered, "Oh, you're not taking my room, Brinley. I'll be right here beside you. Not about to let you out of my sight."

17

Brinley

"So, then Trevan literally picks Pyke up and tosses him out the club's door. He must have slid fifty feet with his face in the dirt."

"Those prospects are nothing but trouble." I could hear Meems tsk it as Elena jabbered to her.

Her voice carrying out into the living room from the kitchen as I crept down the stairs.

A delicious scent wafted out with it, making my mouth water.

Silas had said he needed to take care of some club business, and he'd be right back. To make myself at home, as if I didn't feel the most out of place as I ever had.

So much for him refusing to let me out of his sight. I figured the sleeping situation was just him trying to torment me, thinking I was going to stay in the same room as him.

That man had another thing coming.

I inched forward, my ear inclined.

"And you know Trevan isn't about to stand for backtalk, especially on his birthday." Elena's inflection was pure cheek.

Meems laughed a chortling, wry sound. "Pyke was messing with the wrong man, that's for sure. You'd think he'd have a better head on him if he wants to be a Crow. He has no sense."

"Maybe Trevan will just have to knock it into him." That time it was giggles and awe.

I crept closer, keeping my footsteps quiet. Not because I wanted to eavesdrop but because I was worried I was interrupting.

I peered through the opening.

Meems, which apparently meant 'Grandma' in Mercer, was on the other side of a long counter that segmented a small dining room from the cooking area.

Kai was on this side of it, on the floor playing with blocks with his blue blanket beneath him, babbling to himself.

"And I bet you'd fight for a front-row seat." Meems cast an appraising glance over at Elena who was pulling a salad from the fridge. "Though I imagine you'd fight for a front-row seat to anything that man does."

If Silas thought his Crows' talons were crimson, he should have seen Elena's face.

She hurried to set the salad onto the counter next to the fridge, then ducked back inside, rummaging around like she was looking for the meaning of life.

When she edged back out with a bottle of ketchup, she hiked an innocent shoulder. "Trevan is one of my closest friends. Of course I pay attention to what he does."

"Simple as that?" Speculation infiltrated Meems's tone.

"As simple as that." Elena said it far too bright.

My own speculation sparked.

Holy camole. Did Elena have a crush on that beast of a biker? And why didn't I feel so up in arms about it as when I thought she was married to Silas?

"If you say so," Meems hummed, then Elena grabbed the salad bowl in one arm, ketchup in the other, and turned to carry it to the table.

Her face broke out in a giant smile when she noticed me standing there.

"Brinley, you made it. I was about to shout for you to get your cute little butt down here. I thought you might be hiding from us."

Kai's head popped up. "*Bwinwey*!"

I cleared the thickness from my throat. "Nope. No hiding here. I'm actually starving."

It'd been a long fricking day, and I hadn't gotten the chance to devour my snacks the way I'd planned to.

I wondered if Elena had any idea of what had gone down while we'd been in town. If Silas shared those things with her. Or maybe to them, those types of incidents were wholly routine.

"It's a good thing because I made enough to feed an army," Meems said.

Elena set the salad and ketchup on the table. "I told you Meems and Lulu were in straight competition to outdo each other with the food. Not that you're going to find me complaining."

"I no *compwaining*." Kai climbed to his feet, using his hands to push himself up before he came toddling in my direction.

Light, golden brown waves framing his adorable face.

The kid's grin was ridiculous. So melty and sweet.

He came right up to me and lifted his arms over his head.

I looked around for help.

Elena chuckled. "That one is not shy."

So, I, uh, was supposed to pick him up?

Apparently, since he popped up on his toes and made little grabby hands in the air.

All right then.

I swept him up.

It turned out, holding him was even meltier.

The child was heavier than he looked, and there was something about his weight in my arms that made me pull him closer.

Kai laughed and smacked at my cheeks. "You eat, *Bwinwey*?"

"Yep. I'm going to eat." The words were croaked and soggy.

Emotion lifting. Like flowers pushing up from a grave.

Or maybe it was just that the day had been long and strenuous.

That and I was still basically a prisoner in this place, no matter how welcoming they were being.

Trapped due to circumstances not my own.

But I was feeling less and less like I wanted to escape.

Maybe this was exactly how Stockholm Syndrome was formed.

Delicious food and adorable babies.

Definitely not grumbly, bossy bikers.

Nuh-uh, no sir, no way.

"What can I do to help?" I peeped, shoving off the wistfulness.

"Just make yourself whatever you want to drink." Meems ticked her gray bun toward the refrigerator. "There's tea and soda. Wine and beer. Silas is going to be back with milk from the club's stock in just a minute if that's more your flavor."

She waddled around the counter with a large casserole dish.

It smelled as near to heaven as I could imagine.

Kai grabbed me by both cheeks and pushed in so close that our noses touched. His eyes were wide and emphatic. "*Appwe juiwse.*"

"Is that what you want to drink? Apple juice?" I basically cooed it. Apparently, I had *sucker* tattooed across my forehead because I was pretty sure I'd give this kid anything he wanted.

He nodded vehemently.

I looked to Elena for approval before my foolish gaze went hunting around the room like I was looking for clues.

Where was his mom, anyway?

"He can have half a cup," she said before she looked at Kai. "So you don't get your belly full of juice too fast."

"Kai's *bewwy* is *hungee*." He grabbed his chubby belly and squeezed it.

I choked over a laugh.

No doubt, this child had every person on the property wrapped around his finger.

I carried him into the kitchen, hooked on my hip, then pulled the bottle of apple juice from the fridge.

"Glasses are in the cabinet on the left," Elena told me.

I found a plastic one with a lid for Kai, grabbed a glass one for me, filled his half full, then decided to do the same with mine.

"We match." Kai bobbed his head, peeking up at me for affirmation.

My chest pulsed and spasmed. "I guess we do, don't we?"

"Can you hold that?" I asked, handing him his cup.

"I am big."

Sufficient answer, and I was mumbling, "You're a big boy, aren't you?" as I carried him into the little dining area.

I set my glass on the table, then went for his highchair. He suddenly scrambled up in my hold, wrapping one arm around my neck as he plastered himself against me.

"I sit *wit Bwinwey*."

"Oh, no," Elena cried. "Did you pick another new favorite?" She smacked her palm over her chest dramatically, acting like he'd delivered a mortal wound.

It must have been a familiar game because Kai giggled like mad before he hid his face in my neck. "No, *Wena*."

She came dancing over, poking little love jabs into his sides. "Yes, Lena, yes, Lena!"

He howled with laughter, and I found myself swinging him away from her, getting swept up in their game.

Elena gasped. "Not you, too."

I whirled all the way around, my hand on the back of Kai's head like I was protecting him. "Well, I need someone to like me around here."

It was purely playful and far too easy. Clearly, I should be working harder at keeping up my guard.

"Oh, I think it's clear a few people around here like you plenty fine." Meems claimed it just as the front door clattered open.

The sound of Silas tromping through the living room echoed through the space before he appeared in the archway.

A gallon of milk dangled from one hand, and he was still dressed in his Henley and cut, hair messier than normal from the frantic ride we had taken.

The man was so viciously beautiful it was unreal.

Dark and delicious and looking at me in a way that sent my pulse crashing through my woefully deprived body.

"And there he is," Meems muttered under her breath.

Mmm…yeah…no.

None of us should be thinking such blasphemies.

Kai's head popped up, and he held his cup toward Silas. "I got *juiwse*."

It was the only thing that seemed to tear Silas's attention from me, and all that fierce ferocity dissolved as he turned his attention to Kai. "What, you got juice? And here I went all the way over to the club to get you milk."

Silas lifted it like proof.

Kai giggled more, again snuggling up against me, his little dimples peeking out on both cheeks. "I get *mewk* when I go nigh-night."

"Ah, well, I guess it's a good thing I went, then."

Silas strode through, brushing my upper arm as he angled into the kitchen.

Chills lifted at the connection point, and the breath was heaving out of me without my permission.

Meems peeked my way.

So sly.

Whatever she was thinking was clearly a terrible, bad idea.

It wasn't going to happen, but I guess no one could blame me for having a reaction.

I could only imagine he had it on ninety-nine percent of the population.

That commanding aura that made you look twice. In interest or fear, it didn't really matter.

The man held the force of a blackened sun.

He placed the milk into the refrigerator and pulled out a beer.

"Before you go opening that, grab those potatoes from the stove and bring them to the table," Meems instructed.

"Yes, ma'am."

Clearly, she was not one of the ninety-nine percent.

Then she gestured at a chair. "Brinley, take a seat, love, and get yourself something to eat."

I sat down with Kai still in my arms since it was apparent there was no chance he was letting go.

I didn't mind so much.

Elena settled on the chair to my left.

Silas sauntered over with a big pot of mashed potatoes. He leaned over the side of me, really freaking close as he set them in the middle.

Was that on purpose?

Did he keep *barely* touching me to drive me out of my mind?

He took the seat to my right.

Meems settled next to Elena, leaving one chair open.

"Where is that scoundrel of a brother of yours?" Meems asked. Not so much with judgement but affection.

"Passed him on my way back," Silas rumbled as he took a big heaping pile of mashed potatoes, but rather than filling his plate, he splatted it onto mine. "He was finishing up a task for me, then he'll be here."

That was when the door banged open again, and a few seconds later, a guy came striding through the archway like a whirlwind that tore through and left everything in shambles.

All smirks and grins and cockiness.

As handsome as Silas but in an entirely different way.

Brown hair and similar eyes, though his were a couple of shades darker. Where Silas was covered in ink, only a few individual tattoos dotted his arms.

I would say he had to be at least ten years younger than Silas.

All sharp edges, too, but where Silas's gleamed like razors, his were softened with a cool easiness that made him appear a whole lot more harmless than he undoubtedly was.

When he saw me sitting at the table, he came to a jolting standstill, surprise jetting through his distinct features, before his mouth broke out in a smug grin. “Ah, so this is the one who’s causing such an uproar around here.”

His gaze raked over me before it drifted to his brother. “Gotta admit, the details are becoming a whole lot clearer on why.”

18

Brinley

"Are you sure you have everything you need?" Elena poked her head through the doorway of Silas's bedroom.

I looked up at her from where I rested against the black leather headboard with a leg curled under me. I'd been staring at my stupid phone for the last twenty minutes, praying for it to vibrate with a message after I'd sent yet another text to Dereck.

Another he hadn't bothered to respond to.

Only a dull lamp glowed from the nightstand, but I could still see well enough to know Elena had gotten ready for bed.

Her deep brown hair was twisted up at the top of her head in a messy knot, and she'd changed into a cute black pajama set. A long-sleeved top with matching shorts.

Her smile was sly and soft. I wasn't sure how she pulled it off.

"I think I'm good, thank you."

"Are you sure? You ask for it, and I'll see that it's delivered." She wagged her brows, clearly tempting me into some sort of gluttony.

I let go of a light giggle. "If you're trying to offer me more food, then you are looking at the wrong woman. I pretty much had to crawl up the stairs, I'm so full."

That meal of creamy pesto chicken and mashed potatoes had tasted even better than the heaven it'd smelled like.

I was stuffed.

And confused.

Trying to orient myself to yet another change I didn't fully comprehend.

It was nearing ten, and by some grand mercy, Silas had remained downstairs when I'd come up to get ready for bed, the confounding man sending Meems off as well and promising to clean up the kitchen.

Who freaking knew bikers were so damned helpful.

Kai was long asleep, zonking out halfway through dinner.

Silas had pushed from his chair and swept him off my lap to take him to his room.

A loaded awareness had rippled around us as he'd pulled the sleeping baby into his massive arms, freezing to stare down at me for two elongated beats before he'd turned, snatched his blanket from the floor, and carried him upstairs.

I was still trying to process that one.

The child constantly trying to give me bites of his food.

His sweet laugh.

His even sweeter face.

The way it made me feel when he called me *Bwinwey.* Something that felt like it might both heal and hurt. But maybe I needed it. Maybe I needed to feel something I hadn't ever allowed myself to feel.

Elena's smile widened. "Meems has that way about her."

"You mean making you feel like you've been a part of her family your entire life when you just met her?"

Elena giggled and shuffled deeper into the room. "Give her five minutes, and you're hers forever. That is, if she likes you."

"Did I pass the test?" I tried to play it as a quip. I really didn't care one way or the other.

At least that was what I was telling myself.

But if I was being honest, I felt like I'd witnessed something special during dinner.

Something unexpected.

Something that I'd been missing for a long, long time. The vacancy inside me was so aged by now, the wounds thickened by scars and calluses, that it felt almost foreign.

Watching them chat and tease and play through the entire meal. Like they were this normal family when you could not mistake that there was a seedy underbelly.

Those men weren't just wearing those cuts because they liked motorcycles.

I'd *heard* it last night. I had heard the brutish malevolence that had seeped through that rugged door that I imagined protected some sort of dungeon on the other side.

No, I might not have been able to make out the full story, but I knew that story was there.

Locked up like my old diary.

I just had to find a way to crack it.

I'd do best not to get cozy. Blinded by false comfort.

If I wanted to find out if Dereck and I were really going to come out of this thing unscathed, I needed to be proactive.

Not get lulled into a food coma.

Every minute my brother didn't text me back, the more unsettled I became, and as much as Silas kept trying to weasel his way into my senses, making me trust him, I'd be an idiot to fall for it.

"Um, it's fair to say you are *in*." Elena's voice was all conspiratorial exuberance as she settled onto the edge of the bed facing me. Amusement tugged at the edges of her lips. "Don't be surprised if she doesn't let you leave."

Yeah, that's what I was afraid of, though I was pretty sure it wasn't Meems who was my jailer.

"I have to admit, it is pretty nice to have another woman around here," she added. "You can see that we are a bit outnumbered."

She shrugged her shoulder. "And okay, since you're twisting my arm about it, I should also probably admit that I really like you and I think you fit in pretty great with my family."

There was absolutely no arm twisting to it, and the cute, shy, confident thing she did was digging its way through the rocks that clogged my spirit in suspicion.

How was she so unbelievably *nice* when she was surrounded by all these bikers? There was no missing the overbearing masculinity that sucked the oxygen from that clubhouse.

Maybe she was a secret spy that Silas used to infiltrate hearts and minds, and this was all an act.

Then the gold flecks in her hazel eyes were shimmering with moisture, and she glanced away for a beat before she looked back at me with a pinch of pink on her cheeks.

"Honestly, it can get kind of lonely around here. It's like I'm surrounded by all these people whose main job is to make sure that my every need is met, all while I feel like I'm missing so much."

She choked a little sound as her chin trembled. "It's weird having so many people around you and still feeling lonely, you know?"

With her vulnerability, my stomach twisted.

Okay, I sucked.

Was a deplorable, disgusting human being.

Even having an errant derogatory thought about this angel.

Because I was slammed with the torrent of pain that gushed out of her. So deep and heavy it couldn't be feigned.

I tossed my phone on the bed and sat forward so I could take her hand. I squeezed it hard. "I totally get that, Elena."

The second I touched her, a tear streaked from the corner of her eye.

The thing popped out so fast I thought she must have been holding it in for so long she was about to bust from the pressure.

With her free hand, she frantically swatted it away.

"I feel like such a jerk." The quieted words crawled out of her like a dirty secret. "Feeling that way. Like I don't appreciate every single thing my brother has done for me. Everything he's sacrificed for me. For this whole family. But God, sometimes I feel like I'm a bird trapped in a cage."

"You don't need to feel guilty for recognizing that you're lacking something." The words clawed from my mouth, low in emphasis. "Even if you want more, it doesn't mean you don't appreciate what you have."

Emotion wrestled through her features.

Shame and guilt.

Hope and belief.

She leaned closer, desperation cracking on the plea. "But then when I try to go after it, I end up making really terrible mistakes that put my entire family in danger."

My chest squeezed to the point of breaking.

I was sure what she was referring to.

I hesitated, warred, worried I was about to invade a space that she didn't want me to enter.

My tongue swept over my suddenly dry lips before I decided to take a chance. "Silas told me that something bad happened to you. That you were kidnapped."

Surprise jolted her back an inch, a hot gust of air leaving her lungs before another tear slipped free.

"It was my fault."

I released her hand so I could set my palm on her cheek.

"It's not your fault."

It didn't matter the circumstances or what she thought she might have done. Whoever they were, those sick sadists were responsible.

I could feel it, as sharp as a blade driven into my soul.

It was the kind of hurt that went bone deep and never could be eradicated or erased.

Elena paused before she whispered, "I wasn't kidnapped. I was duped. I thought this guy who found me on TikTok really liked me, and I was so lonely, I fell for it. Willingly snuck out to meet him, having no idea who he was until he shoved me into the trunk of a car then locked me in a dirty room."

"Oh God." The horrified response punched out of me.

How awful. How terrifying.

I sat for a moment in her torment, trying to figure out if I should press for details or if she just needed quiet, undeterred support.

"Did they…" I finally managed, though I couldn't bring myself to fully say it.

She sniffled and gave a tiny shake of her head, clearly knowing what I was implying. "They beat me up. Taunted me. Laughed at me for being so stupid. But they didn't do that."

I couldn't help it.

Relief heaved out of me.

What had happened to her was appalling, but…

That time she was squeezing my hand. "I'm still afraid sometimes, but I'm okay. I promise. I just feel ignorant and embarrassed. Devastated that I put my brother and the rest of the guys in that position."

My nod was frantic. "I think it can be really easy to put ourselves in risky situations when we're trying to find ourselves."

Then my voice turned urgent. "Most of the time, those risks are worth it. They are life-changing in the best ways. But it is also true that sometimes those risks backfire in such a catastrophic way that we think it will ruin us."

Another tear slipped down her cheek, her eyes bright in the dim light of Silas's room.

I edged forward another inch and set my other hand on her opposite cheek.

Framing her face.

"But without those risks, we aren't going anywhere. We aren't discovering what we really need or who we are meant to be."

I angled my head with significance. "Don't you dare blame yourself for taking one of those risks. The blame lies on those who take advantage of you taking those risks."

I really hoped I wasn't giving horrible advice. God knew all the advice I attempted to beat into Dereck's brain hadn't worked.

But it wasn't like he'd actually listened.

Hell, most of the time he'd run out and done the opposite.

Elena nodded frantically as if she were trying to draw the faith I had in her deep down into her spirit before she suddenly threw herself at me.

For a second I was shocked, then I gave into the embrace.

Let her hug me so zealously I thought she might squeeze the life out of me.

Eager gratefulness rolled out with her words. "I won't, Brinley. I promise, I won't."

I hugged her back with as much fervor. "Just be careful doing it, okay?"

I tacked on the last because I couldn't stand the thought that she might run out and do something reckless.

Because it wasn't about taking unnecessary risks. It was about taking the ones that meant something.

I guess maybe it was time I started to listen to my own advice.

"How will I know?" she asked. Desperation poured out of her.

I curled my arms even tighter and whispered, "Your heart will know."

She nodded in my hold, both of us hugging the crap out of each other before we broke apart when we heard a throat clearing from the doorway.

Caught off guard, Elena whipped around.

I guess I wasn't so shocked to find Silas there, leaning against the jamb like the crooked king that he was, a paper bag dangling from a big hand.

Maybe somewhere deep inside myself, I'd felt him coming.

A shockwave that blasted my senses.

"What the hell, Silas?" Elena hissed. "That was mean, sneaking up on us like that."

The arch of his brow nearly touched his hairline. "You're in my room."

Elena sent him a scowl. "Well, this is where Brinley is."

I guess it was probably that second he noticed that she'd been crying, because his bare irritation flipped.

In a beat, his features were gripped by dread and worry.

An instant ball of simmering rage. His eyes darted to me.

Demanding to know what was going on.

If I was the one who was responsible for it.

Without a doubt, if he disliked me before, he'd hate me if I'd harmed her in some way.

I'd end up on the chopping block out back. I imagined there had to be some sort of torture chamber on the property.

You'll have to find a better reason to off me, buddy.

Because I really wanted to wrap Elena up and protect her, too.

Crap, I guess Silas Mercer and I had something in common, after all.

Well, that and the scorching energy that blistered through the air whenever he got within a hundred-mile radius of me. I doubted something so powerful could be one-sided.

And okay, I really liked his little boy.

And Meems was pretty freaking great, too. I might have even developed a little soft spot for Brody.

Silas crossed his tattooed arms over his chest.

The man all sinewy strength and concern.

The expression he wore right then made it exponentially worse.

Being in his space and thinking he might be something different than the treacherous biker who'd wrangled my brother into a position he hadn't intended.

"What happened?" Silas glanced between us with the demand.

Clearly, he thought whatever it was, he had to fix it.

Elena huffed as she slipped off the bed. "Am I not allowed to have a private conversation with my best friend?"

Best friend?

I didn't think I'd ever been promoted so fast.

"Best friend?" Silas repeated exactly what I was thinking.

Elena lifted her arms out to the sides, palms up, a razzing accusation twisting across her face as she gestured around the room. "Do you see any other friends around here?"

"Wow, and here I thought I was special." It came out playful.

She looked back at me with a grin. "Oh, believe me, Brinley, you are special. Even if every one of those girls who hang out at the club decided they actually liked me, you'd still be my number one."

I gave her a teasing scowl. "I'd better be."

"You can count on it."

Then she reached out, the sudden playfulness we'd been tossing around caught up in something intense.

That grief and hope shining bright in her eyes.

I wavered for a beat before I took her offered hand. She swung it around. "Sometimes our hearts just know."

Emotion raced my throat. Thick and sticky.

Then she gave my hand a little tug. "Why don't you come stay in my room so you don't have to be by this bossy brute?"

Silas pushed from the wall. "Not going to happen."

Elena pouted. "Why not?"

He strolled in like a snarly viper. "Go to bed, Elena. We already talked about this."

"Ugh, fine." She turned back and wrapped her arms around me again. Hard.

Her mouth at my ear.

"Thank you."

"Anytime and always," I whispered.

Big, big promises I shouldn't make.

She nodded again before she pulled away, pranced over to her brother, and lifted up on her tippy toes to peck a kiss to his cheek.

Then she was out the door with it clicking shut behind her.

"Huh. I guess she wasn't so mad, was she?" I mused quietly.

Silas didn't answer. Instead, he stalked over, and he dropped the bag he was carrying to the floor on his way. A wraith slipping through the dancing shadows of his room.

Severity fired from him in a way I hadn't seen it do before.

He leaned in close, and he planted both hands on the bed on either side of me.

I might as well have been taking a big gulp of whiskey-soaked cherries.

I needed to be careful, or I'd get drunk on that scent.

"What was going on in here?" he demanded in that growly, surly voice.

I blinked. Stunned for a moment by his proximity before I found my footing.

"Other than you being overbearing and bossy, as usual?" I sent him as much sass as I could muster.

Irritation rolled out of him. "With Elena."

"We were just talking."

"About what?"

Cripes, was this man nosey.

"That was bestie talk." I lifted my chin like I was going to prove some kind of point.

Show him that Elena deserved at least a modicum of privacy.

Some grace and belief.

"I'm not playing, Brinley. You think I didn't notice she was crying?"

I got his worry, but I didn't think he comprehended that he was sheltering her in a way that left no room for growth.

"News for you, *King*," I snarked, hoping he'd get the clue. "You don't need to know every little move your sister makes."

Some emotion I couldn't quite pinpoint crashed out of him. Banged at the walls and battered against my chest.

"You don't get it, do you? How dangerous these people are?"

The intensity that flash-fired from him blasted me back. My head hit the pillow, and a gush of air ripped from my lungs as Silas crawled over the top of me.

He pinned me without any part of us even touching.

"How could I when I have no idea who you're talking about?" The words creaked.

It was a wonder I could even release them.

The normal green in his eyes glowed red. I should have been terrified by the sheer hatred they contained.

But I guess I was wholly distracted by the way it seemed muddled by fear.

By fierce loyalty.

A secreted part of him that I couldn't discern.

Silas seemed to war.

Hesitating as he hovered high, his body pitching back and forth with the ruthless energy he radiated.

"There are monsters who roam this world, Brinley. People who are so wicked, who have no good in them, that I can't consider them human. And it's my job to protect the vulnerable from them."

No doubt, he was talking about Elena.

The rest of his family.

His club.

Maybe even me.

But I was sure there was something about the statement that went so much deeper than that. Sure that he was leaving out something extraordinarily significant.

A pivotal piece of him that throbbed and begged from the shadows.

My heart jackhammered at my ribs.

So fast and quick it seemed to gather up the oxygen in the air and swirl it into a vortex.

A vortex that threatened to suck us both down into an endless pit.

Because I thought I could see it.

Silas's own confusion. Both of us in disbelief at whatever this feeling was that whipped through the room.

Or maybe it was a normal encounter for the Crimson Crows' president.

A nightly occurrence where he ended up perched over unassuming women laid out in his bed, and I was the only one here who felt like a hurricane was twenty seconds from hitting land.

Except, I was pretty sure I could hear his heart hammering, too.

Heat blistering from his flesh and flickering over mine like a fiery caress.

His reservations were so distinct I could taste them coating my lips.

One more thing about this man that could get me drunk if I wasn't careful.

But I wasn't feeling so careful right then.

This was straight recklessness.

Like maybe I was taking my own risk by not shoving him off.

Silas Mercer was the last man I should want.

But God, there was something about him that drew me in. Like maybe he was inviting me to crawl through his fractures and cracks.

The most terrifying part was I thought maybe he could crawl through mine.

"What does that mean?" I finally managed, going back to what he'd said.

I wanted to know how and why it was his duty to protect the vulnerable when I was pretty sure he was little less than the grim reaper blazing through town.

I needed to understand *this*.

"Why am I really here?" Here I was, the vulnerable one, all but pleading it.

In contemplation, Silas's tongue stroked over his plush bottom lip.

Gaze burning a hole right through the middle of me.

A battle of trepidation and conviction crawling through his expression before he gritted, "Because I have a deal with your brother. I protect you as long as he delivers what I want."

Okay, so I was completely at fault that I was crushed by his answer.

Gutted, really.

I set myself up for it, after all. Letting him swindle his way under my skin.

Bringing me here.

To his family.

Promising me he would protect me like it actually meant something to him.

Anger boiled to the top, snuffing out the hurt.

"So I *am* the means to an end? A bartering chip? A job?" Plainly, it wasn't completely snuffed out considering my stupid, unreliable voice cracked on *job*.

I rammed my hands against his chest to shove him off.

A frenzy took me over as I fought to get away.

I had to get out of this place before he completely wrecked me.

I was already showing severe signs of terminal spinelessness.

Only he grabbed me by the wrists, and he pinned them to the pillow on either side of my head.

A scream rolled my throat, but I subdued it since it wasn't his family's fault that this guy was a complete bastard, and instead, it left me on a hushed shriek.

"You might as well let me go," I spat between clenched teeth, thrashing below him. "I'm as good as dead, anyway, aren't I? I'll make it easy on you so once you're done with my brother, you don't have to make the effort to drag me off your property to throw me to the wolves."

I expected defamation and slander considering he was finally being halfway honest with me.

Not for him to angle in closer, fury whipping off his tongue. "Never. I will never fucking let them get to you."

It ripped all the reproach and blame I wanted to hurl at him right out of my lungs, and I sucked in a shattered breath when he dropped his forehead to mine.

I was pretty sure it was pain bleeding out of him as he murmured, "Wildfire."

Shocked, I froze, all the fight I was trying to dispatch arrested by the promise he made.

I was fully aware I should try to reassemble that fight.

This time, for wholly different reasons. Or unholy, really.

Because heat was suddenly saturating me through.

Need barreling through my senses, zinging through my veins, and throbbing between my thighs.

Our breaths were shallow.

Haggard and desperate.

If he thought I was a wildfire, Silas Mercer was an atomic bomb.

A detonation right in the middle of me.

He rocked his forehead against mine, and our noses brushed, our lips not quite making contact.

It still might have been the most intimate caress I'd ever experienced.

And I wasn't afraid.

I wasn't afraid.

He kept my hands pinned to the mattress, and I realized I was completely submitted to his will.

He wasn't quite moving, but I could still feel him everywhere.

I had the very unfortunate response of spreading my legs.

A silent plea for the bulge I could feel in his jeans to make contact with my pulsing, aching center.

I had no idea that desire could be as flammable as this. Without a question, with one simple brush, I would go up in flames.

I'd be consumed.

Incinerated.

Ash.

"*King.*" I whispered it at his lips. A shivery, shaky plea.

What the crap? Had I just called him that without it being a sneer?

Apparently, I had since Silas sucked in the sharpest breath, and every muscle in his wicked body tensed.

A moment held.

Then he was flying off me and was standing two feet from the end of the bed before I could even process that he moved.

A foreboding silhouette in the middle of his room.

Demon or angel, I couldn't tell.

He let his gaze travel over my panting, quivering form.

That hot, unrelenting gaze had me pressing my thighs together, searching for friction.

I couldn't fathom that I was doing it. That this man had the power to evoke this reaction in me.

Pare me down to nothing but a needy mess in the middle of his bed.

Then one second later, the intensity shifted, and he reached down and grabbed the bag that he had left on the floor.

Disoriented, I slowly pushed up to sitting.

His expression that only moments ago had brimmed with possession twisted into a cruel smirk. "Guess it's a good thing I brought you a present."

He dumped the bag upside down and poured the contents onto the foot of the bed.

My jaw basically hit the floor.

You could call it affronted disbelief.

It was a giant vibrator, my taunt from earlier coming back to bite me in the ass.

He leaned forward like a beast who could so easily strike me dead.

But I saw it…I saw the way he fisted the comforter as if it was the only thing keeping him from crawling back to me.

"I have a meeting and will be gone for at least two hours. Think it would be prudent if you use that while I'm gone. It's new and sterilized and ready."

How freaking *thoughtful* of him.

Then Silas turned on his heel and strode for the door.

"You really are an asshole, aren't you?" I snarled as I snatched the vibrator. I had every intention of beaning him in the back of the arrogant head with it.

"Yup," he grunted as he took hold of the doorknob.

I thought he was going to stride right out, only he paused and looked back.

Cruel viciousness poured out.

The *King* showing off who was in command.

Only I swore it was covering something else.

"You should remember it." He delivered the last with a punch before the door snapped shut behind him.

Fury and frustration bubbled under the surface of my skin. A horrible concoction of hate and need.

Livid, I almost threw the vibrator at the closed door, mourning the fact that I hadn't taken the shot while I had the chance.

But it wouldn't do any good.

Silas was long gone.

Besides, I supposed there were far better uses for it, and I refused to think of it as a win for the jerk when I pushed off the bed, stormed to the bathroom, and locked the door behind me.

Refused to think of him altogether as I shimmied out of my sleep pants and underwear and set one foot on the edge of the bathtub.

My free hand reached out to the wall for support.

Lucky for Silas, I had plenty of experience in getting myself off.

Unlucky for me, it was his vicious face I saw when I shoved it inside me.

19

Silas

"Motherfucker."

What the fuck did I think I was doing?

I barely slowed to nab my cut from the back of the chair before I stumbled out of the house like I'd been trapped in noxious fumes and was in desperate need of a fresh breath of air.

Ripping at my hair and blundering around like a fool.

How could this woman affect me this way when no one else had ever held the power?

I had enough on my fucking shoulders to last fifteen lifetimes.

Enough baggage that nothing else would fit.

Enough vileness running through my contaminated veins that I knew never to get close.

I would only desolate and destroy.

Not to mention she was so off-limits, it wasn't funny.

Even looking at her was a crime against my own law, and I'd never taken myself as one of those pathetic hypocrites who meted rules but didn't follow them himself.

I'd already drilled it into my entire crew. Had warned them of the dire consequences of turning their attention toward our special *guest*.

Because Brinley was right.

She *was* a job.

A means to an end.

Because of her, we had the chance to rid the earth of that entire group of scum.

She had one thing wrong, though.

I'd never let anyone touch her. I would protect her to my last breath.

It was an oath I made.

A promise.

And that meant something to me.

What I hadn't been prepared for was everything that she turned out to be.

That smart mouth almost as keen as her sharp-witted mind that I could see working at a thousand miles a minute.

Way those eyes toiled and whirled with that unrelenting curiosity, pilfering through the bare facts I'd given her like she still might be capable of coming up with the sum.

But it was the tender, genuine care underneath it that made her stand out.

What made her shine in some kind of rarely seen brilliance.

The way she worried about her brother was a true testament to her character.

I mean, fuck, I'd nearly been blown back into the wall when I'd come into the kitchen and found her holding Kai. Expression verging between bewildered and awed, and her heart gushing out onto the floor.

I'd had to shove down the awe myself.

Then I'd had to sit through that torturous meal with her.

Had to sit and watch her hold that baby. Had to watch her soft smiles and listen to her sweet coos.

Things had gotten insurmountably worse with her groaning and moaning over Meems's delicious dinner.

Woman humming around her fork every time she placed it into her pouty, sex-pot mouth.

It was a very unfortunate side effect that my cock had pulsed to the point of agony with each little mewl.

It was so bad I had to hide my raging erection under the table for an entire goddamn hour.

But when I found her taking care of my sister in my room? I guess that was when I cracked.

When something had fractured. Watching Brinley lift that fiery chin like she was protecting Elena from me. Protecting her secrets and her needs and whatever confessions Elena had given her.

Brinley fully invested in it in a beat. Barely knowing my sister and still so clearly willing to put up a fight for her.

I should have been pissed by the insubordination. People didn't talk to me that way and get away with it.

But was I mad?

Nah.

I was fucking floored.

Maybe even inspired.

All while I was wholly terrified of letting that control go. Terrified that I might miss something again, which was why I basically kept my sister under lock and key.

Admittedly, snatching that new vibrator from the stash of condoms and toys that were kept in a storage cabinet in the club might have been a bad idea.

But after that dinner?

I thought she might have been hurting as badly as me.

See.

I wasn't a total sadist.

Only a masochist, apparently.

Because I looked back at the house as I fumbled out into the night.

Gaze climbing for the second floor and landing on my bedroom window.

The curtains were drawn, so I couldn't see anything but the glow from a dim light coming from within.

But it was the silhouette of the lush, gorgeous woman that appeared in the smaller bathroom window that captured me like I'd stepped directly into a grizzly trap.

Teeth clamping and breaking skin.

It was just a faint outline. Nothing that I could make out other than knowing she was there.

It shouldn't matter. Shouldn't count for anything. But there was something about seeing her that way that made me feel like I might be standing on something profound.

If I were looking for logic, I'd accept she was likely in there ranting and raving about what a jerk I was, which honestly was fully warranted since I'd acted like a total prick on my way out.

Trying to toss up more walls because I couldn't allow her the power to get to me.

Couldn't allow her to continue creeping under my skin and winding her way into the places I never allowed anyone to go.

It had been my only option. I had to force some barriers back between us before we collided in a catastrophic way.

I needed to make her hate me.

Fear me.

Realize I was nothing but a dead end because I was pretty sure she and I had been a couple of haphazard seconds from rushing full steam ahead.

But since this woman seemed to steal all logic, I was standing there under the cover of trees wondering if it'd gone the opposite way.

Imagining she was making full use of my gift.

Imagining she was making the same desirous sounds she'd been making at the dinner table.

Would it be my name slipping out of that smart mouth as she came?

Fuck me. This wasn't helping, and I had business to attend to.

You know, just the *insignificant* task of keeping her and Elena alive.

This whole family alive.

Both my blood and the men who were under my charge.

I scrubbed my palms over my face, hoping it would eradicate the visions from my mind, and I sucked a clearing breath into my lungs before I turned on my heel and forced myself to move.

Night gathered thick, and stars glinted through the breaks in the trees as I trudged across the property in the direction of the clubhouse.

In the distance, I could hear the hoots and hollers of my crew. The dull thud of heavy music echoed through the forest. The drumbeat chanting its depravity that they were undoubtedly losing themselves in.

With each step that I took, the volume increased. It might as well have been the driving force for the way my heart took to hammering at my ribcage.

Every cell in my body hardened as I prepared to take on the severity I wore as Crimson Crows' president.

No, it wasn't a façade, per se.

I guess it was just allowing who I really was to rise to the surface.

The second I broke out of the cover of the trees, the clubhouse came into view. My boots thudded on the ground as I crossed over the gravel road that cut through to the back part of the land and led to the houses I'd just left behind.

Lights glowed from the enormous building, and a bonfire leapt high into the darkened sky.

Licking flames that stirred the air like a warning of what was coming.

Omens of blood and death and perversion.

A slew of motorcycles were parked in a semi-circle around the entire boundary, gleaming against the flames, and about a dozen guys drank beers around the fire.

They were laughing and jesting. Giving each other shit the way they always did. My men might have oozed peril, but they were the closest of friends. Sworn to have each other's backs.

There were no women tonight. They were forbidden on Church nights.

When Dice saw me coming, he put two fingers into his mouth and gave a shrill whistle.

"Yo, President," he shouted behind it.

Everyone's heads swiveled my way.

"Ah, the man of the hour," Brody called, full tease in his voice.

"That's the man of every hour," Trevan corrected with a grin.

"Ah, he likes to think so, but his younger brother just might steal some of the limelight." Brody was all cocky arrogance but with that goodness interlacing it.

I fought a smirk. "You think so, huh?"

"Gonna give it a good go."

"You've got big shoes to fill," Phoenix tossed out with his normal grumble.

"But my dick's just as big, soooo…"

"I think you've mistaken it for your head," Trevan razzed.

"Well, obviously," Brody deadpanned.

A riot of laughter broke out, and I let a smile go before my mood shifted.

"All right, time for Church."

Second I said it, the mood changed.

Standing a little straighter, my main guys drained their beers before everyone broke apart like the soldiers they were, getting into formation behind me as I strode through the main club door.

The bar was the same as ever, barring the fact that the women who normally decorated it were missing, the walls plain and drab.

Couldn't help but think about the way that Little Wildfire had set fire to the place last night, desperate for escape when she thought I was out to do her in.

I thought in that moment, it was the most vibrant it'd ever been.

Flames and light and life filling the space.

Energy alive.

My pulse racing in a way that it never had.

The only female there was Lulu. Mouthwatering aromas wafting from the kitchen as she prepped for tomorrow.

This was her home, so she had an exemption.

Always working late because she'd once told me it was the only thing she could do. Needing to keep her hands busy and thoughts diverted from the pain and the loss, though I could only imagine every time she saw one of us wearing our cuts it reminded her of her husband.

Her husband who'd given his life to further our mission.

Without him, she was alone, so I'd given her a permanent place that would always be hers.

She was the one who insisted on the food. Doing her part to care for us the way she said we were caring for her.

Another twenty or so Crows were inside, along with a handful of prospects.

Every patched-in Crow gathered at my back while the prospects scrambled off to their posts.

Their duty during Church was to guard this compound to the last breath of their bodies. It was where they proved their worth and their right.

We strode through the bar and pushed into the long hall that led to the cavernous room at the end.

Exact same spot where that sneak had been doing what she did best last night—clearly trying to gain intel when I couldn't afford for her to have it.

Didn't know what the fuck was wrong with me because I couldn't stuff down the slog of guilt that lifted every time she asked a question. Questions I had to shut down with some vague, pathetic answers that she still did her best to decipher.

Every time I looked at her, I felt like I was going to bust and spew every secret. Or maybe I was just worried she had the power to infiltrate my thoughts. Dig her fingers around in my mind and discover my secrets. Pluck them free and make them her own.

Clearly, I needed to get my shit together.

Redefine the boundaries between us before I did something reckless like devour that delicious body and lay myself bare.

Tossing open the twelve-foot high wooden doors seared with the Crimson Crows insignia, I strode into Church.

Every Crow poured in behind me.

It was a long room that ran horizontally.

A worn, rambling wooden table sat in the center, and twenty high-backed wooden chairs surrounded it.

The room was dark, the antique chandelier hanging from the cavernous ceiling above sending shadows scattering in the flare of its light.

A pathetic illumination attempting to chase away the ghosts that had followed us into this room.

There was no chance of it succeeding.

The walls were covered in dark, gruesome paintings—paintings spun from our Madman's hands. It was the only way for Phoenix to purge the demons from his brain.

I'd given him free reign.

My crew took their chairs, except for the newest members who would stand until they fully earned their seat.

I was at the head.

Trevan to my right and Phoenix to my left.

Seventeen others took up the rest of the chairs, and another ten hovered on the fringes.

I slammed the gavel down onto the worn, rustic wood of the table. "I call to order this meeting of Crimson Crows."

Trevan gave a dip of his chin. "I second it."

"Good," I said as I glanced around at my army.

The lot of them were unruly and wild. Shaped by wounds and traumas. Scars that had been carved on their spirits and minds.

Driven by the rage that had coated their souls in sin and barbarity. Twisted by the thirst to right some of the wrongs that had been meted by tyrants and oppressors.

I wouldn't have anyone else beside me.

Their devotion was unwavering and complete, and their utter commitment to our cause had written them as my brothers.

Every bit as permanent as the tattoos on my body.

They were family.

No, they didn't know what our club really stood for when they became prospects. We needed to establish their complete loyalty before we could take them there.

Which was why the prospects were currently guarding us without a clue of what we were actually meeting about until the time came when we gave them a peek at what Crimson Crows was really about.

Those we never came to trust were plucked out and weeded.

"Have some important updates tonight," I started with. "Going to need each of you to be all in. Focused and ready."

A raucous of "ayes" went up around the room.

They agreed without having any indication of the details.

Exactly what was required of them.

"First and foremost, tonight's job. Are we set?"

I looked to Fuse.

Dude was as fucking smart as they came, the scary kind of smart that verged on diabolical. He had a photographic memory. Permanently cataloging every face and name he encountered. Dates and times and details embedded in his wicked brain.

He lifted his trimmed, blond beard, blue eyes hard as he stared back at me. "Team is en route."

We'd been getting intel coming in about constant deals taking place near a southern town in Oregon.

Guns and fentanyl.

Even though we were neck deep in the bullshit with Kent Ellison, we couldn't turn a blind eye.

It was close enough that we could be in and out without notice, small enough that we only needed a handful of men to carry it out. But what we were stopping was atrocious enough that it was worth the expenditure.

Our duty always prevailed.

"Do you foresee any issues?" I asked.

Fuse was in charge of intel. In organizing every facet of every job. Piecing them together like a disordered puzzle that only made sense in his mind.

His hacking skills were almost as good as Cash's, though directed at different things.

"No. This one should be cut and dry. In and out. Easy."

But the impact would be astronomical.

"Good. Keep me apprised."

His tongue swiped out to wet his dry lips. "I'll let you know as soon as I hear it's done."

I dipped my head then pulled in a steeling breath, ready to dive into the larger matter at hand.

"You all know the girl is here." I tried to keep my tone in check. Last thing I needed was a mention of Brinley rumbling out like possession.

"We might have noticed." Tamping it was a failure since a smack of suggestion filled Trevan's voice, all while he capped it with a question mark.

A razzing challenge lifting in his dark gaze.

Yeah, she'd made quite the impression last night.

A wildfire streaking through the night.

But that could be written off as expected.

What could absolutely not be written off?

Fact that I'd had her on the back of my bike when I'd taken her into town earlier today.

Assholes were going to make it something it wasn't.

Something it couldn't be.

"No question she made a bit of a stir when she tried to run last night." I played it off like Trevan wasn't referring to something else.

A bunch of speculative nods woven with muted amusement rolled through the Crows.

It'd been quite the scene.

Like she was actually going to make it over that fence before I got to her.

"She thought she was here as a prisoner," I continued. "Thought we were basically holding her against her will and holding her over her brother's head. Thought she was marked for dead."

"Thought?" Phoenix's low, raspy voice curled into the room, his hands in fists on the table.

Mad was written across the knuckles of his right hand and *Man* was on the left.

Each pinky capped with a jester's face.

My chest tightened, and I looked at him point blank. "I at least owed it to her to let her know that she's safe here. Protected. We aren't in the business of tormenting innocent women."

"Not a whole lot about her that looks innocent to me." Colby cracked it like any of this was a fucking joke.

I was not prepared for the way a wave of anger punched me in the face. Possessiveness clutching me by the throat.

My teeth ground, and I leaned back in my seat, searching for cool when I was five seconds from snapping.

"You say something like that about her again, you lose your tongue." I attempted to keep the words easy. They still came out a blade.

Dude knew it wasn't a euphemism, and he inhaled an unnerved breath as he roughed a hand through his long, dirty-blond hair.

Colby blazed through women faster than the last one had time to roll out of his bed, and it wasn't uncommon to find a few of them there.

"Meant no disrespect." It cracked as it left him.

"Don't let it happen again." I stared him down for a beat before my gaze drifted over my men.

"It applies to all of you. Already warned you she was off-limits, and that includes talking about her unless it's directly related to the job. Do you understand?"

Yeah, we were an MC, but we were governed by our own playbook. Our rules were formed around our mission.

It blurred some lines since we had bunnies running rampant, and we allowed some of the typical MC behaviors. We had to look legit, and on a whole lot of levels, we were.

These guys were originally drawn to the club for a reason. It wasn't like they were going to sit around being subject to the conventional laws of society.

Every single one of us was violent and brutal.

Destructive to the extreme.

We just took those propensities and morphed them into something different.

Bigger.

It was the little good we had to offer after lifetimes of corruption.

But I wasn't feeling so *good* right then. Not when I wanted to reach halfway down the table and snap Colby's neck. Not when I wanted to crawl inside that woman, sift around in all she was, discover that thing I could feel simmering under the surface.

A disconcerted rumble of assent went around since it was rare anyone evoked that type of reaction from me.

Trevan looked at me all the harder.

Prodding gaze burning a hole in my cheek all while some kind of smirk edged the corner of his mouth.

Like the fucker thought he knew something I didn't.

I only grunted at him before I turned back to the table.

"Cash is continuing to gather intel. He thinks we should be ready to roll in the next two to three weeks. I need every single one of you ready for when that happens. This will be the largest job we have ever undertaken, and it is not going to come without risk."

Without risk?

What a joke.

This was fucking perilous.

A death wish.

Hatred bound my guts in coils of white-hot fury. Rage curling my hands into fists.

God knew how desperately I was wishing for death, but not for anyone else but the monsters who had stolen so much from me. From my family.

No clue who I really was. Trying to push me into a corner. Trying to bend me to their will like I was going to cave. Thinking I was some two-bit criminal. Nothing but a mule to haul their poison across the country.

Motherfucker had no idea who he was dealing with, but he was about to.

I'd been trying to infiltrate their organization for years, ever since I discovered who they really were, and it was time to bring it to fruition.

Aggression and anxiety blustered through the enclosed space. None of my brothers were immune to the stakes.

"How many?" Phoenix growled it from the side.

My chest tightened. "At least eighty men spread out over multiple locations."

It would require a massive amount of coordination.

Perfect coordination.

There was no room for missteps or miscalculations.

I watched as the magnitude of what we were undertaking sank in. Their expressions shifting through a million things.

Dread and determination.

Ferocity and fear.

Always, always landing on the oath that we had taken.

"We have to be precise. We can't afford any mistakes," I gritted.

Even if we only made one of them, we'd all be dead.

"And do we trust the intel Cash is gathering?" There was a grumble of suspicion from Styx, a guy in his early fifties who'd followed me over from my days in the Iron Owls MC in LA.

Days when I'd given myself over to greed and gluttony.

To sin and a reign of terror.

When that crew had splintered, I'd formed Crimson Crows. Along with a handful of others—Trevan, who I'd known from childhood, and Phoenix, who'd been an Owl—Styx had followed.

His question wasn't because he doubted Cash.

Cash and the rest of the Sovereign Sanctum crew were loyal. Steadfast to the extreme.

Our brothers in arms.

This was all about the weaselly little fuck who was so duplicitous he might as well have had traitor stamped on his forehead.

"He was solid when he came forward to give info on Elena, and we have to trust he's going to be solid now."

I basically had to force the words out since they weighed heavier than lies.

At least three of my men scoffed.

Yeah, there was no love lost there.

"And if he isn't?" Phoenix demanded.

"You know Cash is covering all the bases. If he flips, we're gonna know. And his sister is here. That has to count for something."

My throat narrowed when I said it. Clotting off in foreboding and more of that possession that would only serve to make me weak.

No doubt, this bullshit I was feeling was one of those *mistakes* we couldn't afford to make. One that would trip me up and send me failing.

"And you think he really gives a fuck about her? You think she's anything more than bait or a decoy?" he pressed.

Rage clouded my eyes, a violent storm that blackened the edges of my sight.

"He knows what will happen then." The words were so hard they nearly cracked my teeth.

The air was charged as Trevan rocked back in his chair. Usually, he was my voice of reason. The guy who told me things were going to turn out just fine. Chill and smooth as fuck.

Of course, it had to go and be now when he got critical. "Yet you packed her up and moved her to your house this afternoon? Means you think something else is up."

A heavy sigh pilfered from my nostrils. Should have known this would be coming. Their questions hanging stiff and suffocating in the air.

I hadn't debriefed them on what went down this afternoon, but it was time I did.

"There was a guy in town, in the parking lot of the drugstore I took Brinley to."

On my left, Phoenix stirred, violence skimming his tattooed flesh. Darkness radiating from his being.

Always fucking ready to draw blood.

Agitation rolled through our Madman.

More so than normal. Brinley's presence here on the compound had seemed to stir him into upheaval.

"And?" Trevan urged in a low tone.

"He didn't make a move, but I knew it in the way he was looking at me."

Normal men didn't stare me down. Instinct coerced them into dropping their eyes and hustling their families away.

Not this guy.

"Motherfucker was there to deliver some kind of message."

"You think there's a chance they have a clue what's going down?" Colby whispered it like he was worried if he spoke too loudly, these bastards would be alerted.

"No one knows." It whipped from my tongue.

Crimson Crows' secrets were guarded as closely as Area 51's.

And we didn't leave anyone breathing to divulge it.

"But we also know that Kent Ellison isn't going to just look the other way after what went down. He wants me under his thumb. Running his contraband. He thinks if he exerts enough pressure, I'll bend."

Cash and his crew breaking into his compound to save Elena, slaying one of his guards while doing it, had been a huge fuck you to his face. He was likely torn between wanting me dead and using my skills. We had the reputation of being the best.

I just wasn't sure on which side he was going to land.

"So you think someone is watching, and your gut reaction is to take her to your house?" There was a prodding to Trevan's words. An undercut of the *I told you so* rolling from his smug-ass demeanor.

Except there would have been no warning loud enough to prepare me for whatever the fuck I was feeling. The greed and volatility. The pull of something I didn't understand.

"I'm not taking any chances. If something happened to her, this whole thing falls apart."

And this mission was personal.

Vengeance.

Vindication.

The whole problem was that wildfire had to go and dump gasoline on the simmering mayhem.

"And you think this scumbag is going to give us everything we need to get this job done?" Cynicism rolled out of Styx.

I gripped onto the edge of the table. My sister's face flashed through the back of my mind. Her body bruised and broken. Used as a tool to control me and my crew.

"I have to trust that he will. We have no other choice."

I looked around the table. My glare was so pointed it probably drew blood.

"We know the devastation they breed. Know the sickness they pour out on this world. It's our duty to stop them."

A rustle of agreement rolled through, the pack of vicious bikers roiling with loathing and disdain.

My teeth clenched and I fisted my hands on top of the table.

"Born in chaos. Forged by iron. Sworn to vengeance." I uttered the words with all the significance they held.

Crimson Crows' pact.

Everyone banged a fist on the table as they repeated the oath they had made. "Born in chaos. Forged by iron. Sworn to vengeance."

And none of us would stop until we saw it through.

20

Silas

I crept into my room like a wraith haunting the night. A dark shadow emanating from within and wisping out in front of me.

Guilt and gluttony vied for dominance.

A tugging at my insides as I slipped into the energy that filled the walls, pressing into her presence that glowed and radiated from where she slept in my bed.

Yeah, I knew full well I could have approached this differently.

I could have set her up with Trevan. It would have made more sense.

All of us knew it.

Bringing her here, taking her under my roof and into my bed, wasn't doing anything but inviting trouble. Welcoming it with open arms.

No question about it as I gazed at her through the lapping darkness of the room.

Like autumn had descended and was sprawled out on the left side of my bed.

Calm for the first time since she'd come here.

A cascade of brunette locks streaked with golds and reds strewn over my pillow.

Only a simmer of that explosive energy emitted from her soft, sensuous flesh.

One side of her face was barely visible where she was curled on her side, that delicious body barely covered by the thin sheet that was only pulled up low on her waist.

Woman wearing a lacy camisole. A riot sent to rock my mind and to decimate my senses.

She was a test.

She had to be.

One that seemed futile and impossible to pass as I kicked off my boots and peeled myself out of my jeans and tee.

I needed to plant my ass on the couch. Or better yet, at one of the empty rooms at the clubhouse.

But no.

I crawled in beside her like a thief intending on stealing what he could never afford.

Heat radiated from her soft skin, and I swore I could feel her spirit crawling the walls of the room.

I forced myself to keep to my side. Eyes on the ceiling.

Should have known they were going to drift.

I shifted my head so I was staring at her through the shadows.

Stared at the distinct lines of her face. Watched her eyes flutter beneath her lids.

I reached out and traced my fingertips down her cheek. Voice the scrape of a murmur. “I won’t let anyone hurt you. I won’t fail you like I failed everyone else.”

21

Silas

Twelve Years Old

"Stop bein' such a little pussy and do it. It's about time you learned to be a little more like your old man."

Silas's father looked across at him from where he sat in the driver's seat of his beat-up pickup truck. Grinning that disgusting smile that drove into Silas like rusted nails.

He hated it.

He hated what his stomach felt like as he sat on the passenger side, one hand hanging onto the door handle like it might be able to stop him from having to unlatch it.

His molars ground so hard it was giving him a headache as he warred with what to do.

His momma would be so disappointed in him if she knew what his dad was putting him up to. He knew it was wrong all the way down to his bones.

"I don't want to," he finally mustered up the courage to say.

His dad laughed a boisterous sound like he thought it was hysterical before the back of his hand came out and cracked at the side of Silas's mouth.

Silas flinched hard with the impact. A splutter of pain and the taste of blood.

He shouldn't have been caught off guard. He should have known exactly what would be coming for him if he disobeyed his father.

But his momma had always told him to do what was right. To stand his ground against anyone who would try to persuade him into drifting onto a dangerous route.

He figured his dad was included.

"Didn't ask if you wanted to, boy. I told you. Now get your scrawny ass out of the truck and do it before I give you the kind of whooping that will leave you unable to sit for the next week."

Nausea boiled in his guts, and his skin felt hot and sticky, his breaths coming hard as his heart pounded with fear.

Anger bubbled on the underside of it. He wanted to lash out the same way as his father had done. Strike him across the face. Maybe take the brick he clutched in his opposite hand and smash him on the side of the head with it.

His dad must have been able to see it because he swept in close, his voice cutting like razors across Silas's face. "You want me to take your disobedience out on your momma for raising such a pathetic piece of shit?"

Silas bowed with the words. Terror ripped through him at bringing more attention to his mom. He tried his best to protect her. To stand in the way when their dad was coming for her.

Things had been good when their mom had kicked him out. Months of peace and his momma smiling, joy in her as she took care of him and his little sister and brother.

Meems had told her it was right. Called it taking out the trash.

But when the *trash* had come back, pounding at the door and demanding to be let inside, his momma had called the police.

They told her that she had no right to keep him out.

He was on the lease, and she had no papers saying he couldn't be there.

Silas knew to his guts it was bullshit. Wrong that she had to let him back in. Wrong that he'd *won* again.

"Don't sit there and act like you're better than me," his father sneered. "You got my blood running right through you. It's time to use it. Now get out before I beat the man into you."

Hatred boiled in that blood. The blood that Silas hated. He clenched his teeth, sucked for a bunch of breaths, and tried to shove off the fear.

But it chased him like a swarm of bees as he finally shoved open the door. His ears rang with adrenaline. A concoction of terror and hate and disgust.

He ran across the road and bashed the window of the car rather than his *daddy's* head.

Glass shattered, little splinters that went everywhere.

But he wasn't prepared for when an alarm started blaring. Shocked, he jolted back, eyes skating back and forth to see a bunch of people turning to look at him. Panicking, he started to run back for the truck.

But not before a guy came busting out from a store, right behind him in a flash.

Tackling him to the hard pavement below. His chest pressed so hard to the road that he thought it was going to cave in as the man pinned him down.

"You little shit. Did you just try to rob me? You bust my car window? You're gonna pay for that."

Silas struggled to break free, and for once, he was thankful his dad was there, that he could get this guy off him because he was crushing him bad.

Putting so much weight on him it was hard to breathe.

Only his attention cut to the opposite side of the road when the engine of his dad's old truck suddenly roared, tires peeling out, the tail of his truck disappearing as it swerved down the street.

• • •

His momma stormed with him out of the Crimson Creek police station. She had his hand locked in hers, like he was four and she was marching him out of a store after throwing a tantrum.

The sun shone bright, and he blinked against the jarring rays. Jarred from sitting on a hard chair in a dark office for what had felt like an entire week, then the next released into the cool spring air.

He wanted to fall to his knees from the relief, but he tried to force his chest and chin up. To pretend like he hadn't been the most scared in his life. That his heart hadn't felt like it'd been stretched and mashed like Play-Doh.

The worst part was his mom. The way he could feel her entire body quaking. Her head held high too as she rushed with him down the five steps of the big building and around to the side of it.

There, she whipped him around, and she bent the smallest fraction since he was almost as tall as her, getting right in his face. "Tell me what happened."

"I already told you." He basically stammered it, though he tried to make it sound hard. Mean like his dad's voice.

He wasn't great at telling his mom lies. But no way was he going to let on that his dad had forced him to do it.

Not when he knew she would confront him, which would turn into a big fight, and she'd end up getting hurt.

He would never be responsible for that. Would never let it happen. It was his job to take care of her.

It was what he'd been made to do. He knew it all the way down into his soul.

"Don't lie to me, Silas. I know you're not telling the truth."

Redness flushed his skin, and the scrapes on his face from being pushed down onto the pavement burned, but not as hot as his shame.

"I told you. I saw that there was a wallet in the cupholder, and I figured there had to be money in it."

Air huffed out of her mouth, and she inched closer to him, but her words came out soft. In all the belief that she always gave him. "You're not a thief, Silas. I know you didn't come up with that plan yourself. You can tell me whatever you need to."

He wavered, looking away and gnawing at the inside of his cheek like it might be able to keep the truth from bleeding out.

"Please tell me, baby." Sadness oozed out with it, and he looked that way just as she whispered, "I know it was him, wasn't it? Did your dad put you up to it?"

Put him up to it?

Moisture bleared in his eyes, and in discomfort, he shuffled on his feet, trying to fight the hurt that blazed across him like the strike of a leather belt.

"Tell me, Silas. You're not going to get into trouble. I just need to know."

"He made me." He hated that he sounded like a sniffling little baby when he said it, but he couldn't help it. Couldn't help the icky feeling that slicked through his veins.

"Because I'm like him," he whispered like a horrible secret.

His mom took him by the outside of the arms. "You are nothing like him. Nothing."

She almost shook him as she wheezed the last.

"You are kind and good and care about those around you. You love, Silas. You love with every cell inside this body, and it doesn't matter if you've got his blood, you've got Silas's heart."

She said it as she set her hand over the thunder of it.

"It's your heart." The words gushed out of him. She was who he wanted to be like.

Tears blurred her eyes, the soft green sad. "No more of this, baby. It's done. It's over."

He wanted to ask her what that meant, but she suddenly shot upright, taking his hand again, glancing both ways before she darted them across the tree-lined street to where their minivan was parked on the opposite side.

Confusion bound him when he saw that Meems was sitting in the front passenger seat, and when his mom ripped open the sliding back door, his brother and sister's car seats were both buckled onto each side of the middle row with an empty spot left right in the middle.

There was no place to sit in the back seat since the whole thing was stuffed with their things.

"Get in, baby," his mother whispered.

His nerves scattered.

Excitement and relief and more of that confusion as he tried to process exactly what was happening.

"Hi, *Sigh-us*, my *brover*!" Brody kicked his tiny feet as Silas squeezed by to get into the middle, and he could barely return a, "Hi, buddy," around the lump in his throat as he settled into the middle.

On the opposite side, Elena reached around her car seat, a big smile on her dimpled face as she gripped his arm. "We're goin' to Meems's house."

His heart felt like it was going to explode, and his grandmother shifted around to give him a soft smile. "That's right. We're going to Meems's house."

Bewildered, he met his mother's gaze through the rearview mirror.

He thought he was going to be grounded forever.

Or maybe his dad would have been the one to give him his punishment, even though his mom never told him when he was in trouble so that wouldn't happen. Still, his dad didn't seem to care that much about it when he found out, that was, if he was even around.

But instead, his mother said, "And we aren't coming back."

22

Brinley

"Come on, Dereck, we have to hurry." Brinley grabbed his hand as he scurried out the school gates, their feet rushed as she led him down the street.

"How was school?" she finally asked.

"Fine," he muttered.

"What did you get on your math test?"

He sent her a grin. "I only got five wrong."

"Out of how many?"

"A hundred."

"That's a good job. A really good job."

"Only because you helped me study."

They'd spent two hours working on it yesterday afternoon.

They rounded the corner and rushed across the street, traveling the four blocks to get to their house.

The exterior was worn and the lawn overgrown.

She inhaled a steadying breath, knowing she'd have to do something about that.

She rummaged through her backpack and got out the key.

Turned it in the lock and let them inside.

"Take off your shoes," she instructed Dereck as they both dumped their things onto the scroungy linoleum floor.

He didn't listen, just ran through the house leaving a trail of mud.

Frustration ballooned in her chest, but she tried to remember he was just a kid. He didn't think not to bang the cabinet doors or climb all over the furniture.

Besides, she had worse things to worry about.

She crept down the hall. The door was ajar by an inch. The same way as she left it this morning.

Her heart sank, and she had to steel herself before she finally pushed open the door.

Her mother's eyes were closed, but they barely fluttered open to the sound of her. "There's my girl."

She spoke so quietly Brinley could barely hear it. The words croaked and uneven.

Brinley tiptoed up to her side, put the back of her hand on her forehead like her temperature was going to make any difference.

"How are you feeling?"

Her mother forced an ashen smile, her lips a cold, weathered gray. Her head that once had boasted the same brunette curls as Brinley's was now bald, her body wilting away beneath a green striped bedspread.

"It's not so bad today."

Brinley knew it was a lie. It was always bad.

"Is there anything I can do?" Brinley would give anything to take it away.

Her mother reached for her hand and twined her spindly fingers with Brinley's. "You do more than enough. I hate that this burden has fallen on you."

Fighting the burn at the back of her eyes, Brinley ferociously shook her head. "It's not a burden. I don't want you to worry about anything. We have it under control."

Her mom unwound her hand and softly touched her cheek with her fingertips. "You're sixteen. You should be running free and wild, not looking after me and your brother."

"I wouldn't want to be doing anything else."

Her mother's smile was tweaked in sadness. "I'm so sorry, sweetheart. I tried so hard."

Grief clotted Brinley's throat, and she gathered her mother's hand back up in hers, her words rushed, "Please don't apologize. It's fine. It's going to be fine. I promise."

"You'll take good care of him?" Pain broke from her mother's tongue.

Brinley wanted to drop to her knees at the side of her bed, throw herself over her and weep, but she forced herself to nod. "You know that I will. I promise."

Her mother nodded, and a tear slid free. "My sweet girl. So beautiful. So selfless. I want you to promise me that you'll take care of you, too. Use those math skills to their fullest." For one flash of a second, her mother's yellowed eyes twinkled. "Become a doctor or an astronaut."

"I'm scared of blood and of flying." Brinley stumbled over the tease.

"Okay, fine, an accountant."

Brinley's eyes squeezed tight for a beat. "I will, Mom."

"I love you so much."

"I love you more than you know," Brinley choked.

"I think I need to rest," her mother said, and Brinley nodded, touched her forehead again before she crept back out.

Her footsteps laden with the weight.

Dereck was in the kitchen, peering through the pantry door.

"I need to leave for work," she told him. "I need you to make sure you have your homework done and your room cleaned before I get home."

"What's for dinner?" he asked.

She went to the fridge, cringed when she opened it up and there was an inch of milk at the bottom of the gallon. A couple of apples. Ham and cheese.

"You're going to have to have a ham sandwich until I can get to the store after I get paid tomorrow."

"I hate ham sandwiches," Dereck groaned.

"I know, Dere, I know. I'll figure out something better soon."

She slung her arm around his shoulder and kissed his temple before she headed for the door, slipping into her shoes and grabbing her bag before she stepped out and locked the door behind her.

She took her phone from her pocket, stared at it, anger rising up so fierce inside her. But right then, she didn't have time for pride.

So she tapped out the message.

Brinley: *Dad, please call me back. We're in a bad way. We need your help.*

But he hadn't cared before, so she should have known he wouldn't care then.

I startled awake, though not in a full panic the way I normally did.

I guess maybe it was the heavy heat that saturated me through that kept it contained.

Like I was wearing a ten-thousand-pound security blanket.

A blaze of warmth that filled the cold, dead places inside me as I blinked my eyes open to the bare, fluttery light that cast the room in glittering motes as morning climbed to the sky and streaked through the thin drapes.

I had the urge to snuggle deeper into that comfort, only I froze when it became very apparent the blanket I was wearing was a breathing, living thing.

Deep, long breaths panted into the nape of my neck. A tattooed arm draped around my waist. A strong, foreboding body plastered to my backside.

My heart rate increased. Sped and raced and thudded at my chest. Right where he had one of those malicious hands spread over the spot, as if maybe even in his sleep, he was trying to hold it in.

But I knew better than to think Silas was doing any of this out of care. I needed to remember his secure arm was a shackle.

Holding me in place and keeping me prisoner to his will.

With that in mind, I tried to slip from under his grasp, only his arm tightened as gruff, sleep-weary words whispered from his lips.

"I've got you. I've got you."

Surprise locked me in place, his tone rippling over me like a raspy caress. The confusion and need he evoked in me zapped like a downed powerline across my flesh.

He pressed himself closer, and a tiny gasp catapulted out of me when I felt his cock pressing against the cleft of my ass.

The thinnest amount of fabric separated us. It didn't come close to being enough to conceal the granite, desperate length of him.

I should be terrified.

Freak out.

Break out of his hold.

Fight him.

Fight this.

Fight the sensation that swamped me like murky, muddy bog.

What did I do instead? I sank back into the comfort I shouldn't feel, no consideration as to what it would cost.

Into the steady pound of Silas's heart that somehow slowed the mania that toiled in my spirit.

I shouldn't find respite in him.

He was the enemy. A liar. A bad man.

I knew it as well as I recognized my own reflection, which even that seemed to be becoming warped right then.

Because he pulled me closer and nuzzled his nose into the side of my neck, both arms cinching tighter around me as he moaned a disoriented sound.

Deep and gruff and decadent.

The fear I expected was there, but it was fuzzy and distorted. Mangled and contorted by the buzz of need that licked just beneath the surface of my skin.

Because I wanted this.

"Wildfire, burning me alive," he mumbled close to incoherently, though I heard it clearly.

Felt it singe through me the same as the hand that was splaying wider across my belly. The other still holding onto my heart like he could be the one to keep it from splintering apart.

Mend it when I was pretty sure he was going to be the one responsible for the complete decimation I could feel crawling up from the horizons of hell.

The meager bandages I'd placed on our lives getting ready to be ripped away by whatever Dereck had done.

I was only allowing myself to be lulled into a false sense of security. Hypnotized by a guy who screamed duplicity.

Maybe he was right. Maybe I was totally looking for trouble.

Because a stupid moan got free when he rubbed his cock against my bottom. Desire boiling up through the vat of self-preservation that had served to keep me whole for all these years. Oozing through the cracks to seep into my bloodstream.

A shiver of terror and need ripped up my spine. Each sensation was so at odds that I all out shook, and my hand grasped onto the sheet like it could serve as an anchor.

It was clear which of the battling emotions won out since I pushed my ass harder against his rigid thickness.

I shouldn't like it.

Shouldn't like the thrill I felt when the low growl rumbled up his throat before it curled into the dense, disordered air.

Arms cinching even tighter, he began to rock against me, and our breaths became short and shallow as lust billowed in the atmosphere.

Inciting a storm. A war that magnified every thought.

My questions and my uncertainty and the stupid, reckless need he somehow managed to arouse in me.

My center throbbed, and crap, I thought I might be done for.

"What do you think you're doing to me, Little Wildfire?" He was fully awake by then. There was no mistaking it.

The severity that rocketed.

Zaps of lightning sheared through the room as the rasping, rugged words cut from his mouth.

"Was this the plan the whole time? Send in this siren to distract me? Seduce me? Sing me your intoxicating song so I'd be caught unaware?"

A puff of incredulous laughter shot from my tongue. The sound mixed with the desire that coated every surface of his room. "You're the one playing games, Silas Mercer. You're the one who insisted on me sleeping in your bed."

I didn't know what in the world I thought I was doing, but I rolled my hips, rubbing myself against him, notching the hunger just a smidgeon higher.

My stomach was both light and heavy, toppling and turning over, the same as the emotion did in my chest as I reached for something inside me that had been missing for so long.

Only flickers of apprehension tickled in the periphery. Muted by whatever power Silas held over me.

He shocked me by suddenly shifting and rolling me onto my back. He climbed up to hover over me, his big body pinning me to the bed.

His vicious, beautiful face suddenly filled my vision.

Every carved, slashed angle was inscribed with ferocity.

The gold flecks in his eyes ignited in a fit of need and something that looked decidedly close to dread.

"I'm not playing games, Brinley, but clearly, I am playing with fire. Barely even touching you, and I've crossed so many lines. Committed a thousand crimes."

He had both hands planted on either side of my head, and I became painfully aware that he'd wound himself between my thighs. The weight of his cock pressed to that spot that had begun to ache and glow.

A fool, I arched toward him, and both my hands fisted in the sheet below like it could keep me from reaching out.

A skirmish between what I wanted and what I knew would destroy me clashed in the middle.

"Yet it's me who's going to get burned, isn't it?" I choked out what I hoped sounded like an accusation. "You who's going to toy with me? You who's going to use me until you get what you want?"

He'd fully admitted it last night. I was a means. A tool. A pawn.

Nothing more.

I needed to remember it.

His chuckle was rough. Filled with biting disbelief. "Nah, baby, it's you who can bring me to my knees. You who has me crawling with a flick of your fingers. You could ask anything of me, and I'd be helpless but to give it to you."

He rocked against me once.

Fire lancinated up my spine.

On instinct, my hands shot out, and I gripped onto his waist. "Answers. Then give me answers."

Darkness gathered, furrowing his brow into a stark, slashing V.

Both of us were stuck in that position.

Teetering on the edge of a bottomless chasm that churned below us. Threatening to set us off balance and toss us into its abyss.

"I just need you to trust me, Brinley," he finally said.

"What if that's not good enough for me?"

"It's going to have to be. My only objective here is keeping you safe, and I won't jeopardize that." The words ground off his tongue.

A soft scoff ripped free. "Isn't that what I'm in? Jeopardy?"

"Not with me standing in front of you."

Another one of those gritted promises.

Stone toppling from his mouth as if it could build a new foundation.

Did I believe him? Trust him? How could I?

But there was something in the roil of his expression that made me see his truth.

"I don't like being left in the dark." It was close to a plea.

He almost smirked. But it was soft. "That's because you're always in control. Fighting for yourself. For your brother. The fierce lioness that you are. Going it alone because there's no one there to have your back. But this time, you're giving that fight to me."

Fear and hope clattered around in my spirit. How could he know that about me? My throat was nearly closed off when I whispered, "And what if you fail me?"

That darkness flashed a hundredfold, and he curled his hands around my wrists and pressed them to the bed. He dipped down so close that I tasted the words.

"I won't."

The little thumps low on the door startled us, and Silas pushed off, rolling over so he was sitting up in the bed just as the door clattered open.

While I lay there panting toward the ceiling, trying to gather my bearings enough to sit up, too.

I did just in time to see Kai toddle through, only wearing a diaper.

Adorable dimples denting his cheeks and his eyes that were the same color as Silas's shining in the glinting rays of morning light.

"*Siwas*!" He pointed a chubby finger at the man who roughed a tattooed hand through the mess of his hair, and my brow pinched, realizing it was the first time I'd ever heard Kai call him anything.

Silas.

Not Dad or Daddy.

But that confusion was getting batted away by a surge of affection when Kai turned that sweetness on me. Basically dancing as he shifted to point a little finger at me. "*Bwinwey!* You stay Kai's house?"

I gathered the sheet and brought it to my chest. It wasn't like I was naked or anything, but I still felt like I'd been caught in a scandal.

Bare and vulnerable.

That didn't seem to keep the smile from tweaking at the edge of my mouth, though. "I did."

"You got sweet *dweams*? I got sweet *dweams*." He patted his chest as he kept coming right up to the end of the bed.

Without reservation, Silas shifted so he could reach for him.

The man only wore his underwear. The length of his broad back bare, though completely covered in twisting, black ink.

Two winged creatures sat in the middle facing each other, their foreheads touching in a clear standoff.

One angelic and one demonic.

Black tendrils wisped out from their fingers and chests to duel and twine. As if their spirits were battling not to be tied together.

Silas plucked Kai from the floor and pulled him into those arms he'd just had around me.

Arms I was having trouble imagining as anything other than refuge right then.

"That's because I wished them on you when I tucked you into bed last night, remember?" Silas snuggled him close, tickling him and making him howl with laughter.

Kai grappled for his face, clutching onto his cheeks as he leaned in close and ferociously shook his head as if he were trying to convey something super important. "I no *scawed* nigh-night."

Silas's flinch was almost imperceptible. A wince that seemed to come from the deepest recesses of his soul. If I hadn't been watching so closely, I would have missed it.

But maybe I would have felt it, anyway. Sensed the way he pulled the child a fraction closer, breathing in as he buried his nose in Kai's golden-brown locks.

Every word gravel as he pushed it from his throat. "That's right. You don't have to be afraid to go to sleep. Not anymore. You're safe. You're safe."

My stomach clenched and something just as deep inside me began to ache.

In question, I cut my eye toward Silas.

God, I wished there was a way I could see inside him the way he seemed to be able to see inside of me.

Without separating from Kai an inch, Silas still managed to glance at me from the corner of his eye.

In that brief, fleeting moment, I swore he was flayed open wide.

Love. Pain. Hate. Determination.

A maelstrom that raged inside him.

Immune to the intensity, Kai wiggled his way free, his grin so big it took up the entirety of his precious face. "Kai eat?"

"Yeah, buddy, I bet Meems is whipping up something delicious downstairs," Silas told him.

"My Meems?" He patted his chest again, though he seemed to be asking Silas for confirmation.

"That's right, your Meems, too."

"My *Siwas*?" Insecurity filled that question, and I felt myself breaking apart a little as I watched the interaction.

As I watched Silas tremble with undeniable grief.

He took Kai's little hand and spread it over his chest so Kai could feel the beat of his heart. "Your Silas. Always, Kai. Always."

Kai nodded, back to grinning as he scrambled off Silas's lap and turned onto his belly so he could slide off the end of the bed, shouting, "I get *Wena*," as he raced through the door.

He left a swath of emotion in his wake.

Anguish.

Love.

Despair.

Affliction.

Silas sat far enough forward that I was basically looking at his back, but I could still feel every single one of those things writhe in his being.

"I thought he was your son," I finally whispered into the stagnant silence.

His head barely shook. "No. He's our baby brother."

My throat closed off, and my chest felt like it might cave. It was a horribly dangerous reaction to have to him.

Because I didn't just want his touch to give me some imprudent pleasure that I was pretty sure would only cause another scar.

No.

I wanted to climb to my knees so I could wrap myself around him and soothe his pain.

I wondered if I would ever learn my lesson.

But reservations meant little when someone was bleeding this way.

"And...you're raising him?" My voice barely broke the disordered hush.

A heaving sigh worked out of him, and he roughed a hand down his face. "I didn't know he existed until two months ago."

Surprise shot from my nose, but I didn't have time to respond before Silas continued.

"Had hoped my father was dead. Turned out he was just destroying the innocent again."

"Silas." His name was a crushed breath, and I reached for him, my hand fluttering out between us in uncertainty.

Silas pressed on. "I got a call from one of my friends in the middle of the night. Cash," he said by way of explanation. "He told me he'd gotten a report about a little boy in the emergency room with my same last name. Blood type was a match. He figured he needed to give me a call to make sure we weren't somehow related."

A boatload of questions arose from that statement alone. I wasn't fool enough to assume this Cash guy was a first responder or medical professional. And I seriously doubted Silas had cop friends unless they were of the dirty kind.

There was something there, hidden in the confession, something I was sure was an intrinsic, concealed part of him. One that was likely another blight.

But those things seemed to matter not in the moment. When I could feel the fractures segmenting Silas in two.

Like he didn't know if he wanted to weep or rave.

His head dropped lower between his shoulders, and regret gushed from him like a ruptured well. "Kid clearly neglected and abused."

Weeping sounded really good right about then. A clog of it balled at the base of my throat.

That time, I did reach for him, my fingertips tracing over the sharp edges of the creatures warring on his back.

Silas shivered, his spine curving as he wrapped both arms around the back of his neck.

"I should have ended that bastard years ago when I had the chance. When he stamped out every beautiful thing I'd ever known in my life. Nothing but a pathetic alcoholic who doesn't deserve to breathe."

He croaked over every syllable.

"Silas…"

He gave a harsh shake of his head. "And after all of that, there's no question I should have ended him the night I went to save Kai from his grips, but I didn't, thinking I'd lose the last shred of humanity that I possessed. And now that fucker and junkie bitch think they're actually going to get him back."

I gasped when Silas suddenly whirled, and in a blurry instant, he was on his feet and standing at the end of the bed.

Wearing only his underwear. Chest bare. Scars littered his body, and the morbid, grotesque faces on his throat wound down with the rest of the ink that covered the entirety of his chest and abdomen.

That similar depiction of the crows on the grave all of his motorcycle club wore was painted across his chest, though the scene was embellished. Crows flying through the air and carrying corpses.

Stamped right in the middle of it was *It's Your Heart*, the letters dripping blood over a date from fifteen years ago onto the grave below it.

He clearly believed his was hopeless.

But after what he had just told me? Did I believe that?

He gripped the sheets on either side of me, and he dove in close, our noses bumping as he did. "I won't let it happen, Brinley. I won't let anyone hurt that little boy. Won't let anyone hurt Elena. Won't let anyone hurt *you*. I'll lose every last shred of humanity that I have to see it through. Good thing since there's not much of it left, anyway."

Then he whipped away, snatching his jeans from the floor and shoving into them, doing the same with his shirt, before he snagged his boots from the floor and stomped out without looking back.

The door slammed shut behind him right as gutting pain slashed through my middle.

Pain for Kai.

Pain for Elena.

Pain for *the man*.

Crap.

I was in so much trouble.

• • •

I inched down the stairs, freshly showered and ready for the day. Unsure that I could face the people I could feel rustling around on the bottom floor, their laughter and voices carrying from the kitchen.

Not with everything that had been revealed, even though I was fully aware there were a thousand more concealed secrets lingering in the corners.

I kept easing down, my footsteps quieted on the wooden planks.

A television droned quietly from the living room, and as I stepped onto the bottom landing, I paused, caught by the news story playing out on the screen.

A male reporter stood in front of yellow tape that cordoned off an area near the shore.

His voice was muted by the volume level, but it was still loud enough that I could make out what he was saying.

"I'm here in Southern Oregon, twelve miles south of Harrisburg Beach where the bodies of five men were discovered early this morning by local fishermen. At this time, neither the cause of death nor the victims' identities have been released, but we are told this is being considered a homicide investigation."

He gestured behind him. "As you see, we've had constant activity by law enforcement agents, but so far, no official statement has been made."

He returned facing forward. "But a local resident who wanted to remain anonymous spoke with me, telling a sordid story about this corridor being used for drug trafficking, their small community wrought with a string of fentanyl overdoses. While we have no confirmation of a connection, there is speculation that this morning's grisly discovery may be related. We'll bring you more details as we have them."

The camera cut to the female reporter in the studio. "Thank you, Greg. And after this break, we'll be back with your weather forecast..."

The peel of giggles coming from the kitchen ripped my attention away, and I shook off the chills that slid down my spine.

I hated it.

Hated the violence and cruelness and the horrible things that infiltrated our homes and communities.

The things that destroyed our families.

That shiver cut deeper, the sickening thought of Dereck getting involved in something so deplorable turning my stomach. Last night, every scenario had spun through my brain as I tried to piece together what he had done that was so awful.

I just couldn't imagine it or accept it. Not after he'd promised he would clean his life up. That he'd never repeat his mistakes.

But he hadn't exactly been honest about that, had he?

I inhaled a cleansing breath, forcing it off, then fortified my armor again as I inched toward the kitchen archway.

Stalling at the threshold, I peeked inside.

Meems was on the other side of the bar, dumping ingredients for what looked to be a dessert into a big mixing bowl, while Elena was beside her with Kai in her arms.

She swayed and danced with him, the little boy's soft curls bouncing around his chubby, pink cheeks, his eyes full of joy and mirth as she spun him around, nonstop giggles rolling out of his precious cherub mouth.

My heart squeezed. Squeezed so fiercely I didn't recognize the sensation.

Sorrow and hope and this perception of protectiveness that came completely unbidden.

Silas had it all wrong. His determination to fight for that little boy with everything he had was what *made* him human.

I should be afraid of it. Of the clear threat that he had made. But standing right there, I realized the lengths I would go, too.

Because that little grin only grew when Kai noticed me, and he reached a hand in my direction.

"*Bwinwey*!"

Elena stopped spinning him, and her expression brightened even further when she turned toward me. "Well, good morning, sleepyhead."

I arched a brow. "It's not even eight."

She giggled. "We're early risers around here. You're going to have to get used to it."

For real? There was a biker club across the property. You'd think everyone would be dead to the world until two.

And I would not be getting used to it. I wasn't going to be around that long. This had to end, and it had to end soon. I wasn't sure how much longer I could take it.

Not when Silas kept confusing every rationality that I possessed.

"We're almost ready for breakfast dessert," Elena added with a grin.

"Breakfast dessert?" I asked in a cloud of amused perplexity.

Meems hummed as she started to mix the batter. "I always figured there was no reason for holding off on the best things in life, so rather than capping the day off with sweets, we tend to start them that way."

A single one of my brows arched for the sky. "I do remember the cherry pie we capped the night off with last night."

It was probably the reason Silas smelled like cherries all the time. Decadently sweet while the man dripped with poison.

He was nothing but confliction.

Meems chuckled. "Well, that is because we had a very special guest at the table, and besides, we do a whole lot of indulging around here. You might as well sample the good if it's sitting right out in front of you."

My stomach twisted. I wanted that. To live that way. To reach out and take a little of what I wanted when it was offered to me.

Too bad that offering usually bit me on the hand.

"And was a little good going down in that bedroom last night?" Elena wagged her brows.

Pure suggestion.

My throat grew thick.

"Um…no. Absolutely not."

Whatever had gone down between Silas and me last night and this morning definitely could not be considered *good*.

At best, it was greed and gluttony and dipping your toes in dangerous waters. That was if you were one of those 'look on the bright side', positive sorts of people.

Tantamount to tossing around a nuclear grenade if we were at all being practical.

Because I was pretty sure the small amount of safety I'd built around myself was close to being blasted to smithereens.

Kaboom.

Obliterated with a brush of his malicious hands.

Meems's gaze swept over me, looking me up and down, as if she could see the imprint of her grandson's hands plastered all over my body.

Not that we'd really gotten up to much, but to me, it felt illicit since I hadn't experienced anything close to that in a long, long time.

In discomfort, I shifted on my feet.

"It sure looks like someone wanted it to," she speculated.

Did this woman read minds?

I huffed. "No way."

"Yes, way!" Kai peeped like it was a game, holding onto Elena's neck with both hands as he leaned back and beamed my way.

Elena laughed. "I think it's written all over you, Brinley Webber."

"And what's that?"

"That you have a thing for my brother."

"No, I'm not, *I can't…*"

I didn't mean for the last to come out, and I wrung my hands when I realized the way it sounded.

Exactly the way I meant it.

But I didn't need either of them privy to that. No one got that piece of me, not that there was ever anyone there to hold it.

Except everything slowed, and the playfulness drained as Meems set her mixing spoon aside.

The woman looked at me as if she'd known me my entire life.

Like she cared about me.

Wanted the best for me.

"You are worth every good thing in this world, sweet one. Don't you ever question it or let anyone make you believe that you don't deserve it."

"I..." I couldn't force real words out around the lump in my throat, but I finally managed to whisper, "You don't even know me."

She eased around the counter, and there was no stopping the burn at the back of my eyes as she approached.

She simply took my hand and squeezed it. "But I can see you. Hear you. Feel you. And I feel your pain the same way as I've had to feel it in every single one of my grandchildren."

Sorrow wisped through her aged features. "I couldn't stop it, though Lord knows I wish I could have, but somehow I've been blessed enough to get the chance to try to see them through the other side of it."

A rush of tenderness and understanding gushed out of Elena, and she held Kai tighter as she stepped toward us like she was drawn.

That same pain that I'd sensed in her last night was present, but it was muddled by the type of hope that her grandmother was talking about.

"And no, I can never take away the atrocities that were inflicted on them. Can never erase the horrors or the memories or the scars. But I can love them through it. I can be there to urge them to accept every *good* thing that is set in front of them rather than them rejecting it because they're afraid of it being ripped away."

She squeezed my hand a bit tighter. "Trauma does that to you. It tries to steal the joy from your future, too."

Her voice shifted to a desperate wheeze. "You can't let it."

A tear slipped free. I didn't even know it was there. I'd never felt so vulnerable or exposed in all my life.

It appeared the harsh façade I normally wore had been left at this house's front door.

Part of me wanted to run out and grab it. Don it the way I did my clothes and shoes.

Protect myself the only way I knew how.

But Elena was looking at me with her spirit splayed wide, soft hazel eyes shining with moisture, and she was hugging that little boy.

I was still reeling from the bare glimpse Silas had given me into what the child had likely suffered.

"Meems is right, just like you were last night," Elena prodded, dragging me back to when I'd been trying to give her encouragement. And there they were, turning around and doing the same for me.

"Your heart will know," she emphasized.

Then she laughed a tinkling sound. "And I'm not saying it's my brother who will make you feel that way because that man is about as overbearing as they come and you can do a million times better..."

Playfulness ridged her brows, and I knew she wasn't truly trashing Silas since she grinned this wry, overindulgent grin as she mumbled out of the side of her mouth, "But I can't help but feel a little *somethin' somethin'* when the two of you are in the room together."

"Oh, you aren't the only one," Meems agreed. "Two of them are nothing but flame and gasoline."

"You should have felt it, Meems, when Silas came waltzing back late last night and I was in there having a chat with our Brinley? The energy was as heavy as a bomb."

Kaboom.

Obliterated.

Just like I'd worried.

"There's nothing between us," I defended on a shaky breath. "I'm only here until we get this thing sorted with my brother."

Whatever the hell that was.

"Mmhmm...well, you might as well take a little *good* while you're here." It was pure suggestion out of the mouth of Silas's grandmother.

I choked over a disoriented laugh. Was she actually suggesting what I thought she was?

But I didn't have a grandmother or an anyone to give me crap, and I'd be a liar if I denied that I loved it just a little bit.

And that was the whole problem.

I was pretty sure I could love far too easily when it came to them.

Reckless girl, just begging to get her heart bashed in a little more.

I lifted my chin and tried to shove all the emotion down, playing it light, an attempt at a joke as I forced out the rebuttal. "I think I'll have to pass on that certain kind of indulgence, thank you very much. I'm usually a safe road kind of girl."

And I wasn't about to allow myself to be a doormat anymore.

I forced a giant grin. "But I will take a little something of whatever you're getting ready to bake over there."

Meems chuckled as she started to waddle back toward the kitchen area. "We'll see about that. But at least you're taking a little of the good that I have to offer."

Then she paused and looked back. "It doesn't matter where it comes from, Brinley. The good. The joy. Don't be afraid of it. Don't shun it. Live it."

I stood there dazed for a moment before I was being jolted back in surprise when chubby hands were suddenly reaching for me.

Kai basically jumped out of Elena's hold and into mine. Giggling and wiggling as he wrapped his little arms around my neck.

His weight so perfect and right, and my heart was getting filled to capacity again. If I wasn't careful, it would burst from the pressure.

Then he edged back so he could see my face, his tiny palm patting his chest. "My *Bwinwey*?"

More of that insecurity. More of his fear that he was going to be forgotten or left behind. But in spite of it, he was still brave enough to ask for what his little soul needed.

One of my hands curled up to cup the back of his head as I held him close, and I pressed a kiss to his temple, fighting the words that broke loose in a jagged whisper. "Yeah, baby, your Brinley."

23

Silas

I planted my palms on the rugged table inside of Church. It was the middle of the day, but darkness still reigned in the windowless, cavernous room, the shadows barely broken by the faint glow of the chandelier that dangled from the ceiling.

Phoenix and Trevan were on either side of me as I angled toward the five Crows who had gathered on the opposite side.

Everyone remained standing.

Still itching and twitching with the violence that charged through their veins.

"Give me the details," I demanded, voice hoarse.

Regan, lead of last night's detachment, canted his head. Red hair wild and untamed by the wind.

A big, burly motherfucker who was as vicious as they came.

"Mission accomplished. As if you expected anything less."

He set a briefcase onto the table and slid it my way.

Throat growing thick, I opened it. Stacks of cash were laid inside, just as we knew they would be.

"You count it?" I asked.

He gave a sharp shake of his head. "No. We got in, left them the way they deserved to be, and got out. But it looks to me like it will land on the five mil mark, exactly as anticipated."

I gave a tight nod as I snapped the case shut and passed it off to Trevan before I asked, "How many men?"

"Five."

"Any issues?"

"Job was clean, but we made sure to make it hurt plenty before it was done."

Vengeance.

My blood roared with it.

"Good."

"It's the least we can do." A smirk took to Regan's face.

Air huffed from my nose, and my chuckle was razor-sharp. "Always know I can count on you. All of you." I glanced at the rest as I said it.

Their eyes gleamed with the destruction they'd meted.

A bid for Hell and absolution.

"Rest up. We have a big job ahead of us, and I'm going to need everyone at their best."

Regan roughed a meaty hand over his cheek, mouth tweaking at the side. "Resting up isn't exactly what we had in mind, Prez."

Laughter scraped free. Bloodlust usually led to lust. "Do what you need to do. Just be ready for when I need you."

"We always are."

They turned on their motorcycle boots, tossing open the heavy door. Each banged the heel of their fist on the threshold as they passed, chanting, "Born in chaos. Forged by iron. Sworn to vengeance."

24

Brinley

I wondered if I'd ever get used to the feel of him sweeping in behind me. His presence overpowering as it blasted through the stuffy office.

Potent, delicious heat.

I really shouldn't like it, but after last night and this morning? He was getting places I couldn't let him.

"How are you?" That gruff, low voice hit me like the calluses on his fingertips.

A shiver raced.

I peeked at Silas from over my shoulder.

My stomach toppled over.

God, he was pretty.

Violently so.

"Just as frustrated as I was yesterday morning with this computer." I managed to put a little snark into it. "If you actually want me to make any progress here, I'm going to need the correct tools."

The barest smirk lit the edge of his plush lips. "It's not sufficient for you?"

Clearly, he knew it was a pile of crap.

"This thing is as old as I am."

Amusement drifted across his face. "You really think you're going to whip this place into shape?"

"That's why I'm here, isn't it?"

Obviously, I knew that wasn't true, but sometimes it was easier to pretend.

"Bookkeeping?" He said it droll, a question tacked to it. Head inclining like maybe he was trying to piece my job together with my personality.

It wasn't quite what I'd promised my mother. Close, but with about ninety-five percent less pay. I was sure I was making her super proud, that and the fact that I'd allowed Dereck to go astray.

I hiked an indifferent shoulder. "What can I say? I'm good with numbers."

Something passed through his features. Something calculating. Then he gave a clipped nod. "I'll see what I can manage."

"Thank you." It left me far too fast and wispy. What was I thinking, getting soft on this guy?

As if aiming to prove my point, his expression hardened like dried clay. "I'll be back. Stay out of trouble while I'm gone."

I gave him a salute, and I was the fricking fool who giggled when he left.

• • •

"Passcode to get in is 85641." Silas leaned over my shoulder, orating the numbers at the same time as he punched them into the keypad of the laptop he showed up with.

I quirked a wry brow. "Is that the code to get into everything around here?"

He huffed a disbelieving sound, as if he were offended I thought so little of him. "Just making it simple for you."

I bristled. Now I was the one who was offended.

He chuckled a little, and his breath skated over my cheek. I had to stop myself from clenching my thighs. "Don't worry, Little Wildfire, there's nothing in here that will land you in hot water. Just a bunch of old files and the software we used back in Moonlit Ridge. It should streamline things a bit."

He clicked into the program, and I nearly jumped with joy. "I guess bikers do know how to run businesses, after all."

He lifted his hand and dragged the back of it down the angle of my jaw, his mouth so close that I could nearly taste him. "I can think of a few more things I'm pretty good at."

The words dripped sex.

Goosebumps raced.

I should shove him off. The most astounding thing was that I didn't want to. My mind blown that rather than fighting back, I wanted to sink into the indulgent promise he was clearly making.

Wondering if it was a little of the *good* that Meems had been talking about.

I nearly scoffed at myself.

I knew how horribly bad it would be, but God, I wanted to bottle up this feeling, keep whatever he had seduced in me and put it on a shelf as proof that it existed.

The main door swinging open had Silas stumbling back, and I tried to shove off the reaction, totally flustered and probably flaming red since my blood raced at ten thousand degrees.

"Well, hello, dear brother." Elena's voice was full of an accusatory laugh. I couldn't see her from where I was sitting, but if I could, I was sure her expression would contain a gleeful allegation. "I hope we're not interrupting?"

"Hi, my *Siwas*."

Kai was with her, and there was no stopping the soft smile that started somewhere in my heart and lifted to my mouth.

Silas grunted behind me. "Not interrupting a thing. Just was showing Brinley how to get into the laptop I brought her so she can make herself useful while she's here."

It could have hurt. Stabbed deep enough to cause a wound. But I knew he was covering. Covering for what he didn't want to feel, either.

There was no way this was one-sided.

"Huh. I thought I heard some heavy panting in here."

"Don't be crass, Elena."

"Crass? I live at an MC compound. That was hardly crass."

"*Cwass*." Kai giggled, and my spirit thrummed, and I was fighting a wild grin as I finally gathered myself enough to push to my feet.

"Oh, there she is." Elena drew it out, her eyes widening with the tease.

"Here I am and totally breathing normally."

It was a lie.

I'd been two seconds from hyperventilating from the mere brush of Silas's hand.

"Mmhmmm."

"What do you want, Elena?" Silas scuffed.

"Kai and I were bored and thought we'd come see what Brinley was up to. We thought she might need some help. We're about to go bonkers inside that house, you know, since you won't let me get a job."

"You don't need a job," he grunted.

"Well, maybe I want one. I have a freaking bachelor's in business and there's absolutely nothing to do with it."

My eyes must have bugged out of their sockets from the surprise because Elena sent me a pout. "Received online and without interacting with a soul. Shocker, right?"

"Don't need this today, Elena," Silas rumbled, agitation flashing through his body.

But it was hurt flashing through Elena's. "I'm not a little girl anymore, Silas."

"We'll discuss it later."

"We'll always, 'discuss it later'."

Pain rebounded between them. Silas because he so clearly wanted to shield her from every horrible thing in the world and Elena because she so clearly needed to be set free.

A clear conundrum since I doubted there was a really good solution for either of them.

Silas finally sighed. "You can help Brinley out here in the office today."

Elena squealed like she was that little girl that she wasn't close to being.

"That is if Brinley doesn't mind."

Now he was asking for my opinion?

"Um, obviously that's a yes from me," I said, trying to coerce the thickness from my voice.

"Because we're besties, obvi," Elena added, grinning conspiratorially my way.

At this point, I wasn't even sure that was an exaggeration.

Silas hesitated, narrowed attention pitching between us, before he shook his head and turned on his heel and walked out into the shop, Elena's overeagerness robbing him of a response.

Then she laughed. "God, he's so easy to rile up."

"It's only because he cares about you."

Elena swayed Kai as she strode around the high counter, a smirk lighting her pretty face. "Ah, how the tables have turned. Now you're the one sticking up for him?"

"Me? Sticking up for him?" I hooked a thumb toward the shop. "No way."

Kai mimicked me, giggling as he gurgled, "No way!"

Crap, this kid could melt the polar icecaps.

"I just want the best for you." I shrugged, like it was no big deal that I meant it.

"You want me to have a little of that *good*?" She wagged her brows the way she'd done earlier in the kitchen.

Amusement had me shaking my head as I plunked myself down in the chair in front of the laptop.

"And what *good* is it you're looking for?" I deflected.

Elena pulled up another chair and plopped Kai onto her lap. "I want to own a gift shop. Maybe have a man who looks at me the way my brother looks at you. You know, the simple things in life."

I could feel her rolling her eyes, like the thought of them was impossible.

With Silas, they just might be.

My mood turned serious as I looked across at her, taking us back to our conversation last night. "Are those some of the risks you're willing to take?"

Air puffed from her nose, and I saw the flash of sorrow blanket her. "They are, but I doubt anyone would be brave enough to take one of those risks on me."

I reached out and squeezed her hand. "I don't think your brother would stop you from finding joy, Elena. He might be protective, but he's not cruel."

Well, at least toward her. I had a hunch the man could be sadistic.

"I think everyone around here is too terrified to find out." Her breath hitched when she said it, and I was sure she wasn't speaking ambiguously, but about someone specific.

"I doubt I'm worth dying for." She attempted to play it as a joke. I fully knew better.

"I'm pretty sure you're worth everything, Elena. Don't you dare give up on what you want. No matter what happened in the past."

Kai was all snuggled up under her chin. Her chin that wobbled.

I probably shouldn't have pushed, but I couldn't help myself as I glanced over my shoulder to make sure we were in the clear before my gaze was back on her. "It's related, isn't it? What's going on with me and what happened to you?"

She blanched, and she sniffled against the emotion. "I don't know that for certain, Brinley. Silas doesn't let me in on those things. He says it's safer if I don't know what's going on."

She hesitated then rushed, "But everything changed after I was held hostage. Silas was quick to pack us up and move to another state. Now everything is more hushed, the guys always whispering and glancing my way, the secrets feeling like they might suffocate."

She let go of a heavy exhale. "My brother has always been on edge, but there is something even more rigid about him now. And with you being here…"

She shrugged a little, but it wasn't indifferent, her eyes pinching in urgency. "They're really bad people, Brinley, and if it is related, then you are in the right place. My brother won't let anything happen to you."

I didn't mean to feel deflated when she admitted it. I hoped that maybe I could glean something from her, some idea of what the hell was going on with Dereck, but I didn't want to manipulate or use her, either.

Because I liked her. Far more than I should. All of them really. Verging on a negligent way.

There was my heart, dangling at the opening of a shredder.

I turned to the laptop and clicked around, trying to orient myself. Mostly it was folders with a ton of old files containing Talon & Torque documents for at least seven years.

I figured the best I could do would be to get their current payables and receivables up to date, send out late invoices to the umpteen service invoices that remained unpaid, and make sure their accounts were balanced.

I wasn't sure how they stayed afloat, but I had an inkling the shop wasn't their only source of income.

Those boys bad, even though it was getting harder and harder to view them that way.

Elena kept rocking Kai who was steadily drifting to sleep. The child seemed to be able to conk out wherever he was.

"So, what's on today's to-dos?" she asked, also trying to clear the heaviness away, a bright smile tacked to her face.

I made an annoyed sound at the back of my throat. "Getting all of those handwritten invoices into the system."

I gestured at a giant stack I'd already sorted.

"Eww, why did I volunteer?" she teased.

"This is no gift shop," I returned. "You won't find any glitter around here."

I got it then. All the notes and the cute things. It fit her perfectly.

"But one day you'll have a store full of it."

"I hope so," she whispered, then both of us jolted with the clatter of activity that suddenly echoed through the air.

All the machinery clipped off in the shop while a bunch of shouts lifted.

Elena shot to her feet. I couldn't stop her before she rushed out the entrance door.

I was right behind her.

"Goddamn it, Elena, get back in the office, right now," Silas growled, halfway across the lot and heading in the direction of the big open gate.

Only she was frozen.

Pale and ashen.

So clearly going weak.

I pulled Kai out of her arms and stepped in front of her, trying to make sense of what was happening as a bunch of Crows went stalking toward a middle-aged guy who stood out on the other side of the gate.

Maybe in his mid-fifties. Salt and pepper hair and beard. Scruffy and mean.

He didn't step over the boundary line.

I was pretty sure he was aware if he did, he'd be writing his own obituary.

Energy blasted and shook. Hate shivering through the rays of sunlight and setting them askew.

Both Silas and Brody were at the front of the pack, while Trevan and six other bikers I didn't know the names of came up at their rear and sides.

The guy sneered, though he lifted his hands and shouted, "Want to see Kai."

That was all it took for me to know. For my own hatred to blister like a forest fire through my veins.

A wave of protection rose over me, and I curled an arm tighter around Kai, somehow managing to grab Elena's hand with the other.

"We need to go." The whispered frenzy of my voice finally breaking her out of the trance.

I was taken over by the urge to flee. To protect. To break the cycle the way Silas was so desperate to do.

I wouldn't let that bastard have him, either.

I didn't take them back into the office.

I wanted to get them as far away from this asshole as possible.

So, I rushed with haggard breaths around the side of the shop, hauling Elena along behind me as I balanced Kai in one arm.

My single destination the house tucked at the back of the property.

Toward that structure that felt like a haven.

Like no one would have the chance to get to any of them there.

I didn't follow the gravel road. I hit the path that cut through the cover of trees since it was about half the distance.

Brush and shrubs rose up beneath. A maze of woods that hugged like shelter.

I did my best to run with Kai in my arms.

He was still asleep, and he bounced against my chest, my efforts slowed by my heels that kept sinking into the soft earth.

I finally kicked off the hindrance and dropped onto my bare feet.

Then I ran. Ignoring the pricks of sticks and rocks that cut into the soles of my feet.

None of that mattered.

The only thing that did was getting them to the house.

Elena let go of my hand so I could hold onto Kai better and raced up to my side, a blur of tears on her face.

"Silas won't let him get to him," I promised on a rasp, a hand cupping the back of Kai's head, pouring that same oath into him.

Elena choked with a nod, and I ignored the sharp bite of pain as my foot was pierced by a particularly sharp rock, sucking it down with the anger that had come at me from out of nowhere.

I wondered if Meems could feel it. If she'd felt the horror strike in the heavens because she was shuffling out onto the porch at the same second we broke out of the thicket.

Dread and ferocity on her face.

A shotgun held across her body.

We barreled up the steps, and she lowered the gun so Elena could throw herself into her arms.

Her grandmother so clearly her safe place, while Meems gave me a knowing look over her head.

25

Silas

"I'd turn around, get back in your truck, and go back to where you came from unless you want to find yourself buried on this property." I growled it, jutting my chin toward the hunk of metal sitting alongside the road.

My insides a riot of rage and bad fucking memories.

It was the same fucking truck.

It would have brought me to my knees if I hadn't been driven by hate.

Hate for the man responsible for everything.

None of this would have happened if it weren't for him. Not the tragedy nor the spiral.

He laughed a callous sound, sneer ripping between me and Brody. "Came here for what's owed to me."

I tried to stop myself, but there was nothing I could do but let my attention skate over my shoulder, praying Elena would do what I told her and take Kai back inside.

Terrified she wouldn't since I saw the look on her face.

The way she'd gone cold, color draining from her face like the last drops of blood from a body.

Her own traumas had begun right here with this piece of shit, too.

Surprise nearly reared me back when I saw Brinley holding Kai, and she was dragging Elena along behind her with her other hand.

Hustling them away and out of sight.

I couldn't even grasp the feeling that rose up in me then.

Complex and complete.

Chest tightening and stomach swimming.

She was protecting them.

I turned back to the scum standing at the edge of my property, hands curled into fists to stop myself from reaching out and choking the life out of him.

That one memory spinning through my brain on a circuit was his only saving grace.

It's your heart. It's your heart.

But I wasn't feeling so graceful right then. The sight of him enough to stamp out that last bit of humanity.

Knew Brody had none of it. Not with the way every muscle in his body was strung like a bow.

An arrow set on a course to impale.

He was barely old enough to remember, and it was this shitbag who'd robbed him of the opportunity for those memories.

I cocked my head. "And what is it you think is owed to you?"

"The kid or money. You know the score. You don't get what you don't pay for."

I scoffed. "Fucking rich from the likes of you."

He let his gaze roam the front of the property, over the row of bikes and the gathering of my men. I nearly came out of my fucking skin with him even possessing that bare knowledge, but I forced myself to toss out a stance of not giving a fuck.

He turned his scorn back on me. "Looks to me like you turned out like your pop, after all."

My spirit howled, but I kept up that quickly disintegrating cool. "Nah, doubt something so insignificant could make much of an impact."

"Huh. Funny since you're making an awful big stir about this."

"Not about you. It's about that kid. He's what matters. And I'm going to tell you once more, and after that, there will be no further warnings."

I took one menacing step toward him.

My entire crew did the same, edging closer, making sure he knew the threat of death was looming.

"You're going to turn around, drive back to California, and forget that any of us exist. You will haul your pathetic ass out of my town, and you won't look back. You're owed nothing but a death sentence, so count yourself lucky that I'm allowing you to walk away. Next time, I won't be feeling so benevolent. You got me?"

He smirked a mouthful of rotten teeth. "Wonder what your momma would have to say about that."

I nearly cracked. Ended him right there on the street. That was just as a random car drove by, slowing to gawk.

Trevan took me by the elbow to stop me, same as Dice did to Brody, that cool we'd barely been fronting dissipating to sweltering mist.

"I think it's time you get on your way," Trevan issued in his genial but lethal way, his attention pinned on PJ when he said it. "No need for things to get messy, but I promise you, they're about to."

Air puffed out of PJ, affronted and the pathetic stench of a man who only had concern about himself.

He looked back at me. "This is far from over. One way or another, I'm going to make you pay."

My mind spun through our altercation the night I'd flown in my truck to the hospital where Kai had been. In Northern California, in a city about two hours outside of Moonlit Ridge.

The way he'd demanded that I was going to pay for Kai. That nothing came for free.

"I owe you nothing." It was a snarl. "Now get the fuck out of here before you no longer have the ability to walk."

He took a step back, smirking harder. "You're gonna regret disrespecting your daddy that way."

"Un-fucking-likely," I spat.

We all stood ground until he tucked tail to his truck. The sound of it roaring when he turned over the ignition nearly leveled me with the memories.

One of those sensory things that you could never purge from your mind.

None of us moved an inch until he turned a U in the road and the echo of it disappeared in the distance.

"Colby, Dice, trail his ass out of town and make sure he's gone," I commanded.

"On it, Prez."

Colby clapped Dice on the back and the two of them went running for their bikes, while the rest of the group dismantled.

All except for Phoenix, Trevan, Brody, and myself.

"You okay?" I finally asked my brother.

Brody shook, the normal easy arrogance he wore crushed by grief. "Don't know why you leave him standing."

I didn't fucking know, either.

"What do you think his game is?" Trevan asked.

"Same as it always is. An easy dollar. And Kai isn't up for fucking sale. Bastard isn't getting anything else out of me."

He'd already stolen enough.

My frayed nerves zapped, not fucking sure where I was supposed to go from here. The last thing I wanted was Kai raised in this life. He deserved so much better. Deserved so much better than me bringing him out of abuse and right into something just as wicked.

The same as Brody and Elena.

Every choice I made only dragged them deeper into the foulness of my life.

I felt lost.

So fucking lost.

I scrubbed both palms over my face, struggling to keep my shit together.

Mind spiraling through so many things.

This bullshit and the task at hand.

Brinley.

Fucking Brinley who was wrecking my head.

Running with Elena and Kai.

Protecting them the same way as she'd been so protective of my little sister last night.

I whipped my attention to Trevan. "Check with Colby and Dice and make sure he gets out of town." Then I looked between all three men. "He comes back, and he doesn't leave."

They knew exactly what I meant.

"You sure?" Trevan pressed.

Phoenix stirred, the Madman placated by the news.

I looked at Brody. Searching for what he felt. For what he needed. This wasn't only about me.

His throat bobbed heavily, eyes wild, before he gave me a tight nod.

I looked back at Trevan. "Yeah, we're sure."

"All right, then."

"I'm going to go check on Elena and Kai," I told them.

Trevan inclined his head. "You want the gates locked up?"

"No. We need to appear like everything is normal. If Kent is watching, we need him to think nothing is amiss, and we're business as usual."

We couldn't afford for it to look like we were gearing up or hunkering down. Couldn't afford for PJ to cost us this gig.

We needed to continue on like it was another normal criminal day.

"Crows ride tonight at ten. Through town. We go to Keg & Creek." It was a local dive I was looking into purchasing. One that held so much consequence for me I couldn't stop myself from going back there right after I came back here.

The original owner long gone.

Its sordid history erased as if it'd never happened.

"If we're hiding out in these walls, it's going to raise red flags. Let everyone know."

Trevan dipped his head in assent.

Then I was moving.

Storming around the shop in the direction Brinley had taken them. Toward the little footpath I somehow knew she'd followed.

Like I could scent her.

That almond and apple scent mixed with terror and care.

I dipped under the shade of the trees, my heart that had been pounding hard now careening.

My gaze snagged on the same peep-toe shoes she loved to tempt me with that had been kicked off and left on the path. I ducked down and picked them up, my pace increasing as I moved through the stir of energy toward the house.

It was denser the closer I got. A whir of it that spun around the walls.

I clumped up the stairs, wondering what the fuck I thought I was doing, so fucking drawn I couldn't think straight.

I tossed open the door to the flurry of activity going on inside.

"I said I'm fine." At Brinley's wheezed words coming from the kitchen, my screaming heart jumped to my throat. I flew through the archway.

She was in a chair turned out from the dining table, holding a bloodied damp rag to her foot.

Fury splintered.

"Are you hurt?" I demanded.

"She cut her foot up real good," Meems confirmed, her gaze slanting to me.

Tortured and pained.

Full of an apology.

I gritted my teeth, trying to feel none of it, my attention slanting to Elena who was on her knees in front of Brinley. Her hands flitted all over like she wanted to do something but had no idea what.

"I'm worried she needs stitches." I could hear the tears in Elena's voice.

"I'm fine," Brinley huffed again, then she pinned those fiery eyes on me. "Is he gone?"

That was her concern.

"Yeah, he's gone, and he's not coming back."

I dropped my focus to Elena, offering it like a promise.

She nodded at me, the normal sass and irritation she watched me with replaced with trust and pain.

Like she got my reasoning for keeping her sheltered, but there was still no erasing the pain of it.

"Where's Kai?" I gritted.

"Sleeping in his playpen. He didn't even wake up." Elena's laugh was soggy.

My nod was sharp.

Eyes dragging back to Brinley who peeled back the rag to get a look at her foot.

More blood gushed, and she winced, quick to cover it up.

"Fuck," I grumbled, and I was scooching Elena aside and sweeping Brinley from the chair, one arm under her legs and the other behind her upper back.

"What the heck, Silas?" she gasped as the rag splatted to the ground.

I didn't answer.

I just carried her up the stairs and into the bathroom in my room, likely leaving a trail of blood behind us.

It wouldn't be the first time I'd done it.

I didn't stop until I had her settled on the counter before I knelt in front of her so I could inspect her foot. One hand on the outside of her calf as I carefully studied her sole.

She winced, though she didn't make a sound as I gently prodded the flesh.

"It's not that deep," I rumbled, though it was a hundred percent in relief. "Don't think stitches are going to be required."

"See, I told everyone it was fine." She huffed it, though her hands were clinging to the edge of the counter.

Not close to fine and it didn't have anything to do with her injury.

I met her gaze.

Was trapped by it, really.

"You protected them." Could barely get the words out around the dryness of my mouth, and they still sounded like praise.

"I…" Her tongue stroked over her lips. "I can't bear the thought of someone getting to them. I don't even know them and…"

She trailed off. Unable to vocalize this thing that neither of us could understand.

"He's gone?" she finally asked again, though quieter, like it was a secret she was asking me to trust her with.

"He's gone."

"He wants to take him back?" She gulped around the fear. Like it was hers as much as it was mine.

Disquiet rolled with the hate. "He just wants money."

Her brow pinched. "Did you give it to him?"

I stared up at her from where I was kneeling on a single knee, still clinging to the side of her calf. "He's never taking anything from me again."

Understanding passed between us. Fierce and vehement.

Mutual respect and something deeper.

I could barely move as I forced myself to stand and go to the cabinet where I pulled out the first aid kit and a fresh washcloth, my guts a tangle as I warmed it under water then knelt back in front of her.

Tenderly lifting her foot so I could clean it.

Those eyes were on me the whole time.

Sifting and penetrating and cutting me through.

Her skin so fucking soft and her spirit so fucking right.

Bright and blinding and a little dark. I wanted to explore every facet. See what made her glow and discover what had caused the hardened places.

I dabbed ointment on the cut then fully wrapped her foot so it would be secure.

I looked up at her.

Found the awed, confused expression on her gorgeous face.

And there was nothing I could do but turn my head and press my lips just to the inside of her knee and whisper, "Thank you."

• • •

The roar of motorcycles filled the heavy summer night. Humidity clinging to the air and sweat drenching my skin.

Me at the helm as we rode into town, my crew in formation behind me.

Trevan and Phoenix were a fraction back and side by side. The others gathered at the rear.

The showing heavy and malicious.

People parted, eyes swinging our way as we passed through Crimson Creek. The diner and bakery and the eclectic shops, though most of them were closed for the night.

I'd left twenty men to guard the compound, but it wasn't enough to quell the anxiety that prickled through my senses.

The feeling that something was off.

Not quite right.

We made the left at Cutter Lane and wound down to the area by the river and pulled into the dirt lot in front of Keg & Creek, a wood-paneled building that looked like it hailed from the 1890s.

I gritted my teeth at the sight. Memories assailing.

I forced it all down, knowing vengeance was soon at hand, and we rolled inside like we owned it. Wearing our cuts, voices boisterous and loud, drinks flowing, my men carousing.

But the whole time I itched.

Unsettled.

Antsy.

And that feeling never settled until I stood in my room five hours later, staring down at her sleeping in the middle of my bed.

Wild brunette curls strewn around her.

No peace until I peeled off my tee and jeans and crawled into my bed next to her, wrapped her in my arms, and pulled her back to my chest.

26

Brinley

Four days had passed since I started staying in Silas's house. Four days of sleeping with him wrapped around me like that was where he was meant to be.

He said it was so he could protect me. Be right there to stand in front of any threat that might make itself known, but I was pretty sure there wasn't a soul who could make it onto the property who wasn't supposed to be there and come out with their lives intact.

I was highly doubting that I was in any actual danger within the compound walls.

The only real threat was the man who still wouldn't budge or give me answers, but who was steadily chipping away at every reserve.

The brittle bricks guarding my spirit and body crumbling a little more with each harsh, vicious look.

I didn't know if it was those or the gentle ones that were getting to me more.

The man both predatory and tender.

I had no idea what to make of him.

The contrast and complexity.

The intimidation and the care.

The way he'd tended to my foot then stood up and walked out like he couldn't stand to be in the same room as me for a second longer.

The brash, greedy way in which he talked to me and the softness of his breath that he'd exhale into my nape when he was holding me.

He didn't push it beyond that.

He'd crawl into bed long after I'd fallen asleep, the man a vat of whiskey and cherries that I'd float in for the night, and he'd be gone when

I woke each morning.

Without fail, I'd be sticky and sweaty and pulsing with need.

My dreams had become both vivid and surreal.

In them, I allowed him to touch me.

To take me.

To own me the way he'd admitted that he wanted to.

I didn't know how it'd happened, but I'd allowed myself to fall into the strange, terrifying comfort of this place.

Every free minute was spent hanging out in the kitchen with Elena, Kai, and Meems. Falling for them more with each beat.

Care coming on severely every time I glanced their way, that foreign sense that they felt the same way when they looked at me.

Like I mattered, and it kept filling up places that I hadn't realized had been empty.

I probably would have completely submitted to the comfort of this place—convinced myself nothing was amiss and I was here by choice and not because I'd been forced to be—if it wasn't for the fact I still hadn't heard from Dereck.

The only reason I knew he was still alive was because I asked Silas and he told me. It pissed me off that those bubbles were no longer popping up to at least give me an indication that he was still breathing every time I stared at my latest unanswered text.

He was such a jerk.

So thoughtless.

And the longer I was there, the more my anger grew toward my little brother.

It wasn't right, the way he used me. I wanted to take care of him. Support him. But how the hell was I supposed to do that when he never met me in the middle? I mean, had I even crossed his mind since he'd dropped me here?

I was still watching and waiting for answers, listening in close to conversations and trying to pick up on any intonation or trace.

Hoping one of the bikers at the shop would slip and reveal something they weren't supposed to.

It turned out, the Crimson Crows were freaking tight-lipped. No sinking ships around here.

So, now I sat at the desk behind the counter in the office, inputting a stack of accounts receivable invoices and trying to make them match up against the payments Torque & Talon had received.

It was kind of a mess.

The move seemed to be the culprit of the disaster, like they'd just picked up and shoved everything into boxes without care or thought.

It didn't exactly sit right since over the week that I'd been working here, I had come to realize that these bikers actually took the business seriously.

Without fail, they showed up at eight each morning and worked in the shop for hours.

Was it dumb that I'd taken some sort of pride in sorting out their financials? Wanting to help Silas? To fix something for him when I could feel the weight of burden pressing down on his shoulders?

Probably, but at least it kept me busy.

Kept me from succumbing to the frenzy that buzzed at the back of my spirit and mind. A distraction from the dread and worry that sat like a barbed-wire ball at the backside of my heart.

It didn't matter that I could hear hoots and laughter and distorted voices seeping through the brick walls of the office.

I could still feel the tension that tugged and curdled the air. Every Crow carved in a razor-sharp edge.

Like something was coming.

A dull threat on the horizon.

Each of them ready for all hell to break loose.

Or maybe because of the lifestyle they lived, that was just the way they always were, and it had nothing to do with my situation.

But there was something about the way Silas hovered over me that told me that wasn't quite right.

Metal and power tools echoed through the walls, a muddle of warped voices and indistinct conversations that carried as I studied an invoice then inputted the numbers into the correct column.

A shiver rocked over me when the door between the shop and office swept open behind me, the same way it did every time Silas came into the room.

I wanted it to be a reaction to the fear I should feel.

Nope.

In its place was shimmery anticipation.

A buzz of energy that slashed and struck, lifting the fine hairs at the nape of my neck.

Silas's footsteps were long yet slowed, his boots thudding on the dingy floor, and my stomach twisted as I felt the overwhelming weight of his presence ease up to me from behind.

His breath fluttered a piece of my hair over my cheek as he reached around and set a plate covered in foil on the desk.

"Eat."

Coarse, raspy care.

Bossy to the extreme.

King.

"I couldn't eat another bite."

Meems had already stuffed me before I came into work this morning.

Eggs and bacon and toast dripping with butter and homemade jam.

His chuckle was scraping and low, and God, my stupid belly did a thousand flips. "Pretty sure you're going to want a taste of what's under there."

"You think you know me so well."

It was a quiet taunt.

Begging him for the attention.

"I think I'm figuring it out." His fingertips lightly trailed up the opposite side of my jaw, scattering goosebumps as they went.

One of those safe touches that I pretended didn't mean anything.

The profile of his face just came into view in my periphery on the other side.

So close.

Smelling like an old-fashioned at ten-thirty in the morning.

Dang it, was that scent addictive.

"Why are you bothering?" I wanted it to come out as snark, but it reeked of desperation.

Those sinewy muscles bunched as he stalled out.

Hesitation blowing through him like the howl of the wind.

Even though he wouldn't give me any details, we both knew what was coming.

I'd either be dead, perish to whatever secret he was keeping, or I'd be right back in the same place.

By myself.

Fighting.

Fighting for Dereck.

Fighting to protect myself.

Fighting to survive.

Except something had to change. It was time. I couldn't keep doing this with Dereck, even though the thought of disappointing my mother destroyed me.

I couldn't keep allowing him to ruin my life again and again.

That was if he didn't...

I crushed the thought in its tracks. I refused to even contemplate it.

"I don't know, Brinley, but I can't seem to stop."

The fingers that had been slipping along my cheek slid into my hair. Fisting into the locks as his nose ran the length of my opposite jaw.

Flames tore through my body.

"If we don't stop, I'm pretty sure it will destroy us both," I rasped.

"Probably," he grunted. "But I think it might be worth it."

Worth it.

"I think I've been hurt enough." It was a shaky defense.

His hand in my hair slipped down until he was holding me by the front of the neck.

Need flooded my veins, as well as a flicker of the old terror that worked to hold me back.

A prisoner.

Was that what I was always going to be?

His mouth pressed close to my jaw. Voice drenched in chaos. "And I'm the fool who wants to take away your pain."

"I don't know if there's anyone who can do that," I wheezed. I shouldn't have released it. It sounded far too much like an admission.

"And I'm nothing but the selfish bastard who wants to try. Not supposed to touch you. Can't touch you..." He murmured the roughened words up and down my jaw.

Trembles rolled and the desire that I'd been battling broke free.

Making me gasp as he let his lips come close to my mouth.

"Doesn't stop the way I want to, though, does it?" he rumbled. "Way I want to peel you apart, layer by layer, then be the one to piece you back together?"

"I'm not broken."

But clearly, I was begging to be with the way I leaned farther into his hold.

Because I wanted to feel.

I wanted to feel something different from what I'd been subjected to for so long.

I was tired of the cold and the vacancy.

And whenever Silas entered the room? I felt alive.

"Nah, baby, you aren't close to being broken. You're a force. A storm. A *Wildfire*. And I want to burn. Even though doing it might prove to be the death of me."

"And I'm ready to live." It was a whisper. A secret. Maybe one I was trying to claim for myself.

"Gonna see to it that you will," he murmured before he reached over to peel the foil from the plate.

Once again, he commanded, "Eat."

I nearly choked over a laugh when I saw it was breakfast dessert.

Okay, dessert concealed as breakfast.

A mountain of pancakes piled high with cherries and whipped cream.

Silas dug his finger into the cherries and cream and brought it to my lips.

Stupid, foolish girl, sucking it into my mouth.

He slowly pulled it out, then he walked away, muttering, "Fuckin' Wildfire. What are you doing to me?"

• • •

Funny how I thought I couldn't eat another bite, and I'd scarfed down the entire plate.

But with the realization that it was time for me to make a change, I decided to go ahead and take a little of the *good*.

That *good* might have made me feel like I was going to burst, but it was worth it.

A strange satisfaction glided through me as I sat there an hour later, making a dent in the stack of invoices.

I should have been off kilter after the earlier interaction with Silas, the way it felt like we were on the brink of a catastrophic explosion, but it was an easy smile climbing to my face when the main door swung open to the lobby.

Probably a smidge too peppy as I stood to welcome the customer.

A man strode through before the glinting glass pane drifted shut behind him.

He looked simple.

Innocuous.

Safe enough.

But the blood drained from my head and my limbs went weak as recognition bowled me over.

It was the same guy from the drugstore parking lot.

Terror bubbled up to the surface, and nausea twisted my stomach into painful knots.

My attention darted in every direction, trying to gauge the best escape route.

Could I make it to the shop doors before he got to me? Did Silas have any clue that he was there?

He cocked an easy grin with a tilt of his chin, casual enough to suggest that he was only there to request a simple oil change.

But it was the gleam in his eye that told me he was there for devious things.

Fear clutched, and I tried to swallow. To stand my ground and not let this asshole know I was shaking.

His brow pinched like he was confused, but I knew full well that it was feigned. "You know…you look awful familiar. Kind of like this guy I know."

A piercing pain stabbed into my chest.

Dereck.

He was talking about Dereck.

I didn't have time to run or spit in his face or demand answers or any of the thousand things I wanted before he moved.

A blur as he jumped over the counter.

Terror screamed through my senses, so loud I thought it would burst my eardrums.

My senses whirring into disarray.

Wanting to fight because fighting was the only thing I had.

But he had an arm locked around my waist from behind and a knife pressed to my throat before I even knew what happened.

My knees sagged when he gritted in my ear, "You're coming with me, bitch."

27

Silas

From where I was in the paint booth, I tore off the respirator so I could inspect the first coat that I'd applied.

The sounds of the rest of the shop were subdued by the insulated partitions.

I examined my handiwork.

The black paint shined, gleaming and pristine on the old Ford Mustang that I was restoring.

Once left for dead after a crash, but the owner who'd plucked it out of a junkyard was trusting me to breathe it back to life.

Reforming mangled metal into something that in the end would eclipse the original.

Pride welled in my chest while my guts continued to be snarled and tangled.

All thanks to one fiery brunette who'd left me in shambles.

Swore to fuck, she was going to do me in.

Raze every restraint.

So fucking off-limits yet she'd begun to feel like the Holy Grail.

A tantalizing treasure I was never worthy of touching, but if I didn't, it made me feel like I might be facing down death.

No matter what I did, I wasn't going to win.

Blowing out a sigh, I studied the hood a little closer. Tracing the defined lines with my eyes.

Deciding I was happy with the results of the first coat, I tossed the mask aside, shucked off my gloves, then pulled open the door and strode out into the main part of the shop.

Heavy metal blared from the speakers, and five of my guys were head down and absorbed in their tasks, the sound of high-pitched power tools becoming one with the deafening beat.

Didn't know what it was, but the guard I always wore sharpened.

Prickles that shot down my spine in spikes of awareness.

My heart started to thump.

Hard and manic.

My gaze jumped to the open bays, scanning quick. As quick as my boots carried me that way.

"Where's Pearce?" I shouted as I tore through the shop.

Pearce was the prospect I'd put on guard at the lobby door.

Dice hiked a shoulder, his arms lifted above his head as he worked below a Toyota on a lift. "Dunno, Prez. Probably off somewhere stealing himself a piece of ass."

That was all it took to have Trevan whirling around and tossing his drill, instantly picking up on the turmoil that whipped me into a squall.

I did my best to keep my cool. A wasted effort since I immediately felt like I was being burned at the stake.

That's exactly what it felt like when I realized there was a car parked in front that hadn't been there before.

A gold, metallic sedan.

The same car that had been in that lot.

Dread spiraled through the middle of me. A slick of alarm so thick that I nearly tripped on it.

"Fuck," heaved out from my throat before I was shouting, "Trespasser!"

It was the one word that would have everyone within earshot on their feet and armed in a flash.

"Lobby, now!" I commanded as I whipped my gun from the holster hidden inside my coveralls, guts a riot as I edged for the interior door.

I wanted to go barreling in, but I needed to be prepared. Do this the right way. There was no room for mistakes.

Trevan was right behind me, his own gun drawn.

Aggression cracked on his clenched teeth, though he was giving me his steadying voice the way he always did. "Careful, Prez."

I felt Phoenix move, a roil of darkness that coasted from the shop like a wraith, followed by Colby and Dice who ran out of a bay to head off the front door.

My men were trained like soldiers, knowing exactly what to do when evil came calling.

"Brinley's in there." It ground off my tongue.

I didn't even realize I said it aloud until Trevan mumbled, "Know it, man. We'll get her. Just keep your cool and don't do anything rash."

But there was no cool to be had.

Not when I felt myself splintering like an axe struck through a brittle piece of wood.

A dominating wave of possession sweeping through me that had no place, one that had been coming on ever since she'd run my sister and baby brother to safety.

A possession I had no right to feel.

But it was there.

Suffocating.

As thick as the fear that saturated my spirit.

I told her I'd protect her. I couldn't fucking fail her the way I'd failed everyone else.

I gripped the butt of the gun in both hands, finger trembling on the trigger.

Sweat dripped down my back.

I cut my attention to the right. To where I knew Styx would be in position, in the line of sight between us and the guys at the front.

Our eyes and ears for both teams.

I watched as five Crows came hustling up from out of nowhere, three parting to the front door and two coming up behind me and Trevan.

I gave the count.

Three ticks of my chin.

Then Styx gave the signal to the guys at the front as soon as I did.

We all busted in at the same time, my crew piling into the office and poised for a fight.

My heart sank to the pit of my stomach when I took in the scene.

That motherfucker was in the middle of the room on this side of the counter.

Brinley's back pinned to his chest and a knife to her throat.

My ribs squeezed around my hemorrhaging heart.

"Stay the fuck away or she's done," he snarled, spinning a fraction as he hauled her back in the direction of the door.

Every eye in the place flashed toward me, my crew looking to me for the next move.

Wondering how I wanted them to handle this.

Safe.

I just wanted her safe.

If it was only us, this would be a bloodbath.

But not when an innocent's life was on the line.

An innocent whose face was so full of terror it knocked my fucking knees.

Bile climbed my throat as that protectiveness bound up my insides in a ball of aggression.

I wouldn't allow anyone to hurt her.

I promised her.

Fucking promised her.

"I mean it!" he shouted. The tip of that gleaming blade dug deeper into the delicate flesh of Brinley's throat.

A droplet of blood dripped from the wound.

"Everyone out of my fucking way, or she dies."

Rage screamed, and my blood ran hot.

The group of my guys at the front wavered, never ones to stand down, before they split apart, unwilling to take the chance that he wouldn't drive that knife deeper if they didn't let him through.

The piece of shit grinned at me from over her shoulder.

Agony licked across my insides.

A howl of misery and determination.

"Drop the fucking knife," I growled, swiveling a step farther into the room.

Dude was a fool for coming here like this.

A dead man walking.

No question, he was nothing but an expendable messenger.

Kent Ellison didn't exactly have a reputation for cherishing the sanctity of life.

Which was why I couldn't fucking wait to end his.

The lowlife in front of me paid no heed, just kept yanking Brinley backward toward the main door.

Every cell in my being writhed, the thirst for vengeance coating my tongue.

Brinley was stiff in his clutches, those eyes that were pinned on me a hurricane of desperation.

Pleading.

A stir of hate and obstinacy rolled through me, and I willed myself not to charge in their direction.

Instead trying to convey to her with my eyes that she was going to be okay.

I wouldn't let anyone hurt her.

"Stop right there or you're dead." Violence was carved into my words.

He already was. The fuckwit had to know it.

But maybe he was stupid enough to think he was going to get away with this because he chuckled a low sound and pressed the knife deeper against her throat.

Blood trickled from the tiny gash.

I couldn't fucking swallow, my pulse thundering, a fucking freight train of urgency that barreled through my veins.

"Nah. Don't think so. I'm going to walk right out of here and you're going to let me," he sneered.

"And how do you suppose? You're surrounded." I said it casually. Like the result had already been exposed.

"Because I have what you want."

I scoffed and tried to play it off. "And what's that?"

"Her."

He was right. Utterly, completely right. And for all the fucking wrong reasons.

"Let her go, and I might let you live."

He smirked. "It's funny that you think you're the one in control here. The one calling the shots. Kent asked that I leave a little message for you."

I huffed like I didn't give a shit what that prick had to say, all while my finger itched on the trigger, waiting for a clear shot.

Ready to take it the second I had it.

"He wants you to know that you have one more chance." Deviant sneered it. "He'll forgive you for that little stunt you pulled with your sister, but when you come crawling back, you know you're his and you bring Elena with you. He said to consider it part of your debt."

Rage hit me so hard it was blinding.

Disgust and hate and the truth that I would never let anyone get to my sister again.

"I'm going to take this one with me as a little extra bonus."

It was all I could take.

I snapped.

Surging forward with the intent of tearing the fucker apart with my bare hands, but Trevan grabbed me by the elbow and dragged me back just as the creep yanked Brinley all the way out the front door.

The two of them were swallowed by the swell of gleaming sun before the door swung shut behind them.

Fury combusted, a deafening roar in my ears.

Wildfire.

Wildfire.

"What the fuck?" I snarled, trying to break out of Trevan's hold.

"Just wait," he gritted.

I thrashed, and he tightened his hold. "Trust me, brother, wait."

That was right when a single gunshot rang out, followed by an ear-splitting scream out of Brinley.

It pierced my chest like a flaming arrow.

That was right when Trevan released me, and I went barreling through the lobby, shoving through my guys and out into the glaring light.

Brinley was on the ground, her knees and hands scraping the gravel as she dragged herself back in my direction.

Juts of horror and disbelief hurled from her quivering, mortified mouth.

Locks of autumn-spun hair wild and disheveled around her stunning face.

An indecipherable emotion rose up in me as I watched the agony and determination rip through her distinct, unforgettable features.

Brinley Webber looked like she was crawling out of a pit.

Rising from the ashes.

Bastard was on the ground howling, holding onto his upper thigh where he'd clearly been hit.

Brody stood thirty feet away, his gun hanging limply at his side.

The playful cockiness he normally wore was covered by the murderous viciousness that contorted his face.

The same as it had done when that pile of garbage PJ had shown up here.

My spirit twined in both regret and praise, sure that he had been the one who'd taken the shot. The one who'd saved Brinley.

Four Crows raced to the sleaze on the ground and hauled him up by both arms.

I barely even registered him fighting them since all my attention was locked on Brinley.

Brinley who was clamoring for me.

I went running her way.

Scooping her off the ground and into my arms.

Relief slammed me so hard I could barely stand.

"I've got you. I've got you. You're okay. I've got you," I mumbled into her hair.

A sob hitched from her throat, and she locked her arms around my neck as I carried her back toward the lobby door.

Trevan stood outside it, eyeing me firm and fierce.

I lifted my chin at him.

An unspoken thank you.

Because he fucking knew what was going down in the middle of the mayhem. He knew my men had it covered and would easily take the fucker down without putting anyone in unnecessary danger, when I had let myself lose sight.

Willing to run headlong into the fire.

Without a plan or foresight.

So fucking reckless and wrong.

But that seemed to be exactly what this woman was doing to me.

Making me reckless.

Angling toward things I shouldn't touch. Wanting things that I sure as hell couldn't keep.

He gave a quick flick of his head toward the asshole that the guys were dragging in the direction of the clubhouse.

A silent promise that the swine would be ready for me when I was ready to deal with him.

And deal with him I would.

But right then the only thing that mattered was Brinley.

Brinley who was shaking in my hold.

A fist of rage threatened to crush my breastbone, fury and violence still hot on my hands.

Fuck.

What I wouldn't give to hop on my bike and destroy the beast who had set this into motion. Turn around and end anything or anyone who would threaten to do her harm.

Say fuck it to the whole plan and end him myself.

But I couldn't let her go, either.

Couldn't do anything but carry her back into the lobby and around the counter where I carefully settled her onto the desk.

She gasped and choked, hands still clinging to my neck as I inched back so I could take her in.

Almost dropped to my knees when she tipped her face toward me.

Tears soaked her cheeks.

Confusion and dread and terror toiling in those harvest eyes.

I gripped her by each side of the jaw, trying to wipe away the stains like it might be enough to erase the intent that had been perpetuated today.

"Are you hurt? Did he get you anywhere else?" With my thumb, I swept up the trickle of blood from her neck.

"No." She gulped, and she squeezed her eyes closed for a beat, like she was trying to bring herself back to reality.

Problem was, this *was* her reality.

I hated it.

Hated that this nightmare was real.

Hated that she had been sucked into her brother's mess and that I was a twisted part of it.

"You're okay. You're okay," I rumbled again.

Trying to make it true.

Wishing I had the power to take it away.

That I could make it better.

That *I* could be better.

"Am I?" Brinley basically begged as she gripped onto my wrists. "Am I really okay?"

"Yes. Because I'm here. I'm right fucking here." It was the only answer I could give.

She gulped. "Who was that?"

"Not sure, but we'll find out." Brutality curled out with the words.

"He...he wanted to take me. He knew Dereck." It tumbled out of her mouth.

I kept running my thumbs over the tears that slipped down her cheeks.

"I know."

"I don't understand any of this, Silas. I didn't ask to be a part of it. I don't want to be a part of it."

"I don't want you to be, either, and I'm going to make sure to get you out of it. I promise you."

I wouldn't stop until I made it fact.

"That's why you're here," I grated. "You're here so I can protect you from it."

Even though we were obviously doing a terrible job.

How the fuck that bastard got in here unnoticed, I didn't know.

Pearce's ass was mine, but that was going to have to wait.

Because I was rooted.

Fucking stuck.

Stuck on this woman who was making me want things I had no right to want.

Nothing but a selfish bastard who had nothing to give but pain and grief.

And there I stood, wanting to devour the temptation in front of me.

My grandmother had always urged me to go after the good things in life. To take it when it was presented because we never knew when we would no longer have the chance.

Problem was, the only thing I would do was taint it.

Ruin and spoil and desolate.

"I'm scared, Silas." Brinley hiccupped as the admission slid between her plush, pouty lips.

Her simple words gripped me in a chokehold.

Energy lashed.

Since the moment I met her, she had always been harsh. Fierce and volatile. A hurricane rushing in to make landfall.

And now she was laying herself bare, allowing vulnerability to come spilling out.

Like she trusted me to hold her insecurities. Hold the things that had shaped her into this little fighter who refused to let anyone get to her.

"I'll ruin you, baby."

It was a warning for both of us.

Because I could feel the distinct break that had been made. Something inside of Brinley had shattered apart when that monster had come through the door, same way as it'd done me.

"Why don't I care? Why do I want you to?" she whispered through the torment.

"Because maybe you're as reckless as me."

Wild curls framed her gorgeous, stunning face, tight body clad in another one of those tiny dresses that had been slowly driving me out of my mind.

Cream colored fabric hugging her curves, her trembling legs swinging off the edge of the desk.

A glutton, I slowly wedged myself between them.

There was so much confliction in her gaze, I couldn't quite make sense of it.

A whirring of convoluted air that spun her into mayhem.

Need and desperation and something that looked far too close to trepidation.

Those wild eyes devouring.

Both eager and afraid.

My chest tightened in a fist, tighter than it ever had, fully aware that she was exposing something that she hadn't before.

I just couldn't quite put my finger on it.

A good man would tear himself away. Get the fuck out of there before he crossed a line he couldn't undo.

But I wasn't close to one of those, and with her, I'd been crossing them all along.

A captive to the gravity that she emitted.

"I shouldn't be here like this with you, Brinley. Shouldn't be touching you at all. But I don't know how to stop when it comes to you. The way you make me feel..."

Electricity crackled in the air. A connection that burned where I held her on either side of the face.

Her sweet breaths panted into my face.

Apples and almonds and cream.

So delectably sweet that I knew I was touching on some kind of innocence that I hadn't recognized in her before.

Her lips parted on a rush of desire.

"I'll ruin you," I gritted again.

Those eyes were so wide as she begged, "I want to know what that feels like."

Fuck it.

Fuck the questions and the consequences.

I dove in. Our mouths and souls colliding.

It was a clash of desperation and the pent-up desire that had been working between us since the moment she descended like a storm onto my property.

Full scale combustion.

Tongues and lips and teeth.

All while these wayward specks inside me ached to become something different.

Wishing that I was different than the man I'd become.

A man who'd do anything to be good enough to stand at her side. Good enough to call her mine.

It's your heart. It's your heart.

That thought alone should send me running out the door.

Instead, I drove my fingers into her hair, gripping onto the erratic curls, driving the madness higher. Brinley's lips were so fucking soft, so fucking delicious, that I knew they had to be coated in poison.

Had to be with the way I'd gone delirious.

Caught on a rush of dizziness that took me whole as I pushed the kiss further, the surging of something massive and overpowering that ballooned in my chest.

Something brighter than I'd ever experienced before.

Needy fingers fisted in the shirt beneath my coveralls that were partially unzipped, and she gasped these short, whimpered breaths into my mouth as I shifted my head from side to side, devouring her mouth and wishing that I could sink all the way inside.

Brinley parted.

Opening to me.

Body, spirit, and soul.

Her head tipped back and the desirous sound that rolled up her throat was nothing but a plea.

Tugging her a little from the desk, I wound myself all the way between her thighs.

A frenzy lit as I pressed my hard, aching cock to the mind-boggling heat that radiated from her pussy.

Far too many clothes divided us to leave either of us satisfied.

I wanted to erase it. Erase every barrier that separated us. Own her the way I needed to.

"Is that what you want, Brinley? You want me to peel you apart? Fuck you so good that the only name you know is mine?"

My tongue swept between her lips at the same time as I rocked against her.

Our tongues stroking and tangling and inciting a mania that spun the room.

Walls whirring at warp speed as I kissed her with everything that I had to give.

Intensity blistered. Scorching our flesh.

Flames licking up from the well of attraction that had me hooked from the moment I saw her.

When I'd somehow known this girl was going to change everything.

Brinley rasped. A mewl of hunger that was bound up with this confusion that rained and battered at our senses.

A hurricane that hit land.

She struggled to get closer, whimpering and whining as she rubbed herself against my raging hard dick.

"Wildfire," I mumbled at her mouth.

"King."

How the fuck it sounded like affection sliding off her tongue and onto mine, I didn't know.

The words slipping between us in a frantic appeal as her fingers rushed up my shirt to grip onto my shoulders.

"Please," she begged like I could be something that she had been missing.

I wanted to be.

I wanted to fix whatever went dark in her gaze. Calm those flickers of fear that sparked from her spirit whenever she hit me with all that feral, stormy heat.

Nothing but a fool who wanted to discover all that she was.

"Want you like I've never wanted anything in my life. In a way that makes me question all that I know. How is it you hold that power?" I rambled it against her mouth, sucking down the nonexistent air.

Drawing her essence into my lungs instead.

Had the very dangerous thought that she might hold the power to breathe life into all the vacant places that had long gone dead.

Resurrect a piece that had been lost.

One hand slid from her face to the back of her neck so I could control the kiss, while the other took a path down her front.

Hand palming one perfect tit, my thumb stroking over the hard, peaked nub of her nipple, swirling it and making her arch and moan.

"How? How? I don't understand," she mumbled, nearly incoherent as she pressed herself closer, and a growl was ripping free as I was assaulted with a lust unlike anything I'd ever known.

Piercing as deep as a bullet.

It was something that verged on deranged. A tipping point that once it spilled over, we both were going to drown.

My hand kept traveling south, gliding down her side and to her hip.

I palmed the outside of her thigh, using the leverage to rock against her, tiny sparks lighting up behind my eyes.

Greed taking me over, I edged back an inch so I could glide my hand under the thin fabric of her dress.

Dress that was pushed up high, exposing the silken tops of her lush legs.

Sight of it was enough that I nearly came in my pants. My mind lost.

All fucking rationale and purpose and knowledge of who I was evaporating in a beat.

Guts knotted in need, I brushed my fingertips over her soaked panties.

I couldn't wait until I got to fully sink inside.

Fuck the consequences and the promises I had made. Let my crew shove my head under a guillotine.

I pushed her underwear aside.

Brinley suddenly flinched, and every molecule in her body froze for a flash.

I didn't know how I recognized it through the haze of lust that saturated the air, but I did.

I recognized it like a smack across the face.

Like another mark slashed into my soul.

Her hands that had been grappling to get closer tightened in a way that told me she was trying to keep herself grounded.

To keep herself from spiraling into a place she was terrified to go.

Sucked back into a darkness that threatened to swallow her whole.

I wanted to go on a rampage. Demand that she make me a list.

A list of names of every single person who'd ever hurt her so I could eradicate the stain of them from the earth.

Panting, I checked myself, framing her face in my hands and trying to slow the haphazard pounding of my heart.

"Brinley," I grunted, her name jagged shards of glass.

In restraint, I rocked my forehead against hers.

Her eyes were still closed tight, hands steel bands where they were bound in my shirt.

She only squeezed her eyes tighter, her words thin rasps. "Don't stop. I don't want to hurt anymore."

"And it would kill me to hurt you, and I refuse to be one of the bastards who has."

"Don't you want me?" Her voice was something I didn't recognize.

Small.

Ashamed.

I pulled back, gripping onto her face. "Want you more than I've ever wanted anything in my life, which is clearly an indication that I shouldn't have you. Won't be another monster taking advantage of you."

I didn't know who they were, but I knew they were there. Could see the grim history stretching out like an eternal road at the backs of her bleak gaze.

Drawing me down it like a beast searching for prey.

I'd hunt them.

I'd hunt every fucking one of them.

She hesitated, blinking as she tried to dip her gaze.

"You weren't supposed to see me this way. No one was. I'm so sick of it, Silas. I'm so sick of being pathetic and weak."

"There isn't a single thing weak about you, baby. Not one."

I brushed my thumbs across the hollows of her eyes. "You just had a deviant dragging you out the door with a knife pressed to your throat. You are one of the strongest people I know. This force that *forced* its way right into my life. Shaking up everything that I thought I knew and making me see something else."

I was worried right then that she might be the only one who could see *me*.

"I'm going to take you back to the house," I finally forced out, peeling myself from her gravity, though I still couldn't seem to let go of her face.

Needing the connection.

To feel the life beat of her under my palms.

Shaking her head, she swiped away some of the moisture from her cheeks with the back of her hand.

"I need to work."

"Not happening. You need to rest."

And I needed to get far the hell away from her.

Clear my fucking head.

Put about three states between us because the only thing I wanted to do was dive back in.

That need was almost as excruciating as the thirst to spill the blood of the wicked.

And spilling blood seemed like a really good plan right about then.

Brinley peered up at me.

Face tear-stained and this bright hope shining through the torment that she'd suffered.

Girl nothing but light.

That connection I felt to her spun and churned and worked itself into something different than it'd been.

My soul shifting to understanding.

"Please, don't fight me on this," I murmured. "Let me take you back to the house so you can wash that scum off your body. Can't fucking handle that he had his hands on you."

If I thought I'd felt protective of her before? That need had bloomed into something desperate and complete.

Like maybe it was the one fucking reason I'd been born.

To be there.

Right then.

To set her free.

Brinley sniffled. "Okay. Getting out of these clothes is probably a decent idea. I'm kind of a mess."

Was she really agreeing that easily? I wondered how messed up it was that I wanted her to fight me.

"I kinda like the mess you are." I knew with the way my smile went soft that I was completely fucked.

She shook her head. Sadness filling the motion.

No doubt, she was aware that she and I were teetering on a very precarious cliff.

Getting attached in a way that we couldn't.

And fuck me. I wanted to keep her.

Claim her.

Put a property patch on her back and make her mine.

My mother's face flashed through my mind.

My guts toiled.

Hatred burned and guilt constricted.

I couldn't do that.

My life was destruction, and I refused to cause her harm the way I did with everything that I touched.

Refused to subject her to a life of heartache.

To pain and suffering and horror.

I made a silent promise right then that I would somehow find a way to shield her from it.

From her brother.

From the old wounds that held her hostage.

Most of all, from me.

28

Silas

Fifteen Years Old

Sweat dripped down Silas's spine as he pushed the shopping cart across the parking lot of Crimson Creek Market & Deli. The elderly lady hobbled slowly at his side, and he forced himself into keeping her pace.

He angled the cart up to the trunk of her car and loaded her groceries in. She patted his arm as she placed a few coins into his palm, her wrinkled face tripping up in a genuine smile. "Here you go, young man. I sure appreciate you helping me out."

"Thank you, ma'am," he mumbled, trying not to eye how much she was giving him because he didn't want to be like that, but it was really difficult to stop himself.

Money was tight.

No matter how much his momma and Meems told him money didn't matter, he could feel the stress rolling off them.

Could hear them muttering under their breaths about the rent being late again, and he didn't think there could be enough coupons clipped in the world that would cover the cost of feeding him and his siblings, though he'd taken to sneaking the expired food his boss tossed into the dumpster each night into his backpack.

Most of it seemed decent.

His momma worked at the steakhouse almost every night, but it was the slow season for tourists, so the owner kept sending her home.

So Silas had taken it upon himself to pick up every extra shift that he could, and he made sure to walk every person out just in case they'd give him an extra tip.

He was pretty sure the thirty cents the old lady had given him wasn't going to make a dent, but he figured she probably didn't have a whole lot extra, either.

He made sure she was safely settled into the driver's seat of her car before he turned to push the cart back toward the sliding door of the market.

The building was wood with a pitched roof like most of those around town, its awning painted red.

He was halfway there when he heard a rumble that made the hairs lift on the nape of his neck.

He knew that sound.

It was a sound that made his skin crawl.

He didn't want to turn around when the truck came to idle behind him but, for some reason, he couldn't stop himself.

He turned, and the passenger-side window was rolled down, his dad grinning at him through the opening. "There's my boy."

Silas wanted to scoff.

He wasn't his boy. He didn't want anything to do with him. Silas hadn't seen him around town in at least a year. That was the way he wanted it.

"What are you doin' spending your summer vacation slogging away here for?"

Silas didn't answer him. His dad didn't have any right to know what was going on with them. Not when he hadn't given his momma a penny in all these years.

"Got something for your momma."

Silas cringed, silently berating himself for even thinking about her in front of him, like maybe he'd plucked her face right out of his mind.

"She doesn't want anything from you." Silas hoped his voice didn't shake when he said it.

"Ah, I'm pretty sure she's gonna want this."

Silas wanted to tell him to go to hell, but he got caught on the small paper bag his dad waved between them.

He looked around the parking lot, his thrumming heart rising to his throat, feeling like he was doing something illicit as he reluctantly edged forward and accepted the bag through the window.

The paper crinkled as he slowly peeled it open to look at its contents.

His stomach flipped over.

There had to be five hundred dollars inside.

"Whole lot more where that came from." His dad paused like he was waiting for Silas to say something before he filled in the silence. "My boy shouldn't be working at a place like this. Working his fingers to the bone without any reward. You gotta be smart like your old man."

Smart was about the last thing Silas had ever considered his father, but he couldn't deny the relief he felt at holding all that money.

"I'll be back next week with more. Probably shouldn't tell your momma where you got that, but I'm trusting that you make sure she gets it."

It was the first time Silas thought maybe his dad had something good in him, giving him this and thinking about their family.

"I will," he finally managed.

"That's my boy," his father said before he drove away.

• • •

A clatter of voices and laughter carried through the small house as Silas stepped through the door.

He scuffed the mud off his boots before he went clomping into the kitchen.

"Silas! You're home!" Elena ditched the big bowl of dough she was working with her hands, jumping off the small stool where she stood beside Meems.

She threw herself against him, the way she did every time he came home.

His chest felt full as he hugged her back. "Hey, Lena."

"How was your day? Did you make a lot of money? Meems and I are making cherry pie for dessert. We know it's your favorite."

Elena's head was up to his waist, his little sister getting ready to turn eight.

Meems hummed from where she swayed at the counter. "That's right. We figured our Silas has been working hard all day, so he deserves a special treat."

Unease rolled through his stomach, the money he had hidden at the bottom of his backpack feeling like it weighed a hundred pounds. He swallowed it down and ignored it.

"What do you think?" Elena beamed.

"I think it's the best surprise ever," he told her.

She laughed before she went blazing back to their grandmother's side and climbed onto the short stool so she could reach.

"Hi, Silas!" Brody came running into the kitchen, two Transformers in his hands. "You want to play?"

"Give your brother a minute to relax, Brody. He's been working outside most of the day and he needs a little breather," Meems instructed.

"Ah, man," Brody whined.

Silas roughed his fingers through his little brother's hair. "How about after I take a shower we go play ball out front?"

"Deal!" Brody went running right back out.

Meems tsked. "That boy has so much energy he's liable to tear down the house."

Chuckling, Silas shuffled the rest of the way into the kitchen and pecked a kiss to Meems's cheek.

"Missed you," she said.

His chest tightened as he dipped into the fridge and pulled out the almost empty bottle of orange juice.

One he'd snagged from the dumpster two days ago.

"Missed you, too. Where's Mom?" he mumbled.

"Getting ready for her shift."

He spun the cap off the bottle and tossed the whole thing back, guzzling down the cold juice in three big gulps.

He sent Meems a big grin when he saw that she was giving him the side-eye. "Already almost empty," he said, tossing it in the trash before he ducked out and went wandering down the hall toward his mother's room at the back.

He poked his head inside the open door.

She was at the mirror, pulling the big curlers from her hair. She was dressed in black jeans and a black undershirt, but she hadn't put on the black western shirt that was part of her uniform yet.

"There's my sweet Silas," she said with her soft smile through the mirror.

"Hey, Mom," he muttered, not sure why he felt so nervous as he stepped inside and crossed the room, welcoming her tight hug.

"How was your day?"

"It was really good." He pretty much stammered it.

She must have sensed it because she pulled back with a frown, studying his face. She had to look up now since he was an inch taller than her.

"What's going on?" She'd always been able to tell when something was up with him.

When he was upset or sad or secretly excited.

He wavered, unsure what to do or what to say. He'd always hated lying to her. He knew he wasn't good at it and knew even more that it wasn't right.

But he knew she needed this even though she'd refuse it if she knew where it came from.

So he tried to twist his mouth into a genuine grin. "I got a big bonus today."

Her frown deepened, but not in a bad way. "A bonus?"

"Yep. Mr. Barker said I was doing such a good job that he wanted to give me something extra."

"That's amazing, Silas. Of course he thinks you're doing a good job. You're the hardest working, most caring person I know."

His chest stretched with guilt, and he hid his face by kneeling to set his backpack onto the worn carpet, his hands shaking as he unzipped it and dug to the bottom to pull out the bag.

Standing, he extended it to her.

Confusion traipsed through her expression as her eyes darted between the bag and his face.

"Take it," he urged, and she seemed wary as she took it.

A soft breath of surprise left her when she peeked inside.

"Silas, this is…" She couldn't seem to find the right words before she was looking at him deep. "This is a lot of money."

He shifted uncomfortably on his feet. "It's for you."

Her frown deepened. "No, honey, you've been working hard this whole summer and you deserve this."

"No way, Mom. It's for our family. I know we need it."

Moisture made her eyes glassy, and the guilt made him feel like he was going to pass out.

But she needed it badly. He knew she did. So any guilt he felt was worth it.

"Please, Mom…I need you to take it. You work so hard to take care of all of us."

She reached out and set her hand on his chest. Whispered, "Silas, my sweet boy. It's your heart."

That heart felt like it was going to bust.

29

Silas

The room was dank and stale.

Clad in gloom and shadows.

Hidden in the depths of the clubhouse.

Walls so fucking thick there wasn't a chance that anyone else could hear the wails coming from within.

And wails there were.

I dragged the tip of the blade across the bastard's chest, opening up the flesh.

Motherfucker howled where he was bound to a wooden chair, his wrists tied to the armrests and his ankles to the legs.

His entire body arched from the chair.

Like he was stupid enough to think that he might be able to escape the fate he had condemned himself to.

Blood gushed from the wound, a wave slicking down his chest in a sheet. It thinned out in streaks that dribbled onto his bare stomach, mixing with the wound that had been made there, too.

I leaned in close to his face and demanded, "Not gonna ask you again. What does Kent know?"

Motherfucker angled back and spat in my face. "I'm not telling you shit."

Rage surged, and I lifted my arm and wiped the blight off with my shoulder, teeth grinding as I attempted to keep the fury reined.

The thoughts of Brinley that kept invading made it damned near impossible. The memory of her trapped with that knife to her throat leaving me close to unhinged.

He was going to feel that same fear and pain a hundredfold.

But first, I needed answers.

"Bad idea, acting like that in the position you're in, don't you think?"

He squirmed as I played the tip of the knife around a spot that I'd already opened on his shoulder, but he only clenched his jaw, trapping the words I knew wanted to get free.

Phoenix itched behind me. A barely held frenzy licking across his flesh. A phantom waiting in the shadows. Demon begging to come out to play.

Wanting to dig his talons into this asshole and make him pay the way he deserved.

Phoenix could play with him later.

Right then, I had to extract whatever secrets and dirty deeds this piece of shit was hiding.

Everything was riding on this.

If Kent had any indication of what was coming for him, we were dead.

Every single one of us.

And I wasn't sure if this scum coming here was a warning that Kent had a suspicion, or if the deviant was just giving another go at putting me and my crew under his thumb.

The latter didn't fit.

Not when it was clear he was here for Brinley.

This was about Dereck.

If that motherfucker had flipped…

Anger boiled, closing off my throat, and I dug the knife in a little deeper.

Dickbag gritted his teeth, specks of spittle flying from his mouth as he tried to guard himself from the pain.

"If you don't start talking, I'm going to let my friend here have a little visit with you." I tipped my head toward Phoenix. "And I promise you, you don't want that. I'm much nicer than him."

I gave him a smile.

All teeth.

He thrashed, yanking at his bindings.

"Fighting isn't going to help you. Confessions are. Now why did Kent really send you?"

When he didn't answer, I slashed the knife across his cheek.

Deep.

Agony blistered from his being, and he finally shouted, "To deliver his message!"

His breaths heaved, his skin drenched with sweat and blood and pee. The stank of his fear filling up the room. "He wants you to know there is no escaping him. Wants you to know that you belong to him."

"And why were you taking Brinley?"

Asshole went mute.

I lifted my arm and hacked the knife three times into the top of his thigh.

Howls of agony banged and ricocheted against the walls before the words began to tumble from his mouth.

"Because I recognized her when I saw her with you, and I knew that slimy prick Dereck was up to something. Figured the boss would be happy to see me show up with something extra."

Fuck.

Fuck, fuck, fuck.

I kept the knife poised high, words slashing demands from my mouth. "You tell him she's here already?"

Did Kent know we were coming for him?

For all of them?

Were the pieces coming together and Kent was realizing Dereck was about to mete the kind of betrayal that could never be taken back?

Sweat poured from the scum's hairline. "No. I…I did it on my own," he rasped.

He was now nearly completely covered in blood.

Streams dripping to the ground below him.

"I thought he'd move me up from this grunt position to the place where I belong once he saw the initiative I was taking."

Initiative.

Fucking twisted bastard.

The rage that had held me in chains since my sister had been taken spun me into tumult.

Lawlessness singeing my already frayed nerves.

"Are you lying to me?"

"No, I swear. I fucking swear."

"You're sure?"

"On my life. And I swear I won't tell anyone that Brinley is here. Your secret is safe with me."

"Yeah, it's definitely safe with you."

I slowly stood, wiping the blood from both sides of the blade onto my pant leg.

Then I turned to Phoenix and gestured at the piece of shit tied to the chair with my chin. "Do your thing and get rid of him when you're finished."

I stalked to the door and ripped it open, the wailing screams and pleas that suddenly filled the room clipping off as it slammed shut behind me.

30

Brinley

In the distance, the bonfire leapt toward the blackened sky, the flames close to kissing the bottoms of the branches that stretched out in a canopy over the front of the clubhouse.

The trees soared to a height that made them appear as if they touched the stars that were strewn into eternity.

Sentries that stood guard over the property, the same way as the riot of men who were gathered around the bonfire did.

Wearing their cuts, beer bottles in their hands, their laughter echoing through the cool, summer night.

There was no missing the fact that there was also a horde of women present tonight. No shortage of leather and lace, but I guess I was offering a bit of that, too.

Dressing myself up like my clothing was armor as I stalked my way toward the party.

I refused to cower or hide in Silas's room after what had happened earlier today.

I was no shrinking violet.

I refused to let the incident be a stumbling block, and I'd be damned if I allowed it to send me tumbling all the way back to five years ago.

I refused to be *her*, even though I'd been foolish enough to let Silas get a peek of her.

Time to rectify that.

I honestly thought the fear I'd been holding at bay for years would keep its stupid mouth shut since it'd been close to nonexistent every time Silas came in the room.

Desire taking its place.

But for one flash of a second, the terror had sucked me under and panic had hit.

Blackened waters that rose to cover my face.

But somewhere inside, I'd also known I could reach out and find safety.

I knew Silas wouldn't let me drown.

I thought he wouldn't notice that flicker.

Really, he shouldn't have.

It really wasn't that big of a reaction, and I knew I would have been able to tame it if I'd been given a couple of seconds.

Leave it to the foreboding man to be the one to see right through me.

Like he was an extension of me.

The terror zapping from my nerves and becoming one with his.

It was wild that I found so much comfort in it.

Never once in my life had I felt as secure as I did the moment he was holding me by the face.

His breaths mine.

His care distinct.

Reading a piece of me I never left exposed.

A week ago, the last person I would have attributed those qualities to was Silas Mercer.

From the get-go, I'd deemed him wholly wicked and cruel.

A part of him was.

I wasn't blind.

I could only fathom what had happened to the man who had tried to kidnap me.

I could feel the violence skimming from Silas's hands just as sure as he'd been able to feel the horror rippling from mine.

Maybe I had taken a quick jaunt into becoming a horrible person because I wasn't so sure that I could even count the retaliation as unjust.

"Are you sure this is a good idea? Don't get me wrong, your girl here is always down for a party. But after what happened today, I'm not so sure my brother is going to be all that welcoming."

I was jarred out of my spiraling thoughts by Elena who stumbled along at my side, trying to keep up.

You know, since I was basically marching toward my destruction.

"You can go back," I told her offhandedly, but inside, I was hoping that she wouldn't.

I needed backup.

A pal.

Or if I really got myself into trouble, a cell mate.

"Ha. You want my brother really mad at me? That is not going to happen."

She'd dressed up, too.

Wearing a cute floral dress that hit her mid-thigh and white sneakers on her feet. It was a whole lot more country than biker.

Me, I'd gone full biker babe. At least, I hoped that's what I was pulling off since I didn't have a lick of leather in my closet.

A short black dress.

Fitted up top and frilly at the bottom.

Hoping to fit in with these other women and no one would really notice.

"Then we're in this together." Grabbing her hand, I weaved our fingers together.

I was thankful for the support, even though I wasn't quite sure what my intentions were other than proving to myself that I could walk out the door without crumbling.

I'd already spent two hours in the shower bawling.

No more of that.

Elena swung our entwined hands between us and sent an adorable grin my way. "So, you basically need an accomplice?"

She nailed it. Spot on.

"Is this a crime?" In innocence, I widened my eyes.

She arched a brow. "Have you met my brother?"

I let go of a shallow laugh. "Unfortunately, I have."

"Unfortunately?" Both her brows lifted that time, like I'd been caught with my hand in the cookie jar and had chocolate smeared all over my face.

Okay, fine, that kiss wasn't terrible.

Not even close.

If I was being honest, it was wonderful and exhilarating and probably the best thing I'd ever felt.

Because it was raw and unbridled and not muffled by the voices that would forever haunt my mind.

I mean, they'd obviously been there. Lurking in the background and waiting around for the opportune time to gobble me up.

It'd been there with that instinct to freeze, the memories swarming me for a flash.

But they hadn't owned me the way they normally did.

I huffed. "I guess he's kind of growing on me."

She laughed, then frowned, our pace slowing as she peered at me through the wisping darkness that held us in the cover of the trees. "I can't believe someone got on the property today. That he…"

Grimness gripped her expression.

"I'm fine," I promised her, probably a little too quickly.

I just couldn't stand the direction her mind had clearly gone.

Tears blurred her eyes. "It was horrible, Brinley, when they had me. I didn't think I'd ever get out. If something like that happened to you…"

Her throat tremored.

My spirit flailed in a way that made me want to weep.

Desperation had me squeezing her hand in a vise. "I'm so sorry, Elena. I'm so sorry."

Memories threatened to rise up and wipe me out like a hundred-year flood.

She shook her head. "I can't stand the idea of someone hurting you. I hate it, Brinley. I'm so sorry."

I guess we both were thinking the same.

She swiped at a tear that got free. "And I know my brother is freaking out that someone got to you. That the asshole even got that close."

"They saved me." It was a whisper.

Awe.

Confusion.

My mind was boggled because those bikers had fallen into form like they were a trained army. Taking this guy out like they were old pros and not some rag-tag group of thieves running the streets.

Elena let go of a soggy huff. "Of course, they saved you. There was no chance Silas was going to let that creep steal you off this property."

"Should I trust him? Should I really trust him?"

I realized I was pleading.

Trusting her to tell me the truth.

She looked around, gaze sifting through the shadows, like she was worried we were going to be caught doing something scandalous.

No doubt, in Silas's eyes, we were totally up to no good.

She turned back to me, her nearly black ponytail falling around her shoulder as she angled her head close.

Eyes the same color as his swirled with emphasis. “There is no one you should trust more.”

It was a punch.

Glee.

Relief.

More of that confusion.

“He’s a criminal.” It was a bare, fleeting argument. “The president of a freaking motorcycle club. And I’m pretty sure that patch they wear on their backs isn’t just for show.”

I’d bet my very meager life savings that if you messed with them, those crows would be dancing on your grave.

Violent.

Brutal.

Savage.

She glanced around again, her chest shuddering, her voice fully a whisper. “You don’t have to be afraid of him, Brinley. Not in that way. He would never hurt you. But I’m not so sure about what he could do to your heart. Those boys have a way of trampling all over them.”

She choked over the last. Eyes shimmering. Opening herself wide to a new source of her pain.

One we were going to have to address later, but there were so many questions whirling through my mind right then that I couldn’t keep them tapped.

“Did they kill that guy?”

Air huffed from her nose. “Is that something you really want to know?”

“Yes.”

I regretted it the second I said it. But it was knee-jerk. Reflex. So I supposed it had to be the truth.

A little scowl twisted up her brow. “I think that’s something you’re going to have to ask Silas.”

I huffed. “Your brother won’t tell me a thing.”

Except I couldn’t block the memory of what he had said.

The gruff, needy words he’d rumbled into my flesh as he kissed me into a puddle.

Admitting that he wanted me the way I wanted him.

In a terrifying, overwhelming way.

But something severe was stopping him.

A darkness that made him look even more menacing than usual, which was saying a whole lot.

Elena tossed me a sassy grin. “Oh, I think you could probably work your magic on him.”

“I think it’s entirely the other way around and it’s him who’s working his magic on me. He’s the one who’s casting spells.”

She shifted and snuggled up to my side as we started to walk again. “So, you’re saying you do like him?”

“So you’re saying you do like Trevan?”

Deflection was the best defense.

She fumbled over a step, heaving out a breath before she slung out what I knew she hoped to be a casual response. “I didn’t say a thing.”

“You don’t need to when your face does all the talking.”

She snuggled closer, her head basically buried in my shoulder as she whispered, “Like I said, these boys have a way of trampling all over our hearts. I think I should probably leave it at that.”

And maybe I could already feel mine breaking as we stepped out from the cover of trees and headed for the toiling group of bodies that appeared as silhouettes and shadows around the firelight.

Because I swore I felt it cracking beneath the pressure as I looked across the flames to the only one I could really see.

Silas Mercer staring back.

What the hell had I let this man do to me?

31

Silas

The fire curled and licked toward the underbelly of the trees. Shooting sparks that danced higher before they turned to ash and fluttered to the ground.

I sat rocked back in a chair, entranced by the flames while my crew joked around me.

"Did you see me in action?" Brody gestured at himself. Amped after today's unfortunate incident.

"What I saw was you ducking for cover," Trevan razzed behind a sip of his beer.

Brody gasped in mock offense. "Are you kidding me? I went straight hero today."

Brody stretched out his arms like he was the prize.

Phoenix grunted the way he always did. Seldom amused.

"Hero, huh?" Trevan's brow lifted with the tease.

"Don't you know not all heroes wear capes?" Brody tossed out.

Trevan cracked up. "Nah, heroes wear cuts."

I fought a chuckle, but my words were serious as I told Brody, "You did good today."

He looked my way, seriousness taking over him too. "Wouldn't have let that bastard get away with what he planned. This club's mission is my mission."

"I know," I affirmed.

Meaning it.

He might have messed around nonstop, but when it came down to it, Brody knew what was important.

The same as the rest of my MC.

This mismatched family that fought for what was right.

It was me who'd gone askew. The one who'd fucked up. Fucked up so bad, letting myself get lost in her.

She was abso-fucking-lutely off-limits.

A job.

A woman under my protection who was basically being used as a pawn.

And I'd let that purpose spiral.

Splinter as she not so slowly seeped beneath my skin.

I mean, fuck, she might as well have been a drug injected directly into my veins.

Whittling her way through muscle and bone and getting to the marrow.

Casting a glow somewhere at the center of my being.

She was this riotous light that I was drawn to. As hot as the sparks that flitted from the flames.

Wildfire.

Kindling that had lit something deep.

Warming my long-dead spirit.

I needed to put out that fucking fire stat.

Extinguish it before it destroyed the oath that I had made.

But I was only getting struck by another lash of severity.

Awareness crawled across my flesh and piqued every cell in my body in keen, desperate attention.

My guts tangled in a fit of greed as I watched her come stumbling out from the cover of trees with my baby sister in tow.

What the ever-lovin' fuck did they think they were doing?

And what the fuck was she wearing?

Brinley dressed up in one of those tempting short dresses. This one black with capped sleeves and a plunging neckline, flowy skirt to match.

Thighs that I'd had my hands all over earlier exposed, legs for a fucking week.

Waltzing in like a conquering queen on those black peep-toe sky-high heels that could make even a good man commit obscene things.

And I was not a good man.

A swell of possessiveness rushed in, something that verged on irate as every last Crow standing around the fire took note.

It wasn't like I could blame them.

She was a flash of lightning striking on parched land. A storm rolling in to quench a ten-year drought.

Trevan's attention cut to Elena, exactly the way it was supposed to, and he stood, already lumbering her way.

He wasn't only my second in command when it came to the MC. He was second in command at watching over my sister.

Charged with her safety in the moments I couldn't be near her, an obligation I'd given him after she'd been rescued from Kent Ellison's clutches.

One he took fucking seriously. Always watching and hovering close.

Elena pulled away from where she was tacked to Brinley's side and instead grabbed her hand and pulled her into the fray of men and women already devolving into depravity.

The party slanting toward unruly.

Styx fingering some chick where he sat at a picnic table while another was on her knees sucking his dick.

A few others were scattered about clearly deteriorating in that direction.

My cock hardened at the thought of Brinley doing the same.

Getting on her knees right out in front of everyone so they would know she was mine, all while I wanted to gouge out their goddamn eyes if they caught sight of her doing it.

No one could say I was being rational.

From over the fire, I watched as a few of my men moved up to Brinley, checking on her, gruff assholes still exerting their care.

"Thank fuck she's okay," Brody rumbled before he moved in her direction, ducking into a cooler on his way and extending it to her like a peace offering.

Something heavy clouded him, even though I could see him trying to front his easy, arrogant smile.

She accepted the bottle, and I couldn't make out what they were saying, but Brinley's gorgeous face was all pinched up in gratitude.

I hated that Brody'd had to draw blood, but I knew full well that venom already pumped through Brody's veins.

It was coming.

Inevitable.

They say you can leave, but you are always where you came from.

And I was going to have to accept that he was cursed like the rest of us.

Brinley suddenly lunged for Brody, hugging him tight before she stepped back and tried to straighten herself out, unable to believe she'd allowed herself to expose her vulnerability that way.

The fear and horror I knew still clung on, acting like all was good as she cracked her beer and brought the rim of the bottle to her lips.

Those lush, distracting lips.

Fuck, I couldn't sit still for a second longer. I needed to put an end to this. Command she and Elena go home.

This wasn't the place for them tonight.

Not any night.

I pushed from my chair, telling myself it had nothing to do with the fact that I needed to get closer.

No fucking stopping myself.

Drawn.

Brinley Webber nothing but gravity.

The kind that was so powerful it could drag you across galaxies and you knew full well it'd crush you when you collided.

I started to move, basically stalking along the fringes of the gathering since Brinley and Elena had once again begun to move, Elena holding Brinley by the hand as she led her toward the clubhouse.

They disappeared inside, the door swinging shut behind them.

Trevan didn't hesitate to follow.

They'd be fine with him watching over them, but I couldn't stomach the thought of letting Brinley out of my sight.

Not with the vibe that had taken over the MC tonight. The high of the kill still saturated the oxygen, turning the pack wild and rabid.

A shivery sense of mayhem and unruliness urging their souls into upheaval.

Music pumped extra loud and undulated through our senses.

I felt half mad in it. Deranged as I cut through my men, heading directly for the door.

It might as well have had *Destruction* stamped on a sign hanging over the top. A call to Hell since I knew that was exactly where I was headed.

Going after the one thing that I was as sure of as my guilt was off-limits.

A thousand times so after what I discovered earlier today.

The truth that a whole lot of that brash impetuousness that Brinley wore was a cover. A cover she wore so well. One I wanted to sink my dirty claws into so I could expose everything underneath.

Nothing but a bastard for wanting to do it.

I tossed open the door and stepped into the raving fray of the clubhouse bar.

Music blared at a deafening level, the lights dimmed, though the strobes over the dance floor had been set to high.

A haze of smoke and rebellion clouding the atmosphere.

Crows wearing cuts loitered all around, but there had to be at least three women to every man.

It was the perfect way to feed the frenzy.

The air charged.

Fuel for the insanity.

I shouldered through the crush, and a few Crows clapped me on the back as I went.

"Prez, how's it going?"

"Good job today."

"Took that fucker out."

I gave them slight nods and grunted responses, never slowing as I followed the energy that glowed and called.

Elena and Brinley had taken up a spot at a high-top table near the back right corner of the bar. Both were sipping beers, their gazes taking in the decadence and debauchery unfolding in front of them.

Fuck. I wanted to shield my sister. Cover her eyes and her heart. Send her back to the house and shove her back into that cage, clip her wings the way I'd been doing for so long.

It was utterly wrong, but I didn't know anything else.

How to protect her when I forever felt our safety slipping away.

Knowing I was traversing treacherous ground, I turned course and beat a path to the main bar.

Tonight, Lulu was slinging drinks behind it, her grin both warm and sly. Her weathered face arched in knowing speculation as I slipped onto a stool.

She immediately set an old-fashioned in front of me. A sugar cube and cherry floated in the amber whiskey.

"It's been a day, honey." Care filled her tone.

"Yeah," I mumbled, wrapping both hands around the glittering tumbler like it might serve as a lifeline.

She cut a glance at Brinley and Elena.

"She okay?" she asked.

A huff puffed free as I brought the tumbler to my lips, soaking my tongue with the sweetness, relishing the burn as it slid down my throat.

I hoped it would soothe the chaos, but it only poured gas on the flames that raged in my stomach.

Amid it, there was nothing I could do but slant my attention to the two who had their heads pressed together. Giggling and whispering.

As thick as thieves.

Like they'd been friends forever.

Wasn't exactly sure what tightened my chest at the sight of it. That same wayward emotion that had detonated inside me when she'd run Kai and Elena to safety a few days ago.

I turned back to Lulu. "Doubt it. Who would be after going through what she did today?"

She hummed as she wiped a rag over the gleaming bar top. "Well, I'm sure it definitely made a mark, but I can also say she's doing a whole hell of a lot better right now than she would have been otherwise."

Rage burned hot, and I attempted to swallow around the shards of glass that rolled around at the base of my throat. "Bastard never should have gotten that close to her."

"No, but you did what counted and because of that, she is sitting right over there tonight."

"That doesn't mean I didn't almost fail."

"Key word here is *almost*." Lulu said it wryly. Almost a tease.

I grunted, and she laughed. "Sorry to break it to you, honey, but you weren't close to failing. There is zero chance that scoundrel would have gotten her off this property the way he intended. Idiot would have had twenty-five Crows chasing down his tail in nothing flat."

"She shouldn't have been here for the chance of that to happen in the first place."

She shouldn't be subject to me or any of this bullshit that would ruin her life.

Lulu arched a brow, her wrinkled features deepening with disbelief. "Like that's your fault when you stepped in to protect her? Took on that extra burden, invited more danger into your life? God knows where she'd be right now if it weren't for you."

A growl got free with the toil of hate the thought spurned, and I gripped the glass tighter, so hard I was surprised it didn't shatter.

"And that reaction right there tells me that girl is exactly where she is supposed to be." Lulu bobbed a finger at me, like my expression alone offered up proof.

Handed it to her on a silver platter.

My jaw clenched in restraint. Refusing to claim it myself. "She shouldn't be within five states of this place."

"And tell me you want her to be anywhere else?" Lulu was all challenge and snark.

"I just want all of this over with." To put an end to Kent Ellison and his foul, sickening reign.

Ensure my sister was safe from his clutches.

Set Brinley free.

My guts twisted into a snarl of possession with the last.

Soul lashing out in refusal of the idea of her leaving this place.

Because the only real place I wanted her was in my bed.

Lulu angled her head. "And there isn't a thing else you want to come of it?"

"Nope." I popped the *p* before I took another swig of my old-fashioned. Hoping it might cover the blatant lie.

Of course, Lulu picked up on it, anyway. Woman as insightful as they came. She never hesitated to make sure I knew it, either. "You just go on tellin' yourself that, sugar. You think I don't see it written all over you?"

Disbelief shot from my chest. "And what's that?"

"Somethin' that hasn't ever been there before, that's what. Somethin' you've been missing since the day I met you. Somethin' I'm sure has been missing for a long, long time."

My chest stretched in a flurry of pain and regret.

"You're seeing things," I grumbled.

"I sure am, as plain as day. You're the one who's not paying attention."

My head shook. "I don't know what you're angling at, but you might as well drop it. Nothing is going to come of it."

"And why not?"

My teeth ground, and the words were spilling free before I had the good sense to tamp them. "Because I refuse to condemn another person to the calamity that I am."

I couldn't believe I let it slide from my mouth. But Lulu had that way about her. Always plucking and picking until she'd peeled the skin back to expose what was rotten underneath.

She scoffed. "Condemn them, huh? Like you did me, coming in to rescue me when I was at my lowest? Saving me and supporting me when I lost my husband? Giving me a home?"

"That's because we take care of family."

"And maybe that girl right there needs one, too. Maybe she's missing that same piece so many of us are when we come here."

My insides stirred.

Swam and thundered with the music that pounded from the speakers.

Shoving it off, I ground out, "She's been hurt enough. I refuse to be another. Besides, the last thing I need is another burden on my shoulders."

I added the last like it could mask what had basically amounted to a confession.

"Huh..." Lulu's musing cut off the hazardous spiral of thoughts. Only they got so much worse when she muttered, "Maybe someone else will fill that hole for her."

I whipped around to find Brinley in the middle of the floor, dancing with two prospects.

Two prospects who wanted to get dead.

Lights strobed over her lush, perfect body. Brunette curls so fucking wild around her face. Red and gold streaks glinting beneath the strikes of colored light that kissed over her soft skin.

Wearing those heels and that dress.

Each of the prospects held one of her hands, beers in their other, their cuts saying "Prospect" across the back since they'd yet to patch in.

They definitely weren't winning any points toward making that happen, either. As far as I was concerned, they had reached a quick, defining deficit.

Nah, it didn't seem to matter that they were all laughing and joking and dancing a bit goofy.

Completely innocent.

No harm, no foul.

Everything about it still felt indecent.

A landslide of greed slammed me, and I nearly climbed to my feet, though I forced myself to remain sitting when Elena joined her, Brinley stepping away from the guys so she could dance with my sister.

Elena giggled as she tried to match Brinley's perfect beat, her ponytail whipping around her, her laughter rising above the din.

I needed to let them be. Let them have some fun. Blow off some steam.

God knew Brinley deserved it after what went down this afternoon. Elena just as much with all the bullshit she'd been through.

But what Brinley was engaged in didn't quite add up with her reaction from earlier.

Storming her way into the club with her head held high.

I got the unsettled sense that she had armored up again and was trying to prove something.

That should be of no concern of mine.

I needed to turn away. Get up and get on my bike and just fucking ride.

They were safe and fine. Trevan wasn't more than three feet from my sister.

She was being closely looked after, and I knew he would do the same for Brinley.

But I was ensnared.

Hooked on the hypnotizing sway of Brinley's hips and the tantalizing roll of her body.

Energy thrashed and streaked. Carried on the lights that flashed through the clubhouse bar.

A ton of women had moved onto the floor. Flirting and dancing with my men.

But Brinley was the only thing I could see.

The chick who was dancing with Fuse shifted around, rubbing her ass on his dick while she reached for Brinley. She slid a hand down Brinley's bare thigh, no question inviting her to join in on the *fun* they were about to deteriorate into.

Brinley didn't quite oblige, dancing out in front of her, though that gaze snapped toward me.

A beacon.

An invitation.

A trap.

Her lips parted, and the desire that had coated her expression earlier in the office had grown tenfold.

And fuck, I was hammered with another swell of possession. Feet knocked out from underneath me, body tossed and toppling in the tide that sucked me under and dragged me into a sea of greed.

So thick it might as well have been quicksand.

I drained my drink and slammed the empty onto the bar as I stood.

Could barely make out Lulu's chuckle from behind and her muttered, "That's what I thought," as I stalked in Brinley's direction.

The woman's gaze seared a hole through the middle of me as I approached.

Brinley swayed.

All sultry like, teasing away my restraints.

My stride was slow and measured, like in the space and time that separated us I might be able to squash whatever the fuck it was that I was feeling.

No chance of it because it was only multiplying with each step that brought us closer.

When she was within two feet of me, I snatched her by the wrist and hauled her against me.

All that soft, decadent flesh against every hard inch at the front of my body.

So fucking sweet.

Brinley gasped, eyes going wide, lust running rampant through their depths.

I growled as I wound an arm around her waist and tugged her even tighter against me, mouth pressed to her ear so only she could hear. "What the fuck do you think you're doing?"

It was grit.

Gravel.

Rutted breaths heaved from her, and with each jagged exhale, it pressed her tits against my chest.

Tendrils of her aura slipped through my nostrils and wound into my lungs.

Apples and almonds and cream.

I wanted to take a giant bite. Now that I'd had a taste, I was terrified I would never get my fill.

"Dancing." It wisped from her. Both a challenge and a plea.

"You're not supposed to be here."

She lifted that defiant chin. "You told me I could go anywhere on this property except for the places it was clear I shouldn't be."

"And you should know full well this isn't one of those places."

"You said I was allowed in the clubhouse."

"Not if you're looking for trouble."

"And what kind of trouble am I looking for, Silas Mercer?" Both brows lifted as she dispatched what was nothing less than a taunt.

"You know exactly what kind of trouble you're looking for. Know exactly what you're doing to me."

My nose hit the angle of her jaw as I mumbled it, and I was only faintly aware that I was breaking at least a hundred of my own rules by doing it.

Right out in the open and in plain sight of my crew.

Guilty as fuck, and I'd be the first to deliver the verdict.

My palm splayed out over the silky fabric at the small of her back.

She edged forward, hiking up on her toes and pressing that tempting mouth to my ear. "And maybe that's exactly what I want. Maybe I'm looking for that exact kind of trouble. Maybe I came here looking for you."

The growl that ripped from me was so explosive it was a wonder the walls of the building didn't crumble.

A wonder every person there didn't scatter to take cover.

"Believe me, baby. You don't want what I have to offer," I warned.

"You're wrong. I think I want to experience every single thing that you are."

"You don't know what you're asking."

She lifted that brazen face. "I don't care."

"You'd care when you found out the depths of my depravity. You'd care when I left you mangled and broken."

I already promised her that I would.

"Now I want you to take my little sister and go back to the house where you belong." I breathed it a little too close to her mouth, my cock straining so hard in my jeans there was no chance she didn't feel it begging at her belly.

A shiver rolled down her spine.

A shiver that raced up my arm, my palm still firmly pressed to that sweet spot, a fiend who kept her locked tight against me after I just told her to get lost.

She curled closer like she had no intention of listening, and I rumbled, "That's an order."

I forced myself to release her.

Brinley stumbled back a step, expression full of a scoff and disbelief.

She cocked her head.

Sheer provocation.

"You know," she drew out like she was musing it. "I think I'll stick around and see if anyone else is interested."

Then she turned on those heels and strutted her way back into the melee, like there was a chance she belonged in the middle of it.

It was not going to fucking happen.

I was on her tail, shoving through the crowd. Surprise choked out of her when I grabbed her by the hand and spun her around.

Her entire being morphed into victorious glee, no doubt thinking she'd won some sort of seductress medal.

Then she squealed in shock when I had her off her feet and tossed over my shoulder before she knew what hit her.

"What the hell do you think you're doing?" she rasped, frantic hands trying to grip onto the rigid leather of my cut but never finding purchase.

There was no need for her to hang on since there was no chance I was letting her go.

I prowled toward the main door.

Didn't give a fuck that every eye in the bar swung in our direction, that one action lifting a ramble of speculation. Their mouths wagging with the rumors that were going to fly.

There weren't a whole lot of shits to give when Trevan gave me that look, either.

Smirk seated firmly on his face.

I told you so.

I didn't give a fuck about much of anything except giving this girl a little of what she was asking for.

32

Silas

"What do you think you're doing? Silas, put me down."

Brinley squirmed as I stormed with her out into the babbling night. My boots ate up the ground as I hooked a quick left to carry her into the dense cover of trees that separated the club from my house.

Some speck of my conscience screamed to set her onto her feet and send her on her way.

But something else was screaming so much louder. "No."

Her body jostled and bounced as I stalked through the shadows, a cataclysm of greed and stupidity rushing my steps.

"I'm not some little girl you need to lock up and hide away behind a closed door." Coarse, jagged words rushed from Brinley.

"No, you aren't, are you?"

Her ass was in the air, that short, flowy skirt blowing up in the breeze and exposing the perfect round globes of her butt cheeks.

So ripe and juicy and right at the side of my face that it took everything I had not to turn my head and take a bite.

Instead, I sank the fingers of my free hand into one curvy mound.

Palming and kneading.

A gasp rocked from her. In an instant, I could scent her arousal soaking her through, a shockwave of her blistering through my body and ratcheting the lust gripping my guts.

"This what you want, Brinley? You want a little of what I have to give?" I growled it.

"I…what are you doing? Silas." It was confusion spiked with need.

"Say it," I demanded. "Do you want it?"

"Yes."

That was all I needed to hear.

I increased my pace, boots a thunder as I carried her through the woods.

Her little breaths hitting the air and driving the madness higher.

Each step amping the anticipation as I hauled her toward the house.

I didn't pause or set her down when I climbed the porch steps, and there was no wavering or faltering as I ferried her through the wispy darkness of the living room and up the stairs to my room.

I just marched forward on a full-scale suicide mission.

Her rasps and pants spurring me forward.

I clicked the door shut behind us before I edged through the shadows that crawled the walls of my room.

I didn't take her to my bed.

I set her down on the black leather sofa under the window.

A goddess sitting in the silvered, fluttery rays of moonlight that filtered in through the thin drapes.

Her chest jacking with each strained breath and eyes doing avid, feral things.

A thrill bolted from her being in shocks of electricity that blasted through the room.

Dressed in black, that flimsy, silken skirt hiked up high around her thighs.

Long, toned legs draped out in front of her, bent at the knees with those heels planted on my floor.

Knees just spread.

Trembles rocked through her with the furor of an earthquake.

This goddess? I was pretty sure she would prove lethal. Touching her condemnation and blame. But there I was, sinking to my knees in front of her.

Nothing but a beggar at her feet.

But it was Brinley who was going to be doing the begging tonight.

My palms landed on her knees.

Flames flashed.

In a surge of desire, she arched from the couch. Body bowing in a petition.

"Silas..."

My name wisped out into the night and curled around me like a lucid dream.

There was something deeper and more profound in that single word coming from her mouth than any other that had ever touched my ears before it.

Like it might mean something.

Like I might mean something to her.

Guilt tried to rise to the surface. To force me back into the order where I knew I should stay.

But there was something about Brinley Webber that had me pinned.

I couldn't help but think maybe I might have a little more to offer. Giving her *this.*

Dominance and control capped off in a blitz of pleasure.

"You want this, Brinley?" My voice was low and raw. Cutting through the charged air in the slice of a warning. "You want me to wipe away that flash of terror you were feeling today? Replace it with everything that I am?"

Her gaze darkened, toiled with old wounds and debilitating horrors and sheer, absolute want.

She knew I wasn't referring to the fuckwit who tried to drag her off but rather whatever'd had her recoiling at my touch.

Referring to the ancient fear that would glint at the farthest recesses of her fierce, ferocious gaze.

Something she guarded like family jewels that had been tarnished.

And somehow, I was able to see it.

Maybe it was sick that I wanted to be the one to hold it.

Sick that I wanted to be the one to have the honor of sending her soaring. The one who would cause her to give in and let go.

Realizing in it, she was the one who held all the power. Because I knew I couldn't erase it or be the one to fix her, but maybe through me she'd see how fucking strong she was. See she could rise above the brutalities that had been committed to her.

"Yes, I want to feel you. I want to feel everything," she rasped, squirming on that leather cushion.

"You're going to let me give you this? The little that I have?"

Fire flamed in those harvest eyes, and Brinley kept flipping between innocent and vixen. "And what's that, Silas? What is it you have to give?"

"Pleasure and the promise that you're in control while I'm giving it to you. Just for a little while. While you're here and under my roof. Then, when you walk out of here, safe and whole, you'll realize the sick fuck who hurt you no longer has any control over you."

I gritted my teeth at the mention of the faceless degenerate. I'd try to get her to give me the name later. But not right then.

Not when I was trying to inject her full of belief.

"He has no say in the way you live or the things you want. Has no control over your fantasies or desires."

A wave of that desire flooded from her body, and Brinley's lips parted on a breath of passion and yearning.

Trust filtering out into the fervency that carved the room in lust and something far bigger.

Something I knew should send me running.

Instead, my hands clamped down tighter on her knees as I tried to force myself into a cool that had been obliterated the second this woman had stepped onto my land.

"Don't know what you've done to me, Brinley. Don't know how you have me so spun up. The way you have me ignoring every rule that I've ever made for myself and this club."

She huffed a disconcerted laugh. "It's you, Silas. You who has me so twisted up that I don't recognize myself. I shouldn't be letting you touch me like this. I don't…"

Her eyes squeezed shut as her words trailed off.

My heart took that time to be reckless, stretching out for hers, wanting to assuage the flash of pain that struck through her being.

"You don't let men touch you?" Maybe I was the twisted one since it crawled out like possession.

She gave a little frantic shake of her head, that armor dropping. "No."

"Do you want me to?"

"Yes."

My hands shook where I had them locked on her knees. I didn't know if it was originating from her or me.

"How long has it been? How long has it been since you felt safe with a man?"

A quiver rolled her delicate throat, and she attempted to swallow the heaviness. "Five years."

A growl rolled in my chest, and I splayed my hands wide as I slowly glided them up the tops of her thighs. Attention fixed to her face, searching for any discomfort or fear.

She arched back, and her shoulders hit the backrest of the sofa as the rest of her bowed toward me.

She released a raspy, frenzied breath, and in it, her admission slipped free. "I'm not so sure I feel safe with you."

I froze, a stake to my fucking heart. "Would never hurt you. Not like that."

Her hands were suddenly over mine, urging them farther up her legs, her body arching more with each inch.

"Maybe I'm a total fool for believing it, but I do. It's the rest of you that terrifies me. The way you make me feel every time you come into the room. The way you seem to understand me. See me. I think you could crush me, Silas."

My chest tightened.

"Be clear, Brinley, I'm not worth any of that. There's nothing left inside me that makes me worthy of whatever you think you're feeling. Nothing decent or good. I ruin everyone that gets close."

Something flared in her gaze that made me certain she was going to argue with me, so I ducked down, lips hitting the soft flesh at the top of her right thigh.

A feverish exhalation puffed out of her, and she murmured, "Yes."

A clear invitation.

I slowly kissed over the delicious skin that could compete with the taste of Meems's apple pie, though I'd never dare tell my grandmother.

This woman nothing but a perfect fantasy.

A perfect, torturous dream.

My cock screamed at my zipper.

I beat the lust back and forced myself to focus on what this was all about.

"Tell me where he hurt you, baby, and I'll mark myself right over the top of it. Mark myself so deep that I'll be the only thing you can feel. The only thing you can remember."

I mumbled it as I kept kissing over the golden flesh of her legs.

Fingers wound in my hair, and Brinley arched higher as she yanked at the locks. "Everywhere."

It was pain.

A plea.

Desperation.

Hunger battled with the rage that thrashed at my insides. Both were so stark, I didn't know which was most critical.

Doubted she could never truly forget, but fuck, I was going to try.

A balm for the scars that had never fully healed.

Show her she no longer had to be a prisoner.

She was fucking free.

Free in me.

Those fingers curled tighter in my hair, right on time as I kissed higher.

I barely recognized my own voice as I spread her knees and murmured my lips up the inside of her thigh. "I'm going to make you feel so good, Brinley. Write myself all over you. Sink so deep that you're going to forget what it was like before I met you."

Claim you.

Put a property patch on her back so the whole fucking world would know who she belonged to.

I knew a whole hell of a lot better than that. Knew what it would cause.

Not to mention I was tangling with the club's collateral.

But right then I couldn't seem to convince myself otherwise.

Brinley let go of this desirous whimper as I edged higher, a gush of her words slipping off her tongue. "Give me everything you can."

"Wildfire. Trying to do me in."

"I think it's me who's done in."

I chuckled as I ran my nose along the edge of her lace underwear, nearly knocked out by the lust-inducing scent.

Guts in knots as I confessed, "Nah, baby, I knew you were going to do me in the second you climbed out of your brother's car."

"I wanted to hate you." It was a whisper she released into the dense, lapping air.

"You should still hate me," I warned.

"I wish that I did."

And I could feel both of us teetering on that ledge. Tripping in a direction neither of us could afford to go.

I forced myself to look up at her so she could see the truth of what I was saying.

"I'm not a good man, Brinley."

She made a 'no shit' sound. Clearly, I'd already more than proven it.

But she didn't know the lengths.

"That doesn't seem to matter, does it?" she pressed. "Because no matter how hard I fight it, it only grows. This burn that lights me up every time you get near me. It's big and powerful, and there's absolutely nothing I can do to stop it."

A shock of dubious laughter rocked from me. "You think you're not having the exact same effect? The fact I have you in this room alone is enough to warn me to stay far the fuck away from you, and I'm powerless to do it."

"Maybe we're both what the other needs."

There was far too much hope lining the underside of those words.

I should shun the suggestion, but it lit something in the coldest place inside me.

And did she stop?

No.

Not this one.

"Maybe you need reminding that there is good inside you, too." Her eyes flared with enough vehemence to sear it into my flesh, as hot as an iron prod.

Fuck.

Brinley Webber might be perfect for me. Carved of the same battered, brutalized stone.

I forced myself to edge back a fraction, rising up high on my knees as I gripped the outside of her thighs.

Giving her space to change her mind.

Waiting for her to resurrect the walls that once had stood like a mile-high barrier.

But they'd been felled.

Rubble in a wasteland.

Her expression begged me to put her out of the misery that had built between us, while her spirit begged for something bigger.

And fuck, I didn't know how there was some piece inside that wanted to return it.

"If I had a soul, a piece of myself left to give, I'd give it to you. But you should know there's none of that left. Need to be sure you're good with that," I told her.

She quivered from her chest to her chin as she stared up at me, then lifted that chin higher and issued the whispered demand, "Show me what it feels like to be free. I want to experience it. I want to know what it's like when the pain goes away. I want to know what it feels like not to be alone. To not be the only one fighting for myself. I want you to hold it, even if it's just for a little while. Wreck me like you promised."

Possession thrashed, and the words turned coarse and jagged. "Don't worry, baby. I plan to. Going to show you that you're not alone and you are not the only one fighting for yourself. Going to show you that you *count.* And when you leave this place, you'll know exactly what to demand from a man."

My spirit howled at the thought of another man touching her, my hands gripping on tighter like I might not ever have to let her go.

And I knew, right then, it was Brinley who was going to wreck me.

Not even that was enough to stop this train that had sped out of control, and she was trembling so hard I thought the sofa might take flight as I slipped my hands higher beneath that frilly black skirt, and I hooked my fingers into the edges of her underwear.

"You gonna let me have a taste of you?"

She squirmed and lifted her ass from the couch. "Please."

I peeled the slip of lace down her lush, curvy thighs, dragging them all the way down her legs and unwinding them from those heels.

I tossed them to the side and was right back to gripping her by the knees, spreading her wide so I could get a good look at all the deliciousness I'd been fantasizing about.

Need thundered through my bloodstream at the sight of her pink and bare. Her slit soaked with desire.

My mouth watered, and I felt like I was being burned up.

Scorched alive.

My eyes devoured, roving over the curves of her body. Gaze flicking from the stunning, unforgettable edges of her face, down over her trembling, jutting chest, and dipping down to the sweet spot between her thighs.

Brinley exposed. So utterly indecent and so perfectly right.

Because I was the one who was foul.

Staining her perfection this way. Letting myself weave even a thread of my depravity into her.

Knew I was nothing but a bastard because I couldn't wait to leave my mark.

"Wildfire," I rumbled. "Seductress. So fucking sexy. Making me lose my mind. Making me want things I can never keep."

There they went, perilous words slipping from my mouth.

Brinley arched and sighed. "Silas."

"You're stunning, Brinley. Fucking gorgeous. Nothing but a tease of paradise."

"You're the tease, Silas Mercer." She choked it.

"Are you an eager girl? You need my mouth on you?"

"Yes." The thickened word braided through the charged air.

Energy lashing and whipping.

I dipped in and stroked my tongue through her cunt.

I nearly came in my pants.

But it was Brinley almost hitting the ceiling that had me freezing, thinking I'd freaked her out, worried I'd sent that fear sailing through her again, but her hands were back in my hair, urging me on, "Silas," leaving her on a whimper.

"Wildfire. Fuck. Knew your pussy was going to be so damned sweet."

Soft and slick and hypnotizing as I wound my arms under her legs, gathering her up so I could angle her just right as I dove back in.

The taste of her had me boiling over.

Brinley rasped and moaned as I licked deep into her folds. "I like that."

I couldn't even suppress the chuckle as I eased back a fraction. Chest stretching in something that felt far too close to affection. "You like me licking this sweet cunt, baby?"

Leave it to Brinley to press herself closer to my face. "Yes…don't stop."

"Made you a promise. Plan on keeping it."

I drove my tongue deep between her lips then swept higher so I could get to her needy, engorged clit.

She bucked and gasped, fingers pleading in my hair. "Oh…Silas…I…"

"You're free in me," I mumbled as I swirled and stroked my tongue.

"That's where I want to be."

And I knew we'd both been taken someplace we didn't know as I fully gave in, laving and lapping my tongue at her clit as she whimpered these guttural sounds that landed on my ears like prayers.

Woman injecting me full of something that didn't belong there. Sparks of long dead embers threatening to flicker to life.

I got twisted inside out as I spread her wider, tongue fucking into her cunt before I was back to eating up that throbbing nub.

The sounds and scent of her were driving me mad.

Pleas.

My name.

Praise.

I swirled just the tips of my two fingers at her entrance, asking for permission.

She spread herself wider, grip unyielding and tugging at my hair.

A pleasured pain rocketed down my spine.

Tightening my balls and pulsing my cock in my jeans.

That's exactly what she was.

Pleasured pain.

Because I knew I was doing everything wrong. Touching this woman who was forbidden to touch.

But I'd take any penalty coming my way if it meant I got to give her this for even a second.

I thrust both fingers deep. The walls of her pussy spasmed around the intrusion.

"You like that?" I growled.

"Yes." It was half delirious.

"Wait until it's my cock stuffing you full."

A tremor rocked her, and I could feel ecstasy lighting at the edges of her being.

Winding her in tendrils of anticipation that grew with each plunge of my fingers.

Even though I was trying to keep myself in check, take heed, I was getting the sense that this girl liked it hard.

Her hands eager at the back of my head as she tried to spur me on.

A frenzy coming over her as she fully let herself go.

No fear.

No reservation.

I fucked my fingers in a deep, harsh rhythm.

She writhed with each one.

Chanted my name as she pressed her nails into the flesh at the back of my neck.

Needing more.

Desperation rolled from her in spastic juts. "Silas, oh…I'm…I need..."

"Wildfire, let go, give it to me." I thrust my fingers deeper, driving them fast and hard as I licked her into oblivion.

Flames jumped and leapt, and she arched, her chest coming up from the couch as pleasure gathered as fast as a summer storm.

"How does it feel so good?" she rasped.

"Because you deserve it. You deserve to feel good," I rumbled as I shifted, and I curled my fingers and rubbed them against her G-spot.

She went wild.

Brunette curls thrashing around her.

Spirit rushing and racing.

No question, she was about to go off like a ten-ton bomb.

Brinley climbing toward those heights as her muscles tensed and her body bowed.

Then she split.

"King," she moaned as her head rocked on the back of the sofa and the rest of her levitated from the leather.

That nickname she'd given me was muted and coarse and grazing against me like a brutal embrace as she throbbed around my fingers.

And I wanted to be.

I wanted to be the one who ruled this body and this tender soul she was just then exposing.

That inconceivable connection glowed, crackling between us with all her wild turbulence, and fuck, there was something about it that felt like home.

My damned mind bent with the need for it to be my cock that was getting squeezed by her hot, soaked pussy.

But even this was far more than I should take, and I was the selfish fiend who lapped up every last drop of her pleasure.

Sucking her down, imbibing all that she was as she quivered and shook in my hold.

Her grunts and pants were heavy as she continued to hold onto my hair like it was the only thing keeping her from fully floating away as she remained elevated for the longest time.

Flying.

Soaring like I promised.

Bliss saturating her through as she twitched and jerked.

I kept her there for what felt like a lifetime. Until I felt the last of the aftershocks roll through her body, then I slowly settled her bare ass onto the couch and eased my fingers free.

I sat back on my heels and my hands went back to her knees so I could take her in.

"You good?" My voice was the coarsest it'd ever been.

And Brinley? She gave me this loopy, lopsided smile. The girl fully doped up on pleasure.

My chest stretched in pleasure, too, though it was a different kind.

It was the kind that murmured of pride and relief and the simmering of joy.

So fucking reckless it wasn't funny, but fuck me, there was some stupid part inside me that wanted to make her happy.

I was fucked.

So fucking fucked.

"That was the best thing I've ever felt," she mumbled around that dopey grin.

I cocked a smirk. "Told you I was going to take care of you."

Redness touched her cheeks, Brinley going fully vulnerable.

"It turns out, I like the way you take care of me, Silas Mercer."

"That's good because I plan on doing it again and again."

Her teeth clamped down on her bottom lip, and she sat up, that fall of hair raining around her shoulders, eyes firing with greed and interest and the barest flickers of uncertainty as she slid a hand from my stomach down to my aching cock.

Rubbing me over my jeans, she barely peeked up at my face. "It seems like maybe I need to take care of you, too."

I choked, nearly knocked from my feet by the greed that surged through my body.

Gritting my teeth, I curled my hand around her wrist, stopping her. I knew if my dick got free of its confines, I was going to fuck her senseless, and I wasn't positive she was ready for that.

Hell, I wasn't sure either of us were ready for that or if we would ever really be.

My dick strained, wailing in reproach, hating that the bare specks of my conscience were cutting this off while the rest of me felt like we were just getting started.

But I had to admit, even touching her this way was bliss, and that was going to have to be enough.

"No, baby."

Her face pinched. "You don't…?"

I could feel the questions.

The hurt and the rejection.

I shot forward and framed her face in my hands.

The feel of her against my palms singed me all over again.

"If you think I don't want you, Brinley, you're horribly mistaken. I've never wanted anything more in all my life. But you, Little Wildfire, are a treasure, and I fucking refuse to tarnish that."

The fingers of her left hand swept over the back of my hand. "That's funny since every time you touch me, everything feels a little bit better."

More of the vulnerability.

Trust.

Truth.

Amber gaze churning with every dangerous emotion she shouldn't feel.

Or maybe it was only my heart that was slanting toward the treacherous.

And I shouldn't fucking do it. I knew it. But I eased forward and took that tempting mouth.

Only this time I kissed her slow.

Desperate and deep and with the few shards of myself that I had left to give.

A call of my spirit and a plea of my tongue.

Brinley kissed me back.

Every bit as ardently.

I felt cracks splintering the floor below me.

I forced myself to pull back, except my next action was every bit as reckless since I gathered her up, pulled her into my arms, and carried her to my bed.

I propped her on the side of it, then snatched a tee from my dresser, my eyes on her the whole time as I returned to her. Reaching out, I slowly, carefully, peeled her out of her dress then worked my tee over her head.

She swam in it, and there was something brand new stretching across my chest as I stared down at her sitting there wearing my shirt.

Wild curls cascading around her. A softness I'd never seen before etched on her face.

I stripped down to my underwear, then climbed onto the bed, nestled her in at my side so we were looking at each other.

Face-to-face.

Staring at each other through the ghosts that frolicked in the night.

I took her hand and held it up between us as I threaded my fingers through hers and murmured, "Tell me, I need to know."

33

Silas

"Are you sure you want to hear my sob story?" She attempted to play it light, but I wasn't blind. I could see her mouth tweak down on the side.

Could feel the way her entire being shook with the thought of having to conjure what I was pretty sure she'd tried to bury beneath a castle tower.

But I figured it was futile. No stopping or altering the collision we were headed for.

Fuck, she was so pretty. No way to get enough, my eyes flicked all over her face.

Squandering the sight.

Knowing it was fleeting, no chance of something so good meant for me.

So I memorized every line and curve and divot instead. Tucking it down into those vacant places that I held for the ones who meant something to me.

Listening to the way her heart thundered and battered in the space between us, mine doing its best to match.

To keep up.

To keep time.

Insane the number of beasts I'd faced down, and I was positive it was going to be this beautiful creature who would be my demise.

"Is it wrong that I want to know every single thing about you?" I murmured as I played with one of those curls before I let my fingertips trail down the angle of her jaw.

"That would be a whole lot to unload on you, King." It was nothing but a soggy tease.

My chest stretched tight, and I splayed my hand over her cheek, my thumb brushing back and forth along the hollow of her eye.

"What, do I look weak to you? You think I can't handle all that you are?" There I went, doing my best to play it light, too.

A fool's game since I already carried the weight of the world on my shoulders.

Her expression dimmed, harvest eyes caressing over me like she was trying to memorize me the same way. "You look like the kind of strength that I could get lost in. Someone who could make me let down my guard. Someone I could come to rely on if I'm not careful."

I saw the rest of what was written there. The truth that the only person she could rely on was herself.

"Would it be so bad to rely on me?"

"For just a little while? This mess requires a whole lot more than a few weeks." Sadness weaved its way into Brinley's tone as she repeated the warning I'd already issued.

This was temporary.

Whatever this was had an expiration date.

It was the day I put Kent Ellison six feet underground.

"Though a few more of those orgasms might be nice." Another joke to deflect, her seductive mouth stretching into a taunt that was riddled with affection.

Affection I could never earn the right for her to feel, but there it was. Potent and disorienting.

"I'd hold it all if I could, but I'm asking you to let me hold this."

This was what I could. The strength I bore.

Vengeance. Revenge. The drawing of blood.

Wasn't so sure I'd consider it a gift, but right then, maybe it was.

Her strong brow pinched, and the pad of my thumb went to tracing along that spot, too. Trying to soothe, wishing there was a way to completely take it away.

"I've never let anyone go there before."

"Are you afraid of taking me there?"

She scoffed a small sound. "I'm afraid of everything, Silas."

Fury clawed through my insides, though I kept it tapped, stored it up for when I could hunt down the motherfucker who'd caused the pain that roiled in her being.

It'd be my honor to flay the skin from his bones.

I wasn't above torture.

Hell, half the time, I took pleasure in it.

"Who was he?" I didn't mean to let it come out a command, but that's exactly what it was.

A flurry of rage skimming beneath the surface of my skin and ushering me toward mayhem. The thirst for retribution rocking my hands.

Brinley flinched, but I knew it wasn't because she was afraid of me.

She was terrified of being taken back.

Terrified of lowering the walls enough that I could see over them.

Moisture filled her eyes, a hurricane of browns and golds and reds drawing me deep into her storm.

"Silas..." She trembled, and I knew she was getting dragged back.

Terror breaking the cracks that had been made in her façade.

I set both hands on each side of her face, anchoring her to me as I whispered, "I'm right here. You're not alone."

34

Brinley

Twenty-One Years Old

Brinley sat at the small island in the kitchen. A bleary light hung from overhead, and her temples throbbed as she sorted through the pile of bills that had grown so high they were going to bury her.

Her stomach was in knots as she tried to figure out how the hell she was going to make a dent in them.

She'd been close.

Close to finally catching up.

Paying off the debts that had hung over her head like an anvil.

She and Dereck had lived with their aunt for a year after their mother had passed, but when Dereck had started getting into trouble at school, she'd kicked them out.

Brinley had been seventeen.

Lost.

Grieving.

The hole inside her so big she didn't know how she hadn't bled out.

But she'd had to figure it out. Take care of Dereck because there was no one else to do it. Their father had only gone so far as to say they were living with him on paper since she'd literally gotten onto her knees and begged him.

She made it simple enough for him that the paperwork was already filled out so he didn't have to put in the effort that he couldn't seem to find the energy for.

She'd scrounged and saved and worked three jobs.

It was never enough. Food was in short supply, and the hungrier

Dereck got, the further he'd seemed to spiral.

Stealing, fights, and God knew what else.

Brinley had finally found a decent bookkeeping job at an attorney's office, and it brought in enough to cover rent for a two-bedroom apartment, utilities, and food, that and nursing her mom's old car along and praying it wouldn't finally go kaput.

Then Dereck had been arrested, and she'd had to take out a loan to get him out, bartering with one of the attorneys at her office to help them, selling her soul once again to keep the promise she'd made to her mother.

Pain pressed against the underside of her flesh, and she looked up at the microwave clock.

Five past midnight.

Unease churned in her guts.

Dereck promised. He promised he'd be home by eleven. Told her not to worry. That he was keeping his nose clean. That he'd never make a mistake like that again.

Brinley tried to steady herself. To find the hope of this life. Something good in it.

But she wasn't sure how that would happen when she thought the loneliness might swallow her.

The ache consumed.

She missed her mother so much.

Missed her belief. Her faith. Her praise and her hugs and the soft way in which she looked at her.

"I'm trying, Mom. I'm trying so hard, and I don't know what I'm doing wrong."

Her phone vibrated on the imitation granite countertop beside her.

Dereck.

Freaking finally.

Only her stomach dropped when she read what the text said.

Dereck: *I'm in trouble. I need you to come and get me.*

There was an address beneath it.

Sickness crawled through her like a dose of venom. She wavered, gaze rushing around the tiny kitchen like it might give her an answer. Take this away.

She quickly tapped across the screen.

Brinley: *What's going on?*

Dereck: *I'll explain once you get here.*

God, why did he continually do this to her?

"Mom, please help me."

She waffled, then pushed from the stool and stomped to the door where she grabbed her purse and keys, then hurried down the steps to the parking lot below.

Her mother's old car chugged and moaned before it finally sputtered to life.

She threw it into reverse and blew out of the lot, following the directions on her phone, winding her way into the scummiest part of town.

It wasn't like they were living at the Ritz, but there was something about the darkened house that sent chills crawling through her being as she came to idle at the curb.

Dread twisted her stomach.

Trepidation and fear.

She fumbled through a text.

Brinley: *I'm here.*

Nothing. No response.

She itched, her knee bouncing a million miles a minute while she waited. Trepidation dragged across her skin like sharp, jagged talons.

Brinley: *Hello?*

Her phone remained silent.

Her head swiveled back and forth as she peered through the night, irritation lighting her up as the stilled darkness echoed back.

She should leave. Put the car into drive and get the hell out of there.

Every molecule in her body knew it.

But those words spun through her mind.

I promise.

They were the last ones she'd ever spoken to her mother. She'd been gone when she got back from work that night.

Trembling as hard as an off-balance washer, she clicked open the door and climbed from the car, sucking down steadying breaths as she crept up the cracked, pitted walkway to the dilapidated house.

The wooden boards creaked as she edged up the two steps, and her heart hammered as she moved to the door.

Her knock was slow and unsure.

Somehow, she knew to run. Could feel the evil seeping through the thin walls.

But when she turned to do it, it was too late.

The door opened, and she was being hauled inside.

A hand over her mouth as she was dragged into the darkness.

Her eyes wide in the pitch of the room. But she guessed she didn't need to see them to know there were three of them.

She could taste the vileness coming from two other men who invaded from the corners of the room.

The one behind her murmured filth at her ear, a severing of her broken heart, knowing a part of her was going to die there even if they spared her life. "Seems your brother thinks he's going to get away with not paying what's owed to me. I think it's time we taught him a lesson."

35

Brinley

My mind spun through the horror of memories while I lay there in the sanctuary of Silas's arms. I wanted to give it all to him, but I wasn't sure that I could force the details from my tongue.

I wasn't ready. I didn't know if I'd ever be.

But I had to give him something.

I wanted to.

My mouth felt sticky and dry, but I managed to force out, "Dereck owed these guys money..."

I guess those few words were loaded with enough implication that Silas felt the full force of them.

Because he flinched then pulled me closer, hazel eyes waiting. Searching my face.

"They used me to punish him."

"Fuck. Brinley." It was a brutal grunt. Every muscle in Silas's body curled with aggression.

His arms were locked so tight, and I got the sense he was desperate to make me understand that I wasn't alone.

Or maybe that he was willing to crush anyone who'd ever hurt me in my past.

Tears blurred my eyes. I hadn't had someone care for me this way in so many years. And then? It'd been my mother. Which was a whole different experience from this.

I felt overwhelmed by it.

Struck.

Like I could maybe...let go.

"It's okay, baby, I'm right here," he murmured, then hedged, "What happened?"

"All three of them attacked me, used me, and I think they had the intention of killing me..."

I couldn't believe that I let that much out. That I trusted this man who was supposed to be the last person I could trust with my darkest secret.

My chest stretched as he somehow gathered me closer.

Rage blistered through him while this tender care soaked right through the middle of it.

"I actually lost consciousness," I told him, "which I guess was a blessing."

I choked over it, so awkwardly. Giving this part of myself to someone felt foreign.

Strange.

Even the fragments that remained jagged in my mind.

"I woke up in the hospital. I don't even know how I got there."

"Who were they?" Fury curled around his growl, and his massive hands fisted at my back. No question, it caused him physical pain not to get out of this bed and release it.

My head barely shook. "I don't even know."

I'd woken up to Dereck at my side. Holding my hand and promising it would never happen again.

They'd stolen his phone and used it to lure me. He swore he had no idea they would do something so despicable. Swore he was sorrier than he'd ever been. Swore that he would never get himself into that kind of trouble again.

But he'd also begged me not to give the police details or else he was dead.

It was the hardest thing I'd ever done. Protecting him after what he'd caused.

But I couldn't be the reason for his death sentence.

And after that, he'd been...better.

Still a mess. Constantly losing jobs and not having enough for rent. But that was minimal in comparison.

We'd been halfway normal until now.

"But Dereck knows," Silas seethed. It wasn't even a question. It was a straight shot of judgement.

I swallowed around the tears. "Yes. But I didn't want to know. I didn't want the burden of knowing who they were and knowing they were out there if I couldn't do anything about it. Dereck was dead if I went after them."

"I can do something about it." There was a promise behind it. Like that was exactly what he intended.

My head barely shook. "It's in the past, Silas. I just want to live. Put all of this behind us. Ensure my brother is safe, then I want to live life. Finally, truly live it."

He didn't look convinced. I was pretty sure the next chance he got he was going to shake the names out of Dereck.

Probably right before he put a bullet in my brother's brain.

I scratched my fingertips over the stubble on his cheek. "I need you to promise me that you'll let this go."

His jaw clenched. "Not sure that I can. Idea of someone hurting you makes me want to go on a rampage. I want to end anyone who's ever hurt you. Destroy them the way they deserve to be."

He brushed back a curl from my face, twining it around his finger as he stared at me through the dancing shadows.

"You want to fight for me, King?" I meant for it to come out playful, but it was brimming with emotion.

The pad of his thumb stroked my cheek. "Yeah, Brinley, it's become blatantly apparent that I do."

"I just want this all behind me."

He inhaled a cleansing breath like he was packing away the little I revealed, but I had the sense he planned on ripping it wide open later.

"And what does that look like, Brinley? If you were fighting for you? Living a little for yourself and not sacrificing everything for your brother?"

I shrugged a little. "I don't know. Maybe I'd go back to school. I always had this dream of being an accountant."

His soft chuckle was surprised. "An accountant? I thought most girls dreamed of being librarians or doctors or, if you're Elena, opening an adorable store."

His eyes widened a smidgeon with the tease.

I could feel the redness pink my cheeks. It seemed once I let a wall down, the vulnerability came flooding out. "I don't know...I just...like piecing numbers together. It's like a puzzle that I'm solving. And I like the idea that I might be able to help people save money, maybe? Take some of the strain off their lives."

"Which is why you're taking that job out in the office so seriously?" he surmised.

I sent him a playful glower. "I don't do anything half-assed. What did you expect?"

He shocked me by suddenly rolling onto his back and pulling me on top of him. His fingers weaved into the fall of my hair as he gazed up at me. "What I didn't expect was you."

36

Silas

I stared up at Brinley. Her eyes glinted with unshed tears and with a belief that seemed impossible that she could feel.

After learning the tiny bit she revealed about what had happened to her, I couldn't believe that she was here.

She hadn't divulged much, but I could feel the magnitude of it.

The way it'd shaped her.

Scarred her.

Tormented her mind.

I wanted to demand more information. Jump out of this bed and drive straight to Dereck and force the little prick to give me their names.

Couldn't believe he'd get himself tangled with another monster after that.

And it was clear right then that Brinley was too good. Too giving. Too right.

I wanted to protect and avenge every part of that.

I gazed up at her stunning face.

I didn't know how to process what I was feeling.

How to handle it.

This was so far beyond what I was equipped for it wasn't funny.

I was the destroyer, and the only thing I wanted to do was resurrect what she'd lost.

Well, and do a little destroying, too.

Guilt crept into my throat. "Hate the way I treated you when you came here. Threatening you. Trying to make you afraid."

Every word cracked.

"Every one of my men was commanded not to touch you. I want you to know that wouldn't have happened here."

Even though I was the bastard who implied it. Attempting to bend her to my will to keep her safe.

But not all good intentions are right.

She huffed a breath, glanced away before looking back at me. "It's weird. I was terrified. Terrified of coming here. Of Dereck involving me in something I didn't understand. In something that would put me in danger again."

She chewed at her bottom lip, contemplating as those eyes moved over my face. "But I don't think I was ever actually afraid of you. Just of the reaction I had to you. And I think this afternoon I wasn't flinching because I was scared of you touching me, but because I wasn't. Because I wanted you."

"It's safe to say I was a little freaked out by the reaction I had to you, too."

She paused, her mind rolling before it came to a standstill.

Nerves rattled her through before she finally whispered, "Can you tell me what's really going on with my brother?"

Dread thrummed, a cold slick that slipped down my spine.

Fuck. It was getting harder and harder to keep secrets from her.

Who I was and what I was involved in.

But this secret was for her. Because I fucking cared and I wanted her to make it through this unblemished, though today had proven that was a failing goal.

"Can't let you go there, Brinley, but I can tell you that he brought you here because he does care about you. Because he cares about your safety and trusted me to protect you until we put this to an end."

Was that bullshit? Was he only doing it out of self-preservation? And was I only saying it to erase some of the hurt etched on her stunning face?

But when I'd had my gun stuffed down his throat, it'd been her name he was garbling. Was it his heart or was he low enough to use her against me?

After what I learned tonight? I was thinking he might be the biggest piece of scum that existed.

Right up there with my father.

"Put what to an end?" she demanded.

I warred before I said, "The bad guys he got himself mixed up in.

That's as much as I can tell you."

Fear suddenly clawed its way through her expression, and she swallowed hard. "Can you just tell me one thing? Is it the same people who had Elena?"

Malevolence ripped through my body. "Yes."

Despair wrenched through her, the confirmation stabbing through her like a rusted blade.

Like she was sinking into the awareness that Dereck likely hadn't changed.

"I guess I see what's riding on this," she muttered through grieved disbelief.

But she couldn't.

She had no idea what we were really undertaking, and there was no way I could guide her into those places, even though I was somehow tempted to do it.

Drag her down into my darkness.

Invite her in.

Keep her.

I slipped both hands to her neck.

Hovered. Wavered. Wanted.

So close to giving in.

The wail coming from the other room stopped me in my tracks.

"No! No! No!" Little cries echoed, then Kai was begging, "*Siwas*!"

Heart fisting, I moved Brinley off me and was on my feet.

37

Brinley

Kai's cries echoing from the other room nearly broke me in two, and I shot upright, head spinning as I was dragged from whatever the fever was that had been blistering between me and Silas and to Kai's reality.

Soul wrenched when I felt the terror radiating from his room.

I didn't think that part of me could break any farther as I watched Silas blaze out the door, the cries breaking off a moment later.

Silas's soft voice echoed, then came closer as he returned to the doorway of his room.

Kai was in the security of his arms. The tiny baby tucked close, his head burrowed up under his chin. As close to him as he could get because he knew he was safe there.

I guess I somehow knew that's where I was safe, too. That no matter how hard and battle-clad Silas was, he was a haven.

A haven for his men.

A haven for his family.

I had a hunch he was the only one who didn't know it.

Kai's cries shifted.

Quieted.

Soothed as Silas slowly rocked him and kept running his hand down his back.

"I've got you. I've got you."

"My *Siwas*?" Kai hiccupped through his tears.

"Yeah, buddy. Your Silas. And I'm not going anywhere."

"Ohhhh-kay," that baby mumbled into his chest.

Crushing.

It was absolutely soul crushing.

The amount of sorrow and love that suddenly splintered out from the middle of me.

A breaking apart and a coming together.

Brittle pieces knocked free and a knitting of something profound winding itself into the vacant, harrowed places.

I thought Silas must have felt the impact because that ferocious, unrelenting gaze fell on me.

Sadness and devotion and something that looked like his own terror poured out.

It turned out he was right all along. I was looking for trouble.

I was in so much of it.

Because I knew right then he would destroy me.

He was nothing but a bomb dropped right in the middle of barricades and levees I'd built up to protect myself.

Atomic.

Complete annihilation.

Silas slowly shuffled over to the bed and crawled in beside me with Kai still in his arms.

He laid down with the little boy, and I followed suit.

No restraints or securities left.

Not after him touching me and showing me that I could *be*. That I had the power to ask for what I wanted. For what I needed.

Not after he'd held me after.

And sure as hell not after this.

Kai nestled in the sanctuary between us. His little thumb went to his mouth, and he hugged his blanket to his chest as he released a jutting sigh, the horror of the nightmare that had woken him expelled into the calm swells of the lapping night.

He made little grunting noises as he snuggled deeper, and Silas stared across at me from over his head.

Jaw clenched, eyes wide and fathomless.

Letting me see all the way to the bottom.

Where maybe he was every bit as afraid as the rest of us.

Another stuttered breath filtered out of Kai, and he rolled around to face me, still sucking his thumb as he curled into my chest, his free hand fisting up in Silas's shirt that I wore.

On instinct, my hand went to his back to pull him closer. Wanting to shield and guard him, too. Or maybe it was just a bare, blatant promise that I would.

A toil of brand-new intensity suddenly blazed out of Silas, and his palm slipped to my cheek.

And I guess that was the point when everything cracked.

When there was no ground left below me.

When I stumbled.

When I fell.

Already sure I'd be crushed at the bottom.

38

Silas

Darkness reigned and ghosts crawled the walls. The gloom that had always painted my life rimming the edges of the room, poised and ready to devour.

But a light held it at bay.

Flames around her.

Brinley Webber in my bed with that little boy tucked up against her chest.

Wildfire.

I set my hand on her cheek.

I was scorched.

Charred.

Ash.

Staggering in a direction that would tip me over the edge.

Drawn to a cliff like it exerted five thousand tons of gravity.

A force I wasn't sure I had the will to fight.

But I had to.

I had to remember who I was.

39

Silas

Fifteen Years Old

His dad returned the next week just like he promised, the rumble of his truck again lifting the hairs at the back of Silas's neck.

Yeah, he still wanted to punch him in the face, but there was some dark place inside him that was eager for what he had.

Silas figured he owed it. That every dollar the jerk ever made should be given to Silas's mom. She was the one who had earned it. Worked and toiled to put a roof over their heads when this scumbag never gave a crap.

"There's my boy." His voice clawed at Silas's ear, though he still turned to look at his father through the open passenger window. His dad leaned across the seat with another bag.

Silas eyed it warily while his tongue salivated. He had the urge to snatch it out of his hand.

"Told you I'd be back," he said with a grin. Silas couldn't tell if it was affable or malicious.

Silas took the bag, his heart beating fast, the sun shining down hard and sweat slicking his flesh when he peeked inside and saw there was even more money in there that time.

"You're gonna have to earn the next one," his dad said.

Silas's stomach dropped to the ground. "And how am I going to do that?"

"You're gonna meet me at the back door of Keg & Creek Tavern at midnight. And you don't tell your momma."

• • •

It was easy. He didn't have to do a whole lot.

Take the backpack that was always hidden in the overgrown brush along the river and run it through the cover of the woods to the back of Keg & Creek.

Take the bag that was waiting for him there and run it back to the same spot.

Shove it into the hole near the bank and cover it with branches and leaves.

There'd be an envelope just for him in the side pocket, one that he'd split the contents of with his dad back where he always waited at the end of the road.

He didn't even have to see the guys who were in a boat on the river who came for it, the sound of the garbled boat engine only hitting his ears after he disappeared back into the forest.

Yeah, he knew what was in those bags. He might have been an idiot for doing this, but he wasn't a moron.

But it was hard to care when he'd seen the weight sliding off his mother's shoulders. The bags under her eyes not so deep.

He was halfway through the woods when he heard the telltale sound of the muted boat engine, one that idled in the place it sought every three nights.

Out of breath, he paused beneath the glow of the moon, his mind spinning and his stomach sour.

He set his hand over his heart where it beat.

Knowing whatever the cost, it was worth it.

40

Brinley

I was prodded from sleep by giggles and a little hand smacking against my face.

Okay, not prodded.

Knocked.

"*Bwinwey.* You got eyes?"

One of my lids was being peeled back, and my one-sided sight was filled with a cherub face that was peering into my eyeball like he might be able to see into my brain.

I released a sleepy laugh, forcing myself to blink all the way open.

Kai was on his knees at my side.

Shocker, the spot where Silas had slept was empty.

A deluge of memories came flooding back.

Silas's mouth on me, his head between my thighs.

No fear.

No terror.

No shame.

I only wanted more.

More than anything, I was sure I'd feel regret for sharing what I had. Sure I'd want to go running from his property, which was only asking for more humiliation since there was no doubt he'd only come dragging me back.

But there was none.

No embarrassment or disgrace.

Kai knocked me out of the trance by patting both my cheeks.

"You '*wake*?"

I cleared the roughness from my throat. "Yeah, baby, I'm awake."

"My *Bwinwey*?" He bobbed that sweet head.

My chest again felt like it would cave.

Mush.

Shaking the drowsiness off, I forced myself up to sitting.

He scrambled right onto my lap, chubby arms locked around my neck as he bounced on his knees.

"I eat?" He nodded.

It was so emphatic, there was no question he considered this an emergency.

I curled my arms around him and stood, my heart pressing fiercely against my ribs as I rocked him back and forth.

"I think we should probably change this pee-pee diaper first," I teased around the fervor that had taken me hostage.

A riot of giggles erupted from him. "I not got pee-pee."

"Are you sure?" I spun him around.

Another outbreak of giggles. A song of joy that banged the walls, ricocheting back to penetrate a spot inside me that I didn't know existed.

I kept swaying and swinging him as I carried him from Silas's room and into his.

The upper floor was quiet, no one around, the clear life of the house apparent in the faint drone of the television and distant voices that rose up from below.

I inclined my ear.

Was Silas down there? Did I want him to be? I wasn't sure I could face him, not when there was a heavy chance that what I was feeling would be painted all over my expression.

No way to conceal it.

Rays of morning light poured in through Kai's window, a spray of motes dancing merrily and lighting up the adorable decorations.

Illustrated trucks and tractors and trains were stuck to the walls, and the bedding in his crib matched.

A giant 'Kai' was painted over his changing table and a smaller swirl of 'You are loved' was beneath it.

Affection gripped and pulsed, and the emotion welled as I carried him to his changing table.

Realizing what Silas, Elena, and Meems were trying to portray to him. Knowing that they wanted him to feel safe every time he entered this room.

I settled him onto the cushion, and he giggled some more, the terror from last night long gone in the light of the day.

Every cell in my body rose in defense of him. Wanting to show him that.

Love.

My spirit clogged because I was sure I wouldn't ever want to stop.

I peeled back the tabs of his diaper, and he scratched the nail of his little index finger over the words that had been written for him.

"*Wove*?" he sang, half melody, half question.

No doubt, he'd been read the statement over and over as the rest of his family had stood in this exact same spot with him.

"That's right, Kai." My voice was thready and thin. "You are loved. So much."

"Kai *wove*!" He beamed at me.

My broken heart flailed, and the words wheezed out of me.

"And I love Kai. So much."

My hands shook as I finished changing him into a fresh diaper.

I pumped sanitizer onto my hands, rubbed them together, then he was back in my arms.

He peered up at me. "Meems got yummy?"

I choked over a laugh. "I bet she does."

I carried him downstairs. The morning news droned from the television, the volume set nearly to mute.

I assumed it was used as background noise.

Habit, maybe.

They hardly needed it.

Not when Elena's laughter resonated from the kitchen.

Ricocheting from the tiles and rebounding in the type of joy that I thought would have been crushed by what had happened to her.

But it was real and alive. Filled with hope and belief even when someone had tried to stamp it out.

And maybe it was all because of them that I felt a flicker of that hope bluster up inside me.

Maybe I really would leave this place remembering who I once wanted to be. Maybe they were forcing me to see something so much greater than the demons that fought to keep me chained.

Because as I padded out on bare feet onto the cool floors, I felt freer than I had in a long time.

No doubt set on a collision course that was going to destroy a piece of me, but maybe the pieces I'd reclaim would be worth the pain.

Or maybe I was just really good at telling myself lies.

Glee lit Elena's face when she saw us walk in. She was sitting on the far counter, facing us, her legs swinging as they dangled over the side.

Her dark brown hair piled on her head and her pretty face void of makeup.

"Well, good morning." Suggestion oozed out of her mouth.

She said it at the exact same time as Meems was mumbling, "Speak of the devil," into the dough that she was mixing in a big metal bowl.

I hooked Kai onto my hip. "Are you all admitting that you were talking about me behind my back?"

I cocked my head like I was really pissed off by the idea. Too bad it was punctured with lightness.

It seemed it was catching when it came to them.

As if what happened between Silas and me last night hadn't been the most exceptional thing I'd ever experienced.

"Behind your back? No way. Everything we have to say, we say to your face. You will find no backstabbing around here." Elena grinned.

Yeah. The only thing you found around here were secrets and skeletons tucked under rugs and hidden in closets.

"And what is it you have to say?" I challenged, pure sass.

Giggling, Kai pointed an innocent, accusatory finger. "Say!"

Meems arched a brow. "I think your attire says plenty enough."

She let her gaze wander down my body, a burden of proof. And it was just then I was realizing I stood there in nothing but Silas's T-shirt.

Barefoot and itching as the fabric swam around me.

It hit me at the middle of the thighs, quite a bit longer than half the skirts and dresses I normally wore.

Their faces promised I'd never donned anything so scandalous.

Redness rushed my cheeks.

I never took myself as being shy, but I felt like covering under their scrutiny.

"Oh, well, I ran out of pajamas. You know, I didn't get to bring that many of my things here, so I just grabbed the first thing I could find."

I'd run out of something, all right. My sanity.

Meems's brows lifted higher. "And the pile of laundry I left folded for you on top of Silas's dresser yesterday wouldn't do?"

She might as well have been delivering a closing argument. The jury convinced.

Guilty.

Of course, that jury only consisted of one.

Elena, whose expression filled with triumph. "Did you get naked with my brother?"

I choked over the knot of surprise that clotted off my throat. Leave it to Elena to go straight for the jugular.

"I don't know what you're talking about," I spluttered, hanging onto Kai like he was a wall I could hide behind.

"Oh, come on, Brinley. Silas literally *carried* you out of the clubhouse last night. Tossed you right over his shoulder. Caveman style. It was clearly a man setting out to make his claim."

Heat crawled up my neck.

Tendrils that wrapped around to constrict.

"No, no, you have it all wrong. He said you and I were breaking the rules, going to the clubhouse last night. When he told me to come back here and I refused, he carried me. Can you believe the audacity? That man is nothing but a brute."

There, my own closing statement.

Maybe I'd swayed her judgement.

"And he left me there?" she opposed.

Right, there was that.

I glowered at her though there was zero heat behind it, my own dare twisting my voice with a distinct insinuation. "You had Trevan to watch over you."

"He never even looked my way," she countered.

"Liar."

She glared back. "You got naked with my brother. You might as well fess it up because I see it written all over you."

This girl had no filter or boundaries.

"I did not sleep with him."

"Kai *sweep Siwas* and *Bwinwey.*" The sweet boy patted his chest.

A huff of befuddlement and awkward amusement shot from my mouth.

Elena cracked up then basically whined, "Come on, admit it, Brinley.

You're supposed to tell your best friend everything."

"We didn't sleep together," I reiterated, my voice croaking as I lowered it with emphasis. I don't know why I was so choked up about it.

Apparently, orgasms given by men who looked like gods and had wicked fingers made you emotional.

That vibrator definitely didn't hold up.

Elena looked crestfallen. "But something happened," she insisted. "The man looked like he'd embarked on his life's mission."

I wavered.

She must have taken it as confirmation because she jumped off the counter and shouted, "Ah-ha!"

A celebration of victory.

Like she was the one who won the medal when it was undeniably Silas who deserved a gold star.

"I knew it."

"It wasn't like that." I shuffled on my feet.

Meems's grayed brow ticked higher, so close to becoming one with her hairline. "And what exactly was it like? Because it appeared to me with the way Silas went running out of the house first thing this mornin', he was every bit as terrified over whatever it *was* as you."

My throat felt too tight, nerves firing and getting into a tangle that I wouldn't be able to undo.

"He's just seeing to it that I'm cared for while I'm here."

"Oh, I bet he's taking care of you," she drew out.

"No different than I'm sure he does with all the other girls falling all over him around here."

It was purely a defense.

It wasn't like I didn't notice all the women who kept slanting their gazes his way last night. Aiming to garner his attention as he sat at that bar and gruffed and glowered at me like I was the bane of his existence.

No one could blame me for rubbing it in a little bit out there on the dance floor.

He totally deserved it for busting through my reserves.

I guess we'd both been pushed up against a wall. Neither of us left with any restraint.

My chest tightened.

Strike that.

Silas had.

He'd slammed the brakes on the direction I'd been heading before things between us had really gotten out of hand.

Meems laughed an incredulous sound. "You're talking about the bunnies running around here?"

I shifted Kai around to my other hip, the little boy playing with my hair, taking giant pieces and hiding his face behind them like he was playing his own game of hide and seek.

"Obviously." I shrugged, nonchalant and like the thought of it didn't sting.

A dull blade driven right through the middle of my sternum.

Visions flashing of three or four of those women crawling all over him.

Jealousy was such an ugly emotion, and right then, it was *crawling all over* me.

I finally got myself together enough to walk deeper into the kitchen.

The old lady chuckled low as she cracked an egg into the mixture. "You think whatever is going on between the two of you is no different than the nonsense that goes on over there at that clubhouse?"

"Isn't it?" I said it like it was no big deal as I wound around Elena so I could get to the cupboard that held the coffee cups.

You know, just making myself at home.

One step closer to that decimated heart.

A total fool because my spirit leapt when Meems shifted to look at me from over her shoulder and said, "Not even close, sweet one."

In defense, I huffed while ensuring Kai's limbs were out of reach when I pulled out the carafe and poured a steaming cup of coffee. "And how's it any different?"

Elena laughed like I was dense. "How is it different?"

"Yeah."

"The fact he brought you through that door right there means it's different." Answering for her, Meems pointed toward the front entrance.

Kai wiggled. "Down."

I set him onto his feet, then I took a quick sip of my coffee, wincing as the piping hot liquid hit my tongue.

"He only brought me here to keep an eye on me," I defended.

"Oh, I bet he wants to keep an eye on you. That boy looks like he wants to eat you up every time he glances your way." Meems hummed with a shake of her head.

My guard slipped, and I gnawed at my bottom lip as I looked at Kai who started pushing his toy motorcycle across the floor at my feet. "There is no future there, if that's what you two are thinking."

"And why not?" Elena almost pouted.

I didn't even want a relationship. Had no need for one. I did just fine by myself, thank you very much.

Except…

Air whispered from my lungs. "I think Silas might be as broken as me."

With the irresponsible confession, Meems settled the bowl onto the counter. She turned around. When she did, tenderness had fully taken her over.

Affection and care brimming in the aged lines of her expression. "You're right, Brinley. He's been broken and traumatized. He's been struggling to survive since before he was even a man and doing his best to protect his family while he did it."

My spirit flailed and thrashed.

I wanted to know that part of him. To understand what all of it meant.

"And he's made some bad decisions. Horrible ones. No question about it, and he counts himself to blame for all of it. Thinks he's unworthy when he's probably one of the worthiest people I've ever met."

My chest stretched to the point of exploding, listening to her talk about her grandson with unflinching admiration.

It was only more difficult to stand beneath the weight of it since Elena's expression morphed into that tortured innocence that promised she had endured the same trauma, too.

So much more appalling than the tidbits I'd gleaned.

"But that man is good, through and through," Meems continued, love gushing out on a river of awe. "I've seen it time and again. His sacrifice. And that's not being biased. It's just the plain and simple truth."

She inched forward, and she reached out and touched below my chin, her gaze penetrating as she stared me down. "So good and beaten down by the world that he's always trying to stay one step ahead of it, forever putting up a fight. Broken, but refusing to surrender."

She tilted my chin up further. "I'd bet a whole lot like you. And maybe I'm wrong, but I'm thinking those broken pieces just might fit."

A tremble rolled through me. "I'm not sure about that."

Elena reached out and squeezed my hand. "Your heart will know."

I choked over a strangled sound. Man, was that one coming back to bite me in the ass.

"I don't think Silas nor I are ready for any of that, but maybe we are what the other needs right now."

While I was here, like he said.

It was going to have to be enough.

I could see the red flag waving in my periphery.

A warning tolling at the back of my mind.

If that was the way it was going to be, then I needed to stop allowing myself to get attached.

Easier said than done when I was surrounded by these amazing people.

Elena and Meems.

Kai at my feet.

Silas's ferocity vibrating from someplace outside the door.

The home I didn't have.

41

Brinley

King: *How are you feeling this morning?*

I glanced down at my phone that sat on the bathroom counter for what had to be the twentieth time, wondering how in the hell he expected me to respond to the text.

Talk about a loaded freaking question.

What words were there to say when last night had shifted an intrinsic part inside me? Set something that had been wronged back to right?

Like I know how to dream again seemed like a really imprudent way to start the day.

I leaned back toward the mirror to finish applying mascara, figuring no response was better than the one I wanted to surrender.

My phone vibrated again.

King: *If you don't respond to this in thirty seconds, I'm going to leave the clubhouse to come check on you, and I have important business to attend to. Having to walk out of here on my crew is not going to make me happy.*

I couldn't help but grin.

Surly bear.

Me: *So grumpy at 7:45 in the morning. It seems you must be feeling a little less satisfied than me.*

I pressed send before I could think better of it. They say not to poke the devil and, here I was, trying to rile the beast.

King: *I'll take it that you're feeling extra good this morning, then.*

Gone was the intensity that we'd fallen asleep to last night. The chaotic storm of emotions that had swelled and throbbed as he'd stared across at me while I had Kai tucked to my chest.

Now? I felt a surge of electricity strike all the way from the clubhouse.

Me: *You can rest assured that I am quite chipper this morning.*

There I went, laying down bets on a clearly unfavorable hand. Clearly, I was at the disadvantage. No chance of winning.

King: *Glad you feel that way because I already miss the taste of you on my tongue. This coffee is not going to do.*

Need sailed through my senses. A tumult of butterfly wings that flapped haphazardly in my belly.

Me: *Are you thinking about me when you should be paying attention to that "important business" you were attending to?*

King: *That's the whole problem, Brinley. Can't get you off my mind. You're becoming a distraction that I can't afford, and I think I'm willing to pay the consequences, anyway.*

That time, the butterflies that toppled and turned were of an entirely different variety. A different breed.

Foolish ones that wanted to fly right into the flames.

King: *Can't wait to touch you again. Mark myself a little deeper.*

My thighs trembled.

Me: *I'll be waiting with eager anticipation.*

Was I really so readily admitting it? But there was a whole lot of peace in surrender.

Me: *I'd better go. I need to finish getting ready. It's almost eight.*

King: *And just where do you think you're going?*

Me: *Work. I need to pay my dues for my stay, remember? Someone once told me I'm quite the handful, and that office is still a mess. I have yet to fully work my magic on it.*

Flickers of fear from yesterday licked in the periphery.

But I tamped them down.

I wasn't going to allow myself to become trapped again. Wouldn't let some deranged villain set me back to start.

Not when I was finally starting to feel free.

A response immediately blipped through.

King: *Not a fucking chance that you're stepping foot in that office again.*

A huff of indignation puffed from my mouth, all while my stupid heart pattered with his care.

God, I really was weak when it came to him. But sometimes you had to whittle yourself all the way down to the nub to give way for healthy growth.

Me: *I've got news for you, King. I'm not going to be a prisoner in this room.*

I might as well have stamped my five-inch heel.

My phone immediately vibrated in my hand.

King: *And I won't allow you to be in unnecessary danger.*

Me: *Tell me there aren't at least three men now guarding the gate?*

I sent it with the full force of a challenge.

King: *Gates are locked up tight. If someone wants in, they are going through security first.*

A little relief hit me at the confirmation, not that I expected anything less.

Silas was clearly not to be toyed with, and I knew that trespasser from yesterday had put him over the edge.

Broke something in him, too.

Me: *Exactly as I thought.*

King: *Doesn't change a thing.*

Me: *Sure it does, King. And this girl isn't conceding. There's work to be done.*

A surge of determination rolled through me, and I set my phone aside, dug through my makeup bag, then leaned forward to apply pink gloss to my lips.

I sat back and took in my reflection.

Eyes bright and curls barely tamed.

And for the first time in years, I was almost able to recognize myself.

42

Brinley

It took all of five minutes for that energy to enclose behind me. A blanket of red-hot severity engulfing me where I leaned forward at the desk, flipping the lid on the laptop and pressing it on.

There was no question that it was Silas who came to stand just inside the door between the office and shop.

I could feel him standing there with his sinewy arms crossed over his chest.

Oozing that special brand of volatility.

An inferno of irritation and barely tapped lust.

He would have beaten me there had Brody not given me a ride over in his truck.

I guess Silas had taken my response as a challenge.

A duel.

Or maybe I'd just delivered it as one.

Maybe I wanted to fight it out with this temperamental, infuriating man because there was something about doing it that exposed the remnants of who I used to be.

Something about it that made me feel real and raw and important.

The first time in years that I wasn't the only one fighting for myself.

Some might call it counterproductive.

A contradiction.

I figured anything that made me feel this alive should be considered therapy.

The one thing I knew for sure as I stood there facing away from him was every hair on my body stood on end.

My body hewn in anticipation.

Shivers raced far and fast, and my heart catapulted into warp speed.

I could feel him lingering behind me, the searing severity of his gaze making a slow path down my backside.

There wasn't a casual thing about it.

"What the fuck are you wearing?" he grunted. "Wildfire, doing your best to do me in."

I bent over a little farther, hoping to give him a little peep show of my bottom.

This morning, I'd suited up in my favorite denim dress, the top fitted and the short skirt flowy, hemmed in a matching denim ruffle.

Nude heels to match.

It always made me feel powerful.

Powerful when my control was slipping.

I had none of it then when I straightened and began to slowly turn in his direction, bracing myself to look at him.

I didn't know why I bothered. I already knew I was going to get swept away by the undertow.

A riptide at my feet.

My knees knocked the second I caught sight of Silas standing in the same spot where he always stood glowering at me.

Though now I recognized that glowering for what it was.

Pure, unfiltered want.

Okay, fine. There was a little hate there, too. I wasn't a total fool.

Hate that he wanted me so badly. It was the type of hate that I completely understood because I felt a bit of it, myself.

No question, both our spirits were a bit peeved over the fact that one single person could affect us this way.

We were opposites, me playing it safe and him living on the edge.

We sure as hell didn't match.

Natural born enemies.

Neither of us could really fit into the other's life, even if we wanted to.

I felt all of it as sure as I felt the tremor rock through me as I took him in.

He wore jeans and a tight white tee and his cut over the top. Worn motorcycle boots on his feet.

All his harsh, serrated edges were honed in the morning light. Eyes gold-edged daggers that cut me right down the middle.

Too violently beautiful to be real.

Okay, maybe I was off base with this dangerous game I was playing.

Because right then, he actually looked mad.

Really freaking mad.

"Told you I didn't want you down here by yourself." Silas gritted it, his jaw clenched. Every muscle in his rigid body fired with severity.

"And I told you I'm not going to allow some creep to force me back into a corner." I flung my hand in the direction of the door.

Didn't he get it after what I told him last night?

Besides, I was surrounded by an army. There had been at least four men posted along the front perimeter when Brody had dropped me off, and those were just the ones who were visible.

I had a suspicion the entire club was on duty.

He winced, then that anger was making a resurgence when he stepped forward.

His presence slammed me like a landslide.

I lifted my chin against it. Or maybe I was only lifting it toward it. A masochist who wanted to feel the brunt force of his impact.

"So what? You plan to run headlong into danger for the sake of proving a point? Is that what you want?" He basically sneered it.

"Apparently, since I keep putting myself directly in front of you."

I guess there was no reason to beat around the bush. We both already knew what he was going to do to me, and I couldn't seem to do anything but beg him for it.

Silas chuckled a wry, self-deprecating sound. "I think it's me who's standing in the front row of the firing squad, Brinley. Me who's gonna get burned because I can't fuckin' think straight when it comes to you. Driving me out of my mind. Pushing me through every boundary that I've ever set. Making me want things I can never have."

My heart took that opportune time to flip in my chest, liking the sound of that far too much.

I gripped onto the desk behind me like it could keep me standing. Keep me on my feet so I wouldn't go crawling for him.

Shock slammed me when he suddenly growled, "Turn around and bend over the desk."

How it was possible for those words to send arousal careening through my body, I didn't know.

But there it was.

Throbbing with every pulse of my blood. Heart running manically to carry it to every cell.

My teeth clamped down on my bottom lip.

Normally, I'd be afraid and lash out.

Take it as a threat rather than a temptation.

Not with Silas Mercer.

I felt emboldened.

"Is that my punishment, *King*?" I drew his nickname out like spite, even though there was an avalanche of desire behind it.

It was a wonder the walls didn't come crashing to the ground.

Cocking his head to the side, Silas stalked forward three steps, sending the floor undulating below his feet.

"No, Brinley. It's my punishment." He punched his chest right over his heart, and his words were jagged fragments of strained breath.

Harsh and hard.

"Touching you and knowing that it's only temporary is my sheer and utter punishment. Nothing but a penalty knowing what a treasure you are. How beautiful you are. This fucking gorgeous body and this wild, untamed heart. How's it you managed to get under my skin this way?"

My inhalation was strangled.

He took another step forward, and the scent of him smacked me in the face.

Cherries drenched in whiskey.

I had to be drunk.

"A sentence for this sin," he continued. "Taking this bit of you that I could never deserve. Taking it and knowing I will never get enough. And even with that bare taste, I know I'm still going to have the memory of you scored on my soul for the rest of my life. I don't know how you got there, but there's going to be no getting you out."

I almost laughed. It was me who was going to be marked.

He angled in close, his mouth at my ear. "Now why don't you be a good girl and actually listen to me for once and turn around and bend over the desk. Unless you want me to walk out that door because you know I will. It would be best if I did."

He was giving me an out.

Asking for consent as he took a step back.

I heaved another tremulous breath and slowly fumbled around.

A shot of greed puffed from his nose.

"Bend over."

It said a whole lot with the way I hastily complied. My fingers trying to find purchase on the smooth, slippery surface of the desk as I bent over the wood.

Cool air brushed up my backside, and the skirt of my dress rode so high that I felt it tickle over the juncture of my thighs and butt cheeks.

"You have any idea, Brinley? You have any idea what you're doing to me? Walking around my house and sleeping in my bed?"

Silas remained three feet behind, though with the heat radiating off him, he might as well have been touching me.

In it, I felt like I was going to combust.

Waiting in the baited air that swirled and danced between us.

He finally did, his hand landing on the back of my thigh and riding all the way up until he was palming one cheek. "This ass. Sweet fucking torture."

"Silas." I couldn't help but whimper it, and I squeezed my thighs together like it might be enough to quench the desire.

A bare touch of his hand and I was already shaking.

"You need it, Little Wildfire? You need me to send you soaring again?"

I rocked back as he kneaded my bottom. "Yes."

"So eager."

"You already know how much I need it. What I've been missing."

"And what you've been missing is me."

I knew he regretted saying it the second it slipped because he stilled for a beat, like he was silently beating himself back into the corner where he kept himself fettered.

It was painful the way I wanted to draw him out.

"Yes," I said again, the single word a plea. "You're exactly what I've been missing. What I didn't know I needed."

"I'm going to make sure you know it, Brinley. Going to make sure you feel me so deep there will be no erasing what I've done to you. I'm going to mark you as deep as you're marking me."

He swept his fingertips down the cleft of my ass.

I jolted back with a wheeze, and he edged closer, covering me in his shadow.

"Please, don't tease me."

His lips moved to the side of my neck as he shifted my underwear to the side. "Give me one good reason not to make you beg, Little Wildfire. Defying me the way you do."

His voice was all grating and admonishment, but I could hear what else was in it.

His fear over me putting myself in a bad situation.

"I'm sorry." I whimpered it, and I wanted to regret it. Take it back. But I meant it.

He and his men had run out to rescue me yesterday, stood in front of me when all of this was Dereck's doing. They could have been injured or…

I choked off the thought, not even able to contemplate what kind of tragedy it could have been.

"Are you? Are you sorry for what you're doing to me?"

He let his fingertips drag lightly through my folds.

A tease.

"I thought you said you weren't going to punish me?"

"You're right, this punishment is all on me," he grunted.

He suddenly moved, kicking my ankles farther apart and driving two big fingers into me.

At the sudden intrusion, I gasped and clawed at the wood.

He leaned his chest against my back. His free hand came to my throat and pushed up my chin, and he angled my head around until our noses were nearly touching.

He was everywhere all at once and not nearly close enough.

His fingers sure and strong as he thrust them deep.

My gasps filled the air between us, panted into his mouth, our eyes wild as he stirred me into a writhing puddle.

Pleasure sparked and glinted in little flashes that struck in my body.

"Silas. Please." I didn't care that I implored it. Didn't care that we were in the middle of the office and anyone could walk in at any point.

I only cared about this. About him touching me. Freeing me. About the intensity that ripped and tore between us as he drove me into divine disarray.

"You like it? You like me fucking you with my fingers?"

I did. But I wanted so much more.

"I want your cock." I was really asking for it. But I figured if he was going to ruin me, he might as well do it all the way.

His chuckle was almost mean. "You really want to destroy me, Brinley? You want to own me completely and then walk out of here without looking back?"

"Maybe I don't want to walk." It gushed out, entirely without my permission. But I guess that's what truths normally did.

Silas squeezed my jaw tighter, the plunges of his fingers escalating.

I squirmed and moaned as I rocked back to meet him.

Punishment.

Blissful torture.

"I would never do that to you. You don't deserve this life," he growled.

But there was longing in it. I knew it. I could feel it just as sure as I knew he was mad about it. I should be mad about it, too. That I'd even let that thought invade.

Staying.

I barely knew him, yet somehow, I did. Somehow I saw straight through him the way he did me.

The hand at my throat raked down my chest, grabbing hold of a breast as he went, thumb scraping over the sensitive peak before he dragged lower and shoved his hand down the front of my underwear.

A landslide.

An earthquake.

My entire body quaked as he began rubbing my clit as he drove his other fingers into me from behind.

My toes barely touched the floor, and he rocked his hard cock against my bottom with each stroke.

Grunts and huffs wheezed from me, the same as they were puffing from Silas who seemed every bit as desperate as me.

And I wanted it. To surrender it all. My heart getting dragged in a direction that I knew so much better than to allow it to go. But there was something about Silas Mercer that persuaded and coaxed. My spirit stretching out to meet with the ferocity of his.

Twining and twisting in its petition.

Pleasure gathered with it. Tendrils that lapped and whipped and stirred.

Higher and higher with every masterful manipulation of his fingers.

"I feel it, Brinley. I feel you getting ready to blow. Give it to me. I want to feel you come on my fingers. Want to know that I'm the one giving you the pleasure that you can't get anywhere else."

His words were grunted in my ear as he swirled and drove his fingers.

Bliss cracked through the middle of me. Fractures that blistered and blew, striking in every secret recess that I possessed.

Ecstasy hurtled out of me on a cry.

So loud it crashed against the walls, an echo of yielding that reverberated back. Tremors boomeranged through my body as I soared and spun, his name a moan of confusion and desperation. "Silas. Silas."

"That's right, Little Wildfire. You feel it? What only I can give to you?"

I didn't know which one of us the taunt was intended for because possession ground through his voice as he led me through every flicker and twitch of pleasure.

"I feel it. Do you feel it? Do you feel it, King?" It was an appeal.

Because God, I didn't want to be in this thing alone.

I wanted to belong. To have someone fighting for me as hard as I fought for myself.

"It's all I can feel, Brinley. All I can feel is you," he muttered low at my ear.

My heels no longer touched solid ground, held high by the man who had me elevated to a place I'd never been. His hands firm and unflinching and strong.

As gruff and grave as his voice.

I trembled and shook, gasping for the oxygen that had become nonexistent. Lungs failing. Lightheadedness spinning through my brain as I was caught up in the perfect tumult that was Silas Mercer.

Who knew paradise could be so confounding.

He pressed himself against me as he gripped me tight through the tiny zaps and shocks.

I could feel the radiation of his need.

Greed dripping from his flesh and rocking his body, even though he was giving it his all to keep it contained.

And as he settled me onto unsteady feet, I knew he had every intention of walking. So I spun around, and I had his jeans unbuttoned and was on my knees before he even had the chance to anticipate what I had planned. Hazel eyes went wild with lust as I jerked his jeans down around his thighs.

"Fuck...Brinley." His hands went to my face, holding on like he was going to stop me, but I already had his cock freed from his underwear and was gripping the long length of him in my hand.

He was rigid and hard and pierced at the tip.

A shattered breath left me at the sight of him. At the feel of him. At the fact that I was here, kneeling in front of him, and that was exactly where I wanted to be.

Silas hovered high. A foreboding figure that loomed. A brutal fantasy. Body littered in all that gruesome ink.

His teeth ground as he glared down at me. "What do you think you're doing?"

"Tell me you want it, too."

He choked over a harsh laugh. "Don't think I've ever wanted anything more than that smart mouth wrapped around my cock, but I don't deserve that pleasure."

"You told me you were going to mark me. Show me everything I deserved. I deserve this, don't I? To give this of my own free will because I *want* to?"

Maybe it was underhanded.

Manipulative.

Because that was only a tiny part of it.

What I really wanted was to see him undone and completely at my doing.

I wanted to hear him moaning and begging my name.

I wanted him to surrender, too.

He had taps on my intention because his wicked mouth tweaked up at the side. "I think you just want to own me completely."

I tipped my face up at him and gave him the best answer I could find. "I think that's only fair."

43

Silas

Nah, there was nothing fair about this. Brinley on her knees for me. Stunning face tipped up in my direction with all those wild curls raining around her.

Gold-flecked eyes brimming all that fiery intensity.

Once again looking like autumn riding in on a hurricane.

"Wildfire." I mumbled it. Word nothing but guttural praise.

Knew she was going to burn my world down the moment I saw her. There was no longer any question about it.

"Is that what you want? You want my cock stuffed down your throat?" The hungry words scored off my tongue.

Brinley's entire body quaked, and she stroked me from root to tip. Just that bare attention nearly sent me over the edge.

"I want to make you feel as good as you made me." The admission was breathy.

There was the truth. That goodness seeping through the temptress who'd been sent to do me in.

Possession pulsed through my being, and I brushed the pad of my thumb over her lips. "You want me to fuck this smart, sexy mouth?"

She swallowed hard, woman quivering with nerves and greed.

Fuck, I needed to remember to be careful.

She was trying to push herself. So ready to set herself free. That was exactly what I intended, but I couldn't get selfish in the middle of it.

She stroked me again, murmuring, "Yes," before she leaned up and sucked just the head of my dick between her full, lush lips.

I nearly came, and I hissed as I tightened my hands on her jaw. "Fuck, Brinley."

She peered up at me for a blink, held, hesitating maybe, checking herself, before she came to a quick decision and dove all the way in.

Taking me all the way to the back of her throat.

I nearly blacked out from the pleasure. Punched in the face. Kicked in the gut.

She sucked and licked as she drew back out and then plunged back in again.

An electric charge zinged through my body, tightening my muscles and prowling up and down the base of my spine.

"Brinley…shit…so good. How can one mouth feel this fuckin' good?"

She moaned around me, and it sent the vibrations rolling through every molecule in my being.

Chills lifted across my skin.

Fuck. Didn't think I'd ever felt anything as perfect as this.

Her hot tongue and wet mouth.

I let her set the rhythm, which was just fine considering this woman was a phenom at giving head.

Stroking and sucking as she took me as deep as she could.

Rising up on her knees before she sank down to devour me all over again.

She worked me straight into a stupor.

Hijacking my body and mind.

Thoughts captive. Slanting in directions that I knew better than to contemplate.

To places where maybe I might be good enough and I didn't have that bastard's blood running through my veins.

A curse that claimed and haunted all of my days.

"Just like that, Brinley. This smart mouth…so good. So damned good. Have me in the palm of your hand, don't you? Exactly where you want me."

The words that left me were nothing but praise, and I wondered how it was possible that she'd come to own me.

Body and soul and hands and teeth.

The number of bunnies who'd gotten on their knees for me. Climbed on my dick to give me a ride.

There was no comparison to this.

Nothing that could compete with the feel of Brinley's mouth. Her lips slick and gliding over my cock.

Brinley mewled a desperate sound, curled her hand around my base, trying to get more of me in, mumbling a slew of incoherent confessions that I couldn't make out but felt, anyway.

Her own praise and pleas and need that she injected directly into me. Like she held the full tap on this insane connection.

Pleasure flickered and glinted behind my eyes, and her movements turned a bit erratic as she coerced me to the highest heights.

"Brinley…is that what you want to be? My good girl on her knees for me?"

My girl.

A property patch on her back.

I tried to shove that abhorrent thought to the back of my mind. Beat it into submission.

But maybe whatever was happening here was just as stark.

The way our gazes tangled and our souls linked.

My hips began to rock in time with her.

In sync.

Taking every bit of what she was offering.

Knowing I didn't deserve it but wishing I could be that man, anyway. Hoping to give her back a little of what those bastards had stolen.

I took her a fraction deeper with each stroke.

Until she was swallowing and gurgling around me as I thrust into the warm well of her mouth.

Again and again.

Surging as I fucked.

But it was my heart that was fucked.

Way she looked up at me with those eyes in pure vulnerability.

Giving herself.

Her trust.

Her surrender.

So I took it.

I gripped onto her beautiful face as I rocked into her.

Brinley fully surrendered, taking the outsides of my thighs and hanging on as she let me have my way.

"Brinley…fuck me. Fuck me. So good. So good." It tumbled out of me in a torrent.

A confession.

Truth that she had done me in. That I didn't understand any of this and I wanted a piece of it, anyway.

Sweat slicked my skin as I pounded harder.

A claiming.

Possession.

Brinley was moaning and squeezing her thighs together as the energy crashed and thundered.

A storm.

This hurricane we had no chance of stopping.

A flashfire that had come from out of nowhere.

"Wildfire," I choked, body bowing as a dam somewhere inside me broke.

It was a complete rendering as I split.

"Brinley." Her name was nothing but a roar as an orgasm unlike anything I'd ever felt before ruptured from within.

Cock pulsing and pouring as I fractured apart.

She took me as far as she could as I trembled and shook. Woman lapping and licking me through the oblivion.

Some secret part of me cracked open wide as I stared down at the pandemonium that she was.

Turmoil and longing and a wild, free heart.

Eyes a vortex of desire that sucked me down to the pits of who she was. A mirrored screen that gave view to the fiery desperation that had written her in strength and obstinacy.

All while it was so blatantly obvious that need still pounded through her bloodstream.

Stirred back up by what she had given me.

I had her swept off the floor and propped on the edge of her desk before either of us could make sense of the action.

In a flash, I was on my knees and spreading her thighs and shoving her undies aside so I could get to the sweetness underneath.

Mouth delving deep into the sweet heat.

Eating her like she was my last meal, wondering if there was a chance that I could have the same kind of impact on her as she had on me.

Her hands jerked at my hair as my name was whimpered from her tongue.

"King. King."

Except it was that nickname that she'd given me, and my chest was stretching to the point of pain, heart trying to break free of its confines.

My fingers stroked home, my cock that was still hanging from my pants screaming for the chance.

But Brinley's head was already dropping back, and she released the longest moan, body going rigid before it gave way to full-blown tremors.

Rocking and raging as she squeezed and throbbed around my fingers once again.

Her nails sank into my shoulders and ripped at my cut and dug into the nape of my neck.

Perfect, pained bliss.

A frenzy had taken me over.

No rationale or logic left as I kissed up over the fabric of her dress. Belly, chest, and neck. A total fucking fool as I made it to her mouth, on my knees as I kissed her without any sense.

Her heart raced the same stampede as mine, those fingers tugging at my hair as she kissed me back.

Tendrils of something profound wisped around us.

Wrapping us in newfound chains.

A fettering that was only going to make the goodbye so much worse.

But I was pretty sure Brinley Webber would be worth every ounce of pain.

"Silas," she breathed into my mouth.

"Wildfire," I murmured back, sucking that sweetness down.

Almonds and apples and cream.

I held her that way for a little bit before I finally asked, "You good?"

She exhaled a shaky laugh. "I don't think I could even stand right now my muscles are so blissed out."

"Good." I pecked another kiss to her lips, then I curled my arms around her waist and lifted her off the desk. Her legs dangled below her, the tips of her toes barely brushing the ground as I held her against me.

My bare cock still pressed between us as I swayed her back and forth.

Yeah, no one had ever accused me of being romantic.

Except she exhaled this soft sound as she burrowed her face in my neck, warmth saturating me through as she whispered, "You make me feel good, Silas Mercer. Inside and out."

44

Silas

"You really gonna let her stay in that office after what went down yesterday?"

Phoenix uttered it low from where he dug for a wrench in a toolbox near me. Voice muted and hard, casting a ton of speculation my way where I knelt next to my Harley, running a clean cloth over the gleaming black fender that I'd repaired.

My ribs constricted around my heart. It might as well have been his giant, meaty mitt with the way it felt like it was getting pulverized by the thought of her.

That face spinning through my mind on repeat. Of course, that vision had to include her face tipped up at me with my cock stuffed down her throat.

I had been stewing in that memory all fucking day.

"Compound is secure," I growled.

"Yeah, and that's the opposite of what we were going for. We are supposed to be playing it cool, remember? Putting on a front like there isn't a single issue going down at the club? Now you've got this place locked down like a military installation."

Phoenix laid it out like I'd gone dense and it was his duty to educate me.

His dark edges set in a vicious glower.

Unease stirred.

"That bastard was dead for coming here, with or without Brinley in the mix." I threw it out like a defense.

Phoenix cut a sharp shake of his head. "That's bullshit, man, and you know it."

"And what would you expect me to do?" I gritted beneath my breath, hoping to keep the words out of earshot of the rest of the Crows working the shop.

All of us *trying* to keep up that front and obviously failing.

"You should have kept her locked in that room from the get-go and never let her come out."

I scoffed. "She's not a damned prisoner, Phoenix. She needs this."

Phoenix blew back at the emphasis in my voice. He clearly heard what it contained. I could almost see the crop of hairs lifting at his nape, prickles of awareness crawling through his senses.

Intuition kicking in.

"Thought she was off-limits?" It was fully an accusation.

"She is." I basically spat it. Guilt constraining. A boot smashing down on the back of my neck with the intent of snuffing the life out of me.

Phoenix chuckled an ominous sound, ruthlessness rippling around him in black waves. Pitch hair shoved back. His eyes that were just as dark were slit into daggers as he stared me down.

"You really gonna pretend like you aren't dipping your dirty paws into our collateral?"

I was on my feet in a flash, refusal slashing out. "She's not fucking collateral."

With the way I said it, I might as well have been pleading guilty.

Phoenix took it as such, and a huff of air left him on a shot of condemnation. "Is that right?"

I turned away, trying to gather myself, roughing a hand down my face as I mumbled, "That's right. She's under our protection. Nothing less and nothing more."

Visions flashed. Her mouth and my hands and the twisted greed that was chipping away at everything I was supposed to stand for.

He exhaled something heavy at my back. The sound packed with his loyalty to this club, which I clearly had a deficit of at this point.

I might have been president, but our mission was just as important to my crew as it was to me.

"She's the one thing keeping that fuckwit under our thumb," Phoenix gritted. "You really think he wouldn't turn on us if she wasn't here? If he didn't know she was still breathin' because we're allowing her to remain that way?"

A surge of rage had me whirling back, in his face in a nanosecond.

"Allowing her to remain that way?" It was a snarl that erupted from my soul. "It doesn't matter what that piece of shit does, no one will touch a hair on her head."

Our heated conversation finally rippled through the other Crows in the shop, and Trevan, Colby, and Brody shifted our way to take in the animosity.

All patched-in members within earshot except for Brody, and Phoenix knew he was already on the inside.

Brody knew the score and the dirty deeds and was all too ready to partake in them.

Phoenix tossed a disbelieving chuckle out into the tension that distorted the air. "Seems to me someone already has."

I turned away again, nearly fucking convulsing with the tumult that Brinley Webber had incited on my life.

"I'm not fucking her," I grunted low.

Was that enough? Because it sounded like bullshit, even to me.

Brody cracked up, a riotous, unruly sound, likely only picking up on the back half of the conversation. "That woman is sleeping in your bed, brother, and I'm pretty sure there isn't a whole lot of sleeping going on."

I pointed a finger at him. "Don't start."

With an arrogant laugh, he raised his hands in surrender. "Hey, I'm just telling it like it is. It's damned unlikely that I'm the only one around here noticing you basically go rabid whenever she walks into the room. Not that any one of us would blame you."

Insinuation weaved its way in, an extra thread in the cock of his head.

Oh, but there was plenty of blame there.

Trevan glanced between everyone, attempting to temper the mood. "I don't see any reason to be throwing around accusations. Prez says nothing is going on, then nothing is going on."

It did nothing but drive a hot blade of guilt directly through my sternum.

Phoenix slanted tattooed fingers through his hair, doing his best to tamp down his irritation. You'd think he'd still be quenched from yesterday's kill, but no, he was antsy.

Thirsty for blood.

He seemed to gather himself a fraction, his words subdued but hard.

"Worried something is going on here that you've become too blind to see. Am worried she's becoming a liability. We have too much riding on this for intentions to get skewed. What you pulled last night in front of the entire club…?"

He trailed off with the implication.

I wanted to whip around and tell him that what I'd pulled was letting every single asshole there know she was mine.

But she couldn't be.

I was the one who'd given the charge.

Deemed her off-limits, and it was the kind of rule that was delivered with a stamped seal that there would be dire consequences if someone was stupid enough not to comply.

I heaved out a strained sigh, trying to gather my thoughts that had sprinted in every wrong direction. Remind myself why I couldn't continue on the path that I was traveling.

All while I did my best to ignore the energy that seeped from the office, her spirit a hum right at the edges of my consciousness, luring me back toward the moment's paradise that she had given.

Could still feel and taste her all over me.

"She disobeyed me, and I was putting her back into her place. As simple as that. Nothing is clouded. I know the mission and what's riding on it."

It was a miracle I didn't choke to death on the blasphemous words.

Dubiety dented deep into Phoenix's sinister brow. "Do you?"

"Of course, I do."

Everything.

I knew I had to put an end to this obscenity.

Because this was getting so much deeper than just my oath to the club, which was hefty enough. Truth that I'd basically bartered the woman to gain the upper hand on Dereck Webber. The fact that there was a very good chance I was going to have to put the bastard in the ground made it that much worse.

More than anything, the bare specks of my conscience kept screaming to stop being a pillager of the good. Dragging Brinley deeper and deeper into something she didn't want to be a part of.

I couldn't keep dipping my toes into the treachery. Convincing myself I was offering her something good when I was really only stealing for myself.

It was nothing but a scourge of selfishness and greed.

Her spirit whispered out from the office, attempting to become one with mine.

The problem was, I had no fucking clue how to let go.

How to let go of something that made me feel halfway real for the first time in years.

45

Silas

Sixteen Years Old

Silas remained low, his head darting in every direction to make sure no one was looking as he switched out the backpack he'd retrieved along the bank of the river with the one that was hidden behind the industrial icemaker at the back of Keg & Creek Tavern.

Night swam around him, the drone of the country music playing from a jukebox inside seeping through the wooden walls, his thundering heart louder than anything.

It's the way it always was.

His heart beating so hard that he thought it would explode.

He switched out the backpacks then ducked back out into the cover of the forest. Racing like he was trying to outrun the silvered rays of moonlight that speared down through the leaves.

Trying to stay in the shadows and out of sight as he headed back toward the river.

His breaths were rattled gusts as he finally made it back to the drop site, and he snatched the thick envelope stuffed with the cash he'd split with his dad and shoved it into his back pocket before he got onto his knees and pulled back the branches that covered the hole.

Only he froze when he felt the disturbed energy crash over him from behind. Just in the distance, stepping out from behind the trees.

Terror ridged his spine, and he tentatively shifted to peek over his shoulder.

His stomach dropped when he saw who it was.

"What are you doing?" His mother's face was pinched in hurt and disgust, and she wrung her fingers as she took another step toward him.

"I…" His mouth was too dry to force the lie from his tongue.

"I didn't want to believe it. But all that money kept coming in." She choked it, not even waiting for a response or admission from him since she'd already extricated the truth.

"Mom," he finally managed, but she was shucking off the shock, her demeanor shifting to anger and desperation as she started to rush for him.

Her attention whipped in every direction before she demanded, "Put it down right now, Silas. I don't know what you think you're doing, but this ends right now. Where is he?"

She looked around again.

"I don't—"

"Don't you dare lie to me. I've had plenty of them already." Disappointment gushed out.

"I didn't have a choice," Silas choked.

"You didn't have a choice? You always have a choice, Silas, and I know you were trying to make the right one, but this is the worst one you could have made. We don't *stoop* to this."

She snatched the bag from his hold and shook it in his face. "He put you up to this, didn't he?"

Silas blinked, shuffled on his feet, unsure of what he should give her.

"I just wanted to help. You work so hard, and I heard that the rent was late. I had to do something."

She gave a harsh shake of her head. "But not this. Not this, Silas. Please." She'd begun to beg, the horror of what he'd gotten involved in finally catching up to her.

"Okay, I'll stop." He reached for the bag, but she jerked it out of his reach.

"We need to go to the police. Tell them what's happening. We have to put an end to this."

"Mom—" He didn't get to finish the thought before a boat engine suddenly roared.

Right there, hidden in the brush on the river.

He spun around toward it, squinting as a spotlight blinded him.

He put a forearm up to protect himself from it, but there was no protecting them from the riot of gunshots that suddenly rained.

So loud he couldn't hear as dust and debris flew.

He didn't even feel the hot spikes of pain impale his side.

He could only spin around and throw himself over the top of his mother to protect her.

His mind spinning with terror. With the horror of what he'd done.

No question, they saw her and believed her a threat.

Gunshots continued to fire. A slew that sparked and disoriented.

His ears rang so loud when the barrage finally ended, and the boat engine roared as it sped off into the night.

While everything else seemed slowed. The ravaging of his heart and the processing of his brain.

His movements stilted and broken.

His ears rang and rang, and dizziness spun his head.

The oxygen he tried to expel from his lungs felt like it weighed five thousand tons as he pushed himself off his mother.

His mother who was making sounds he couldn't quite make out.

Gurgled and strained.

One sliver of moonlight cut through. Enough to illuminate her face.

Her face that was splattered with blood.

"Oh God. Oh God. No, no, no." He mumbled it, struggling to push to his feet, the toes of his shoes sliding against the loose dirt below him.

She kept making those noises. Noises that rattled with shock and pain.

He finally made it to his knees, and he was begging, "Mom. Please, just hang on. You're gonna be fine. I promise you're gonna be fine."

She had to be.

He somehow managed to get her over his shoulder, his mind spinning and his body bowing as he battled to stand.

He had to get her help.

He turned and staggered down the path toward where his dad would be waiting.

Wishing he could run, go faster, but his right leg was dragging as he fought through the underbrush.

"We're going to get you help. It's okay. It's okay."

She was wheezing then, these thin rasps that he begged to continue.

"You're okay. You're okay."

Sweat drenched his body as he staggered through the woods, mixing with the tears and blood that obscured his sight.

He forced off the darkness that kept trying to enclose. The waves of dizziness that whooshed through his body.

He finally stumbled out from beneath the trees, and his father's truck idled on the deserted dirt road just in the distance.

Relief sliced through him on a gush of fatigue. On the failing that his body was getting ready to surrender to.

They were almost there. They were almost there. He could do this. Just a few more feet.

"Dad," he shouted. "Help!"

The engine turned over, and the lights flashed on.

Except his father didn't climb out to help him.

He shifted into gear and gunned the gas.

The roar of the old engine and the spitting of dirt as the tires peeled out hitting Silas's ears.

His father swerved as he hit the road, his taillights disappearing in the distance.

"No! Come back! You have to help her! Help us!" He screamed it, his voice hoarse and croaked.

He attempted to fumble along behind him.

"No!" he wailed, a sob hitching in his throat.

He stumbled, and his right knee gave out from under him. He fought to right himself, but he fell forward, he and his mother slammed into the dirt.

Blackness flashed, agony clawing through every one of his senses.

Somehow, he managed to get onto his hands and knees, and his chest battered and bashed as he rolled his mother over.

She flopped onto her back, and her kind eyes were wide and terrified.

"Mom. Oh God, Mom, please! Look at me. You're going to be okay."

At the sound of his voice, her eyes flicked to his. The second they did, they softened, an expression coming over her face that he didn't deserve.

Pride and love.

So much love.

"Take care of your brother and sister."

He shook his head. "No. You're fine. You're fine."

She coughed and blood spluttered from her mouth. "Promise me."

Tears poured, and he choked, "Mom."

"Promise me," she wheezed.

"I will always take care of them. Just like I'm going to take care of you." He wanted the words to come out firm. Full of belief. Except the tears that wouldn't stop polluted them.

Sadness tweaked her blood-soaked lips, and she lifted her hand and set it on his chest. "It's your heart. It's your heart."

Then her arm slumped to the ground.

A wail rose from the depths of him. A sonic boom that reverberated in the stillness of the night.

No.

No, no, no, no, no.

He fought to stand, strain burning through his muscles, agony firing through his being as he grabbed her by the arm and tried to drag her.

Desperate shouts of misery cleaved from his mouth. "Help! Help! Someone, please help!"

But there was nothing.

No one to save them. No one to fight for them.

And he was weak.

So weak.

Darkness enclosed, and he fell face first to the damp earth.

The heart she thought he had imploding.

46

Silas

My cell rang from my pocket, and I ripped it out, heaving a relieved breath while my pulse simultaneously skyrocketed.

"It's Cash," I ground out to the guys who were again gathered in the shop, giving the signal of the call's importance.

I strode out the open bay and into the glaring daylight where it was quiet.

The last four days had been torture.

Blissful fucking torture but torture all the same.

Giving Brinley orgasm after orgasm that she insisted on delivering right back, all while knowing the time was fast approaching that I had to end it.

Holding onto it for a few moments more like a glutton, feeding on all her good when I knew I was only going to turn around and ruin.

Getting more and more attached as I did.

Both of us curling up sated and tangled in my sheets, waking up with my head buried between her lush thighs, sending her to those heights all over again.

I never took it beyond that, like not doing so would somehow afford the two of us some kind of amnesty from the coming pain.

I knew it was bullshit, but I couldn't fucking stop. I accepted the call and brought my cell to my ear.

"Cash." It was a low slash of urgency.

We needed to get this thing done, and the more time that passed, the more precarious the situation got.

"Silas," he grunted in his abrupt way.

"Tell me you have news."

Four days ago, I'd texted to update him on what had happened, fact that blood had been spilled. Another body buried deep in the woods and even deeper underground.

The definitive link the bastard had to Kent.

"Dereck called last night. We have a go three nights from now," he said.

My guts tangled in a smack of antsy anticipation and something that felt a little too close to grief.

My attention whipped to the windows that fronted the lobby, no way to stop the trajectory. Mirrored and shimmery, my abhorrent reflection was the only thing I could see staring back.

There was no way to see the beauty through the glass, but I felt her moving around on the other side, anyway.

Likely plucking away at those keys, trying to sculpt Torque & Talon's accounting into some semblance of shape. Actually making progress on the disaster when I really hadn't anticipated her putting any real effort into it.

Not with the way I treated her when she first came here.

Hell, I was lucky she wasn't sabotaging the whole damned thing.

I forced myself to turn away and focus on what was important.

The safety and deliverance of my crew.

Vengeance for my family.

The complete desolation of the foul repugnance that Kent Ellison propagated.

The monster had zero clue who he was messing with. Thinking he had the power to wield his control and we were just going to submit.

I couldn't wait to see his face when I brought him to his end.

But there was something that clenched at the thought. A revolt coming on deep.

"You're sure?" My teeth gnashed as I asked it.

"All his intel says it is, and everything I've found confirms it. There are three different drops occurring on the same night. I have full details and every meeting place. Dereck said every man in Kent's organization is to be on that night. Three groups divvied out over the deals. Additionally, there will be a large contingency standing guard at his compound, plus a handful at another safehouse."

My nerves rattled like a snake. "So we have to hit five different locations?"

We knew this was going to be the largest undertaking that we'd ever endeavored, but I didn't have the full scale of it until then.

"That's right," he confirmed, a thread of uncertainty in his voice. Wondering if I really wanted to take this on. "Dereck said it's a total of about eighty men, an estimation of ten involved in each deal, five at the safehouse, and the rest at the compound."

"He's sure that's it?"

They all had to be taken out at precisely the same time. We couldn't afford for anyone to alert the other, and we sure as hell couldn't leave anyone as a witness.

Sure, there would be those on the fringes. Accomplices and associates. There was no way to strike down every connection.

But we were going for his inner circle. Ensuring that no one in his chain of command remained.

This would be unabridged and nuclear.

Rats included.

All except for Dereck.

Disquiet rolled through my guts. I was still more than skeptical that he could be trusted.

A deranged, perverted part of me hoped he wasn't, then I'd have good reason to make him pay for what he'd caused Brinley.

"He's betting his life on it." Cash's voice was rough.

I huffed a cynical laugh. "He'd better be sure he knows I'll gladly collect."

"He said he knows the score."

"And you trust that?"

Cash scoffed. "Do I trust a sniveling dirtbag only out to save his own ass? Not a fucking chance, but right now, he's the only real chance we've got. Question is, do you want to take that *chance*?"

Dread stuttered the fierce pulsing of my blood, one skipped beat as fear slicked my insides in sludge.

Not for myself.

But for my men who had stepped up. Every one of them pledging their loyalty and sacrifice. Taking my life's obligation as their own duty.

Didn't mean I viewed a single one of them as expendable.

Our bond had meshed us tight as family.

"It's the only thing we can do." I forced out my commitment to the operation.

"Okay then. Details are on their way."

The documents would be sent to the secret shared folder that Cash and I often used to communicate.

He hesitated for a beat then added gruffly, "My crew is in."

Surprise stumbled my steps before the refusal was rocketing off my tongue, "Not a chance, man."

There were five of them in Sovereign Sanctum. Each one brutal. As savage and ruthless as us. Experienced in the type of *delicate matters* that we often undertook.

Wickedly skilled to boot.

Problem was, all of them had gotten their hearts tied. Married or were shacked up with kids.

No way I was letting them put themselves on the line.

"It's already decided," Cash said like there was no room for argument. "I'm in as deep as you, and if Kent catches wind that it was me and my crew who got your sister out, it won't bode well for us. We need him gone just as badly as you do. Just as badly as this world does."

Emphasis was gouged into the last.

Stickiness clogged my throat, the scale of this close to overwhelming. "You're sure?"

"We're in this with you. Same way as all the times you've been in it with us."

Years of connections.

All the way back to the days of riding in the Iron Owls MC. When we rode for ego and greed and heedlessness rather than for the purpose we donned our cuts for now.

Blowing out a haggard sigh, I relented. "Okay."

We sat in a beat of knowing silence before he hedged, "And the girl?"

Anarchy stormed my insides.

"She's safe and clueless. I'm going to assign a seven-man detail to watch over her and the rest of my family during the raids."

Rejection of the idea blared through my senses at no less than one hundred and fifty decibels.

Earsplitting.

Spirit and mind joining forces to shout at my soul that it wasn't enough.

Howling at me not to leave her side.

It was the proof that I'd become so distracted I couldn't see straight, heavy gray clouds sagging low from the heavens, distorting and disorienting.

Judgement skewed.

Exactly as Phoenix had accused.

I was nothing but a fool who'd gone astray.

I knew it, and I knew it was time I ended it.

I couldn't go on like this for a second more. Pretending like I could keep her when she was elemental to our plot.

So I pressed on and dispatched the blow to my stupid, twisted heart. "Then after, I deliver her to her piece of shit brother."

47

Silas

"Meems has stew on the stove. Six o'clock. She said not to be late, or she'll come over here and drag you back by the scruff of your neck."

Elena grinned from where she held onto the outside of the truck's rear door, leaning in my direction. Dark chocolate hair held in a ponytail and swishing around her shoulders, eyes the same color as mine gleaming mirth.

Sweet as pie and obviously up to no good.

It'd been clear as a summer's day when she'd come driving up in my truck with Kai buckled into his car seat in the back, claiming she was there to collect Brinley after a grueling day at work.

It was grueling, all right.

Her spirit echoing from the walls when I knew that spirit was getting ready to be ripped away.

I grunted a non-response at my baby sister from where I remained in the open bay, kneeling as I worked on my bike. The gleaming metal was essentially in perfect condition, but I was desperate to find something to do with my hands.

Trying and failing at not losing my mind.

The conversation with Cash sat like the rubble of a fallen skyscraper on my chest.

The realization of what was coming finally catching up to the indignation that had steered me in this perilous direction in the first place.

In three days' time, my entire crew would be rushing into enemy territory.

Lives and realities and hopes at stake. Every step treacherous and pitted with peril.

Yeah, we faced down demons all the time. Took chances and risks. But this time, it was different.

This time, there was a very good chance some of us would not be coming back.

Then there was Brinley. Brinley who was blurring the lines in beauty and ambiguity. Mucking the straight shot I'd always walked and sending me stumbling to the side.

It wasn't an exaggeration since she nearly knocked me onto my ass when she came strutting through the office door and out into the shop, still clad in that ridiculously sexy dress that this morning I'd had shoved up around her waist while I'd had her bent over the bathroom counter while I ate her out from behind. Then I'd gotten as close to fucking her as I ever had, rocking my dick through her butt cheeks then coming all over her back.

Even though she was trying to front her normal sass right then, I saw the vulnerability swirling in the whorl of golds as her gaze slanted toward me.

The connection we shared flash-fired across the space.

In it was that thing that had grown and changed over the time she'd been here.

Trust.

Affection.

I could feel it bleeding out of her.

The dam we'd tried to keep between us had been completely wiped out, and my stupid, mangled heart hadn't gotten the memo that I had to rebuild it.

I attempted to dip my focus back to my bike like it could be more interesting than her.

After the call with Cash, I made the decision that I'd tell her we had to put an end to whatever we thought we were doing tonight. Put on the brakes and stop this trainwreck before it happened.

Pack her things up in my room and escort her back to the room above the clubhouse.

Right where I should have left her.

The burn of her gaze seared through me as I forced myself not to return her attention.

Too bad she was nothing but persuasion.

Unable to stop myself, I glanced that way, probably looking like a fucking weirdo trying to remain aloof. Itching as I fought with the urge to cross the fucking garage and drive my fingers into the wild locks of her hair.

Claim her in front of everyone.

"*Bwinwey*!" Kai's sweet voice cut through the tension, and her gaze snapped to the back door that gaped open wide.

Kai was trying to lift his head from his backward-facing car seat so he could get a better view.

That baby beaming with every ounce of his innocent little heart, excitement and joy as he waved his hands, same way as he'd done when he'd gotten a look at me when Elena had first opened the door.

The sight of him had wrung my spirit in that thing I kept struggling not to feel.

I'd ruin him, too.

Just like I'd done to Elena and Brody.

I had to figure out a better solution.

Fix this.

Promise me. An echo of my mother's voice clawed through my mind. I swallowed back the sob it nearly elicited.

It's your heart.

She was mistaken because it was thoroughly bad.

Brinley cleared her throat, shucking off the gravity that clawed through the air in a dire fucking effort to merge us together.

"Hi, baby," she wheezed.

"Are you talking to me or Kai?" Elena teased. Her expression shifted through exuberance and that fat needle she kept trying to drive under my skin.

"Oh wait, maybe you're subconsciously talking to my brother because *whoo-ee* me…is it hot out here or what?" She fanned herself. "I'm not sure how I didn't find you both passed out. Deceased. Because this girl can't breathe."

Awesome.

Now she sounded like Meems. Maybe she should spend less of her days locked up in that house.

"It is summer." Brinley was all cheek as she strutted her way toward the truck, those sky-high pumps crunching on the gravel.

"I am aware, but Meems and I just watched the news and there was no indication that there's a heatwave at the precise location of Torque & Talon Autobody Shop. Because it is a thousand degrees hotter here than it was when I stepped out of the house."

I would have laughed at my sister's absurdity if it wasn't for the fact I was actually being burned at the stake.

Flames licking up, my flesh charred as Brinley cast a searching glance over her shoulder back in my direction, trying to play it cool but wondering if we were ever going to fess up about what had been going on with us.

But it was like I told Phoenix. Nothing was going on other than a few mind-blowing orgasms. There couldn't be.

So I turned back to my bike and ignored her like a prick.

She swiveled back in Elena's direction, and her voice hardened. "You're imagining things."

My chest clutched, and my stupid gaze was sliding back that way.

She kept swaying that sweet ass toward the truck.

"*Bwinwey* sit Kai!" Little hands waved in the air, the boy peeking over the side.

Brinley seemed to stumble a step. "Okay, baby, I can sit next to you."

God, why did it feel like she was driving a blade through my guts every time she called him that? Flaying me wide open to the disfigured affection that kept trying to break free underneath.

She climbed into the back seat beside Kai, giving me a peep of her perfect ass, legs long and bare and urging me toward traitorous things.

My stomach twisted, and my freaking little sister smirked when she caught me staring.

Then she slammed the door shut and skipped around to the front of the truck to the driver's side, hopped in, and put it into gear.

And it didn't matter if I put six hundred pounds of torque into it, there was no chance of stopping mine and Brinley's gazes from tangling as they went.

Those bottomless, mesmerizing eyes haunting me.

48

Silas

We were gathered around the table.

Yeah, the plan was to pack Brinley's things and take her back to the club, but I doubted one more meal could hurt all that much.

Seemed a dick move, depriving her of this delicious meal.

God knew Meems would read me the riot act if I did, anyway, and I'd always fancied myself a decently intelligent man.

I knew how to save my own ass, at least.

Brody strolled in five minutes late. Smug smirk on his face when he glanced between me and Brinley who sat on my left.

"Glad to see you could join us." Meems arched a brow at my middle brother.

He gave her that charming smile. "Had a little something I was attending to at the club."

Elena spluttered around a sip of her iced tea. "Something? More like a someone, I'm sure."

He grinned. "A man never tells."

She barked in incredulity. "Oh, I've heard all about your conquests. So gross."

He waltzed to the fridge, grabbed a beer, and guzzled half of it. "You're just sad you aren't getting any."

A growl ripped out of me, and the dude actually had the decency to look contrite. "Sorry, Prez."

"Just eat your dinner," I grunted, and he took his seat while I itched like a fiend in mine.

Trying not to turn my attention to Brinley so I could watch her wrap that tempting mouth around her spoon.

Kept glancing that way, anyway, teetering between the swells of lust that continually erupted when she'd moan around the metal and the fucking gooey feeling I got every time she reached over and helped Kai get a little chunk of food into his mouth.

Most of his stew had spilled out onto his tray, and the kid was using his chubby fingers to try to chase down the little pieces.

Half of them ended up on his shirt.

"Here you go, sweet boy," she murmured as she hand-fed him a piece of carrot.

I wondered if she'd do the same for me.

"*Fank foo*," he told her, showing her the orange, mashed-up mouthful around his tiny, gapped teeth.

"You are welcome, punky boo." She poked his belly from under his tray.

"I no punky boo."

She tickled him a little more. "Yes, you are, you're my little punky boo."

He squealed in delight, and the air was shifting again.

An ebb and flow that only amplified with each pass.

Energy subdued but far too alive.

Thick and murky yet swimming with light.

Brinley groaned and sat back in her chair and set both of her hands over her stomach.

She'd changed clothes, dumped that dress, though what she'd pulled on wasn't any safer for my sanity. Black leggings and an oversized beige tee, cropped and with the neck cut out of it.

One bare shoulder peeked out to taunt me into rebellion.

"Oh my goodness, Meems, I might say this every night, but that one was by far the best. I'm so stuffed I think I could burst," Brinley told her.

Meems beamed.

Brinley might as well have told her she loved her.

"Wait until you try the pie. It's apple."

Of course, it was.

Clearly, my entire family was trying to drive me off a cliff.

Brinley groaned. "Sweet torture."

She didn't know the half of it.

"I'll slice it," Elena offered, jumping up from her seat. She danced into the kitchen, twirling as she went, sliding all over the wooden floors on her fuzzy socks.

Affection had me shaking my head. "You're going to slip and fall on your ass."

She swung open the freezer door and pulled out a gallon of vanilla ice cream as she did a little dip. "Pssh… You know nothing, dear brother. I am the epitome of grace."

Brinley peeked over at me with those hurricane eyes. Amusement and warmth and that protective affinity streamed out of her.

And somehow, she was the one who saw I felt exactly the same.

My chest tightened.

Tightened to a gutting extreme as I got stuck there under the power of her stare.

Brinley finally pulled away, clearing her throat as she pushed from the table. "I'll help."

I did my best not to follow her trail as she moved into the kitchen area.

A vain attempt since Elena tossed the foil cover off the fresh-baked pie, dipped a fork into it, and brought it to Brinley's lips. "Here, taste."

Brinley obliged, taking it into her mouth, the longest groan rolling out of her.

My brain computed it as the same damned sounds she made every time she came. Like what she was actually moaning was my name.

"This is literal heaven," she muttered, trying to cover her mouth as she chewed, and gave Meems her baker's praise.

Meems shrugged, eyes darting to me for a beat before they were back on Brinley. "Stick around for a while and you'll know how to bake one of those for yourself."

My logic recoiled against it while my stupid heart shouted, 'yes, please'.

Brinley lightly chuckled. "I am no baker, Meems. You'd better not get your hopes up so much when it comes to me."

Slyness crept in Meems's features. "Oh, sweet one, my expectations are high."

"I pie!" Kai smacked both hands on his tray, a lucky deterrent from the implications my grandmother was all too eager to toss around.

"Don't worry, it's on its way!" Elena sang, cutting a tiny piece and spooning a dollop of ice cream onto the top.

"I get pie, *Wena*?"

She danced back up to the dining table. Tapped his nose as she set the small serving in front of him. "Absolutely! Because we only get the best things in this house, isn't that right?"

Elena headed back to the counter, and the second she walked away, Kai picked up the little plastic bowl and basically buried his face in it.

Laughing, I reached across Brinley's empty chair so I could help him. "How about we do it like this, buddy?" I situated the chunky plastic baby spoon into his chubby hand.

Then Brinley was back, setting a plate of pie and ice cream in front of Brody. "There you go, Brody."

"You spoil me," he teased with a grin. But it was soft.

No question, Brinley'd had an impact on every person in my family.

"We all deserve to get spoiled every once in a while," she said.

"Be careful, or we're going to get used to it."

He sent her a wink, though there was nothing flirty to it.

Just approval.

The truth that she fit.

She shifted and set one in front of me.

I didn't know if it was her or the mouthwatering scent of the pie that assaulted my senses.

Apples and almonds and cream.

She eased back and started to round my chair.

And I felt the faintest flutter of fingertips running through my hair at the nape of my neck.

The only girl in the world who was gaining the power to touch my soul.

I guess I should have fucking expected this penalty.

• • •

"You don't need to do those," I mumbled as I slowly crept up behind Brinley where she was facing away at the sink, handwashing the dishes.

In that moment, I felt exactly what I was.

The villain.

A wraith.

A reaper sent to slay.

I stopped when there was five feet between us because I wasn't sure I could get any closer and still get out what needed to be said.

Trying to work up the nerve to do what was right when every molecule that made up my being swore that it was wrong.

Half the lights had been cut, and only a bare glow from the fixture over the sink illuminated the space.

Everyone else had piled into the family room to watch a show with Kai before his bedtime, except for Brody who had gone running back to the club so he could devolve back into the revelry he thrived on.

Head down, Brinley shifted on her bare feet. "I don't mind."

Her voice was quieted. Muted. Filled with a timidness I'd never heard in it before.

Like she knew what was coming and she hated it every bit as much as me.

"Didn't bring you here so you had to work." I grunted it into the dense air.

How her laugh was both throaty and tinkling, I didn't know. From over her shoulder, she cast me an affected smile, those wild curls swirling all around her stunning face. "I'm just earning my keep, remember?"

There was no taunt to it. It was a true question. Wondering what was really happening here.

"You are more than sufficient."

She was too much. Too gorgeous and too good and too real.

A frown notched deep into her brow. "But I'm not, though, am I?"

I guess she had figured out how to read me in a way that no one else could. She already knew what was coming.

"It's me who's not enough, Brinley."

She released a choked sound. "That's strange because when I'm with you, I can feel all the empty places that have been aching inside me being filled. And it feels like enough. Like more than I ever hoped or expected."

Torment gnarled my insides.

"I'm not the kind of man you come to rely on, Brinley. Not the kind of man you should tie yourself to."

She huffed with a shake of her head as she rinsed the last pot then set it into the drainer. "Probably not, but that doesn't mean I don't want to."

Fuck. What had we done? Hating each other one minute. Then somehow, in the blink of an eye, we'd ended up here. But I guess that's why we fought each other so hard at the beginning.

Our spirits had known the danger the other posed.

I hesitated.

Warred.

Unsure of what I should tell her.

What I could let her in on.

I refused to burden her with the full truth of who I was, but I knew that I could trust her fully.

And it was time to stop keeping her completely in the dark.

Unaware and unprepared.

I needed her to know that this was coming up on a quick dead end.

"It goes down three nights from now." Every word was gravel.

Brinley bowed, hands curling into the edge of the counter as she faced away.

Breaths shallow as she dealt with what should have been a boatload of relief yet so clearly hit her with the force of a sledgehammer.

Both of us were fully aware of exactly what that statement meant.

I wavered, trying to work up to the words, lips so fucking dry I could barely force them out.

"Think it would be best if we packed your things and took you back to your room above the club. Mission is going to be precarious, and I'm going to need to be at one hundred percent. Can't afford distractions right now."

It was such bullshit.

A pathetic excuse.

Brinley made a strangled sound, and she began to respond, only she clipped off when little feet suddenly pattered into the kitchen.

Kai ambled his way around me and went directly for her, thumb in his mouth as he dragged his blanket behind him.

"Kai *mewk*? Go nigh-night?" He pointed at the stash of bottles that sat in a basket next to the fridge.

"Are you tired, sweet boy?" Brinley's words were strained with emotion. Soft and saturated with affection.

"I *tie-werd*." He bobbed his sweet head.

Her hands shook as she grabbed a bottle and dipped into the refrigerator before she reemerged with a gallon of milk.

"I know he uses the bottle to soothe himself," she started to ramble. "But we're going to have to wean him from it soon and figure something else out that makes him feel safe. Milk isn't good for his teeth at night."

Every word shook.

An avalanche of pain as Brinley fumbled over the words, choking when she gasped, “I mean, you all will have to wean him soon.”

Milk sloshed onto the counter as she tried to pour it into a bottle.

Energy whipped through the air. Striking against my spirit.

Lashes of anguish and affliction.

I took a regretful step forward. “Brinley.”

She held out a hand, squeezing her eyes closed tight for a beat, her voice ragged as she whispered, “I’m fine. I’m fine. Just let me take him.”

I slumped back, nerves marching across my flesh as I watched Brinley finish filling the bottle, twist on the cap, then sweep Kai from his feet.

That little boy who drove a stake through the middle of me tucked to her chest.

She was nearly frantic as she peppered tiny kisses all over his head.

“My *Bwinwey*?”

She choked. “Yeah, baby. Your Brinley and my Kai.”

Agony.

Maybe before this very second, I didn’t really know what that meant.

She turned and started across the floor with him.

Trying to subdue it.

To contain it.

A quiet storm that swelled and whirled as she approached. A slow, babbling rain that still created a flashflood.

She had her hand on the back of his head as she passed, and she sent me this somber, understanding smile.

Like she got it.

No anger or blame, just the devastating acceptance that this was our lot.

I felt like I couldn’t breathe.

Is this what getting your heart broken felt like?

I had to force myself to remain rooted to the spot as I listened to her carrying Kai to my grandmother then my sister in the living room. Each of them kissed him and wished him goodnight.

His little squeals were subdued by his sleepiness, and when Elena offered to tuck him into bed, Brinley whispered, “No, I’d like to do it, if that’s okay?”

“Of course.” Meems’s voice was a low rumble as she flicked off the television. "I'm heading up to bed, too."

"Same," Elena said.

Meems and Elena headed upstairs.

Brinley was a few steps behind them.

My breaths jutted as the muted thud of her bare feet began to echo through the air as she ascended the stairs.

Retreating.

Dimming.

It wouldn't be long before they faded into nothing.

Every piece of me recoiled, ripping and tearing at my consciousness as the faint thuds of them moving around upstairs filtered down to touch my ears.

Or maybe it was just her fingers sinking directly into my soul.

A prod.

A pull.

That fucking gravity that she exerted.

I couldn't help but move.

Something unseen coaxing me into action.

But it was hindered.

Held in the trepidation that blustered through my insides. Warnings and reminders of who I was. Of the things I'd done and what I caused.

It didn't seem to matter because I found myself standing in the hall two feet from Kai's door.

Hazy light spilled out into the hall, and I could hear Brinley murmuring, "There we go," as fabric rustled, and I could imagine her pulling his sleep shirt over his head.

The sleepy smile he'd give her as he squirmed on his changing pad.

This child who I wanted so much more for, too.

"Which one do you want to read tonight?"

"Doggies." Kai giggled, and the book scraped as she pulled it from the small bookshelf, and I could feel her settling with him onto the rocker that Elena had set up in the corner of the room.

Drawn, I lowered with them. My back sliding down the wall as I sank to the floor. My head rocked back as I listened to Brinley begin to read.

Her voice soft and tender and lulling Kai right into a dream.

One where he felt safe and secure and loved. The way he should be. The way I wanted him to be.

And I could almost remember the sound of my mother's voice. Could almost hear it whispering through the dense, rippling air.

It's your heart. It's your heart.

A tremor rocked through me.

Fuck.

I roughed a hand down my face.

What I wouldn't give to be the man my mother had wanted me to be.

Brinley continued to murmur those soothing words, slower and quieter as Kai drifted to sleep.

For a few moments after she came to the story's end, a hushed silence whisked through the atmosphere, then the rocking chair squeaked as she stood and I heard her feet padding across the room.

Overcome, I stood, too, and I shuffled to the doorway to watch as Brinley carefully laid Kai into his crib. Only a dim nightlight glowed in the room.

She stood gazing down at him, but I knew she felt me.

Hell, I was pretty sure she'd known I'd been there all along. It wasn't like either of us were immune to the simmering fire that smoldered at the fringes of our beings.

Her back rose and fell with her uneven breaths, a slow severity rising and falling over me.

A breaking tide that kept crashing, riding higher with each undulation.

I took a single step through the door.

"Brinley." I wheezed it, no way to staunch the flow of grief. I didn't know if it was fueled by hers or if it was wholly mine.

This need that thrummed and throbbed. Something greater than the physical. A part that I didn't recognize.

Brinley took it as an apology, and she sniffled, clearly working to shore up the pain.

"He's so perfect," she whispered, barely turning toward me. The gold flecks of her eyes flashed in the bare radiance of the nightlight. "I had no idea I could feel this way about a child who doesn't belong to me, but God, I love him so much."

The bones in my chest creaked with the pressure.

"Brinley," I said again. That time it was a plea.

She barely shook her head. "It's my fault. I knew. I mean, God, I've only been here for little more than two weeks, and I let myself go. I was the fool who let this place invade. The one who let your family invade. The one who let *you* invade."

Her brow pinched. "But I don't regret it. Sometimes we have to let ourselves feel—wholly and without reserve, the pain and loss included—to find who we really are."

She inhaled a stuttered breath. "And I've been running from the pain for so long, fighting and fighting and barely surviving, that I forgot who I wanted to be. I lost her, Silas. I lost her behind the walls and armor I built around myself. I lost the hope and the belief and the joy of dreaming. And I want to be her, Silas. And maybe because of you all, I finally might be."

"Brinley." Her name hemorrhaged from my mouth, bleeding like a fatal wound, and I took another step forward. I realized I was basically chanting her name, unable to process or formulate the real chaos toiling in my conscience.

Her words were daggers that impaled. Arrowing through to the hidden places that had rotted and festered in the depths of me for what felt like a million years.

A different lifetime.

Sounded about right considering the good parts of me had died the day my mother had.

And fuck, because of Brinley, flickers of them had been rekindled.

"I want to give that to you." The admission was grit, and I fisted my hands at my sides to keep myself from reaching out and taking what felt like mine.

Her lips trembled. "Do you?"

There was her fire.

A challenge in the lilt of her chin.

"If I were different—"

Her huff cut me off.

"If you were different? I don't want you to be different. I fell for the man standing right here in front of me."

I nearly bowed at her confession, and the connection that screamed between us burned a hole through the middle of me.

A keening wire that fought to draw us together.

I got the panicked sense I'd die if I didn't do something to fill it.

She lifted that fierce chin higher. "Because of that man? Standing here? I'm no longer afraid."

It was me who was afraid. Terrified of what she made me feel. Of what she made me want. The outright control she exerted over me.

I was the fucking president of a violent MC. The spearhead of our underbelly. The one who picked and chose who survived and who met death.

I'd cut down a host of demons and razed a legion of monsters. I'd been marked. Had a score of bounties on my head.

And all it took was this one fiery woman to bring me to my knees.

Wildfire.

"That's because you're the strongest woman I know. Most beautiful. Kind and fierce and untamed. Most giving, even when you know it's going to cost you. Willing to do anything for the ones you love even when they don't come close to deserving that love. You're so fucking brave through everything you've been through, I'm the one who's standing here in awe. You deserve every fucking good thing in this world, Brinley Webber."

I'd meant it to come out as a parting. A goodbye. A severing of the bond we'd forged.

Except she stepped forward.

I was slammed by a deluge of fervency.

A torrent of everything she was.

She reached out and set her palm on my cheek.

"You're right, Silas. I do deserve every good thing in this world. The question is, are you brave enough to accept what you deserve? What's standing right in front of you?"

49

Brinley

There was no longer time to tiptoe around this thing. It was do or die.

So I gave him the challenge. Did he feel the same way about me as I did him? Could he see himself as a good man? Could he find himself worthy of love?

Every harsh angle of his handsome face hardened. Razors sharpening in defense.

That severe brow pinched in pain and discipline.

He growled a throaty sound and once again he rumbled my name. “Brinley.”

This one was a warning. A warning for me to back away or else I was going to be standing in the path of a broken dam.

Because I could feel it tremoring all around him.

His restraint was fracturing. The truth spinning like a vortex in his hazel eyes.

“My only job is to keep you safe, and I’ll gladly die seeing that through.” His voice was gravel.

“That’s not what I asked you.”

Grief curled through his expression. “I don’t deserve it, Brinley, I don’t deserve you. But I’ll give everything for you.”

“Except for the parts you think you’re not worthy of giving,” I whispered. “And those are the very best parts.”

“I’m not…the things I’ve done.”

“They don’t matter.”

His scoff was shallow. “But they do, Brinley. Those are the things that define us. And my definition is foul.”

A frown twisted my brow. “I don’t believe that for a second. Do you think I don't see you?"

My fingernails scraped over the fabric of his tee. Right over the erratic thrumming of his heart.

We were swaying, barely moving in the whorls of potency that swirled in the room. Whipping around us in the same volatility as it had the first time he led me to the room above the club.

An undefined connection that had pulled between us from the get-go.

"You only see the parts I've shown you," he grated.

"No, Silas, what you try to keep hidden are the good parts. But they're there, and they keep rising to the surface no matter how hard you try to keep them concealed."

His eyes squeezed closed for a beat. "I don't want to hurt you. Don't want to drag you into this world." His attention skated over my shoulder to Kai's crib. "Just like I'm terrified of having him in it."

"Do you really think you're bad for him? That you'd let anyone or anything hurt him?"

"Never." It slashed out like a blade.

"Then don't be afraid of loving him. Because I'm not sure if you're aware, but that is exactly the meaning of the promise you just made. That's love, Silas."

He flinched so hard I might as well have punched him in the face.

A rake of horrified words spilled into the addled air. "My blood is cursed. Tainted. And I'll do anything to save him from that."

"So you're saying he'd be better off without you?"

His thick throat bobbed as he swallowed, wavering, hesitating, his attention back on the child.

He was so conflicted I was surprised this man didn't cut right in two.

"No."

"Then love him, Silas. Love him with everything you have."

I gulped and pressed forward, laying myself bare.

"Love me." The appeal croaked from my mouth.

Silas froze. Torment seethed in his being, and his eyes pinched closed as he muttered, "I can't."

It was a blade stabbed directly into my heart.

A violent evisceration.

But I expected it, didn't I? I knew there was no place this could go but to its end, and I'd begged for it, anyway.

Somehow, I managed to keep it together enough to nod, though I could barely speak. "Goodbye, Silas."

I hurried across the hall and into his room, frantic as I gathered a few things, stuffing what I could into my duffel and leaving the rest.

I had to get out of there.

Far freaking away.

I wasn't about to go back to the room over the club.

I was going to disappear.

From everything and everyone.

Dereck could fend for himself because it was time I looked after myself.

Time I went after the things that *I deserved* and the things that *I wanted*.

Too bad what I wanted was the man who stood as a dark silhouette in the middle of Kai's doorway when I flew back out of his room.

I nearly stumbled with the look on his face.

Crushed all over again by the absolute devastation carved in the slashed, explicit lines. I guess he was right, after all. We both were going to end up ruined.

I forced myself to drop my head, slinging the strap over my shoulder and beelining for the stairs.

Head down as I raced to the bottom, holding onto the railing to keep myself steady when I felt every inch of me falling apart.

"Brinley," he heaved from over the upper railing.

Misery lancinated out.

I shook my head with the impact, swallowing down the sob that thickened at my throat.

I hit the landing and rushed for the door, trying to keep my movements quiet since Elena and Meems were trying to sleep. I didn't want to disturb them, but I was pretty sure whatever Silas and I were emitting was likely rattling the walls.

I pulled open the door and slipped out into the night. Bugs trilled in the trees, and I could hear the faint echoes of the party happening at the clubhouse in the distance.

I diverted course, ducking under the cover of branches and heading up the shortcut that led to the front of the property.

I knew I was going to have to go toe to toe with some of Silas's men, but they weren't going to stop me.

I was leaving.

Silas had made it clear there was no place for me here.

I realized I didn't want shelter.

I wanted a home.

I was finally almost free, and I didn't want to go anywhere.

The full realization of that bled out. Rolling off me in staggering waves. The thought of never seeing Elena and Meems again splintered my heart.

But the thought of never getting to hold Kai again? Of never seeing Silas again?

It was gutting.

Knowing I'd never get to experience the high I felt when Silas walked into the room. Of never getting to feel that sense of surety. Of completeness. Of someone fully understanding me, and I didn't have to be afraid or ashamed of it.

A sob hooked in my throat, and I attempted to smother it as I ducked through the shadows that played through the night.

That was when I felt a flashfire of heat roll over me from behind.

A shockwave that torched the air.

"Brinley!" The shout hit me from behind, an echo that reverberated through the heavens.

I stumbled a step.

Knowing Silas, he was setting out to stop me. A job he had to see through.

No more.

I hurried faster, the sandals I'd quickly shoved my feet into slipping over the damp grasses below.

My heart thundered and my senses whirled.

His aura caught up in a flash.

"Brinley!" he shouted again, that time closer.

And I got the same sense I had the night he chased me down when I initially tried to escape.

The fear that I was about to be destroyed, but this time it was a completely different form of annihilation.

"Brinley, please. Fucking stop."

I fumbled, and one second later, I felt him like a landslide. His presence was nothing but domination.

Taking hold of the air that shivered with his potency.

White-hot lightning licked across my flesh, and every hair on my body lifted in awareness.

I inhaled a fractured breath, drawing him into the aching well of my chest.

Sweet, liquored cherry always muddling my mind.

I shouldn't have looked back, but I couldn't have stopped myself even if I knew the sight of him would prove lethal.

Not with the way he had a hook in my heart.

I guess it was.

Because a little piece of me died as I stared at him standing beneath the cover of a massive oak.

At one with the shadows that writhed around him like they'd become partner to that untamed volatility.

Swirls of darkness twined and twisted.

His cheeks and jaw carved of steel.

Towering and massive and robbing me of my faculties.

Too ferociously beautiful to be real.

"I warned you that you'd do well to hate me." Every word cleaved from his mouth like splinters of broken glass.

My entire body squeezed in refusal. "I can't."

His big hands fisted at his sides, and those eyes burrowed right through to the secret places that I'd never allowed anyone to go before.

Not even before my belief and confidence had been demolished. Not with any boyfriend or man that had come before him.

It was only Silas. The last man I should want and the first one I'd ever needed.

He took one step closer, and the ground rolled beneath his feet.

His strong features were written in conflict.

"You want this? You really want this?" His words cut through the dense, suffocating air.

Severing through the despair and touching down on that place within me that he had exposed.

"I want it. I want you."

I said it without reservation.

Torment pierced his expression, and he kept moving, a shadowy eclipse that slipped forward until he was standing right in front of me.

Covering me in a blanket of his ferocity.

"You shouldn't." It was close to a growl.

"But I do." I whispered into the force that drew us together.

Silas reached out and took me by both sides of the face. His hold was acute, like he was trying to get me to understand the severity of what he was saying. "You don't know the full of who I am."

"I don't care."

He gave a harsh shake of his head.

"I'm a killer, Brinley. It's what I do." He ground through every word.

My knees knocked, legs going weak. It was Silas's unrelenting hold that kept me standing.

I already knew it. I knew it the second Dereck rolled onto his property. I could feel the violence screaming from his body, and he'd all but admitted it many times over as he'd issued his warnings.

But not like this.

This time, he delivered it like blunt force trauma.

I wondered which of us sustained it the worst.

Me or Silas, who tore himself open wide.

Exposing the underside.

Showing me the places he hadn't wanted me to see. Yet they were painted as distinctly as the horrors he'd painted on his flesh.

"I know." It tumbled off my tongue, and I wondered if I'd completely lost my mind.

Accepting this.

"Do you?" he demanded, eyes merciless in their claim.

Big hands clutched my jaw as he stared down at me. I inhaled his panted breaths, and our hearts raced as wild as the demand he was making.

"Yes. I know. I see it in you, every bit as clear as I see something beautiful trapped inside."

I set my hand over the thunder in his chest.

"It's your heart."

It's what he had tattooed there. I figured he meant it as condemnation, but I issued it like praise.

He nearly bowled over, and a sound of desperation rolled through him.

Feral and thinly hinged.

"Knowing who I am, you still want me? You want this?" It was pure disbelief.

"I see you, Silas. Who you really are. I don't care about the rest."

Dubiety rolled with the relief.

"Are you sure?" he grunted. "Because once I take you to my bed, I'm not letting you leave it. Once I take you there, you're mine."

And I knew we were on a precipice. Standing on a cliff, ground crumbling below us. But I still had time. I could scramble back and run to safety.

But I no longer had any fear of the fall, and I grabbed onto his wrists and pushed myself higher on my toes so my lips brushed against his.

And I whispered, "Yes."

50

Brinley

"Brinley." That time when he murmured my name it was in surrender. A complete giving that surged through him, so distinct I felt his body bow.

It was directly followed by a hammering of possession that seeped from his hands and into my bloodstream as he dragged me the rest of the way against him.

Walls toppled as he crushed his mouth against mine.

It was a dizzying assault that spun me into a jumble of need and relief and joy.

This kiss?

It was desperate and freed.

Wild and untamed and really freaking messy.

Almost as messy as this situation, I was sure, but those were the little details that didn't matter much right then.

His kiss was close to aggressive in its demand, the muscles in his big body flexing in their need to get me closer.

But there was a smile behind that kiss, both of ours, I thought. A dancing light licking against the darkness that surrounded us.

My heart pressed so full against my chest that I couldn't breathe. I could only feel, given over to the perfect delirium that thudded through my veins.

Silas choked a laugh into the kiss, and a big palm settled on the side of my head so he could angle me just right as he alternated between kissing me deeper and mumbling, "Is this real, baby? Is this real?"

"It's real," I whispered back. "It's the realest thing I've ever felt."

"How'd we get here?" His arms curled around my waist, and he spun us, lifting me a fraction off my feet.

His hold soft and tumultuous.

"Because it's where we're supposed to be."

I had to believe I was brought here for a reason. That I'd been called. That maybe Dereck had been, too. An unknowing partner commissioned to bring me home.

A euphoric giggle rolled up my throat.

It was really difficult to process it, to fully grasp it, my mind spinning with the truth that this was what I wanted.

After I'd chosen to be alone for so long, thinking that hedge I'd surrounded myself was better. That I was stronger that way when I'd never been so certain or powerful right then.

Silas grinned beneath the manic kiss. "What are you laughing about, Little Wildfire?"

My palms skimmed down the rough stubble on his cheeks. Sensation zinged up my arms and streaked through my insides. "That I get this."

Without breaking the kiss, he lifted me fully from the ground and began to carry me back through the woods.

He released garbled words against my lips. "You get all of this. All of me. I don't think there was a chance I could have let you leave."

A needy moan rose in my throat, and my fingers dove into the soft locks of his hair as he kissed me senseless.

He never broke that kiss as he carried me beneath the branches that whisked and rippled above us and to the front door of his house.

He slowed the kiss a fraction as he fumbled around behind me and opened the door with one hand then quietly latched and locked it behind us.

The energy magnified even more as he slowly climbed the stairs, his kiss verging on adoring as he held me with my feet dangling below me into the dusky glow of his room.

The scantest light babbled in from the window and cast the space in a glittery warmth.

Silas laid me down on the plush linens of his bed. He remained at the end of it, gazing down at me where I writhed in anticipation.

We both knew what this had come to.

He appeared a mountainous shadow. Every rocky, abrasive edge of him held in a frailty that I'd never seen him wear before.

"You're sure you want me?"

God, why did that make my heart ache?

"I have never wanted anyone or anything the way I want you, Silas Mercer. Maybe it's inexplicable. Maybe it doesn't make any sense for either of us. But I know where I belong. With you."

"Wildfire."

He murmured it.

Praise.

A claim.

A final decision.

Because when his expression shifted, every crease and corner hardened in domination. He curled his hands in the bottom hem of his tee.

Sparks in his hazel eyes as he slowly peeled his shirt up and over his head.

My breath left me.

A heaving gush as I took him in without a shirt. Solid, packed muscle rippled under his skin. Strength defined in every inch.

My attention went to that tattoo that stood out above all the rest.

It's your heart.

He set one knee onto the bed, and he slowly crawled over me.

My own heart careened as I set my hand over the words.

He bracketed me with his arms, hands planted on either side of my head to hold himself up.

"That's what you are now." His murmur was rough. "My heart."

My nod was as thick as the lump in my throat. "And you're mine." I let a little lightness weave into the heaviness as I brushed my fingertips over his full lips.

"And I'm not about to share you, *King*."

He gruffed a sound of amused rebuttal and nipped his teeth at my fingertips. "You telling the president what to do now?"

"Did you expect anything less?"

"No, baby." He whispered that. Awe fluttering out. "I met my match. The one who was sent to show me my place. Exactly where I was meant to be."

His stare grew vehement, the mood slipping into seriousness, his eyes flicking all over my face as he reached out and brushed back a curl from my face. "I won't be touching anyone else but you for the rest of my life."

My life.

I heard the promise behind it.

"Good because you're the only person I want touching me."

He wrapped his hand around my wrist as my fingers continued to flutter over his lips. He kissed across them, inhaling a deep, tremulous breath. "The ways I'm going to touch you, Brinley. The ways I'm going to have you."

Desire gathered on the horizon. Lighting up my insides in orange and red flames.

"I like the sound of that."

His chuckle was rough, though his words turned reverent. "I'm going to take care of you. Treasure you. Shower you in everything you didn't know you wanted."

My stomach flipped, and my blood pounded.

"I didn't know I wanted any of this. Not until I met you," I admitted.

"And I think somewhere in the back of my head, I did want it. I wanted someone who made me feel this way. But I was never fool enough to dream that I might actually have it."

"It's yours, Silas."

A growl rolled his powerful chest. "That's right, Brinley. You're mine. Mine to cherish. Mine to worship. Mine to adore."

Every word swelled through me on a wave of affection.

He dipped down and kissed along my jaw, and I reached up and lightly threaded my fingers through his hair.

Inhaled everything that he was.

The degeneracy and the righteousness.

The corruption and the integrity.

The brash harshness up against all his sweetness.

He let one hand slide down my side, gliding over the divots of my ribs. The pad of his thumb brushed over my breast.

Sensation pebbled my nipple.

"You're so beautiful, Brinley. Stole the breath right out of my lungs the second you stepped from your brother's car. Knew you were going to be my end when you did. I just didn't know what that meant."

I arched, and the fabric of my tee brushed against the rigid strength of his bare chest, seeking the connection.

To feel the violent ravaging of his heart as he murmured his confessions to me.

"My match. *The match.* The wildfire I didn't see coming. Burning up my world and setting fire to my heart."

"I thought you were the most dangerously gorgeous man I'd ever seen," I whispered into the chaos. "But I never thought in a million years I'd fall in love with you."

I almost regretted letting it go with the way Silas's body went rigid, and everything slowed as he pressed up onto his hands so he was hovering over me.

His beautiful face tortured and severe.

"I guess I should have known I'd fall in love with you. You were a lightning strike in the darkness that ruled my life. A shooting star falling from the heavens and taking me down with you. Warmth in the cold. I've spent so many years allowing hatred to drive me. But this love will be what's driving me now, Brinley. This massive amount of love that I've got for you. You were the only one who could break through the stone, and now, every broken piece belongs to you."

"I love you." I said it straight.

"I'm so fucking in love with you that I've forgotten to breathe without you here. The second you walked out the door…"

His tongue swiped over his lips.

"Even though there was no chance you were getting over the wall…" He quirked an accusatory brow, then the words went gruff, "I knew the wall I'd erected between us was one I couldn't bear."

"Who would have thought the one I believed my captor was my ultimate destination?"

"Guess you should have known all along that you belonged to me." He hooked my leg up over his hip when he said it, just putting enough pressure at my center to feel the hardness that begged back.

He rocked against me, slow but sure.

Tiny fireworks sparked behind my eyes. A promise of what was coming.

I clawed at his shoulders, and he released a low chuckle at my ear. "Not even close to having you yet, and you're already lighting up."

"I need you."

"You have me, baby. And you always will."

Silas carefully edged back and rose up on his knees.

His skin crawled with lust. With desperate, tapped need. He curled his fingers into my tee. "Gonna strip you bare. You good with that?"

"I'm already bare, Silas. Stripped bare because of you."

I sat up a little so he could lift my shirt over my head. Cool air brushed my flesh as he pulled it free and tossed it to the floor.

I wasn't wearing a bra, and he heaved a breath and cupped my left breast. "So damned pretty. So sexy. Nothing but a fantasy that bashed through the armor in my world."

I pushed into his touch, tilting my head back in pure supplication.

"Please," I whispered again. Just in case he didn't get the hint.

"No need to beg, my eager girl," he rumbled into the tension that hung heavy in the room. "It's already yours. Lay back."

It was a soft grunt, and I hurried to comply, the rise and fall of my chest stuttered as my head hit the pillow.

Silas eyed me intently as he hooked his fingers in the waist of my leggings, and his teeth raked his bottom lip like maybe he needed to prepare himself.

I knew this was different for him, too. That neither of us had ever experienced another this way.

This thing that felt so utterly surreal.

So utterly profound.

Silas started to peel them down, taking my underwear with them. A low groan rolled out of him as he edged back and dragged them all the way down my legs.

Slowly.

Like he was savoring every inch that he exposed.

He tossed those aside, too, and then he was rising up high on his knees, staring at me.

A flashfire erupted across my skin. Flames licking hot over my naked body, those eyes searing me all the way through.

"How's it I have a goddess in my bed?"

Redness streaked, and I squirmed.

"You have any idea what you do to me?" His words scraped over me like rough, desperate caresses. "Have any idea the way you flipped everything upside down? Crashing into my life like you did?"

"I doubt it's half of what you did to me."

"Promise you it's a whole lot more than that. I may not deserve you, Brinley Webber, but I'm going to spend my whole life trying to."

Dipping down, his mouth possessed mine, his kiss deep and long and slow. His lips sweeping over mine in fluttery brushes.

His tongue soft and warm and invading.

He wound me into a needy puddle, and the only thing I could do was pant and squirm beneath him.

He picked up a trail going south.

My jaw. My neck. My right breast.

My nipple sucked into his sinful mouth.

My belly.

The tops of my thighs.

His lips adoring every inch as he kissed lower before he scooted all the way off the end of the bed.

He knelt to untie his boots, then he rose high.

Towering over me, his stare unwavering as he popped the button on his jeans and unzipped the fly.

He shoved them down and off his ankles.

And Silas Mercer stood in front of me bare.

Completely naked.

In a way he hadn't since we first started pleasuring each other.

If I thought he was intimidating before…

I pushed up onto my hands so I could take him in.

His cock jutted toward the ceiling, gleaming with the rod that pierced his tip.

His abs trembled and his heart rolled.

Depravity dripped from the demons that crawled across his flesh. A warning of who he really was and what he was capable of.

And I knew what I was asking for. What I was surrendering to. Offering this wickedly dangerous man my body and soul.

"King."

With the way I breathed it, I knew it said everything.

"Wildfire," he grunted.

The connection that had drawn us together from the beginning twisted around us as he climbed back onto the bed and wound himself between my thighs.

A storm that formed at the ends of the earth and gathered to consume us.

His skin skimmed mine.

A stoking of the flames.

Magnifying the severity.

Warm, whiskey eyes were pinned on mine.

"Saw your pills on the counter, and I've been tested. Want you bare," he grunted.

Nothing between us.

I arched up, pressing against his hot, hard length.

Begging for it, too.

A guttural sound rolled in his chest, and he rocked up, his forehead pressed to mine as he tried to temper the lust that screamed.

Volatility shocking through his domineering body.

Clearly he was trying to control himself.

Worried that he was pushing me in a direction that I wasn't ready to go.

My fingers sank into his shoulders, our stares unwavering as I breathed across his lips, "I'm safe with you."

"I promise that you're always going to be." The words came with the force of an earthquake.

Silas reached between us, taking himself in his hand and aligning with my center. The blunt head of him brushed my lips, notching just inside, a pulsing fullness that wasn't close to being enough.

A shaky sound wheezed out of me as he stared down at me for one moment more.

An oath.

A promise.

Our truth.

Then he growled as he drove himself deep.

Every ounce of oxygen fled my lungs. The man so big he overwhelmed. My body stretched to capacity as he took me whole.

My nails scratched at his back as I struggled to adjust to his size. Or maybe I was just struggling to adjust to the sharp shift in my life.

A whimper of yielding curled out of me.

One that Silas swallowed, his words murmured into my mouth. "Brinley, fuck. So good. So good. Nothing in the world like the feel of you."

As if he'd been struck the same way.

Changed in a blink.

In the joining of something that shouldn't be but somehow came into focus in perfect, quick sense.

"Nothing." I clung to him as I said it. Like my life depended on it.

I guess in some way, it did.

Silas slid an arm around my waist, splaying his palm wide at the small of my back as he dragged me close, this man who'd broken down every wall and every reserve.

The one who'd made himself a place in the hollowness and filled it to overflowing.

"You fit me perfectly, baby. Do you feel it the way I do? Like you were made for me. Like you've been embedded in every cell."

"And I'll never be the same."

Silas pulled almost all the way out, and I let go of a whimpered, needy plea, before he surged in as far as he could take me.

"Told you I was going to ruin you," he grunted through the desire that leapt into the room.

"In every way." The words left me on a gust.

"Every way," he rumbled, and he angled down so he could take my mouth.

Kissing me so deeply that he became the air within me as he began to move. Pulling back and thrusting in these slow, rigid, mind-bending strokes that nearly made me pass out with each one.

Pleasure glinted at the edges of my sight. At the edges of my spirit.

Friction and light.

He angled his head back an inch to take me in, his words a coarse scrape. "So tight and perfect. This sweet little cunt. Knew you were going to be perfect. Knew you would do me in."

He kept kissing me, and I was kissing him back. Letting the frenzy take control as we gave ourselves over.

Silas increased his pace. Rocking and snapping his hips in a quickening that blustered through me so dynamically that it almost felt like grief.

Like loss because I was letting a piece of myself go while finally finding myself completely.

I struggled to touch him everywhere.

His face. His sides. His ridiculously perfect ass.

I met him thrust for thrust. Welcoming the streaks of pleasure that speared through me with each urgent jut.

Our names were moans that tumbled from our tongues. Whispering our belief into the other as we submitted to this dizzying dance.

"Brinley."

"Silas."

"Wildfire."

"King."

Our bodies rolled.

Boneless.

Liquid.

Creating a new mold.

And it grew and grew. Shaped and formed and swelled and surged.

"Silas," I panted as he drove me toward the type of bliss I'd never known.

That buzz I'd felt the moment I met him hummed.

Amplifying the connection that strummed between us.

A mystifying song that I didn't know the words to but fully understood.

Silas worked me over. His body undulating in surging, claiming waves.

Skin stretched taut over his muscles, his breaths short and rasping as he fed them to me.

"Nothing like this. Nothing like being in you. The feel of you wrapped around my cock. Don't know myself anymore, Brinley. Don't recognize what it's like to feel this way."

It was a tumble of confusion and dominance.

Ecstasy shimmered through my nerves. Ticking and sparking with each drive of his body.

"It's you. It's us," I rasped.

"It's us," he murmured, and his rhythm shifted. The frenzy that clung to the outskirts winding its way into the connection.

Silas rocked harder and deeper. One arm slid up to hold me from behind the neck while the other wound between us. He stroked my already swollen clit.

All-consuming. Speeding through my senses and igniting in my veins.

This man over me and in me and *with* me.

I came apart at that.

A rupturing.

A sundering.

Bliss barreled through my body. A bullet train that bashed through the last barrier.

I tried to subdue the shout of his name, but I couldn't contain the absolute freedom that I found in him. It coursed between us in my own heedless claim.

Tingles of perfection burned through my insides and across my flesh.

Ecstasy.

There was no other way to describe it.

Silas gripped me tighter. Racing to meet with my orgasm that went on and on. His body coiled and tightened as his hips fucked and snapped.

Hard and rushed.

As rushed as the breaths that heaved from his lungs.

And he was right there, coming apart, his hands adamant as he hung on to me as he came.

"Fuck. Brinley. Fuck."

His mouth dropped open on a silent groan, and his harsh, menacing face contorted in rapture.

And in that moment, he was no longer bound to who he thought he had become.

He was made new by the bonds that we had formed.

In this horrible life that neither of us had asked for, each of us broken in our own way, both willing to hold the other's pieces.

Without question, I was going to hold all of his.

We stayed that way for the longest time, every synapse alive with pleasure, before he finally slumped down, though he kept himself supported on his elbows so he didn't smash me with his giant body.

His smile was almost sloppy as he gazed down at me.

Tenderly, he brushed back a lock of hair that had gotten matted to my temple and tucked it behind my ear.

Then his fingertips fluttered up to run along my cheek and down my jaw.

"Nothing in the world, Brinley Webber. Nothing quite like you."

51

Silas

It was strange when you sentenced yourself to a life of nothingness and all of a sudden you were given everything.

It was like receiving that coveted acquittal when you knew you deserved conviction.

A commuted sentence five days after you'd been condemned to death.

A stay of execution when you had earned every drop of poison they planned to drip into your veins.

My heart throbbed with the gift.

I was going to be sure I didn't squander or waste it.

This chance that I'd been given for something good.

Brinley and I had shifted onto our sides so we were facing each other. Our breaths were discordant and rusty, both still disoriented from the sudden deviation in our lives.

I lifted her hand between us, threaded our fingers together, and gazed at her through the gauzy light that filtered in through the window.

Knowing she was my exoneration.

My liberation.

With our hands joined, I ran the pad of my thumb along the outside of hers, watched over at the dreamy euphoria swimming on her face.

My spirit clutched.

God, she looked sweet this way.

Sated and spent.

Different.

But I guess both of us were.

"How do you feel?" It was a deep tremor that fused with the sanctity that had settled like peace in the room.

Those eyes flitted over my face, her curls wild and a mess, so fucking pretty where she lay on the pillow curled up with me on my bed.

Her teeth raked her bottom lip before she quirked a tease. "Like I made a really good choice on who was going to be my man."

A chuckle rolled, and my heart fucking swelled.

Joy pressed at the places I didn't know existed.

"You're satisfied with the performance, huh?" My words were soft. Riddled with affection as my thumb kept stroking the back of her hand.

"I'd say you exceeded expectations."

I shifted our hands so I could run my knuckles along her jaw. "What I didn't expect was you."

"No, I think it's safe to say neither of us expected this, but I'm so glad it was given."

"Me, too." Satisfaction rumbled with the words. "I've never felt like this before, Brinley. Nothing close to when I'm with you."

A bit of that vulnerability seeped out of her. "What do you feel like?"

"Like I'm falling, and I'll never hit the bottom because I'll forever get deeper and deeper."

Emotion fluttered all over her stunning face. Strikes of life. A never-ending flame. "I feel that way, too."

She paused, hesitated, then her cheeks pinked with that coyness. She turned our hands so she could brush her fingertips over the tattoo she kept touching that covered my heart.

The one I'd gotten to remind myself how easy it was for your meaning to get twisted.

A smile tweaked up at the corner of her lush, sexy mouth as everything about her went playful. "So does this mean I'm your old lady now?"

I choked over a surprised laugh, and my pulse stampeded at the thought.

A slug of possession through my veins.

I snaked my arm around her slight waist and plastered her against me.

She smelled like apple pie and sex.

Suffice it to say it was more than appealing.

I burrowed my face in her neck so I could take a big drink, mouth a rumble at the sweat-tinged flesh. "Have every intention of putting a property patch on your back."

She giggled, and I edged back so I could take in her expression.

She pushed up onto an elbow and arched a defiant brow. "Property patch?"

She was all challenge and sass. Feisty as hell. Just the way I liked her.

I sent her a smirk. "That's right." I gripped onto a handful of her hip and gave her a little jostle. "I told you that you're mine now."

"So that's what that means, huh?" It was wry. No anger to it.

Light laughter filtered out of me. No chance she was into that kind of submission.

She'd been fighting me every step of the way, and I doubted that was going to change now.

I sobered as all the issues we were up against broke into our bubble, and I reached out and hooked my index finger under her chin.

Searching that hopeful face and wondering how the hell she trusted me with it.

"Nothing would make me happier than claiming you in front of everyone."

A frown dented her strong brow, reading deeper into it, just like I knew she would. "But you can't?"

My chest tightened, and I leaned up on my elbow so I could see her better. "Not yet, but I'll find a way to. I'm breaking a thousand of my own rules by touching you. And not just the ones I made for myself that I have to go this life alone. The deal I made with your brother..."

I trailed off. Wanting to lay every single detail out for her on a silver platter.

But I couldn't defy my crew that way. Not when what I was doing was already bad enough. Putting them in the position that I was.

Getting greedy.

"There's a lot riding on this, Brinley..."

Everything.

"I have to make sure I don't cause any distractions in the middle of it."

Her frown cut with worry. "Is it...dangerous?"

God, what was I supposed to say?

"My life is by definition dangerous. What we do..."

Uncertainty swirled through her hypnotizing gaze. No question, her thoughts were back on the confession I'd made.

Not that she hadn't had her suspicions. But there was no way she knew how grim it was.

I knew she wanted to ask exactly what I meant by that, so I brushed the back of my hand over her cheek and started to speak. "But this? It's the most dangerous thing we've ever done. But it has to happen."

Tears blurred. "I can't stand the thought of something happening to you."

"It won't." The oath was out before I could think better of it. I had no right to make it. Not when I knew some of us wouldn't be coming home.

Brinley blinked, horror thinning her voice. "And Dereck?"

I hesitated, at war with the truth that this thing could still go south. "My intention is he's getting out with us."

Her eyes flicked all over my face, searching before she pushed me the way she always did. "And what is this, Silas? What is it you're involved in? This doesn't seem like some beef with another motorcycle club."

I couldn't give that to her.

Not yet.

Not until after all this went down and I met with the club. In Church, I'd tell them the line I'd crossed and let them know I didn't intend on ever turning back.

They were going to have no say in that.

My devotion to Brinley.

But giving her the inside on what Crimson Crows really did?

We'd vote if Brinley could fully be let in, going through the same channels that the rest were approved.

So I gave her what I could.

The bare, blatant truth.

The crux. The beginning. The mission I'd set out on long ago before it landed me here.

"With the help of your brother, I'm finally going to get revenge for my mother's death."

52

Silas

Seventeen Years Old

"Where are you going?"

His grandmother's voice echoing down the short hall stalled him in his tracks, and his hand trembled on the doorknob.

Dimness suffused the dense air, and he struggled to breathe through it.

"Out," he grumbled.

"I see that filth you're wearing."

He'd pulled on his Iron Owls cut right before he'd been ready to slink out.

He wasn't necessarily sneaking. But this was an unending fight with Meems that he wasn't in the mood for.

He slowly swiveled around on his motorcycle boots.

"You're just seeing the *filth*, Meems. It doesn't have a thing to do with the cut." He basically sneered it.

He watched the pain slash across her face, and he shifted on his feet, the regret that tried to flutter up squashed by the anger that had become his constant partner.

"You know better than that, Silas Mercer. We all choose our paths, and the one you're traveling down right now is the wrong one."

He scoffed. "I started down this path two years ago, and there's no getting off it."

Because the path he'd chosen had killed his mother.

"You made a mistake, Silas, but it's in your power to stop making it. This isn't what your mother would want from you."

"I'm thinking what my mother would actually *want* is to be alive."

Grief speared through her being, her features aged by at least a decade over the last year.

He hated it.

That he caused it.

That he was the one who'd destroyed their lives.

His brother and sister without a mother.

Living in this shithole of a house in LA since it was close to Meems's sister and she was going to help out.

Their financial situation far worse than it'd ever been.

But that was the one thing he could do something about. That and avenging his mother.

He'd run into this guy named Deke who introduced him to the club's vice president, Trent.

They stood for everything he needed.

Power and brutality.

He was going to need it when he finally hunted these motherfuckers down. It wouldn't be wise to take them all on himself, though he would if he had to.

It wasn't like he could get any information from his father.

That piece of shit had disappeared that night.

Fucking coward.

Silas guessed the guy was lucky because if that bastard showed his face, Silas would end him himself.

He had no names, but he did know some of the shipments had been coming out of California. He figured if he got in deep enough, he might be able to uncover who they were.

Even if it took fucking years.

Because he wasn't leaving this life until he buried them.

"What your mother would want is her children flourishing. Thriving even after she's gone because she already instilled her belief and hope in them."

Silas's heart throbbed, mangled and torn, every beat distorted. He rubbed the spot over it like he could stop the bleeding.

"You know she wouldn't want this for you," Meems continued, "and I don't, either. She loved you more than life, Silas, and as her mother, as *your* grandmother, I'm begging you not to do this."

He closed his eyes against the onslaught of his grandmother's words, bolstering himself through the trauma.

Gripping onto the hate.

And he gritted as he turned the doorknob and pulled open the door, "Go back to sleep. You don't need to worry about me."

• • •

How easy it was to slide into the life. A pit of corruption that sucked him right to the bottom of the barrel.

Years had passed in a blur of greed and iniquity.

Running drugs and weapons. Killing. Stealing and maiming.

Guilt ate at his insides with every passing day. Gnawing away at any remnants of humanity that remained.

He might have completely lost himself, but that one purpose remained the same—seeking revenge for his mother's death.

He'd watched and listened for years. Desperate to pick up on any trace of the men who'd slain his mother. Ones he was sure had taken her out for the simple fact she was standing there.

Their intent to get rid of him, too, believing they'd been exposed.

When he finally got ahold of them, they were going to wish that they had.

His Harley chugged low as he pulled up in front of the dive in one of the most dangerous areas in LA.

A pack of his brothers' bikes was already parked facing out on the street.

A row of gleaming, malicious metal beneath the vapid city lights.

He did the same, using his boots to propel himself backward before he killed the engine and kicked the stand.

He swung off and strode through the doors into the mayhem of Iron Owls' reign.

Heavy metal music screamed, flashes of light shearing through the smoky dimness that held to the rest of the room.

An army of men donning their cuts, drinking straight from the bottle, snorting piles of coke while others shot up in the corners.

Any women there were considered fair game. Ripe for the taking. Laid out in every erotic position.

Splayed across the bar top.

Stripped and legs spread on a chair.

Tits spilling out onto tabletops while Silas's brothers took turns fucking them from behind.

That was unless they had a property patch on their backs, then that became a whole different story.

It was ludicrous to him. That an Owl would take a woman and tie her to this disgusting life. They might have chosen it, but if they really cared about someone? Would they really drag them into this?

But Silas figured most of them didn't give two real fucks about anything. Only themselves and what they could pillage and thieve. Their women mere possessions.

Silas kept the three people in the world he actually cared about far away from this.

His stomach twisted at the thought of Meems, Elena, and Brody. His grandmother's pleading eyes haunting him every fucking time he walked out the door.

She'd never given up in her begging him to change. Continually told him he was so much better than the life he was living.

But he wasn't.

He deserved this hell.

A few Owls clapped him on the back as he shouldered through the pack, and he slipped onto an empty stool at the bar.

The old bartender behind it lifted his chin in question.

"Old-fashioned," he grunted.

"You got a preference of whiskey?"

"Maker's is fine."

The guy whipped it up and slid it in front of him, and he tossed him a twenty for a tip.

Brought the tumbler to his lips and took a sip.

Relishing the burn, aching for a fire when every fucking thing inside him had gone cold.

The energy shifted when the door swung open, and every eye in the place turned as Trent Lawson strode through.

Their vice president whose mere presence commanded respect.

Things had gotten a little weird as of late. A new tension sliding into the club. There was a rumor that there was some beef between Cutter, their president, and Trent and Jud, who were his sons. Only thing he knew was Cutter was a fucking psychopath, so he couldn't imagine there was any true affection between any of them.

Not that it was any of Silas's business, though he felt a whole lot more loyalty and trust toward Trent than he ever would for Cutter.

He turned and took another sip of his old-fashioned when that same ferocity rolled up behind him.

He shifted to find Trent standing there.

"Can I get a word with you?"

Silas's chest tightened at Trent's tone.

Not in fear.

But because of the urgency laced in the words.

"Of course."

He slipped off the stool and followed Trent into the darkened hall that led to some Owl offices at the back.

Trent stopped halfway down and turned to him. He peered over Silas's shoulder to ensure they were out of earshot before he muttered, "Might have something for you."

Silas's dead heart gave an erratic beat. "What kind of something?"

Trent licked his lips, more agitated than he should be. "Cutter made connections with some runners. Up in Northern California and extending into Southern Oregon."

Silas's blood careened, and he swallowed around the dark thrill that surged through him.

"They've been in the game for at least seven years," Trent continued. "Not a huge organization. Mostly feeding heroin into small towns through their channels, though they're looking to expand, which was why the deal was made with Cutter."

Now Silas knew why Trent was itching.

He was offering inside information Silas shouldn't have.

You didn't know shit around here unless it was directly tied to you.

A job you were given.

It kept everyone in line and Cutter in control.

Trent roughed a tattooed hand through his black hair. "It fits, man."

Silas could barely breathe, and his nod was jerky as he realized the gift Trent was giving.

He was finally going to catch up to them.

"Know you've been looking for these bastards for a long, long time."

"Yeah, I have," Silas finally managed, the words choked. "I appreciate you giving me the details."

Trent inclined closer. "Going to have more for you. Names. Locations. And I'm fucking trusting that this doesn't make it back to Cutter."

"You know it won't."

"Good." Trent wavered, glancing at the ground before his inky gaze was back on Silas. "Things are about to get twisted around here. Want you to be careful. Look out for yourself and for your family. And if things go south, pack up and get the fuck out of this city."

Unease stirred through Silas's spirit. "You about to flip on our Prez?"

"All I can say is I'm about to make a few fucking things right, and I'm hoping to allow you the same as I do it."

53

Silas

"How is it possible I got you in my life?" I lay playing my fingers through Brinley's hair, her head nestled on my shoulder, the night long as we just…talked.

Staying mostly off the hard topics and instead whispering about her hopes and dreams.

Unfortunately, her dreams had amounted to basically the hope of bare survival since her mother had gotten sick when she was fourteen.

Her teen years every bit as rough as mine.

I was going to see to it that she finally had room to dream again. Give her room to chase after every single thing she'd ever wanted.

Crazy as fuck that a big part of what she wanted was me.

My mind was still struggling to come to terms with it.

To accept that this was true. That she was mine and she was always going to be.

I had to wonder if the draw toward each other was because we had so many similarities.

Losing our mothers and the burden of caring for our families falling onto our shoulders.

It had shaped our lives in different ways, but in the end, it'd made both of us fighters.

I watched through the shadows as a soft grin kissed her lush mouth. "I guess you're just lucky like that."

My chest expanded. "I guess I am just one lucky motherfucker, aren't I?"

Her fingertips fluttered down my chest. "Oh, yeah. I'd say you are."

My soul did that buzzing thing. Frantic and flailing, still not sure what I was supposed to do with the magnitude of what I was feeling.

The lightness bled into emphasis. "I was terrified of this, Brinley. Terrified of letting myself go. Of loving a single person again," I admitted.

I'd spent so much time hating myself. The choices I'd made. Who I'd become.

Regret was Karma's most powerful friend.

And I had so much of it that it'd stunted any growth or healing. But lying there with Brinley in my arms, I couldn't regret what Crimson Crows had become.

It was fucking important.

I knew to my soul that it was.

Our means might have been criminal, but expunging the slime from the earth counted as something.

I needed to find a way to tell her. Convince my crew that she needed to be on the inside. I didn't think I could keep it from her for long, even if they overruled me.

Not when she had become the most important part of my life.

She shifted so she could peek up at my face. "You're amazing, Silas Mercer. I see the care you have for every person on this property. But more than that, for your family. There is no question of your love."

"It's always felt like my intentions end up hurting the ones that I love. I try to protect them from it, but..."

Her head shook, and her fingertips kept playing over the words tattooed over my heart. "They all adore you. I'm not sure if you realize the way they look at you with respect and adoration."

"That's when Elena doesn't want to kick my ass." I put as much lightness into it as I could.

Brinley's smile was soft. "Well, you are kind of overbearing. You can't blame her."

"I just want her to be happy. To live a normal life."

"And you think being here is stopping that?" she whispered.

"She's right, it's basically a prison."

"It doesn't have to be."

My insides coiled. "Once this job is finished, I'm going to try to make it right. Fix some of this fucked-up mess that I have us in."

A frown pinched her brow, and she softly ran the pads of her fingers over my bottom lip. "Well, don't fix it too much because there's love here, Silas. There's joy and safety and belief. Even if you have a hard time seeing it."

"You really believe that?"

"I wouldn't be lying here if I didn't."

Emotion pulled tight across my chest, and I forced out what I'd been struggling with for months.

"I was afraid of bringing Kai here. Afraid that I'd be trading one nightmare for another for him." I paused, then admitted, "I was going to ask my hacker friend to fake a birth certificate for him so he could be adopted. Find a good family for him who would love him the way he deserved."

"Silas." It was a wheeze. A question. An accusation.

Pure understanding.

She pushed up onto her elbow. "I get it. The panic. The fear. But he is so loved. That child…"

Her voice drifted off, no need for the words when her love for him was palpable.

Exuding from her spirit.

I reached up and touched her face. "I couldn't do it, Brinley. I've tried to build myself up to it for the last two months, and I just can't. I didn't want to love him, just like I didn't want to love you." I hesitated, then asked, "Did you mean it? That you love him?"

She breathed out a shaky sigh. "I think I fell in love with him the moment I met him."

Significance sharpened the air, and I let my thumb roam the angle of her cheek. "I want us to raise him, Brinley. As ours."

"What about his mother?"

Hatred shook my head. "She's as bad as my father. I'll see to it that she has no rights remaining."

Tears blurred her eyes, and her throat bobbed. "That would be my greatest honor."

Overcome, she climbed up to straddle my waist. Weight on her hands as she gazed down like it was the first time she was really seeing me.

I weaved my fingers into her hair. "Then we do this together. You, me, and Kai."

The enormity of what I was saying almost gutted me. But it was in the most exquisite of ways.

She nodded. Almost frantic. That mesmerizing gaze on me.

The air whirled. Something fierce and knowing and resolute. A weaving of frayed, tattered fabrics into something beautiful.

Fuck me. She was gorgeous.

Wild mane of brown curls kissed in honey raining around her, dripping down around her shoulders and brushing over her perfect round tits.

A vision.

An implosion to my senses.

I gripped her by the waist as she steadied herself on my chest.

Her breaths turned needy and shallow.

"I love you, Silas. I thought I was supposed to hate you, but my heart knew."

I'd thought mine was incapable, but it'd known too.

Recognized the only one who could warm the cold that had taken over my life.

I slowly sat up, drawn to her heat.

"Forged in the fire, you and me." I played with a lock of her hair.

"And it's shaping into something beautiful," she whispered.

Flames licked around us. That approaching fire I'd felt coming was no longer in the distance.

It was here, lapping up the walls and burning our senses.

Molding our souls together.

Brinley exhaled, and I swallowed it, dove in to take her mouth.

Kissed her wild.

My hands bound up in her hair and this battered heart feeling whole for the first time.

She moaned and rubbed her pussy over my cock.

"You want me again, Little Wildfire?"

She edged back, sass taking to the edges of her face. "You told me I was never going to get enough. I think we should probably test it."

A growl ripped free.

Playful possession, and I sent her a smirk.

"You want it? Then get on your hands and knees." I tugged her hair back a little harder, knowing it was going to light the fire inside her.

That hypothesis proved correct when surprise widened her bright eyes before a gush of desire rushed in to darken everything else.

"You want me on my knees for you, *King*?"

Seemed fair since that's where she had me.

"That's right. I want to see that ass in the air so I can get a good peek at all that sweetness dripping for me."

She slowly slipped off my lap and shuffled around, though she kept looking at me from over her shoulder.

Soft skin glowed in the faint moonlight as she bared herself to me.

Her ass was round and full, and her slit was still soaked just like I knew it would be.

Lust smacked me in the face, and my already raging dick twitched with greed.

"You're such a good girl, aren't you, Brinley Webber? Way you ache for me?"

Her thighs quivered, and I slipped from the bed and onto my feet.

Rising to my full height.

She was still there, on all fours but facing to my right. She gave a tiny yelp when I snagged her by the waist and dragged her around so she was hitched to the edge of the bed in front of me.

Hips swaying in a slow, entrancing dance as she gave me the most enticing view of her beautiful backside.

The delicious expanse of skin and the mesmerizing slope of her spine.

I ran my palms up her sides and back down, gliding over the hot flesh.

"I'm going to memorize every part of you, Brinley. Explore you from bottom to top. Mark myself all over every inch. Inside and out."

A shudder rolled through her, and she kept watching me from over her shoulder.

"I'm going to hold you to that."

Fuck, what this woman could do to me.

My being roiled with need. The hunger she elicited insatiable.

I splayed my hands wide, gripping her by the waist and skimming down so I was palming her ass cheeks.

I spread her a little.

Exposing all that pink, swollen flesh.

"Such a pretty pussy."

She gulped and rocked back, the tension that wound between us amplifying.

Kneading her hip with one hand, I let the fingers of the other wander through her lips, barely brushing through the folds and up her cleft.

Brinley whimpered. "Silas…what are you trying to do to me?"

"I'm showing you that you're mine. That you're mine to please." I edged forward, pressing my bare chest to her back so I could mutter in her ear, "And you're going to fucking like it."

Another whimper, and she was pushing back, trying to grind her ass against my cock. "I already like it. I like it so much."

"I'm only getting started with you."

I let my lips take an eager path down her spine while my hands coasted down over her ribs and dipped into the divot at her waist.

Then I shoved two fingers deep into the heat of her cunt.

She gasped and arched.

"Are you mine?" I demanded, voice cut low.

I didn't know why I couldn't stop asking it. Maybe I'd just been so convinced that I couldn't have this that I was terrified I was dreaming it.

Making this shit up because it seemed so much more unrealistic than the preposterous life that I actually lived.

"You know the answer to that, Silas. I'm yours."

I drove them in twice, winding her up. "That's right. You're mine."

She clutched around my fingers, and her hands curled into the tangled sheets. "Silas."

"You want more, Little Wildfire? You want me to burn you up the way you've been burning me?"

"Yes, and I don't ever want you to stop."

She whimpered when I pulled my fingers out, then she was moaning a dazed sound when I spread her again and dove in.

Licking a path from her clit to her ass. Lapping and suckling as I went.

Brinley nearly lost it, her body rocking back in a bid for more. "Oh, fuck, Silas…"

"You taste like I already marked you, baby."

She laughed an incongruent sound, her hair swishing around her, the tips brushing the mattress below. "Why do I get the feeling that marking is going to go a whole lot deeper?"

"Because I'm going to mark you everywhere. I'm going to make sure no one will mistake exactly who you belong to."

Someplace inside me warned that I was making oaths that were going to turn around and strike me like a viper bite, but I didn't give a fuck.

Not when it came to her.

I dove back in, spreading her wider so I could drive my tongue into her pussy. Fucking it in and out before I delved lower so I could get to her throbbing clit that was begging for attention. I let my fingers wander her cleft as I did. Roaming along the sensitive flesh, already knowing it was going to send Brinley out of her mind.

She went feral. Clawing and clutching and grinding herself against my face.

"Silas. Please. I need you."

It was just as I thought.

She liked it hard and everywhere.

"Knew you were my match," I rumbled.

I grabbed my cock and lined it up with her center. I thrust in so deep that she bowed forward on a muted shout.

But it was Brinley who was impaling me.

A total blackout. No sense or reason but the feel of her.

"So fucking tight and good, aren't you, baby?" I could barely speak with the way she knocked the oxygen from my lungs, and my hands fucking shook as I gripped onto her hips to keep myself steady.

I was buried to the hilt. Filling her so full neither of us could breathe.

"Silas…you…I can't…"

She was having trouble speaking, too.

"You like that, Brinley? You like me stuffing you so full that you can't feel anything else?"

"Yes. I don't want to feel anything else."

"It's a good thing because I plan on having you again and again. This pussy belongs to me."

She throbbed at the claim, gasps of acquiescence rolling up her throat as she wound her hands tighter in the blankets. "I'm yours…now fuck me."

Shit.

I couldn't stop the grin from taking to my mouth.

She really was meant for me.

"As you wish, baby."

I pulled out nearly to the tip then slammed back home.

So deep both of us were nearly knocked to our knees.

Brinley swayed forward with a desperate heave.

A grunt left me as I hung on to her hips.

The sight of me buried in her had to be the best thing I'd ever seen.

Tucked so tight in this woman.

My chest stretched to the point of blowing.

Ruined.

I was so fucking ruined.

Brinley bucked back. "Please."

"My eager girl."

"I need you."

She had no shame in admitting it.

"You have me, Wildfire, you have me."

I started to move, driving in and out of her perfect cunt in hard, punishing strokes.

"The way you feel. Nothing in the world. Nothing could compare to this," I grunted as I took her deep and long.

Her ass smacked against me with each thrust.

Gusts of air shot from her with each one, and they quickly turned to the chant of my name as I drove her toward a height that I had only ever reached with her.

Brinley Webber my pinnacle.

She moaned and begged as I fucked her, quickening the rhythm with each demanding stroke.

My balls tightened and pleasure prowled up and down my spine.

A buzz that rushed across my flesh.

"The sight of you like this. Taking my cock the way you were meant to do. So perfect. Way you fit me. The way you take me. You are everything. Everything, baby."

The praises toppled from my mouth as I gave her my sheer and utter truth.

This woman who'd crashed into my world and grabbed my heart with a glance.

And I knew there wasn't a single thing that I wouldn't do for her.

I'd give it all.

Give her my life because she'd given mine back to me.

My spirit alive and screaming out for hers.

That energy twisted around us and wrapped us in chains that I didn't want to be free of.

I leaned over her, taking a fistful of her hair and angling her head around so I could get to that hot mouth.

We clashed in a reckless kiss that equaled the mayhem of my thrusts.

Both of us devolving into an erratic urgency that promised we were never going to get enough.

"So good. Such a good girl. My perfect girl. My match. Wildfire."

I could feel her getting close.

The way she tightened and a shimmery sheen of ecstasy glimmered from her skin.

"Give it to me, Brinley. Give it to me."

She split with a guttural moan, and an earthquake rocked through her body.

"King." That nickname serrated from her tongue.

She might have called me king, but I was the one who was kneeling at her feet.

She throbbed and spasmed around me as an orgasm tore through her body, her arousal slick and hot and dragging me right toward ecstasy.

Pleasure blinding as I stroked twice more before I exploded.

Our tongues tangled as I poured into her.

The bliss that she ignited in my veins and streaked out to touch every place that once was vacant.

Warming all the hollow places.

I kept kissing her mad, needing her close. For her to understand what she'd done to me. That she'd changed me. Opened my eyes. Filled the holes that only she could fit.

"Made for me," I mumbled into the kiss. A kiss that slowed as the aftershocks twitching between us faded.

"Made for me," she whispered back, and I was gathering her up in my arms and carrying her to my shower. Flipping it on and letting it warm before I stepped inside.

Intent on taking care of my girl. Adore her like I promised.

I stepped into the heated spray.

Water pelted and steam surrounded.

I kept Brinley locked in my arms. Refusing to let her go as I washed her hair and body.

She grinned a sloppy grin.

Loved up and dopey.

Cutest fucking thing I'd ever seen.

"Are you resolved on washing your scent off me, Silas Mercer?"

I grinned back. "Don't worry, baby. Give me a minute, and I'll dirty you right back up."

I just prayed I didn't taint her with the blood that stained my hands.

54

Brinley

It was early when the smell of bacon wafting up from the kitchen nudged me from sleep, and the tinkling voices drifting up with it brought a smile to my face.

It was instant.

The rush of joy and satisfaction that sped through me the moment I came to coherency.

I wasn't going to lie. My body felt completely wrung out, but it was in the best of ways.

Like I'd been resculpted by Silas.

I had to admit I really liked his brand of art.

I lay for a little bit, just listening.

Elena's laughter and Kai's little giggle.

A rumble of something deep.

Silas.

He was there, rambling around downstairs.

I bit down on my bottom lip, my heart pressing full, then I slipped out of bed, used the restroom, and went padding downstairs.

Elena was just coming up, and a gentle grin filled her face when she saw me midway down the steps.

She was dressed in sequined pajamas with kissing lips all over them, her dark hair twisted into a braid.

"Well, good morning, bestie." She issued it with all her adorable sass.

My already overflowing heart thrilled.

I got this.

I got to keep her.

I got to keep all of them.

"And good morning to you." It was riddled with emotion.

She stalled out a little, concern twisting into her brow. "Is everything okay?"

"Everything is amazing," I told her.

You know, other than the fact that Silas and his club were going out on some secret mission to avenge his mother that somehow involved my brother.

Something that would protect me and Elena.

It was so convoluted, but I had faith that Silas would help me understand once it was over.

Sweet suspicion wound into Elena's expression. "You seem different."

Her eyes patted me down like she was going to find contraband stashed under my sleep shirt.

"Nope, nothing different here. Is coffee ready?" I peeped, angling for a distraction.

I had a hunch Silas wouldn't want me to be shouting from the heavens about what happened between us last night. Not until he figured out how to handle it.

"Do you think we're heathens?" she deadpanned.

I choked over a laugh. "Have you visited the clubhouse?"

She laughed, too, and she kept ascending the stairs. "Okay, fine, but heathens like their coffee just as much as anyone else."

"Thank God."

She went to go by me, only she grabbed my hand as she passed. "You look happy, Brinley, and that makes me happy, too."

And I wondered how long it'd been since I'd been truly, truly happy. Without the constraints of trying to care for my brother and knowing I was failing.

Failing my mother.

Failing myself.

And I knew I didn't have to bear all of that alone anymore.

I knew I was supported.

Knew I found the piece that I'd been missing.

"I am," I whispered.

Her nod was soft like maybe she understood it, then she went bounding up the rest of the stairs and down the hall.

While I edged closer to the kitchen.

Swells of Silas's aura rippled out of the archway.

A freaking beacon that I couldn't do anything but follow.

I turned through the opening.

I'd thought my heart was at capacity, but God, it ballooned by five sizes. I guess I finally understood what the Grinch was feeling.

Kai was in his highchair, eating these dry little snacks that melted in his mouth, his nose all scrunched up in joy when he saw me. "*Bwinwey*!"

When I walked out of his room last night, I thought it'd be the last time I'd ever see him, and my soul broke free at the sight of his precious face.

The promise of what Silas had asked of me echoing through my spirit.

Filling every empty crevice.

"Hi, baby." I could barely speak it.

"You 'wake?"

"Yep, I'm awake and right here."

"*Oh-kay*," he drew out the way he always did before he used his chubby little fingers to chase down another piece.

Then my attention drifted, drawn to Silas on the other side of the counter.

Standing at the freaking stove flipping bacon.

Hair messy and not wearing a shirt.

Looking like the kind of mayhem that promised you were in deep, deep trouble, but it was the grin he cast me that nearly did me in.

Something wry and gentle and possessive.

Meems must have still been upstairs in her room because she was nowhere to be found.

"Good morning." Silas's voice was growly and deep and carved in a tenderness few would expect from him.

Hazel eyes dragged over me in slow perusal.

Tingles lifted in their wake, and I shifted on my bare feet.

I was wearing a sleep shirt that hit me mid-thigh, my hair a mess from the number of times he'd been tugging on it last night.

"Good morning." It scraped out like I'd found my voice for the first time in twenty years.

A smirk ridged his wicked mouth. "You look…off balance this morning. Did your world get rocked?"

I choked over the surprise, letting the easiness he wore wind into my mood. I started to move toward the kitchen. "I might have experienced an earthquake or two. There's a fair chance it affected my equilibrium."

Holding onto a big fork, he shifted a fraction.

The man stood there covered in all those designs. So freaking hot and menacing.

He looked so out of place that I had to hold back a delirious laugh.

Was this really happening?

"Huh, think I might have experienced an earthquake or two myself," he rumbled, gaze sparking with mirth.

"Is that right?" I murmured as I eased around the counter.

Even though my fingers itched, I didn't move all the way for him.

If I did, I'd probably try to jump him.

"That's right." It rolled out like possession.

The energy radiating off him had my hands shaking as I opened the cabinet so I could grab a mug, then I fumbled as I pulled out the carafe since Silas slowly prowled up behind me.

An imposing force that charged through the middle of me.

His nose hit the side of my neck at the same second his hands curled around my waist, and he tucked me against his hot, bare flesh.

"You have any idea what it does to me, Brinley? Seeing you waltz into this kitchen looking like my favorite treat and knowing I'm going to get to see it every day for the rest of my life?"

A tremble rolled through me, and I released a shaky exhalation. "A treat, huh? And here I thought I meant a whole lot more than that."

I managed the razzing through the need that spun through my body.

I could feel Silas's grin against the side of my neck. "Thought you knew I had a sweet tooth? I'm good with having nothing else."

"You'd better be because you're stuck with me."

He softened and hardened all at the same time, and his hands splayed wide over my abdomen, sending thunderbolts of heat firing through my belly.

He pressed his nose deeper into my neck, inhaling before he mumbled, "You're everything, Brinley. A new beginning and my end."

"You're the home I didn't know I needed."

He slowly turned me around.

The air simmered, a driving song that whispered around us.

Every hair on my body lifted in attention.

His palm slipped to my cheek. "Wildfire."

My hands landed on his bare sides. "King."

An adoring grin flitted over his mouth, our gazes tangling in joy and commitment before he set his other hand on my face and pulled me to him.

His plush lips danced against mine. Featherlight brushes that I felt to my toes.

This kiss was slow.

Penetrating.

Winding right down to our souls.

Dizziness spun through my head, and I gripped onto him tighter.

"I love you." He murmured it as he swept back and forth over my lips.

A frisson of perfection buzzed through me. "I love you. So much."

"Ahhh!" The screech behind us stalled us out, and Silas's spine went rigid.

"I knew it. Oh my God, I knew it." A profusion of giggles rolled out of Elena. "I mean, I've been calling this since day one. The two of you were so obviously going to go boom. You had to be blind not to see it. All I'm saying is it's about time the two of you caught up."

Silas slowly shifted around.

Uncertainty rippled from him. Unsure if he should deny it and pretend like what was clearly happening was not happening or straight fess it up.

I bit down on my bottom lip to stop myself from being the one dishing the juicy details.

It wasn't my place, and I could feel the war go down in the middle of him.

This was brand-new territory for him, too.

Some of the eccentricity drained from Elena, and she looked at me.

"Does your heart know?"

There was so much hope embedded in her words that it made me ache.

I glanced at Kai who was babbling away in his highchair, while I did my best not to reach for Silas again.

But instead, he was the one who was reaching for me, sliding his arm around my waist and drawing me to his side as he murmured, "Yeah, Elena, my heart knows."

Frustration infiltrated his voice. "But this isn't something we can go shouting about right now. Not in the middle of this mess. Situation is delicate enough."

Elena's head barely shook. "Love isn't something you should be ashamed of, Silas."

"I'm not ashamed."

"But you all treat it like it's something that should be. Hedge it up behind rules and ultimatums. It needs to change if any of us are ever going to truly be free."

And I thought maybe Elena was the smartest one of all of us.

55

Silas

"Tomorrow night this goes down."

I looked around at all my patched-in members who filled the dimly-lit room.

Church packed shoulder to shoulder with every one of them.

The single chandelier cast an eerie light over their faces where it hung in the middle of the old, rustic table, the images Madman had painted crawling across the walls and ceiling as if they'd come alive.

Monsters bred for a night like this.

Ansty, my crew shifted in their chairs and on their feet. Like maybe I was delivering a death sentence.

My guts fisted at the dread that for some it likely would be. It made me sick to think about losing any one of them.

But they were in this as deep as me.

I met their unwavering gazes.

Trevan's.

Phoenix's.

Slowly making a path over the rest of the men.

I could feel their loyalty and their devotion radiating from their marrow.

Clearing my throat, I leaned back in the high-backed chair at the head of the table.

Their leader. The one who brought them into battle and the one charged with getting them out on the other side.

"You were patched in as a Crimson Crow knowing our mission," I said, voice rough. "Knowing we weren't just here to wreak havoc. Weren't here to proliferate crime and injustice. You knew you weren't going to be running drugs or arms for the sake of greed. You knew we were infiltrating the filth in this world and doing your best to help eradicate its stain."

Volatility curled through the tension.

"You made an oath to take the violence each one of us already possessed and turn it toward something good. And this job? Crimson Crows was born from it. It was the thing that turned the direction of my purpose and set it on a different course."

I paused, letting my words sink deep. "I have been after this motherfucker since I was sixteen years old, and he's always remained just out of reach. Spreading his vileness on the land."

I would never forget the night that changed everything. When the vengeance I'd sought had been transformed.

Restructured.

Iron Owls had splintered the next month, and I'd taken the few men I trusted and created Crimson Crows.

But we were no longer riding for corruption.

We were riding for liberation.

It's your heart.

It's your heart.

"Tomorrow, that reign ends."

I spun the heel of my tumbler against the wood, the scars carved inside me threatening to bust wide open.

But in a way that promised all of this was right.

That maybe in the end, I was living a life worthy of the belief my mother had in me.

That maybe…maybe this offering was enough.

"You've already been briefed," I said around the rocks in my throat. "You know your missions and your destinations and that our friends from Moonlit Ridge and Redemption Hills will be taking up our backs."

I'd gotten word that it wasn't only Cash and his crew who were joining forces, but the guys from Redemption Hills, including Trent who'd been Iron Owls' vice president.

Old friends coming to our aid to ensure this job was done.

"Everyone has to be their sharpest," I continued. "Their keenest. Their cruelest. There will be no place for mercy for the merciless."

It had to be clean or we would be done.

The same as every other job we enacted, but this one was on a scale none of us had ever faced.

Phoenix rocked beside me, violence skimming his flesh as he fisted a giant hand on the table.

"This mission is big, but I believe in this calling, and I believe in you. Be careful. Be wise. And come home."

A riot of fists banged on the table, and the deep resonation of their chants banged through the room. "Born in chaos. Forged by iron. Sworn to vengeance."

They all stood after they said it, the lot of them flooding out through the door and into the long hall that led to the bar.

Half of them clapped me on the back as they went, murmuring every variation of "We have this."

We did.

We had to.

It couldn't turn out any other way.

My chest tightened as I pushed back from my chair.

Anxious to get back to the house but knowing I needed to keep up appearances. Without a doubt, I'd be out in that bar throwing back old-fashioneds for half the night.

Wanting to be curled up next to Brinley instead.

Tucked into her beauty and held in her faith.

Trevan and Phoenix came to stand beside me.

"You good?" Trevan asked. Concern twisted in his brow.

"Yeah. I've been waiting a long, long time for this."

I failed twice at trying to end them in the past, but this time, our only choice was seeing it through.

"And what are we going to do about the girl and Dereck?" It came as shrapnel from Phoenix's mouth.

Protectiveness bound every inch of me, and I wanted to lay it out. Tell him exactly what I had planned. It was fucking painful to muster the lie. "We're going to do exactly as planned. He keeps his end of the bargain, and he walks."

I couldn't bring myself to specifically mention Brinley.

Speculation traipsed across the dark lines of his face. "I don't trust him, Prez. I think you're making a mistake."

I exhaled a sharp breath, and I delivered the words low and hard. "I made the deal, so the deal stands. Don't fucking question it."

I didn't normally rule with a heavy hand, and I considered Phoenix one of my closest friends, but I couldn't entertain what he was clearly suggesting.

I didn't deal in betrayals, especially not when it had brought Brinley to me.

Phoenix's tattooed hands curled into fists, so clearly trying to temper what he wanted to say. His jaw worked overtime before he gritted, "Understood."

Then he turned on his heel and stormed out. I blew out a sigh, and Trevan squeezed my shoulder. "Tensions are high, brother. Don't fret. It's all gonna work out exactly as it should."

I scraped a palm down my face. "Terrified I'm leading my crew to their deaths."

"Of course, you are, which is why every single one of them will follow you into battle. Now get your ass out there and share a drink with your men."

I gave him a tight nod, then followed him out into the dusky hollow of the hall.

Music vibrated the walls, but it was the frenetic energy blistering the air that singed across my skin.

Awareness thrummed through my veins as Trevan pushed out in front of me and into the bar.

I shouldn't have been surprised to find Elena and Brinley there.

Two of them dressed up for a party, though looking so out of place. Standouts from the rest of the women who pranced around.

Even though we had Church, women had been permitted tonight, knowing the men needed to indulge in that type of revelry before we set out on this mission tomorrow.

It didn't matter how many times I looked at Brinley. Every time, my guts tangled.

Wild curls around her. Wearing that same short, satin skirt that was baby blue and hemmed in beige lace that she'd worn the first morning to the office.

Legs so fucking long, especially with those nude pumps.

A stunner walking around on my property.

The fucking sun that had risen on my life.

I could barely fucking breathe.

Trevan leaned in close to my ear and muttered, "I don't know who the fuck you think you're fooling, I just hope you give up trying to fool yourself."

I'd given that shit up days ago, but I couldn't tell him.

Not yet.

So instead, I waltzed behind the bar and nabbed a bottle of whiskey. Lulu tossed me a knowing wink from where she was hustling to serve about ten of my men, and I strode back out and slinked into the shadows.

I tipped the entire bottle back and took a long pull as I watched Brinley and Elena dance.

Lights strobed all over them, but Brinley was the one who was shining into the darkest corners of my being.

Seeping in the way she did.

Eyes flitting to me every few minutes, seductress tempting me into disorder as I tried to force myself to sit still in my seat.

I kept swilling from the bottle, but there was little hope it would quench the thirst.

It only amped it.

I didn't know how much time had passed when Brinley leaned in and whispered something to Elena before she turned and strode through the swinging door that led into the hall.

It turned out Brinley Webber had a hook directly in my soul because I couldn't do anything but stand.

I set the whiskey bottle on a table as I slinked along the outskirts of the bar.

Trying to play it cool.

Not to draw attention to myself.

I slipped out into the hall thirty seconds behind her.

She was there, standing in the middle of it, staring back at me like she knew I had no choice but to follow.

"What do you think you're doing?" It rolled out like a threat.

"Looking for trouble, apparently." Her voice was pure temptation.

"It's me who has found the trouble since I can't stay away from you. I'm supposed to be standing with my men tonight, rallying them for tomorrow's fight, and the only thing I want is to get inside of you."

The bulge against my jeans was proof.

"I'm sorry. I just missed you. Do you want me to go home?" A moment's sincerity filled her words, and fuck, the way she said home penetrated to the depths.

Truth that she got how important this was.

I took two steps toward her, my voice lowering further. "I don't want you to be anywhere but with me. Right now."

She heaved a breath. "Good because I don't want to be anywhere, either. You're leaving tomorrow..." Worry filtered into it before she forced it off and lifted her chin. "So I need you now."

Pride swelled.

I fucking loved that she asked for what she needed. Wasn't shy about it. No fear or questions between us.

I took another step forward.

Our connection thrashed.

Chains of fire that whipped around us.

I reached out and took a fistful of those wild curls, and I angled in close. "What's it you need?"

She rubbed me over my jeans as she sent me a sly, sexy smirk, though the blaze in her amber eyes promised of the seriousness. "Your heart and your cock."

"Mmm," I hummed, running my nose along her jaw. "Good for you because you get them both."

But it was me who had it good.

She kept jacking me over my jeans. Sending shockwaves of pleasure shearing through my veins. My need for her nearly sent me into a tailspin.

A nosedive into this sweet bedlam.

And I realized we were standing in the middle of the hall and we could be exposed at any time. Funny it wouldn't have mattered if I was fucking any one of the bunnies out in the hall.

It was this one woman who was illicit.

A secret I didn't want to fucking keep.

Still, I grabbed her by the hand and hauled her deeper down the hall.

Passed the bathroom I was pretty sure she'd told Elena she was heading to. I opened the door to the first bedroom only to snap it closed when I found Fuse and Jupe in there with three women.

A soft breath of surprise hit the back of my neck, Brinley catching a glimpse of what was going down inside.

I led her deeper, bypassing every door, not able to picture myself taking her into one of the shared rooms where I'd had uncountable women before.

Yeah. I was fully aware that I was crossing so many lines when I guided her all the way to the end of the hall to the massive Church doors.

The Crimson Crows emblem emblazoned across both sides.

A seal of its sanctity.

One I was about to desecrate.

I stalled for one beat before I tossed one side open and pulled her into the wisping darkness.

Heat saturated the air, and her heels clattered on the hard floor as I dragged her up to the head of the table.

I could feel her attention racing. Trying to categorize everything she was seeing. The grim images painted on the walls, the demons and ghosts more alive than when these men had actually been breathing.

"You see what you've done to me, Brinley? It's forbidden for anyone to be in these walls except for the patched-in members of Crimson Crows. You've made me break every fucking one of my own rules."

And I couldn't bring myself to care.

She exhaled a shaky breath, and I kept hold of her as I dragged the high-backed chair that appeared more like a throne from the head of the table.

Putting her in its place.

"If I'm the fucking king, then you're my queen." It was a scrape of air as I pushed her chest down onto the table.

Her skirt rode up so high, the satiny slip of her underwear bunched up in her soaked pussy.

I knelt behind her, and her long legs shook as I slowly peeled the scrap of material down.

I spread her, licking her into a needy puddle before I flipped her around and planted her ass on the rough wood.

"Heels on the table."

She rushed to comply, those high, high heels hooked to the edge. She leaned back on her hands, her skirt bunched up around her waist and her cunt dripping.

I took a single step back so I could appreciate her trembling in need.

Slowly, I unbuckled my belt while I watched that Little Wildfire burn.

I flicked the button on my jeans and undid the fly, shoving them down enough to free myself.

I stroked myself from root to tip.

"From now on, every time I sit at the head of this table, I'm going to imagine when I fucked you on it."

A mewl rolled from her, and she lifted her ass a little from the wood.

"You want it, Brinley? You want this?"

She shoved her fingers into her pussy then lifted them to my mouth. "Why don't you have a taste for yourself and see?"

Vixen.

Seductress.

I sucked them deep, lapping her up as I fully stepped up to the table.

Committing a thousand sins as I brought my tip to her lips, running the barbell that ran through my head over her clit.

She clawed and clutched at me before I shifted and shoved in.

We both arched.

Knocked the fuck out.

Bliss in a beat.

Her walls throbbed around me as she struggled to adjust.

"Silas," she rasped.

I took her by the knees, still buried deep. "This is so you know you'll have this part of me, too. Just give me a little time, and I promise you, there will be no secrets between us."

"I trust you."

"Good."

Then I fucked her right on Crimson Crows's table. Thrusting into her in rough, rigid strokes.

Knocking the breath out of her with every stroke. Our bodies colliding, rocking and gripping.

Her fingers in my cut and my hands on her hips.

Lifting her every time I surged forward.

Sweat drenched our flesh as the type of pleasure neither of us thought we'd find spun us into ecstasy.

She moaned and shouted and I didn't give a fuck if the whole MC heard.

Because she was mine, and it was fucking time everyone knew it.

56

Silas

I knelt so I could snatch Brinley's underwear from the floor then slowly worked them back up her legs. Staring up at her as I did.

Ragged pants jutted from her chest and wisped from her mouth.

My girl still trembling from the aftershocks.

Aglow.

Aflame.

So hot I was worried she might burn through the polar icecaps.

I resituated her underwear then stood, scraping my palms up and down the outside of her thighs, trying to bring us back down to solid ground.

But there was no tranquility. Not when I knew what had to be done.

Brinley Webber wasn't a fucking secret, and I wouldn't go into tomorrow's raid with any of my men still believing she was a pawn in this game.

"Are you okay?" The words were coarse.

A strangled laugh worked out of her. "I think you're intent on breaking me, Silas Mercer."

I cracked her a soft grin and ran my knuckles along the sharp line of her jaw. "Don't act like you can't handle me. Bravest, fiercest woman I've ever met."

"Made for you," she murmured on a breath.

My knuckles traced the defined ridges of her lips. "That's right. Made for me. Written for me just like I was written for you. Etched so fucking deep that I know you were marked there long ago, and I think I'd been unknowingly searching for you ever since. Swear my soul recognized you the second I saw you."

A wistful smile played across her entire face, and the love that we'd found pounded around us.

A snare.

A base drum.

A beat of life.

"I felt you everywhere. Swirling around me and gliding right under my skin," she whispered.

"Guess it's true what they say. Hearts always find their way home."

"And I'm so thankful I found you."

I swept the pad of my thumb over the sharp cut of her cheek, then I edged back and resituated myself back into my jeans.

Taking her by the hand, I weaved our fingers together. A knitting that couldn't be undone. "Come on."

Her cheeks pinked as she slipped off the table and onto those heels, and one of her lush curls brushed my jaw as she leaned into me. "I'm sorry that we came here. I just…I really needed to see you."

Worry gushed from her spirit.

I turned her to face me and tipped up her chin. "Everything's going to be okay. I promise you."

That oath was cemented inside me.

It had to be. This all had to be put to an end because it was time that all of us lived.

Hurricane eyes flashed, tenderness glistening in the flecks. I stood there in the emotion rustling between us before I swallowed hard and turned on my boot, still holding onto her hand as I led her out the door.

The massive, ominous wood clanged shut behind us, and I squeezed her fingers in mine as I hauled her all the way down the hall and to the swinging door that led into the bar.

I didn't hesitate.

I shoved it open and dragged her through it.

Our fingers bound because our souls were tied.

Everyone there must have felt the gush of crackling flames surge out with it because every eye in the place swiveled toward us.

And I lifted my head in a show of power as I strode with her out onto the floor, shuffled her out in front of me, and wrapped an arm around her chest, bringing her back to the thunder of my heart.

It didn't matter that the music screamed. My voice lifted over it with the claim. "This is your notice. Brinley fucking belongs to me, and she's not going anywhere."

I met the shocked stares of all the men gaping back, a challenge in the lilt of my chin, daring them to say something about it.

Trevan only fucking smirked.

I told you so.

But at the far corner of the bar, I could feel the disappointment radiating back.

Phoenix glaring from the shadows, demanding to know what I'd done.

57

Brinley

The faintest morning light infiltrated the drapes, glittering tendrils of gold that curled through the darkness and brushed across the harsh angles of Silas's foreboding, beautiful face.

I would have never guessed that the time would come when I would find complete comfort in it.

He kept running the pad of his thumb over my cheek as he stared at me through the gauzy light like he was also having a hard time believing that he could look at me this way.

The connection we shared hummed between us.

Commitment.

The claim he had made in front of his entire MC last night twining us together.

But fear was also present.

A feeling that had crept into the room the moment we'd woken tangled with the first rays of morning light.

"I'm scared," I finally admitted on a whisper into the stillness that wrapped us whole.

Everything that had brought us together culminated tonight.

Knowing eyes slowly blinked. "I won't tell you not to be, but I will promise that I will come back to you. There is nothing in this world that could keep me away from you, Brinley Webber. Not when I just found you. I would decimate a fucking army. Topple a thousand cities. Crawl through Hell to get back to you. Nothing will stop me. Not when I finally have this light to guide me home."

Relief swelled, my belief in him, and I scratched my fingernails through the stubble on his jaw.

I was inundated with a rise of old sorrow and pain mixed with the peace of his promise.

My mother's weathered, broken face.

Her one request of me.

Dereck's eager, innocent smile before everything had gone to shit.

I felt overwhelmed by the love I would always have for him, no matter what.

"Bring my brother back to me?" It was a coarse, harrowed plea.

The arrow that slaked down Silas's spine was almost imperceptible, but I felt it like I was the one being staked.

His gaze churned in unease for a beat before his chin dipped. "I promise you."

He paused, attention darting to the wall as he gathered himself, swiping his tongue over his dried lips, before his focus returned.

"You probably won't see me for the rest of the day. We need to prep and prepare before we roll out. I'll have seven Crows here standing guard, plus a bunch of prospects."

He winced with the last. I could tell he hated it. Hated that he had to leave us, and he kept brushing his fingers through my curls like in doing it, he might be able to leave a piece of himself here.

I hated it, too, but I wasn't so selfish that I'd beg him to stay even though I kind of felt like getting onto my knees. Maybe find some handcuffs so I could shackle him to my wrist.

"We'll be fine and waiting for you when you return."

His nod was jerky, and he took my hand and pressed a bunch of kisses to the knuckles. "I love you, Brinley. You are my redemption that I never saw coming."

His eyes flicked all over my face, his hands so tender as they kept weaving through the ringlets of my hair. "I swear I will spend my life cherishing you. Adoring you. Protecting you and uplifting you. Both feeding your desires and satisfying them."

Intensity blazed from him. "I have every intention of putting a property patch on you the second I get back, but what that really means is that I'm yours. Always and fucking forever."

My chest expanded. This love thrashing and pressing within its confines. "I think I'm going to like being your old lady."

I attempted to say it lightly, but it was lumpy and unpolished.

Silas's grin was soft. "Yeah, baby, I'm going to make sure you do."

• • •

I showered and dressed with shaky hands. Wandered downstairs, held Kai and peppered a million kisses over his face.

Uncertain looks were shared with Meems and Elena. Both of them were so much more somber in their morning greetings than normal.

There was no missing the dread and worry that filled each second that passed.

Or maybe we were just feeding it into each other. The way it'd amped and increased in me the second Silas had grabbed his cut from the back of the bedroom sofa and strode out the door.

On a mission I didn't completely understand but supported one hundred percent.

Elena had thought it was strange that I was going into the office, but the truth was, there was no chance I could sit idle in that house for the entire day and night and not completely go out of my mind.

Wondering.

Worrying.

Waiting.

Wanting to know all the answers to the questions swirling in a vortex in my brain.

But I had to trust that Silas would give me all of that once everything was said and done.

Trust that it was better that I remained in the dark until it was over.

So I headed to the shop office, opened the laptop, and set to work.

Trying to organize this aspect of Silas's life while a charged yet bated chaos took to the property. The air thick and heavy as motorcycles came and went.

I focused the best that I could on the receivables that had come in. Depositing checks on the app, marking the accounts as paid, sending out reminder invoices to the few that still hadn't been received.

Anxiety burned through every beat. My skin prickling and my heart pounding.

I tried to focus, but my attention kept snagging on the row of icons at the bottom of the laptop where every few minutes a little folder symbol would pop up before it would recede.

It was clearly a shared folder.

I didn't know what it was, but every time that icon shot into my vision, it felt like a coming implosion.

Awareness came on fast. Pins and needles skittered across my flesh.

There were all those old folders I'd checked out before, and never once had I noticed one of those icons flash before.

I tried to ignore it, clicking into a new program so I could pay some of the shop's bills, only it flashed again.

Disquiet gripped my throat, and I glanced around the empty office. All covert and sneaky.

I hated that it was the same sensation I'd gotten the first night I was here and sneaked out of the room where I'd been placed.

Knowing I was traversing dangerous ground that was about to open from below and swallow me.

Following the path anyway since I was reckless like that.

I wavered, hesitated, before I finally clicked on the icon.

It was easy to tell myself that Silas had given me the laptop and he hadn't given me any instructions about staying out of certain things.

As far as I was concerned, it was free range.

Except this folder?

It came with a passcode.

My stomach twined in a torturous twist, and my heart rattled in my chest.

Why I was so unsettled, I wasn't sure. But some things in life triggered a sixth sense, and this was one of them.

I swept my tongue over my bottom lip. Why couldn't I just freaking trust the way that Silas had asked me to?

I loved the man.

Desperately.

Wholly.

Didn't I?

So why was I looking over my shoulder again to make sure no one was around before I turned back, fingers poised over the keys?

Contemplating.

Adding.

Solving.

My nails clacked over the keys.

Silas's birthdate.

Nope.

Elena's.

Nu-uh.

Kai's.

Frustration spun through me when I found it wasn't his, either.

Crap, I didn't even know Meems's or Brody's birthdays.

I tried a few different variations of Crimson Crows, though I was pretty sure that would be way too generic and obvious.

And then it hit me.

A solid piece of reality.

My heart jackhammered as I typed in the code, already knowing it would grant me access.

It's your heart followed by the date below it.

He never confirmed it, but I knew it was the day his mother had been killed.

A surprised gasp left me when it granted me access, and I realized there had to be a hundred different files inside.

Different than in every other folder that I'd clicked into the moment Silas had originally left me with this laptop, though I'd given up halfway through since there was nothing of value. Assuming they were all the same and contained old invoices, I'd never opened this one.

I clicked into a random file. It was just a regular Word document. In every way, it appeared inconsequential.

Somehow, I knew it was not.

It was a date and a town in central California.

I fumbled for my phone and inputted both into the search.

The results populated, and there was a news article that stood out above the others.

Eight men found slaughtered at a house on the outskirts of town.

My spirit stretched taut like a rubber band, and I inhaled a steadying breath and clicked into another.

Another document.

Another date and town.

Seven men. All dead. Their murders remained an unsolved mystery.

I clicked through more.

More dates and towns.

More dead men.

All with suspected ties to criminal organizations.

Mafia. Cartels. Gangs.

My blood sloshed, a flood that I could feel gushing through my veins.

I knew.

Of course I knew, and I promised him that I didn't care, but seeing this threw me off balance.

Shuddered through me on a torrent of uncertainty.

It was the *whys* that made it so hard to comprehend. No longer could I fathom Silas a cold-blooded killer.

Then there were different documents.

Money.

So much money.

Money so different from the shop money I'd been tasked to track.

Millions and millions.

No documents to indicate its origination or its destination.

Just numbers without dollar signs, though instinct told me what they represented.

I wondered if stacks of cash were buried at the back of the property with a heap of bodies.

I thought I could handle it, everything that Silas was, but right then, my stomach was revolting.

Bile climbing my throat as the horrors were marked like lashes across my conscience.

How deep did this go?

How far?

How *horrible*?

I attempted to tamp it back. Come tomorrow, Silas would explain and everything would be okay.

Or was I only lying to myself?

Falling for a killer and pretending like all was fine and dandy?

No big deal.

Is this how decent people were led astray?

The icon flashed again, and I knew there was a new document being saved to the folder.

Everything trembled.

My hands, my spirit, and my heart.

So far, I'd avoided the ones that had come in today.

Maybe some part of me was aware they were going to change everything.

Maybe instinct told me this new awakening would be crushed at its conception.

I glanced over my shoulder again, even though I knew Silas wasn't anywhere around, the power that normally radiated in from the shop silenced in his absence.

The entire place was eerily quiet. The only sound was the raging of every one of my senses.

Each one hollered inside me. A brutal clanging as I clicked into one of the documents, which was another simple Word file.

I frowned when I read the two sentences the file contained.

It has to happen. Too much liability.

I blew out a sigh, realizing I'd clicked on a random one, so I reorganized the files in descending order so the newest would be at the top, then glided the cursor down to the first one that had been sent this morning, simply saved as "D".

Change of plans. He has to go.

Those two sentences made my organs feel like they were being ripped out of my body.

My mind was quick to add through the clues.

D: *Dereck*

Change of plans: The promise Silas had made.

He has to go: Death.

Silas wouldn't though. I knew him. He would never do that to me.

I was jumping to conclusions. I had to be.

I clicked into the next, not even sure who was saying what, but somehow knowing this was a shared folder and two people were having a conversation.

Are you sure? Intel says he's a go.

The next.

It has to happen. Too much liability.

Hand barely cooperating, I flicked into the next.

This isn't normally the way you play.

I know, but there's too much riding on this. The guy's a liar. A rat. And you know what we do with those.

Trembles rocked through me as I clicked into the last.

Understood. I'll see that it's done.

A blade of misery stabbed through my middle, and I nearly bent in two. A sob clung like a blob of poison at the base of my throat.

How could he? How could he do this to me?

I thought…I thought…

I beat the agony back into submission.

I didn't have time for a broken heart. Besides, I was the idiot here. He already told me he would ruin me.

Throat closing off, I tossed my head over my shoulder, almost certain I'd find a beast behind me, ready to strike and end me, too.

The way I knew from the beginning Silas would do.

When did I become so complacent? So blind? So freaking stupid?

Nothing but a doormat who'd been used again and again.

Manipulated so I'd be thrown off track.

I mean, I'd fully stopped looking for clues. Stopped listening. Stopped asking.

Because I'd fallen into a trap and trusted Silas Mercer.

Bile rolled my throat, acid clawing at the back of my tongue the way it always did a moment before I puked.

This was no time to be sick.

I had to take action.

Frantic, I began to fly through all the documents. Comparing them against other reports.

Desperate to find a connection.

A clue.

A way to fix this betrayal.

I kept clicking through the documents, comparing addresses and numbers to Google searches.

Mentally checking off each one as a job done.

There were two addresses in different files that had been sent earlier this week. I looked them up, and neither of them had numbers beside them.

I could only deduce that these were unfinished jobs. Their slaughters yet to come.

Yet I kept searching, somehow knowing they weren't where Dereck would be. That I was missing something.

I heaved out when I finally found one from five years ago. An address in Northern California.

Next to it was a dash with *Failed* written behind it.

I remembered what Silas had admitted that night.

"With the help of your brother, I'm finally going to get revenge for my mother's death."

Silas was returning to a failed mission.

My heart sprinted. An army of horses' hooves walloping in my chest.

I could barely type the address into my phone, and I squinted at the screen when the only thing I saw was a massive gate.

I put it on satellite mode and zoomed out, and my insides flipped when I saw it was some sort of compound in the middle of the woods.

Remote and isolated.

Dereck would be there.

I knew he would.

I jumped from the office chair, the wheels sending it flying back. My breaths were basically hyperventilations as dizziness spun my mind in a thousand directions.

How the hell was I going to get out of here?

There were at least six men standing guard along the front wall. No question, there were more along the perimeter.

And Kai…

Agony panged my heart. How could I just leave him? My love for the child full and complete.

I couldn't contemplate that right then. My only concern in this moment had to be saving my brother.

I grabbed my purse and slung it over my shoulder, tucked my phone into it, then slipped out into the vacant shop.

The bays were open, though it was empty. No sound of machinery or jesting voices. No question, they were trying to make it look like it was business as usual if someone were to drive by.

It only condensed the quiet that echoed like an omen.

Aching heart in my throat, I hurried to the door at the back of the shop and stepped out.

Praying I could act halfway normal as I came to the few bikers loitering at the back.

But I guess with everything going on, anxious appeared normal because they only gave me understanding juts of their chins as I headed toward the worn trail carved through the thicket that I used whenever I walked from the house to the shop or vice versa.

My spirit swirled and clashed and banged, and pain splintered through me with every step I took.

Unable to comprehend why Silas could commit this sort of treason against me.

I wanted to tear off my heels and run.

Run toward safety.

Toward my brother.

Toward Silas.

Torn in every direction.

Every urge made me feel like I would be ripped apart.

Nagging thoughts told me to go to Silas. To just lay it out and demand to know what was happening. Demand to know if it was all a game.

To know if every single thing between us was fake.

A blade drove right through my chest at that, and it nearly made me stumble over the uneven ground.

It wasn't something I could even contemplate right then.

I needed one focus.

Warning Dereck.

I'd let myself crumble after that.

I made it to the densest part of the grove where I was completely concealed from the rest of the property, and I tossed my attention in every direction. Sure I was alone, I broke right and darted toward the fence line.

Praying I could get there without anyone noticing, or God forbid, one of those Crows waiting on the wall, ready to tear me to shreds then dance all over my grave.

I tried to keep my breaths controlled rather than expelling them like bricks, but it was nearly impossible.

The adrenaline mixing with the torment churned them into choked sobs.

My heels kept sinking into the soft earth, and the thorny brush scraped my legs, spiky limbs gripping on like they'd been grown for the sole purpose of deterring my actions.

But I wouldn't be stopped.

I couldn't be.

I had to find Dereck. Save him. I had to wonder if he'd even had his phone this whole time. If all my pleas had been met with silence because he'd never been given the chance to return them.

I slowed to a crawl when I finally made out the white stucco wall in the distance.

My nerves bucked like electric charges.

Trees grew right up against the barrier, and shrubs and vines crawled up over the sides and top.

I went covert as I slinked beneath the green, lush canopy.

Heart so freaking loud I didn't know how it didn't send the birds scattering for safety.

I slowed almost to a stop as I came up to the wall.

I looked in every direction.

Terrified.

Mortified.

Hurt.

No one was there to stop me.

A wave of relief pummeled me, or maybe it was just an exaggerated billow of grief.

The kind that drummed and churned and made you desperate to run, even though you were fully aware it was going to catch up to you at any moment and overthrow you.

I managed to get ahold of an overhead limb, and I hoisted myself up, using my feet for leverage as I hauled myself up on a branch and started to climb.

I reached the top, and a gasp of surprise that I'd actually done it escaped, before I fumbled back down the same way on the other side.

Free when it was the last thing I wanted to be.

58

Silas

"This is it."

I stood at the head of the worn table, my hands planted on the wood, eyes skating over every Crow in the dim, cavernous room.

Violence and determination buzzed through the air, and every breath was like sucking razors into my lungs.

Bare nicks that only added to the frenzy.

"Everyone has been given their assignments. If there are any questions or reservations, I need to hear them now."

I glanced around again, gauging each of my men.

"Nay," Cliff gritted, clearly speaking for all of them. "We are ready, Prez, and not one of us will stop until we bring these motherfuckers to their end."

"World's gonna burn tonight," Regan added with a grim dip of his red beard.

My attention kept skating, meeting the nods and grunts of affirmation of every Crow in the room.

We'd been in meetings all day, hours spent going over plans in fine detail.

Final strategies.

Techniques.

Memorizing every entry point and guarded crevice within Kent Ellison's compound.

The other jobs would be simple. Straightforward. Types that we undertook on the regular.

In and out without anyone knowing we were there.

It was the compound that loomed like a slaughterhouse.

For years, I'd believed if I died ridding the earth of that monster and his mob, it would be worth it, and on some level, that belief remained.

But now, everything had changed.

I'd promised to come home.

I *needed* to come home.

And I wasn't a man who went back on his promises, and the truth was, the only thing I wanted was to come home to Brinley because I finally understood what home really meant.

"Good," I ground out, then I swallowed around the nails in my throat. "No matter what happens tonight, I'm fucking proud of every single one of you. Proud of what you do and who you are. The commitment and sacrifice you've made. The fact that you came into this MC thinking it was one thing and you stayed when you realized the true mission. You might be brutal. Wrought with rage. But you've proven who you really are, and I'm honored to get to be your leader."

Fists pounded on the table and the walls, the low toll of their voices echoing through the hollow chamber of the room. "Born in chaos. Forged by iron. Sworn to vengeance."

"Then let's fucking do this," I growled on a shout.

Everyone flew to their feet and piled out of Church and down the hall. The normal raucous they exuded was bated and contained. Saved up for the fight that was to come.

We poured out through the bar and into the fading light, darkness creeping in to consume the last vestiges of pinks and blues.

A single star blinked through a break in the trees.

My chest compressed and swelled. True hope hitting me for the very first time. A blossoming of faith and burgeoning of commitment.

I wanted to turn on my boots and hike a path back to the house so I could hug my family. Hold Kai and hug Elena and Meems and kiss the fuck out of Brinley before I went.

But I didn't have time to get distracted right then. Only thing I could do was pull out my phone and shoot off a text to Fuse, one of my most skilled Crows who was heading the detail assigned to keeping our compound safe while we were away.

Me: *Confirm that Brinley is back at the house with the rest of my family.*

It took him all of two seconds to reply.

Fuse: *Hours ago. Pyke and Colby saw her go back to the house just before noon.*

I didn't know what it was about it that took me aback. What set my already twisted stomach into a tumble.

A slick of dread that slipped like ice down my spine.

Me: *Who's watching the house?*

Fuse: *Colby is there now.*

My fingers flew as I typed out a message to Colby.

Me: *Confirm everyone is in the house. My grandmother, Elena, Kai, Brinley.*

Colby: *I've been here for three hours. No one has come or gone.*

Me: *Get eyes on them. Do it now.*

Colby: *Yes, sir.*

My heart ravaged at my ribs while I waited. Waited for too fucking long before my phone rang. I answered it before it made it through the first ring.

"What's happening?" The demand whipped off my tongue.

Distress radiated through the line, dumping directly into me. "Prez…fuck…Brinley isn't in the house. She hasn't been the whole day. I thought…"

"What?" I spat it, turning a circle as my eyes began to race.

"I saw her leave the office at right before noon. She took the trail through the trees the way she always does. I thought—"

I didn't give him time to finish his sentence before I started running for the office, shouting at my crew who was already tromping for their bikes, "Find Brinley now!"

I knew giving that order put a wrench in every plan.

It was time for us to move.

But I could move in only one direction. Toward the last place that Brinley had been.

Brody was standing guard at the backside of the office, and his expression warped into worried confusion as I came blazing up.

"Check the trail between the office and house. Brinley is missing." The command struck like a roll of thunder.

Dread covered his features, and he shook his head once before he jumped into action, his voice ragged when he promised, "We'll find her."

We had to.

I blew in through the back door of the shop, attention skating, knowing I wouldn't find her within the piles of contorted metal and the stench of oil.

I burst through the connecting door.

The one that had brought me to her so many times. Where I'd find her leaned over the desk with her perfect ass exposed.

That's what I was praying for. That she was still here, doing her thing, molding this place into shape.

But it was empty.

Void of the warmth she emitted.

My attention skated the area, and it snagged on the laptop on the desk.

The lid had been left open, something she never did when she left. She always shut it down, closed the lid, and turned off the lights, thoughtful of the way she left things.

My eyes skimmed the room. Over the bright lights that blazed from above and the office chair that sat at an odd angle where it'd been pushed back from the desk.

Heart hammering, I moved for the laptop, finger shaking it as I ran it over the pad.

The screen came to life.

I squinted when I saw the document that was open.

Understood. I'll see that it's done.

Confusion bound me, a frown carving into my brow as my heart pounded harder.

I leaned in and minimized the Word document so I could see where the message had come from.

Ice froze me from the inside out.

It was my shared folder with Cash.

The way we communicated. No real details ever given. Just numbers. Addresses.

I thought I cleared everything of importance off the laptop before I brought it to her.

How had I been so fucking careless?

But that's the way Brinley made me.

Still, she shouldn't have been able to get into it. It was encrypted. Covered by a password.

One that she'd clearly easily flushed out.

I looked back at the note. It'd been sent earlier today, and I scrambled to see its origination, starting from the first from early this morning.

A document that looked like it'd been created by me, simply saved as "D".

Change of plans. He has to go.

Cash had responded a few hours later.

Are you sure? Intel says he's a go.

Frantic, I clicked in and out of the files from that day.

It has to happen. Too much liability.

This isn't normally the way you play.

I know, but there's too much riding on this. The guy's a liar. A rat. And you know what we do with those.

It felt like I'd been disemboweled.

A knife dragged down my abdomen.

Gutting me.

Strained air wheezed from my lungs as I tried to piece it together.

This fucking betrayal that I didn't understand.

A command clearly made to kill Dereck.

Brinley gone.

Oh God, no.

She had to have gone to find him. Warn him.

My head whirled with every implication, and I would have passed out if it wasn't for the fury that blazed through my insides.

Every hair on my body lifted when I felt the presence emerge from behind.

Dark and ominous.

Slowly, I shifted to find Phoenix in the doorway, his black eyes roiling with something I couldn't fathom.

"She wasn't supposed to see that." His words scraped the air that had become acid.

Toxic.

"What? The proof of your treason?" It heaved like stones.

He stepped forward.

I gauged him, prepared to counter his attack, though for once, there was no aggression in his movements.

Just surrender as he lifted his giant hands.

"It had to happen. She blinded you," Phoenix rasped. "I did it to protect you. To protect us."

I felt like I was bound in barbed wire. "You went behind my back? Betrayed me? Because I fucking fell in love?"

"She was collateral," he gritted. "Not to be touched by any one of us, and you fucking claimed her."

A hoarse scoff left me. "And that gave you the right to do this? Do you have any idea what you've done?"

I wanted to crumble, but I took a menacing step forward instead. In it, I felt my heart splintering.

This was Phoenix. With me from the beginning. The one who was there the night everything changed.

"Give me one reason not to put a bullet through your skull." I spat it, though it was thin and wheezing.

He barely shook his head. "Don't you see it, Silas? This is a setup. She was there. It was *her*," he emphasized low, angling toward me, trying to get me to see something that remained blurry.

"The fuck are you talking about?" I demanded.

His jaw went rigid. "It was her. The night we went for Kent."

Flashes came at me in shockwaves.

The energy.

That connection.

I swayed, nearly fucking brought to my knees when it clicked.

Phoenix gripped me by the shoulder, leaning down to get into my face.

"And there's no way it's a fuckin' coincidence that her brother didn't have this thing planned. I don't know why or how, but my gut tells me he's gonna flip, and this whole thing is going to be an ambush. I had to stop him before it was too late."

59

Silas

Five Years Ago

"Are you fucking sure it's them?" Phoenix hissed it beneath his breath where their bikes were hidden behind a giant spruce.

The sweeping darkness and heavy fog camouflaged the menacing metal, the powerful motors silenced two hours ago.

The two of them were concealed in the pitch under the cover of night.

Waiting to ambush the motherfuckers that Silas had been hunting for years.

"Every bit of info Trent provided confirms that it is."

They were the only smugglers in the area of Crimson Creek during the time that his mother had been slaughtered, though their home base was there in San Jose.

A place he'd never visited before and a place he never intended on stepping foot in again.

Plus, he could feel it wafting back.

That same vile energy he'd felt every night as a teenager when he'd stupidly embarked on his runs.

"Five max?" Phoenix growled on a hush, grimness radiating from his being as he inclined his head toward Silas.

"It seems so."

Though Silas knew this monster, Kent Ellison, was trying to make his play.

Expand and take over territory belonging to other dealers.

Silas needed to crush him before that happened.

Before he was too powerful and Silas wouldn't be able to touch him.

Phoenix was the only one of the Owls bloodthirsty enough, or maybe just reckless enough, to take this on. That and the fact that Silas could trust him. He knew Phoenix wasn't pussy enough to rat on Trent if things went south and it was discovered Silas was the one who'd taken Kent out.

Silas couldn't ask Trevan because he would try to stop him.

Phoenix was down for this endeavor, even if they were throwing a fucking grenade into their lives.

Their lives were fucked, anyway.

What did it matter?

Only this.

This one fucking thing Silas had to see through.

Movement stirred in the stagnant air on the other side of the rock wall that surrounded the mansion.

Right smack in the middle of an upscale neighborhood.

Silas struggled to find oxygen, and thick, viscid blood thumped through his long-cold veins, this one need the burn that kept him moving.

"This is it," he rumbled low.

"Yeah," Phoenix agreed. A thunderclap of violence charged from his giant body, and his fisted hands tightened on his handlebars.

Through the foliage, they watched as the ornate gate swung open across the street and headlights came into view.

A second later, a black SUV rolled out.

Silas knew from his surveillance there was an armed guard on the other side of that gate.

He and Phoenix waited until the gate fully closed and the taillights nearly disappeared in the haze as it traveled down the street before they kicked over their motorcycles, their headlights cut as they picked up the SUV's trail.

It'd be a whole lot easier to hit this bastard when he was outside his fortress rather than trying to get to him on the other side.

Silas's mouth watered as they thundered down the streets. His heart running a manic beat as they tracked the beasts through the city.

Using their senses to guide them, shrouding themselves in every darkened swath.

They took a maze of rights and lefts, a short stretch of freeway before they were exiting and were dumped in a more run-down part of town.

They stayed far enough back that they were never noticed.

Phoenix's stalking skills were more than stellar.

A fucking ghost that emerged behind someone who had no clue they were about to find out if the afterlife existed.

Hell ready to swallow them.

The SUV finally made a left into a neighborhood, and they stayed far back, cutting glances at each other.

A warning that this was it.

But they had to be cautious. Not charge when they were itching to do it. Because they had no idea what circumstances they were going to find themselves in.

They waited close to a minute before they took the left into the same neighborhood and hid their motorcycles behind the first hedge they could find.

They killed the engines.

Overwhelming silence swamped the cold, misty air, and only the trill of bugs and a dog barking somewhere in the distance filled their ears.

They crouched low, motorcycle boots quietly thudding as they stuck to the shadows as they moved up the road.

A road that branched off in every direction.

Two inlets running left and right and another straight ahead.

Phoenix lifted his face, a wolf trying to pick up the scent.

"Left," he finally grunted. No question, he was following his warped, gnarled gut.

They dipped across the road, quick to disappear into the shadows.

Creeping behind houses and cars and trees.

Searching.

Hunting.

The two guns tucked into Silas's jeans loaded with liberation.

The street seemed to go on forever in a blurry expanse before it curved to the right, running straight back up the neighborhood.

Ducked low, they hurried up the road through the whisking fog.

Listening.

Feeling.

Watching.

"You sure this was the right way?" Silas grunted on a breath.

"They're here somewhere," Phoenix snarled.

They moved up and down the streets where they branched out.

Silas could feel distress and despondency bleeding out from the homes just as his hope started to dwindle.

"Where the fuck are they?" he wheezed.

It wasn't supposed to go down like this. He was supposed to finally have them.

Vengeance at hand.

"They're close. But even if we don't catch up to them tonight, we'll get them soon," Phoenix rumbled.

But Silas couldn't rest in that.

He prowled through the neighborhood.

A pillager with a single thirst.

One crown he wanted to wear.

Until they finally moved up the very last street on the farthest right side of the neighborhood.

There was a house on the east side of the road.

Surrounded by milky filament.

The yard was overgrown, and the paint on the eaves was peeling from neglect.

A ratty, dinged-up sedan sat at the curb.

The SUV was nowhere to be found.

But there was no mistaking it. No question that the fuckers were behind that door.

His jaw spasmed as his teeth snapped, and he inhaled an unsteady breath as he and Phoenix slowed, hiding themselves behind a row of bushes on the opposite side of the road.

"They're here," Silas muttered, the words clanking out of him like broken bits of steel. "I can feel it."

Phoenix looked in every direction, a frown carved across his prominent brow. "Yeah, air is fucking rancid."

It was more than that.

In it was fear.

Horror.

A terror unlike anything Silas had ever encountered, and he'd been witness and partner to a thousand wicked deeds.

And this was the last *deed* he needed to commit to fulfill his oath of vengeance, and he honestly hoped he would die completing it.

He was ready to put an end to the maliciousness. To the wickedness that reigned in his heart.

Kent Ellison had no clue he was coming for him. He likely didn't even know his name. Or if he had once upon a time, there was little chance he'd remember it.

Silas and his mother were inconsequential.

It didn't matter.

He just wanted blood, then he'd call it done.

"Go around the left side of the house, find a window you can get through. I'll go in on the right." Silas's instruction curled through the crawling night. "Be fucking careful."

"You, too, brother. It's time." He could feel the intensity of Phoenix's stare burning into his cheek.

Silas gave him a clipped nod, and they broke apart, both stealing across the deserted road.

A thick fog covered them, the night deepened by the gloom.

The closer he got, the more he felt it.

Agony.

Agony.

Ignoring it, he gripped onto his purpose.

It wasn't so hard to find a way inside. Half the windows had been broken, anyway. He found one near the back where the glass was completely missing except for a single shard still clinging to the top of the frame.

Angling to the side, he slipped through, the leather of his cut protecting him from the razor-sharp tip he felt drag across his Iron Owls patch.

He remained crouched as his boots hit the trash-strewn floor, and he checked his breaths, ensuring that he didn't make a sound.

He doubted by the voices that any of them would notice, anyway.

Their own bloodlust saturated the suffocating air.

Vileness the only oxygen by which their depravedness was sustained.

"Gonna have her one more time, boss." A voice cackled, amped up, both from drugs and the perversion that reeked in the air.

"No, this is sufficient to send the message I need. That and her body on his doorstep."

Sickness rolled in Silas's stomach. Bile climbing his throat. His heart shifted into overdrive.

A riotous thunder that battered at his ears.

Everything spun.

Hands slicked with sweat, twitching with the need for revenge.

All while something else pressed into his conscience.

Retribution was right there.

He could have them.

But there was something that drew him forward. A call he couldn't help but heed.

He crept forward, cringing when his boot crunched against a sliver of broken glass on the floor.

But it wasn't enough to penetrate their barbarity.

"Pick her up and toss her into the back of the SUV. You'll slit her throat once we get there. I don't want her bleeding out in the back of the Rover. Isius, get rid of her car."

Silas peeked around the doorway and into what was the house's living room. It was nearly pitch, and he was barely able to make out the outline of three men standing in the room.

Except Silas could see only one thing.

The stripped, battered body of a girl on the floor. An indistinct silhouette held in the pall.

It didn't matter that he couldn't really see her.

Silas felt like he got turned inside out.

His guts ripped from his body.

His heart toppled like the garbage on the floor, though it beat out of rhythm, out of time.

A monster moved to pick her up, and Silas didn't think.

He didn't wait for the cue from Phoenix for them to go in at the same time.

He just stepped out and started to shoot.

Going for the bastard who knelt first, refusing to allow him to get his fetid hands on her again.

The fucker howled when he was struck.

Chaos suddenly broke out.

Shots fired back.

The one that struck Silas didn't even bring him to his knees.

The disgust, the fury, the rage were enough to keep him standing.

At the back of the house, he heard glass break. No doubt, Phoenix had heard the commotion and was rushing to make his way in.

Another barrage of bullets.

His and the men's.

Silas was on his stomach, trying to crawl into the room.

Footsteps and shots resounded.

Shouts as the men suddenly ran from the room.

"Get up!" Phoenix shouted from the end of the hall.

An engine suddenly roared and wood crashed as the SUV busted through the garage door.

"They're getting away," Phoenix shouted.

Only Silas remained on his knees. Crawling for the girl.

Dead or unconscious.

He didn't know.

Sirens sang in the distance.

Phoenix gripped him by the back of the shirt. "Get up. We have to get out of here."

"No…I…she needs help." He tried to get to the girl.

To change it.

His mother's face flashed behind his eyes.

Her smile.

Her belief.

Was this someone's mother?

Their sister?

Their daughter?

Pain splintered and shook.

"You have to get up now."

When he couldn't, Phoenix fisted two hands in the front of his cut and hauled him to his feet.

"Fuck, man. We have to get the fuck out of here. Right fucking now." He jostled him. "The police are coming. They'll get her help."

Phoenix forced him back down the hall and through the window that he'd come through, then basically dragged him through the three-foot grasses that clogged the backyard, the toes of Silas's boots cutting through the soil.

Phoenix tossed him through a missing slat in the fence and out into the alley at the back.

Their breaths were jutted and harsh as the sound of sirens approached.

Silas suppressed a wail that threatened to rise from his soul.

"The fuck, man? You just let them go?" Phoenix wheezed it near his face, disbelief threaded into every word. “You were supposed to wait for the cue.”

But in that moment, it wasn’t about vengeance.

It was about setting something right.

Helping an innocent.

Silas didn’t know her name or her face, but he knew there were uncountable others just like her.

Pain finally broke through the disturbance, and he pressed his hand to his side. Felt the warm blood dripping free.

“You’re hit?” Phoenix’s demeanor flipped into concern.

“Yeah. I’ll be fine.”

Phoenix gave him a clipped nod, confusion woven on his expression before he helped Silas to stand.

He kept an arm around Silas’s waist as they fumbled down the alley in the direction of their bikes.

They stayed low the way they always did.

Undetected, pausing for a minute when an ambulance with its lights flashing and siren screaming sped into the neighborhood.

And he knew, standing there cloaked in a blanket of fog, listening to the sirens, that he wouldn’t take it back.

As he climbed onto his bike, wincing from the bullet lodged somewhere near the same spot where he’d been hit the night his mother had been slain, he felt something inside himself break apart and rebuild in a flash.

And he knew there was no going back.

60

Brinley

I'd never been one for grand theft auto. It appeared Silas Mercer was truly rubbing off on me.

Criminal activity catching.

I choked over the thought.

Over the drive of the knife that kept piercing my ribcage, allowing droplets of my soul to dribble out.

Gripping the wheel with trembling hands, I sucked it back and tried to focus.

I could fall apart later. That was if I survived this.

I couldn't bring myself to feel bad about heisting the crappy, unkempt car from the neighbor's back lot.

I had no other choice. It wasn't like I could hitchhike.

Even going as fast as this car would take me, I kept glancing in the rearview mirror, waiting for an army of vicious motorcycles to catch up and surround me from behind.

Night had begun to descend, the pinks twining with wisps of silvered, darkened blue.

The woods flashed by at the edges of my sight, and the branches almost touched overhead.

With each mile I traveled, they seemed to deepen with the promise that they would swallow me.

Lead me down a hollowed-out tunnel to my demise.

I swiped the tears from my face with the back of my hand, trying to see through the torrent that wouldn't stop falling as I sped in the direction of the address on that document.

I'd just passed the California state line, and I'd reach my destination in twenty minutes.

What I would find there, I didn't know.

I tried to call and text Dereck a hundred times since I'd tossed myself over that wall.

Honestly, I'd barely hoped for a reply. It wasn't like I'd gotten any before, so I wasn't shocked when they remained unanswered.

The road twisted and wound into obscurity before I finally made it to the turn-off onto a dirt road.

My pulse careened. Nerves firing in every direction.

Fear telling me to run while despair pushed me forward.

Steeling myself, I slowly drove down the lane. The tires crunched over the gravel as I wound around a bend.

Finally, I came to the same massive iron gate I'd seen on the satellite picture.

Every molecule in my body squeezed.

Silas, what am I doing? What is happening? I don't want to do this alone. Please…

My mind silently pleaded with a man I couldn't trust, except my spirit screamed that was all wrong.

Screamed I didn't understand.

Screamed that I was making a mistake.

All while my mother's face flashed through my mind. *"You'll take good care of him?"*

I squeezed my eyes closed, trying to find courage. Belief. Resiliency.

How could those words on those documents lie? I knew what they meant.

Still, warnings that I was off base and in peril screamed at the back of my mind as I pulled the car off the side of the drive at an angle.

Shutting off the engine, I sucked for the missing air.

Gripping the door handle like it held the answer to all life's secrets.

You can do this.

You can do this.

Sweeping my tongue over my dried lips, I clicked it open.

Terror locked my muscles as I climbed out of the car. Night hung heavy, cut by the dull glow of a half-moon.

A gust of wind blew through the trees, the high branches thrashing above, though in it was an eerie silence that crawled across my flesh like a premonition.

I looked around. Into the sinister silence that echoed back.

This was wrong.

Completely wrong.

I had no plan, no idea where I was, and no clue what was waiting for me on the other side of those walls.

Did I really think I could protect Dereck myself? From whatever this nightmare was?

It all came crashing down on me in that moment. I should never have done this. I should have found Silas. Demanded the truth.

Looked into his eyes and found the truth for myself.

Because what he was.

My truth.

I didn't care what those stupid documents said.

I was missing something.

I had to be and the panic had clouded it.

I turned to run back to the stolen car, set on calling him. Confess what I'd been planning to do and beg him to keep the promise he had made to me this morning.

One that he would bring Dereck home.

Only a figure stepped out from the shadows, stopping me in my tracks.

My heart cracked like thunder. A splintering of lightning as it was severed in two.

I might have never seen his face, but I would recognize the vileness anywhere.

The stench of that night when I nearly lost my life. Where a part of me had died in that vacant, dilapidated house.

But what crushed me was when Dereck appeared at his side.

No.

No, no, no.

He wouldn't do this to me. He would never get re-involved with the ones who had hurt me.

Dereck's face contorted when he saw me, his head barely shaking in horror and disbelief.

"What are you doing here?" He wheezed it quietly like I might be the only one who could hear it.

"I…I came to…"

I couldn't force out the words. Silas would be dead if I did, that was if I hadn't already condemned them.

If I hadn't already exposed them and what they had set out to do.

Because this was Kent Ellison. The man who had killed Silas's mother had also nearly killed me.

They were one and the same.

How?

Regret and confusion spiraled through my senses.

Oh, God. What did I do? What did I do?

Kent Ellison smirked. Dark and foreboding. The grossest kind of wickedness.

"Always the little rescuer, aren't you? But don't worry your pretty face," he tsked softly. "You didn't disclose anything I didn't already know."

He suddenly whipped out a gun and put it to Dereck's head.

I nearly bolted for my brother. Threw myself between him and the gun.

But I was frozen by terror.

"I already knew what your rat brother was up to, thinking he was going to get revenge on me for you when I had only rightfully taken payment for what he owed," Kent sneered.

The blood drained from Dereck's face, the same as it did from mine.

As I realized what my brother had gotten himself involved in.

More so, the why.

This was revenge. His current involvement with this monster was to avenge me.

And his intention had been discovered.

"He should have been grateful that I didn't come back for you later and instead gave mercy and let you live," Kent continued.

Horror and confusion spun.

A whirlwind.

"Did he really think I'd just accept him back? Give him the second chance he'd come begging for? I knew the whole fucking time what he was up to. I'm just very good at being patient."

His demonic grin widened. "But I guess I should thank him for doing me the favor of bringing Silas and his MC to my door."

The knot in my throat closed off oxygen.

Asphyxiating.

Oh God, no.

He knew that Silas was coming here.

And it didn't matter what those documents said, I knew Silas would never betray me.

I was the one who'd betrayed him.

Pain sheared through me, and torment dragged me in every direction.

"Run!" Dereck suddenly shouted.

The last thing I wanted to do was leave him behind, but I knew it was the only thing I could do.

I had to somehow get to Silas. Warn him. *Save him.*

And I knew he was the only one who could save my brother.

Only the second I turned, five men appeared like vapor from the mist.

Surrounding me.

I attempted to dart to the left, but one was behind me in a flash. I screamed as I was shoved to the ground.

My hands bound behind my back as my soul was sundered.

A cry ripped out of me, his name on my tongue as my face was pressed into the dirt. "Silas."

Silas. Silas. Silas. I'm so horribly sorry.

61

Silas

"She wasn't supposed to fuckin' see it." Phoenix's jaw clenched and ticked through the hostility that suffocated the office.

"But she fucking did, didn't she? And now she's—" My teeth snapped shut, not able to say it. Terror fisting my spirit, not sure where she was.

If she was in danger.

All while my head spun with what Phoenix had revealed. The hate I'd held for a man for years multiplying exponentially. Knowing that she was the one broken on that floor.

Fuck.

I couldn't even process that she was the one who'd changed everything.

Set my life on a different trajectory.

I guess I shouldn't have been surprised that she kept doing it. That somehow, she'd end up here and become mine.

The moment in time inscribed in me as deep as the ink on my flesh. As deep as the wounds on my heart.

And she was the only one who could heal them.

"She thinks I ordered it. Thinks I betrayed her the way you betrayed me." My words were shredded.

Accusations and pleas.

Phoenix's tatted throat bobbed. "Would never knowingly hurt you. I was trying to protect you and this entire club. I kept thinking that she was familiar, and after you claimed her last night, I realized where I knew her from. I hacked into some old police records in San Jose. Found her picture and verified it was her. I thought…"

He scrubbed a tattooed hand over his mouth. "I thought there was no chance it was random. One way or another, Dereck has to be up to something. I had to stop him."

"You should have come to me. It wasn't your choice to make," I growled, leaning in his direction. "And because of it, she's out there. Unprotected."

My chest felt like it would cave, all while my thoughts ricocheted in my mind, trying to calculate where she could have gone. How she got out of the compound without anyone knowing.

"I'll personally find her," Phoenix grated. "Bring her back to you. She couldn't have gotten far. But you know Dereck needs to die."

My head shook. It didn't sit right. None of it. "No, Phoenix…"

I turned to pace, roughing an agitated hand through my hair as I clomped across the floor.

"If it was them? The men who hurt her? You think he'd go back? Work for them? You think Kent would just allow it?"

Bile tingled the back of my throat, my twined, gnarled guts squeezing the life out of me.

"I think…I think Dereck was on his own mission." The words began to rush. "It's why he came to us with the intel on Elena. He couldn't stomach that bullshit any more than we could. He wanted revenge for what they did to his sister."

The same way as I wanted it for mine. For Elena. For my mother. For that unknown girl tortured on the dingy floor.

"You think Kent knows." It was a statement, Phoenix's hands curling into vibrating fists.

Awareness taking hold as we came to the quick conclusion that this entire mission was compromised.

Kent likely had known exactly what was happening the entire time.

Had known my goal was him dead.

"He has to. He'd never let Dereck back in otherwise."

Dereck was a fool for thinking it.

"Which means he's fucking waiting for us," I surmised.

He was the one who'd been biding his time. Pretending. Waiting for his chance to destroy us.

And Brinley…she went to warn Dereck. Thinking she could stop this entire trainwreck.

I felt like I was punched in the face.

My heart ripped from my chest.

Phoenix dropped to his knees and bowed his head.

Offering himself.

A penance for his sins.

His betrayal punishable by death.

"Do it," he gritted, his eyes squeezed closed.

"Get the fuck off the floor," I grated. "We have to get my girl."

• • •

I stood in front of a sea of motorcycles and leather cuts, the glinting metal swirling with the threads of the night.

"We're likely compromised." I did my best to keep the tremor from my voice, but I was pretty fucking sure my fear was patent.

Not for myself.

But for Brinley.

Brinley, that reckless, brave, ferocious girl.

"If any one of you wants to sit this out, I understand. It's already the most dangerous undertaking we've endeavored, and it's just become a million times worse."

"Except we now know that Kent is waiting for us," Trevan added from where he stepped up to my side. "If it hadn't happened, we'd be walking straight into an ambush. Every single one of us."

I looked at my oldest friend. The one who'd been there through thick and thin. From the start and to this end.

He cracked a grin and said, "I'm going to call this little mishap a win. And you fucking know I'll be riding at your side. Besides, these motherfuckers don't know who they really are playing with."

Phoenix stepped up on my other side. Head still lowered with shame but that dark brutality oozing from his body. "I'll gladly die for this."

Brody suddenly broke through the crowd, donning his cut with his Prospect patch, his chin fierce as he forced his way to the front. "I'm coming, too. And don't fucking tell me I'm not. This is Brinley we're talking about. And this is retribution for our sister. For our mother. For the innumerable others we don't know about."

Emotion flooded from him, and I found I couldn't refuse. My kid brother who'd become a man.

His own brand of brutality running beneath the surface.

My throat thickened, and I watched as every Crow dipped their heads in a show of agreement then moved to swing onto their bikes. The roar of them kicking over their powerful engines was nothing short of a battle cry.

They pulled back on the throttles. A deep, dark rumble of their loyalty and commitment.

Phoenix shouted above the tumult. "It's time to get our Prez's queen back."

I looked at him. Understanding passed between us.

His true intentions, even though they were wrong. His love for me. His oath to always have my back.

The forgiveness that came on sharp relief.

Then I pulled away, my own determination rolling through me like a rockslide, and I moved to my Harley that sat waiting at the front.

I swung onto the matte black metal, hooked the heel of my boot to the rung, and drove down hard on the kick starter.

It rumbled and growled, and I revved it, my own call that reverberated through my men.

I lifted my hand, giving the signal, and we all flooded out through the gate. An ocean of Crimson Crows cuts and backbones of iron.

We rode through the night.

My body coiled and ready, my pulse thundering as loud as the army of bikes.

We rode for two hours, the night growing long the way we had planned.

The moment we crossed the California state line, Cash and his Sovereign Sanctum crew pulled out from where they were hidden and waiting in the shadows, their motorcycles gliding into formation, the same as Trent Lawson and his brothers did about three miles down the road.

These men I'd known for years. The ones who had helped set this whole thing into motion.

My crew began to segment off.

Teams heading to the different drop sites and the safehouse, while the rest of us barreled toward the compound.

Our only hope was that Kent had no clue about the magnitude of our hit. Had no clue that we intended to completely wipe them out. That we were striking everywhere at once.

Counting on the idea that he likely thought it would only be a handful of my men showing up at his door to rescue Brinley, not the all-out assault that was coming for him.

Ten miles out, we cut our lights. Darkness reigned as we traveled under the cover of night.

Five miles out, we split into thirds, taking the hidden paths that Cash had scoped out so we could completely surround the fenced-in property that covered close to two miles.

All while my heart ravaged and my spirit howled.

Brinley.

Brinley.

I'm coming for you, baby.

This wildfire that had torched my beliefs and brought me back to life.

62

Silas

We basically crawled on our hands and knees up a steep embankment on the most remote side of the property.

As fucking deep as you could get in these woods.

We'd swung a mile out before we made our way up the backside of the land that most would consider untraversable.

Cliffs and boulders and a crush of impenetrable woods that crowded out the heavens above.

Trevan, Phoenix, and Cash were at my side.

Everyone had been divided into groups of four that would steal in at different points. Strategically to take out the guards, their circuits and schedules another element that Cash had mapped out.

Keeping crouched, we made it to the top of the ridge, and it brought us to the boundary we were looking for.

The chain-link fence with the top fortified by razor wire.

Now electrified after Cash and his crew had broken in and rescued Elena.

Something I'd wanted to be the one to do, but now, I somehow understood that I hadn't been ready.

Unprepared for what really had been waiting for us or the way my path was going to veer.

Guess I'd become a new believer in fate.

I peered through the pitchy bleakness, the bare outline of my brothers' faces staring back.

The poison in the darkness was so thick I could taste it.

A vileness creeping through that permanently lifted the hairs at the nape of my neck.

Cash tipped his chin, and he quickly worked with the wiring, killing the electricity running to the fence.

The low hum it'd been emitting fell into silence.

The second it had, I sent the prepared text that went to the lead of each team.

Me: *Go*

And that's what we fucking did.

Cash yanked wire cutters from the back of his jeans and snipped through the links in a blink, shoving them wide enough that we could slip through.

We crouched low as we ran through the forest that was every bit as thick here as it'd been creeping up the side of the mountain.

Weapons in hand, we hurtled through the foliage and underbrush.

Boots quiet on the soft, squishy earth.

Breaths held and silent as ghosts.

My spirit moaned. The old thirst for vengeance completely replaced by a brand-new need.

The anguished need to set her free.

Desperation streaked through my being. A pervasive urge to find her safe and whole and unharmed.

All I could see in the back of my mind was the shape of that unknown body mangled on the ground.

This woman who had changed every fucking thing.

Finally, we came to a halt at the edge of the thicket, still cloaked beneath the overabundant branches.

The air left me on a violent wheeze as the vast expanse of grass and the fortress from where Kent reigned beyond it came into view.

We faced one side of the enormous outpost. It was constructed of metal, Kent's operation run under the façade of a logging company, and on this side, there was a row of semi-trucks lined up like they were waiting on their next haul.

Hazy lights glowed back through the fog, and a baleful stillness echoed through the mist.

Too still.

Too quiet.

I shared a glance with my closest men.

Kent and his ring were waiting for us.

We knew it.

So there was only one fucking thing we could do.

I gave the cue and we ran, ducking through the shadows in an attempt to remain unseen.

In the distance, a gunshot rang out.

No question, one of our other teams had been discovered.

And that was it.

It was instant bedlam.

Blinding lights flicked on to blind our eyes right as a barrage of bullets started to fly.

Two men came rushing around the side of the building. Phoenix had guns in both hands, and he started running toward them like the madman he was, unloading on both motherfuckers with a roar.

They stumbled back, piles of trash that dropped to the ground, while Cash took out three men who came from the other side.

Trevan gave me a look. Our job to stay stealth so we could get inside the building.

Knowing that's where Kent would be. Where Brinley would be.

Shots suddenly pelted the ground right at my side, darts that impaled the earth.

"Sniper on the roof," I shouted, and I dropped into a roll, flinging myself under one of the truck trailers.

Concealed and on my back, I eased out enough so I could take a shot at the sniper who was frantically looking over the side for his next target.

He should have known the target was him.

I pulled the trigger, and his body spasmed as he was struck in the neck.

He toppled off the roof, asshole doing two flips as he plunged to the ground.

Body a mangled bow when he hit the cement beneath.

Shots were being fired everywhere.

Shouts and screams and commands echoing through the air.

Dread twisted through me. Fear that any one of my men might be among the anguished moans.

Trevan was tucked low, his back pressed to a shadowy side of the truck I was underneath.

"You good?" he wheezed.

"Yeah. We need to get inside that building."

"Count of three, and I cover you," he said.

He didn't give me a chance to reject it. He simply pushed his hand low, ticking off his fingers.

One.

Two.

Three.

He swung out from behind the truck just as I rolled onto my feet, guns in both his hands firing in every direction while I kept low and ran for the side door.

It was the spot Cash had believed might be the easiest access point from the ground floor. He didn't think we'd have the chance to make it to the roof and cut our way in the way he did when he came for Elena.

That position would only make us more vulnerable.

Movement suddenly whispered from my right, and I whirled.

A man dressed in all black emerged from the shadows.

Grin on his smug mouth as he lifted his gun like he thought he had me trapped.

Fucker didn't have a chance before mine was going off.

The sneer on his face imploded, body blown back ten feet.

A gush of air rushed from my lungs, a fucking river of sweat pouring down my spine, my heart rate manic as I turned back to the door.

I crouched low as I pulled out the tools stuffed in my back pocket, my fingers adept as I quickly picked two locks.

I could feel the terror radiating out. The same sense I'd gotten all those years ago when I'd slipped into that vacant, decayed house.

The mayhem of that warm spirit calling out.

Brinley.

Brinley.

The last lock finally gave, and my lungs squeezed as I stood, body turned and ear pressed to the door like I might be able to hear any movement from within.

Anticipating a full ambush waiting on the other side.

I put my hand on the knob and slowly turned, and the door creaked as I carefully nudged it open.

Listening for any breath.

A heartbeat.

Only a buzz echoed in my ears, a whirring of stilled silence as I stepped inside while chaos continued to rage outside.

It was even darker here, and I cringed when the sole of my boot squeaked against the hard, slick floor.

The lights were cut, but I could ascertain the room was a storage area.

Boxes stacked high.

I knew this room, and I felt even more certain that Dereck had come through.

This matched the exact layout he'd given.

On the other side of it would be a hall.

A hall that would lead to the inner sanctum of the building where Kent spent most of his time.

His living space.

His office.

Farther down were dingy rooms where he kept his captives.

Where Elena had been held hostage.

Manipulated and trapped.

I carefully crept through the maze, my heart in my throat, my skin drenched by the fear and determination that seeped from my pores.

I fumbled my way along a wall, and I slid my palms over the surface until I finally found the door.

I paused, listened, felt.

Let the extra senses that had kept me alive for all these years bleed out.

A groan of something, a shift of feet.

Someone was there.

I tucked a gun into its holster and pulled my knife from its sleeve, and I locked the air in my lungs as I quietly unlatched the door and slipped out into the dusk of the hall.

A man was ten feet ahead and facing away.

I stole forward, and I had his chin in my hand and the knife dragging across his throat before he even knew I was there.

Blood spurted onto my arm, and I carefully laid his limp body on the ground before I stepped over the pile of garbage and continued to edge down what felt like an endless hall.

Footsteps contained. Blood pumping a rabid, ruthless beat.

Finally, I made it close to its end. Two armed men stood outside the door, one on his phone facing the wood and the other shifted toward me, though his head was angled, clearly trying to listen to the other's conversation.

I slipped forward undetected, and he jolted when he finally noticed me a second before I drove the knife into his gut.

I jerked the blade to the side to spill him out.

The other dropped his phone and started to whirl, and I whipped the knife, slashing deep into his arm.

"Motherfucker, you're dead," he wheezed in shock, stumbling back.

"Nah," I hissed, and I cocked my arm back and threw the knife before he found solid ground.

It flew, meeting its mark at the front of his neck.

He dropped like a boulder.

A decimated thud.

And I knew there was no longer any concealing my presence, so I grabbed both guns and kicked in the door they were guarding.

Ready to rush into the room in a blaze of glory, only I froze when I found the scene inside.

Heart dropping to the floor.

Brinley.

Bound and on her knees. A gag in her mouth. Beautiful hair tangled and matted with dirt and blood.

One eye black and swollen shut.

The other begged a desperate plea.

Dereck was on the other side of her.

In the same position.

His entire face was busted to shit. Gaping cuts on his lip, temple, and cheek.

A wound leaked from his side and soaked his clothes in blood.

But in his eyes?

In them was relief. His trust in *me*.

Except I wasn't feeling so relieved when I found Kent Ellison casually standing over the top of them like a complete showdown wasn't raging outside.

Hair styled and wearing a designer suit.

Smug smirk on his face like he'd already won.

Three men with machine guns strapped across their chests stood guard behind him, and he had his own gun held at the side of Brinley's head.

"Drop your guns or she goes," Kent gritted.

I wanted to rush him. Throw myself on top of Brinley. A living shield who would gladly die to protect the treasure.

But I had to play this smart.

Careful.

I heaved out a strained breath, and my hands fucking shook as I tossed them to the floor three feet in front of me.

My eyes scanned, calculating how I could get to Brinley before Kent had time to react.

Then shock hurled from my lungs when I found my piece-of-shit father itching in the corner.

Confusion almost bowled me over.

A near faceplant into a vat of rage and disgust and hate.

I was stuck there for a prolonged beat, a storm of horror and devastation ripping through me as I stared at his worn, leathery face, trying to make sense of what the fuck he was doing there.

Kent released a condescending tsk that drew my attention back to him. "Silas Mercer. So predictable, aren't we?"

His head canted to the side as he looked me up and down.

It wasn't like I hadn't stood before him before.

Pretending like my MC was interested in running his poison across the Northwest in an attempt to infiltrate his inner circle.

I let my eyes dip to Brinley for a beat.

Just needing to look at her.

To see that she was breathing.

Before I forced my focus back to Kent, knowing it was stupid to draw more attention to her.

Not sure what Kent knew. If he had any idea that she'd been in my compound and under my protection for the last few weeks.

Whittling her way into my heart for the same amount of time.

Air puffed from his pompous nose. "It took me a minute, you know, to figure out who you were. The president of this insignificant motorcycle club playing hard to get. Acting like he was above running my goods. One minute all in and the next withdrawing. Asking too many fucking questions. I thought you were trying to make a play. Strike a better deal for yourself."

Locked aggression buzzed through my body, and my fingers tingled with the need to finally put an end to the monster standing in front of me.

But I waited. Searching for the right moment. Trying to calculate how I could take all three of his guards out and get to him without anyone else being hurt.

Minus my father.

I didn't care if killing him did steal the last bit of my humanity. Just his existence was inhumane.

"So, I thought I'd have a little fun with your sister…" Kent continued.

Violence screamed across my flesh, and Brinley whimpered, knowing this beast who'd hurt her in the worst way possible had also tormented my sister.

"Put you in your place and show you who actually is in control," he snarled.

His expression twisted like he had a hard time putting a finger on it. "It should have been impossible for you to get her out, to know exactly how to get in here and extract her. That's when I knew something was amiss. That I had a rat in my midst."

I refused to glance at Dereck, even though it was clear Kent already knew. Clear he possessed knowledge that he shouldn't have.

Not because of Dereck flipping on us.

But because of my father.

Kent paused and glanced at the pathetic fuck who was sweating near the wall before he swiveled back to me with a malicious grin. "Then your father knocked at my office door. Telling me he had something I might want."

Air puffed from his nose. "Such a funny thing, he recognized this pretty brunette from a job I had him on with me five years ago."

I had to stop myself from bending in two.

Shocked that my father had been involved that night.

Had been culpable in what had happened to Brinley.

Rage blistered, and red glowed at the edges of my sight.

Had he been working with Kent the whole time? I thought the coward had run that night. Disappeared to save his own ass. Leaving my mother there to die.

And he'd run right back to Kent.

"Aww, don't feel so bad for not realizing it, Silas." It was pure condescension. "I didn't know you were PJ's son until that moment, either. He told me my runner in that small town of Crimson Creek had been killed. I didn't think much of it. Men die all the time. Are expendable and easily replaceable. My mistake for not making the connection. My mistake for not realizing that your father lied to me."

He suddenly pulled his gun from Brinley's head and pointed it at my father. In surrender, PJ's hands flew up, and he spluttered, "No, Kent, it wasn't like—"

Kent pulled the trigger. An earsplitting crack ricocheted from the walls at the same second his body slumped to the ground.

A gust of addled air wheezed from my lungs.

Shock at seeing my father face down on the ground in a growing pool of blood.

Hatred and pain vied for dominance.

Brinley screamed against her gag, choking and crying as her shoulders sank forward.

My focus jerked back to her. Every muscle in my body twitched. Ached to get to her. Unbind her. Hold her. See to it that every promise I had made to her was fulfilled.

But I forced myself to remain there. Biding time as the gunshots began to fade outside, becoming more interspersed, praying that it was my men who were coming out on top.

Kent shifted so the gun dangled at his side.

Nonchalance radiated from his frame but venom dripped from his tongue. "That was when it all came together for me. I already knew Dereck was up to something. Coming back here out of the blue after he and his sister escaped with their lives five years ago?"

A huff left him. "Only to find out his sister is on your property. PJ confessing who you really are. Trading your real identity for a measly stack of cash. You and Dereck thinking you were going to overthrow me."

I almost laughed. He thought I wanted to take over his twisted kingdom? I was here to end it.

"I figured I'd let you and your men come to me. Save me the trouble of hunting you down. Thank you for proving my theory and making this easy."

"See, you've got something wrong in the middle of that." It came out a low threat.

Kent seemed almost surprised that I spoke before his mouth twisted into a malicious grin. "How's that?"

My phone vibrated in my front pocket, the specific rhythm Cash had set.

I cracked my own grin. "I'm not here to overthrow your empire. I'm here to burn it to the ground."

That was right when all three doors leading into his inner sanctum burst open.

Cash, River, Theo, and Otto blazed in through one door.

Trent and his crew from another.

Fuse, Trevan, Phoenix, and my brother from the one behind me.

Caught off guard, Kent's guards reared back, though they were quick to lift their guns to raze the room in a spray of bullets.

It happened at the same time as the guys who had always had my back also began to shoot.

In an instant, it was pandemonium.

Gunshots and dust and screams.

And the only thing I could do was throw myself forward, grabbing both my guns from the floor before I crawled for Brinley through the smoke.

My heart convulsed when I felt her skin against mine. The heat. The life. The light.

Her relief saturating. Burning through me like a thousand suns.

Wildfire.

While a barrage of shots continued to rain. I covered her with my body, desperate to keep her shielded while the battle seethed around us.

Dread slithered up my spine when I suddenly felt the abhorrent presence from the side.

Too close.

I shifted my head so I could peer out that way.

Kent was on his knees. A gun aimed at me from a foot away.

I curled myself tighter around Brinley.

"Brinley. Brinley."

I didn't realize I was chanting it aloud.

I just needed her to hear it.

My praise.

My belief.

The unending love that poured out of me.

Just as Kent fired three shots.

63

Brinley

Uncountable gunshots were going off, but there were only three that I really heard.

The ones I knew impaled Silas in the back.

I could feel his big, powerful body jolt with each one.

And God, I wanted to grip onto him. Hold him and protect him and shield him the way he was shielding me, but I couldn't even scream through the shredding agony with the gag in my mouth.

Garbled sobs battering against the soaked, balled fabric.

My hands bound between us, heavy with the hopeless need to wrap them around him.

My voice silenced when the only thing I wanted to do was beg him to be okay. Beg him to forgive me.

Go back to the beginning and trust him with every molecule of my being the way he deserved to be.

It turned out, I was the one who couldn't be trusted. I was the one who let her pain and wounds and traumas cloud what my soul knew was the truth.

And Silas was that truth.

My truth.

An eerie silence suddenly reigned the smoke-clogged room. A shrill echo that rang in my ears. A disturbed lull that charged my heart into mayhem where I was pinned below Silas.

He was suddenly rolled away, and a man I didn't recognize was in front of me, tearing the gag from my mouth and dragging a blade through the ropes that fettered my wrists and ankles.

"Are you okay?" he demanded.

I only had one answer.

"Silas."

It was a plea.

A groan.

Desperation as I managed to roll around, my bruised, battered body protesting as I climbed onto my hands and knees.

Scrambling to where Silas was on his back.

Kent Ellison was dead beside him. His skull opened and spilling onto the floor.

I gasped but kept moving, my hands fumbling for Silas. They were frantic as I ran them over his chest, searching for a pulse.

For this life that we'd just found, even though I didn't deserve it.

But I'd gladly take his hate just to see the glint in the gold flecks of his hazel eyes again.

I choked over a sob, and tears blurred my sight as I hovered over the top of him. Frenzied hands flitting all over his cut.

I jolted when strong fingers started winding into my hair at the side of my head, and a low voice murmured, "Wildfire."

My gaze darted to his face.

To those eyes, bright enough to shine through my tears.

He pushed up to sitting. "Wildfire. Are you hurt? Fuck, please tell me you're okay."

Gasping around the relief, I fumbled to get to him.

"You were shot. You were shot," I mumbled, close to incoherent.

His head barely shook, and with his free hand, he took mine and settled it over his cut. "Bulletproof vest."

"And believe me, that shit fucking hurts." Brody suddenly stepped forward through the dust and debris, and he tore off a mask and helmet as he howled with laughter.

He smacked himself across his chest, acting like it was no big deal where he'd been hit.

Deliverance sped through my veins, a shuddering of shock and disbelief. Of pain and regret.

Another man was cutting through Dereck's bindings, and strained air raked from my brother's throat as he slumped with a groan to the floor.

Though his head was turned, his eyes on me, full of loyalty and an apology.

"Dereck," I croaked.

"Everything will be fine," he gurgled. "Like I promised you."

Love and grief spiraled. Binding me as tightly as the ropes. The anger and burden I'd carried were smashed while my own guilt surged to the surface.

The man who'd cut Dereck's ropes peeled back his shirt and grunted, "He needs medical, stat. And we need to find out how many others we have down and need attention."

The man looked at me. "We have a doctor and my wife Charleigh in an ambulance a mile away. Prepared to do surgery. He'll be fine. I promise you."

He and another man rolled Dereck over and picked him up, one holding him under the shoulders and another by the ankles.

While tremors rocked through me.

Shame and relief and a love so distinct.

My body juddered. Shaking uncontrollably.

"It's okay, baby. It's okay. I've got you. I've got you." Silas's promise wrapped me in a dream.

"She's in shock." An unknown voice curled through the disorder, words warbled as they touched my ears.

Silas was suddenly on his knees in front of me. Big hands framing my jaw and forcing me to look at him. I could only see him through one eye, my entire face throbbing.

All of me was throbbing really.

My body and my heart and my soul.

"You're going to be fine, Brinley. I'm right here. Right here."

A sob finally cracked. Violent in its horror.

And I was being swept up, cradled in his arms, his stride firm and strong as he carried me from the room and down a long hall.

Stepping over bodies, muttering the whole time, "I've got you. I've got you."

He didn't stop as he edged through a rambling, darkened room before we were outside.

Surrounded by the deepest, darkest night.

Shouts echoed around us. Organized mayhem as Crows ran through the carnage, piling fallen bodies, liquids being spilled and dumped, no question erasing all traces of their involvement.

All evidence eradicated.

Once again, they had become soldiers the way I'd thought of them the day that man had come into the office to drag me to Kent as an offering.

Precise and efficient.

This motorcycle club so different than I imagined. Its importance hung on the horizon, tickling at the edge of my awareness and scored on my conscience.

I wanted to beg for Silas's forgiveness, but I couldn't do anything but cling to his neck as he strode with me across a vast lawn. My eyes were wide with shock as I peered over his shoulder.

At the fire that suddenly leapt high, quick to consume that massive building.

Silas didn't stop. He carried me into the thick of the woods and dipped us through a hole that had been cut in the fence, his feet sure and his hold strong as he angled us down an embankment and up the other side.

A second or an hour passed as I clung to him, I couldn't discern, before I was back on his bike, planted in front of him the way he'd had me before.

Fierce, unrelenting arms surrounded me as he gripped onto the handlebars and rode us out of the labyrinth of the twisting, twining forest.

No words were said except for the whispers of his breath that he released into my temple as we rode.

He took the roads like a puzzle. Riding further south into California before he wound around and headed north again.

He didn't slow until we crossed the border, then he pulled off onto a rugged, worn path and weaved us back into the sanctuary of the woods.

The stars were beginning to fade as night slowly gave up its hold.

Silas stopped under a canopy of verdant trees, planted his boots on the ground as he killed the engine, then he shuffled me around. He wrapped my legs around his waist and pulled my chest to his.

His arms unrelenting as he held me against his rigid, perfect frame.

"Brinley."

I never would have thought my name could hold such meaning.

Relief.

Love.

Redemption.

But it was all there, surrounding me like I had earned any one of them.

I crushed myself against him. My own relief. My own redemption.

A love so big and heavy that I feared maybe I'd succumbed from it.

Maybe I'd died back in that room and this meeting was otherworldly.

Because how could Silas shower this kind of mercy on me after what I'd done?

"I'm sorry." It was a muddled, disjointed cry. "I'm so sorry."

Silas's arms only tightened, and his head shook, his stubble brushing over my cheek. "You have nothing to apologize for."

"I almost got you killed. All of you."

His head shook again. "No, baby. We found out he already knew we were coming for him. Your actions actually confirmed it. We would have been walking into a full ambush if all of this hadn't happened."

There was a low, searing pride in his voice before it cracked with dread. "Not that I ever want you to put yourself in that kind of danger. I was so fucking scared."

Tears kept spilling, and I had my face pressed into his neck, his warmth heating me through. "I should have come to you."

"Yeah, you should have. But I was keeping secrets from you, and how is a person supposed to fully trust when they're in the dark?"

I sniffled. "But I should have. You've proven it to me time and again, and I…I panicked. Those letters…"

I trailed off. Still not knowing how to make sense of them. Of what they meant.

A ripple of aggression rolled through Silas. "Wasn't me."

My spine stiffened. I could feel that something was coming.

Something big.

That energy thrashed and thrummed.

"It was Phoenix."

Anger burst in my blood, and Silas pulled back, palms coming to my cheeks as he stared down at me through the faint light that began to suffuse the air.

"I know you're mad, baby. I was fucking furious. Thought I was gonna have to put a bullet in one of my best friends. But—"

He clipped off, hesitating before he rushed, "He truly believed Dereck was setting us up. That this whole thing was somehow a ploy at infiltrating our crew."

I blinked, giving him an invitation to explain.

"You see, I've been trying to get to Kent for years. Ever since he killed my mother, even though at the time, I didn't even know his name. I wanted it out of vengeance. Out of a thirst for revenge. I thought it was the only thing that was left for me, so when my grandmother packed me and my siblings up and moved us to LA where her sister lived, I fell even deeper into the game."

His tongue stroked over his lips as he gazed at me, eyes flicking everywhere like he was looking for understanding.

"I let wickedness take me over. I ran with a brutal MC. Sought that lifestyle out, all while I continued to search for any clue of who it was that had killed my mother. Finally, our vice president of that MC came to me with a name. It was the name of the guy who was the only runner in the area of Crimson Creek at the time my mother was killed."

Pain blistered across his face. "Kent Ellison."

It sent a chill rolling through me. I was still trying to process that the one who had hurt me, destroyed me, intended on killing me because of my brother's debt, was the same man.

Tears kept streaking down my face.

Pain for Silas.

For Elena and the rest of the family.

For me.

"Trent told me Kent was trying to expand his operation, and he'd moved it to San Jose."

A bolt of lightning sheared through my middle.

San Jose was where we lived growing up. While my mother was sick. While I'd struggled and tried to provide for Dereck and myself in the time he had slid.

"I finally was going to catch up to that bastard," Silas spat, clinging to my face as if it was the only thing that kept him grounded.

"Phoenix traveled up there with me. He was the only one I knew and trusted enough to get his hands dirty with me fully for the sake of retribution. I feared Trevan would have tried to stop me. We followed Kent from his mansion and across town to this run-down neighborhood."

My insides shook.

"Only thing I had on my mind that night when we tracked him to this abandoned house was blood. His drained on the floor in front of me. I wanted to fucking bathe in it. What I didn't expect to find was this girl mangled on the ground. I couldn't even see her face. Had no idea how old she was or what she looked like or what her dreams might be…"

Air started to cleave from my lungs.

"But this unseen girl struck me. Pierced me like a fucking arrow. She reminded me that maybe there was a purpose in the world beyond wrath and retaliation, and the only thing that mattered then was stopping them from hurting her more than they already had."

"Silas…" His name knotted in my throat as the significance of what he was saying stole like vapor into my consciousness.

"I couldn't wait for Phoenix to get into position. I knew what these bastards intended, and I had to stop them. And yeah, I fumbled and they got away, but it didn't matter, because that girl was still breathing. It was the only thing that had mattered in that moment. And as her ambulance shouted through the night, a new call settled over me. A new direction."

"Oh God, Silas," I whimpered, trying to form words. To catch up to it. "You were there? I…"

He stroked his thumb over my cheek. "I was meant to be there, Brinley. I know it now. Just like I know you were meant to show up on my property all these years later."

He inhaled a steadying breath. "After that night, I left that MC and started my own. Crimson Crows. Named after the town where my mother was slain. We fronted it like any other MC. Drug and gun runners. Raiding. Stealing. And yeah, there are times we have to see those runs through, but it's a façade for what we really do."

His thick throat tremored, and the brightening heavens shivered around him. "We infiltrate those criminal organizations and decimate them. Track their activity. Hunt them. We chase them down until every single one of them are dead."

His words sharpened to blades.

"We pillage them of all the dirtied riches they possess and anonymously pour those funds into privately run social programs and nonprofits. Women's shelters and rehabs and food banks. Whatever we can pinpoint needs it."

I didn't even know if it was shock that punched through me.

I guess it was just catching up to the reality that had been billowing around me all along. A hazy dream that I hadn't quite been able to see through.

Because I'd long since realized Silas wasn't all cold blood and killer.

The killer part? Obviously. But there wasn't anything cold about him.

"And that whole time, I never forgot about that girl battered on the floor. I used her memory to spur me into action, giving the one thing that I thought I had to offer."

Stunned, I gazed at him. Drank in every foreboding, beautiful facet of his face. Of his soul.

"I can't believe it was you. But how—" My brow pinched as I tried to piece the details together.

His jaw clenched. "I never forgot about Kent Ellison, either. I was sure he still didn't know my identity. He had no idea who was coming for him that night. So we moved to Northern California so I could try to get closer to him. Penetrate his organization and fully end him. But I was a fool, not realizing that I was putting my family at risk. The bastard used Elena's vulnerability to get to me."

He paused, teeth raking his bottom lip, before he rushed, "This guy showed up at the shop in Moonlit Ridge. I recognized him as one of Kent's men, and I had my gun crammed down his throat in a second flat. But he came with information on how to get her out. Swore that he was telling the truth. He told me he wanted to help me ruin Kent. Only thing he asked was that I keep his sister safe."

My spirit moaned.

Dereck.

"He went back to get revenge for me," I murmured.

I hated that he'd been so reckless, but that didn't mean my heart didn't swell. Mended in the truth that he did care. He hadn't been taking advantage of me the way I thought.

Silas offered a slight nod. "Yeah. He never told me that, but it's clear that was his own mission. Looking for his own way to take Kent and his empire down."

Silas's hands tightened on my face, and his thumbs stroked along the hollows beneath my eyes.

"I didn't recognize you when you stepped out of your brother's car, but I know now that my soul felt you. I should have known there was a reason I couldn't stay away from you. You burned up every belief I had, just like you did that night five years ago."

"I felt you too. You were this magnet. A beacon I couldn't resist."

His smile turned soft, though his nod was sad. "But Phoenix did. I guess he got a look at you that night. And in his cynical mind, he couldn't fathom how it was a coincidence. He thought I was blinded, and you'd purposefully been sent to hypnotize me. That Dereck was after me for some reason or really was loyal to Kent. I doubt he'll ever forgive himself for going behind my back, but I need to know if you can forgive him?"

I gulped around the emotion that overflowed my throat, but my chest was already too full.

In it, I was unable to find any anger remaining.

Phoenix was only protecting Silas.

The way Dereck and Silas had been trying to protect me.

"I think the real question is if you can forgive me?"

Air puffed from Silas's nose. "I was never even mad, baby. Just terrified that I lost you. But I should have known better, shouldn't I? Because you're a fighter. The strongest person I know. But now you know you don't have to fight me. We fight this shit together. That's if you'll still take me?"

"Still take you?" I blinked at him through bleary eyes. "The second I jumped over that wall, the only thing I wanted to do was crawl back to you. Because the most inner part of me knew."

My fingers scratched over the middle of his chest. "It's your heart."

He pressed my hand flat over it. "And this heart belongs to you."

64

Brinley

The sun climbed above the landscape of peaked mountains as Silas turned his bike through the Crimson Crows' gate.

Oranges and pinks were strewn into the sky. Colors that painted over the darkness and drew hope across the heavens.

After Silas had pulled off the road, I'd switched spots, and I now was wrapped around him from behind.

Fully and wholly attached.

A bunch of Crows were already back at the compound, their bikes lined in a semi-circle near the clubhouse. They mingled about as Lulu handed out beers as they hooted and popped off shouts of celebration.

Silas's motorcycle rumbled as he traversed over the dirt drive, his men lifting their bottles in a salute as we passed.

He didn't slow.

He only wound us through the trees to the back of the property.

That humble house came into view.

I thought it so odd the first time I saw it. Far too modest for a man I'd believed some sort of deviant criminal.

I remembered the first time I sneered '*king*' at him.

Had I felt the power ripple through him then? The fact that there was something explosive?

Devastatingly mighty.

Great.

Good.

The second we came into the clearing, the screen door burst open.

Elena rushed out, though she fumbled to a stop when she saw Silas pulling his bike into its spot.

A hand over her mouth and tears in her eyes.

Silas kicked the stand, silenced the engine, and carefully helped me to stand before he did the same.

Both of us battle worn.

Damaged but no longer broken.

"Oh God, I was so worried," Elena cried, and she was bounding down the stairs and throwing herself into Silas's arms.

"It's over. It's over," he murmured at the top of her head.

"Is everyone okay?" she begged, her fingers curling into his cut.

"We lost two men. Cliff and Jupe."

A sob leapt out of her. "Oh no, I'm so sorry, Silas. I'm so sorry."

"I am too."

He'd gotten the gutting text with their names an hour ago, his body recoiling with the news, pain bleeding from his pores.

Guilt and another burden I knew he would carry.

Two others had sustained gunshot wounds but were in stable condition, the same as was confirmed for my brother.

All of them had been taken to Moonlit Ridge where there apparently was a secret medical facility set up to care for incidents like this.

Silas hugged and rocked Elena for the longest time, their relief and sorrow explicit, before she peeled herself out of his arms and stumbled over to me.

Swiping at the tears streaming down her face.

Her footsteps harrowed and heavy, though her arms were firm when she wrapped them around me. "I'm so mad at you. Don't you dare do that to me again. I was so scared. So freaking scared."

Emotion pulsed and swam, and I wheezed, "I'm so sorry. I was scared, too."

She sniffled. "I know. I heard what happened. You were just fighting for your family, the same as Silas was fighting for his. But God, I hated every second that you were away."

My nod was soggy. "But that's you now, too. My family. And I never should have left that way. I can never express how devastated I am that I handled this all wrong."

She dug her fingertips into my back. "It's okay. We're all finally going to be okay."

She pulled away, and when I looked up, I found Meems on the porch with a wiggling Kai in her arms.

My heart tried to spring from its confines.

Joy and the most staggering relief.

"*Bwinwey.*"

He pointed at me with his chubby little finger, crooking it like he was calling for me.

But he'd been calling to me all along.

I stumbled up the porch steps.

"Bwinwey owie?" Concern filled his precious face when he saw my eye up close.

My head shook as the tears continued to fall nonstop. "No, my sweet boy, I'm okay. I'm okay."

Elena was right. I finally was.

With trembling hands, I pulled him into my arms.

Hugged him to me so fiercely I couldn't see.

"My sweet boy." I peppered kisses all over his forehead and cheeks. "My sweet boy."

Meems touched my arm.

Tenderly.

Murmured, "Now there's the good."

And I felt the swarm of energy gather from behind.

Solid footsteps sending shockwaves along the wooden planks as Silas slowly climbed the steps.

His presence overpowering.

I'd once been terrified to even look at him, afraid of the way he compelled me.

The man too violently beautiful to be real.

But as I turned, I knew he was all those things.

Violent.

Beautiful.

Real.

Mine.

And as he curled his arms around both of us, I knew I didn't want anything else.

The only thing I wanted was this love that had been forged in the fire.

Epilogues

Silas

What the fuck was she wearing?

My dick stirred as violently as the air when Brinley emerged from the thicket, strutting her way toward the lapping fire where I sat under the shelter of night surrounded by my crew.

She was dressed in this fucking flowy, satiny black skirt that didn't even come to mid-thigh. Soft fabric brushing bare flesh. Toned legs for fucking days, amplified by the sky-high heels that she never failed to don.

A plain black tee with the neck cut out of it draped off one shoulder, fitting her snug since it looked like it was tied in the back.

Wild curls blew around her stunning face. Those long locks threaded with strands the color of harvest leaves wisping around her high-cut cheeks.

Eyes entrancing flames with the single-handed power to lead me out of the dark.

Autumn riding in on a hurricane.

A wildfire sent to torch my senses and incinerate my heart.

A stunner strutting around on my property.

Best fucking sight I'd ever seen.

I played it easy, though, sipped from my old-fashioned like I was hardly affected as I watched her approach. Whiskey hitting my tongue and gliding down my throat to pool in my belly.

My sister was in tow, as per usual, though she was wearing her own black little number, which was something new.

I'd always been amazed at Elena's resilience. Amazed that after everything she'd suffered, she'd maintained this doe-eyed belief.

But in the last three months since everything had gone down with Kent Ellison—his entire fetid organization decimated, the death of him and all eighty-three of his men blamed on a feud with a cartel—a new confidence had emerged in Elena.

It was terrifying, honestly.

I still had this soul-deep need to protect her with everything I had, but I knew I had to give her some space so she could spread her wings.

How, I wasn't sure. But I was trying.

You could say Brinley had been inspiring. Standing for her like a sister. Her best friend. Her closest confidant.

And that was one thing I could take confidence in.

"We're at a stop sign, and this chick just climbs out the window of her husband's car and climbs right onto the back of my bike." Brody stood to the side of me, wielding a bottle of tequila in his hand, dude trading off exaggerated stories with my men. "Said she'd never been with a biker before and wanted a ride."

Dumbass rocked his hips.

"Bullshit," Trevan razzed with a grin. "She climbed onto the back of mine."

"She just didn't know whose bike she was getting on," Brody defended with a pitying scoff. "Once she got a look at your ugly mug, she flew off and was groping at me. Saved the poor thing."

Amusement puffed from my nose. Women pranced all around here, more than happy to oblige, but Brody still seemed to think he needed to rack up every woman he encountered for himself.

"Honestly, I think she just liked the sight of this."

He turned, showing off the patch on the back of his cut.

The Crimson Crows logo stitched into the leather.

Enforcer tacked below.

He might have been messing around then. The mood light.

But he'd fucking earned that patch. Had stepped up, ridden at my side, and fought that battle for his family, every bit the way that I had.

It was just as important to him as it'd been to me.

Dereck chuckled from where he sat on the ground to his side, sipping from a beer, "Prospect" written on the back of his cut.

It only made sense that this place had become his home, too.

"You mean, you scarred her for life," Elena called as she and Brinley strutted the rest of the way up, teasing her brother like they were kids.

"I might have done something, but I wouldn't call it *scarring*, Lena.

But what I can say is you in that dress is scarring my eyes." He turned back to me. "Tell her to go change, Prez. She shouldn't be walking around like that."

Elena dipped into a cooler and pulled out two beers. She handed one to Brinley then twisted the cap off the other for herself. "Sorry to break it to you, Brody, but he's not my president. I make my own rules, thank you very much."

She sent me a challenging glare, daring me to counter her on it.

Trevan twitched where he sat at my side.

Apparently, he didn't like it any more than I did, but I figured as long as she was within the confines of the compound, she was safe.

No one here had a death wish big enough to lay a hand on her.

"Well, you are my sister, and I veto," Brody countered.

"Your veto doesn't count."

A low chuckle skated out of me. Tonight, Elena was all sass.

Brinley met my gaze, emitting that soft fierceness she wore like a brand.

Loved that about her.

How good she was. How gentle she was. All while not minding a bit to let the claws come out.

Elena found herself a spot between Colby and Pyke, chatting lightly, while Brinley wound her way around the fire toward me.

My heart accelerated with her every step.

Brinley Mercer a shockwave.

That's right.

My fucking wife.

I meant it when I told her my life belonged to her, and she was going to have every second of it.

She eased over, some kind of coy, knowing smirk lighting at the edges of her lips as she approached.

Body easy and lithe as she shifted so she could nestle herself right on my lap facing out.

Nearly came undone when I saw what was printed on the back of her shirt, and I arced forward, taking her lush fall of hair and moving it from her shoulder so I could set my lips to the flutter at the side of her neck.

"What do you think you're trying to do to me?" I mumbled at the sweet flesh.

Almonds and apples and cream.

I let my fingertips trace over the Crimson Crows logo that was stamped in the middle of her shirt.

Property of the Prez emblazoned in a circle around it.

Her perfect ass pressed against my hard, aching dick, and she shrugged that bare shoulder like she didn't know exactly the kind of effect she had on me.

My whole being reacting in a beat.

She peeked back with those entrancing eyes.

Everything else faded and blurred into the nothingness.

"You like it? Elena helped me make it with her new vinyl press." Her voice was nothing but whispered seduction.

I'd have to thank my sister later.

Right then, the only *thanking* I had in mind was the kind where I spent hours worshipping my wife's delectable body.

"Yeah, baby, I fucking like it. Whole world needs to know you're mine."

"Don't worry, *King*, I don't think there's any mistaking it." It was temptation and a prod, and my left hand skimmed down her arm, drawing chills, until I was sliding my hand over the top of hers and threading our fingers together.

Bringing attention to the tattoos that we'd gotten at River of Ink in Moonlit Ridge the night of our wedding.

Our oath forever marked on our ring fingers.

Mine a solid black band.

Brinley's dainty and hidden beneath the shiny rock I'd put there too.

I pulled our entwined hands across her so I was tucking her closer. Mouth at her ear. "You're everything, baby."

She wiggled against my cock.

A low groan got free. "You trying to play with fire?"

"Always," she whispered on a breath. "I am married to you."

Need smacked me across the face. "Time to go, baby."

I nudged her off my lap and to standing, though I didn't let her hand go as I pushed to my feet, still wound around her from behind as I shot Trevan a look and ticked my head toward Elena.

A silent command for him to watch over my sister.

His nod was succinct. Didn't really need to tell him, anyway. He knew the drill.

He was second in command to her safety when I couldn't be there, which he'd been having to do a whole lot more lately since Brinley had come into my life.

Since I'd been spending less and less time at the clubhouse and instead tangled up with Brinley in our bed.

Time devoted to Kai, this kid who'd become ours. Hell, I hadn't left the house tonight until after I tucked him in, and even then, I would have had to have been pried away if I hadn't known Brinley would be joining me at the fire.

Turned out, thirty minutes was enough of that when there would never be getting *enough* of my wife.

I stayed behind her as I edged through my men who'd gathered, most muttering, "Goodnight, Prez," as I passed.

But my attention was locked on her.

That mess of hair in my face, her back to my chest, my nose to her neck. I directed her to my bike that sat at the head of the pack, and I swung on.

A squeal ripped out of Brinley when I tugged her sideways across my lap, those legs dangling off to one side and her arms wrapped around my neck.

She giggled as she peeked up at me. "This feels dangerous."

I gave her a ribbing scoff. "Only thing dangerous around here is you. Way you have control over me."

"Funny since you're manhandling me." She grinned.

I squeezed her bare thigh. "Tell me you don't like it."

"Can't." She lifted a nonchalant shrug. "I promised I'd never lie to you."

"That's what I thought."

I let my hand wander, riding up her leg and dipping between her thighs.

She whimpered and spread her legs a little further as I ran my fingertips over her soaked underwear.

I wanted to strip her bare right there, but considering we were only at the edge of the fire, barely concealed by the woods, I instead forced myself to grip the handlebars so I could kick my bike over.

I slowly pulled out while Brinley rose up higher, running her lips in a lust-inducing path up my neck before she was kissing me as I took to the dirt lane that led to the house.

Talk about dangerous.

"You trying to make me crash?" I rumbled into her mouth, not minding the assault a bit.

"I think you can handle it. I've seen you ride. A few kisses aren't going to ruffle you."

She was wrong.

I was feeling really fucking *ruffled*.

I suddenly angled my bike off the path, tires rolling over the damp, high grasses as I shifted course and maneuvered us into the sanctuary of the surrounding forest.

Burying us in the shadows, just the faintest trickle of moonlight spilling through the leaves.

Lighting her flesh as she pulled back when I planted my boots out to the side to balance us on the bike.

"What are you doing?" she rasped.

"Can't go on a second more not being inside you."

Keeping my feet planted, I grabbed her by the waist and shuffled her around.

Woman straddling the bike and facing away so I could get a good look at her shirt while I went to work on my fly.

Shoving my jeans down just enough to free my anguished cock.

Brinley gasped as I jerked her panties aside, that flimsy skirt barely enough to cover her ass. My free hand wound around to the front of her neck as I pulled her back, mouth grunting at her ear.

"Not being inside you is nothing short of pain. Did you know that? Way I fucking ache anytime I'm not with you. Anytime I'm looking at you and you're across the room. Anytime I think of you."

"Then you'd better have me," she wheezed, a needy huff from her lungs permeating the whirring night as I grabbed her under the back of one thigh, lifting her high enough to line her cunt up with my dick.

My fingers kneaded into the lush flesh at the back of her thigh, my swollen head poised at her entrance.

Her breaths held while she waited.

"Don't tease me, Silas. I'm aching, too."

"What do you need, baby?"

"Your cock." It was pure desperation as she squirmed to get closer.

"Good thing it's yours."

I slammed her down on top of me. Taking her so damn deep that we both choked at the impact.

My cock squeezed around her spasming, clutching walls.

"Fuck. So good. So fucking good. Every time." I rambled it into the choppy, heated air as I clutched her against me. "Nothing in the world like the feel of you. Heaven when I never thought I could earn it."

"You belonged here all along," she raked.

God, I liked the sound of that.

Belonging when I never thought I could.

Finding a home when I thought I was only meant for destruction.

"Together," I grunted, my hand fucking shaking where I still held her against the throat, feeling the rapid flutter of her pulse beating against my palm.

Feeling the life. The goodness seeping in and taking over.

I let my palm glide down, riding it over her abdomen and under her shirt so I could get to one full tit.

Pulling the fabric down and toying with her nipple while she ground on top of me.

"Yes. More," she whimpered, her back rubbing against my chest.

"All of it already belongs to you."

Her shirt might have said she was Property of the Prez, but it was me who was in chains.

Hostage.

A prisoner.

The only fucking thing I wanted to be.

My other hand joined the first, and I drew her shirt up higher, exposing both tits to the glinting moon.

Rolling and rubbing the pebbled, hardened buds as she rocked over the top of me.

Pleasure sparked and lit.

I kept gliding my hands upward, guiding her arms up until they were locked around the back of my neck.

I kissed along the shell of her ear, muttered, "Ride me, Little Wildfire. Take what's yours."

And she did.

She rocked and bucked as she drove me to disorder.

To madness.

To ecstasy.

To a place I'd thought unattainable.

Nonexistent.

But it was only this one fiery woman who could show me what was possible.

The one to shine her light into my life.

Reawaken what was lost.

Remind me of my purpose.

I slipped my hand up her skirt and rubbed her clit.

It was seismic, the explosion that went off between us.

Combustion.

Decimation.

But sometimes it takes fire to remold the misshapen.

And as for me?

I would gladly burn for the rest of my life.

• • •

It was quiet as we edged through the darkened house, and the stairs creaked beneath our quieted footsteps as we ascended.

My arm draped around her shoulder and her cheek pressed to my chest.

She was barefoot, her shoes dangling from my fingers. We hit the landing and moved down the hall, and I wasn't surprised at all when she took the left into Kai's room.

His door was cracked open, the same as Meems's, in case he woke in the night.

He rarely did, anymore.

The nightmares distant.

This home his safety.

These walls fortified with love.

I saw to it that his biological mother had enough money that she would never show her face again, rights signed off to me and Brinley.

Brinley who came to stand over his crib.

The kid dressed in motorcycle pajamas, cherub cheeks pink, his thumb in his mouth, sucking away in his peaceful dreams.

“He’s so beautiful. I could stand here and stare at him all night.” Brinley ran tender fingers through his hair. “I never thought I’d get brave enough to allow myself a family.”

From behind, I curled my arms around her waist, hooked my chin on her shoulder, and rocked her slowly as I gazed down at our boy.

“I didn’t think I’d be brave enough, either. Not until you showed me that I could be enough.”

“You’re more than enough,” she whispered.

“That’s what I’m going to be, Brinley. To both of you. To every kid we get lucky enough to make. More than enough because you deserve everything.”

Brinley

I was in the office in my usual spot, tapping at the keys of the laptop. A blaze of sunlight lit the frosted glass panes out front, the lobby empty, though I was in constant company with the sound of teasing jests and laughter that lifted above the heavy metal music that screamed from within the shop.

The mood alive and thrumming through the walls.

I was content in it, but oh boy, there was no denying the thrill that sailed through me when I felt the squall of energy rise behind me.

Every molecule in my body tightened and expanded in anticipation.

A flashflood of it when Silas swung open the door.

It was never necessary to turn around to know it was him.

My husband had his own special brand of volatility.

His boots squeaked on the old linoleum floor as he edged up, and he leaned over the back of me, arms looping around my waist and his nose burrowing into my hair.

“What are you doing, baby?”

“What does it look like? Working.” I tried to play it off like he was an annoyance when the only thing I wanted was to feel those brutal hands gliding all over my body.

He grunted a rough laugh into the side of my neck.

Leave it to Silas to send chills scattering.

He lifted his head a fraction so he could read what was on the screen.

I could feel the awed force of his smile. "My little criminal mastermind."

I huffed as my fingers continued to move across the keys.

"As far as I'm concerned, it's criminal *not* to do it."

Silas chuckled, the sound sinking deep. "I like the way you think."

I'd found everything here.

My family.

My home.

My calling.

I'd become entrenched in Crimson Crows' mission as deeply as Silas and the rest.

Working closely with Cash to move the money each operation brought in.

Funneling it.

Laundering it through a bunch of the businesses I found out Silas owned.

A restaurant and a jewelry store and the bar he'd recently purchased down by the creek. It was the same one where he'd been only an innocent, vulnerable kid who lost himself as a runner for Kent Ellison.

Plus, I was the one who searched for the nonprofits that we sank the money into.

Anonymous gifts that came from out of nowhere.

Cash had been my mentor, and he'd joked that I'd earned the equivalent of a PhD in the five days it'd taken him to show me the ropes.

I'd always been a good student.

Even better with numbers.

Had always believed I wanted to do something with that.

Funny how it turned out that *something* was cooking Crimson Crows' books.

Meems was right.

I was going to be a chef, after all, just not quite the one she imagined. But I had to admit, I'd gotten really good at making Silas's favorite pie.

"You do, huh?" I whispered, trying to focus on the task at hand.

Impossible when my husband started kissing up and down my neck.

"Like everything about you, actually," he murmured against the skin.

A little moan worked free, and I struggled to focus.

"Look." I pointed at the screen. "I found this veterinary center right here in Crimson Creek that's known to give free care to animals belonging to low-income families. They just received a twenty-thousand-dollar grant."

"That's fucking good, baby," he enthused in his low, rough voice.

Though he didn't give up in his needy pursuit, sliding the chair out with me in it, leaning further over so he could drag up the skirt of my dress.

Then he went flying back when the lobby door suddenly opened and a bright wedge of light flooded into the room. Squinting, he ran a flustered hand through his hair, doing his best to appear casual as Elena walked in with Kai.

She smirked. "You might as well drop the act, big brother. Do you actually think I couldn't feel you in here getting handsy from a mile away?"

"Hands, Daddy!" Kai pushed both of his hands out, waving his little fingers in the air.

We both choked over a laugh, though Silas was murmuring, "Hey, little man. That's right, you've got two hands, don't you?"

"One, two, *fee*!" He bounced on Elena's hip, letting go of one of his adorable little squeals.

I stood, shaking myself off a bit.

This was my favorite time of day, after all.

The time when Elena brought Kai to the shop so we could all have lunch together. For most of the summer, we'd had picnics out beneath the trees, but since the weather had begun to cool, we'd taken to either eating here in the lobby or out in the shop.

"Mommy!" He reached for me.

My heart did a somersault in my chest.

Racing as it stretched and expanded.

We thought we'd test it out. Calling Silas 'Daddy Silas' and me 'Mommy Brinley', wondering if it would be awkward.

If it would feel like a lie.

It hadn't because that's what we'd become.

His parents.

Silas and I might have loved each other, body and soul, but this little boy was the light of our lives.

"Hi, my sweet boy." The words were thick with adoration.

"I get Mommy." He kicked his feet in a bid to get down.

"Oh, fine, I see how it is. Ditch Auntie Lena the second your mommy is in the room," she teased, setting him onto his little feet then poking at his belly.

He squealed with laughter, giggling and running in place on his little sneakers. "I *wove* my *Wena.* I *no* ditch."

Warmth swelled from her being, and she peeked over at me before she smiled down at him. "We all get to love each other so much, don't we? No favorites."

My chest squeezed in that unending affection Meems shared with everyone. The way she'd taught her grandchildren to be.

And they'd accepted me right into that fold as if I'd been there all along.

I never dared to imagine having this kind of love in my life again, terrified of it for fear of a broken heart.

But I realized the walls I'd built might have shielded me from the threat of pain and tragedy, but they were also shielding me from the *good.*

And I wanted that good.

I wanted it all.

Kai came scampering around the counter, pure grin on his face, eyes the color of Silas's shining with joy and mirth.

I scooped him up and kissed the crown of his head. "Did you have a good morning with Meems and Auntie Lena?"

"I *pway mowercycle*!" He zoomed his hand through the air. "I go Daddy's *mowercycle*?" He pointed in the direction of the shop.

"After lunch I'll take you for a ride," Silas promised.

Kai turned back to me. "I eat right now!"

Light laughter rippled, and Elena stepped forward and set the big, insulated lunch box onto the counter. "Someone is eager, and it's a good thing because I made spaghetti and meatballs. Silas and Kai's favorite."

She peeked over at her brother when she said it.

He arched a brow. "That seems like a lot of effort for lunch."

She shrugged an innocent shoulder. "Nothing is too much effort if it makes my big brother happy."

Speculation filled his expression, and I bit down on my bottom lip.

I knew this was coming.

Elena and I had stayed up all night three nights ago talking about it.

Weighing the pros and cons.

Her dreams against her fears.

Her need against what her brother wanted.

"Really?" He wasn't buying it.

She paused then sighed, then she pulled the folded piece of paper from her back pocket.

She'd printed out the listing.

Had stared at it in secret for days.

Had contemplated and strategized and visualized herself within its walls.

She spread it out on the counter before she stared her brother down. "I'm opening a store in this location."

She tapped her finger on the sheet.

"With or without your blessing, but I really hope I have it."

"Elena..." Silas drew out.

The subject was touchy. I mean, the man could be crazy overbearing. Overprotective.

But was there ever an 'over' when it came to the people you loved?

I got his hesitation.

His own fear.

It wasn't like we lived a normal lifestyle. It was dangerous enough out there even when you weren't involved in the things that we were.

But that was no excuse for not allowing Elena to live.

She lifted her chin. "I know you're afraid and you think you have to watch over me every second of my life. But I'm not a little girl, Silas. You've loved me and protected me, but you've also kept me caged for years. I don't have my license, I had to get my degree from an online university, and I've been on two dates in my life, both of which you followed me to the restaurant. I need to breathe."

She begged that, her hands clutching her shirt over her heart.

"I need to chase my dreams. I deserve to experience everything this life has to offer."

My attention ping-ponged between them.

A tremor rocked through Silas, and Elena inhaled a staggered breath. "Brinley helped me set up a business plan. I have everything together. I just need five thousand dollars to get started. I don't even want to ask that of you, but because you didn't let me work, I don't have any money saved. You'll be repaid within three months."

Silas's overwrought gaze slid to me.

Terror and uncertainty.

I dipped my head in soft encouragement.

He looked back at her, words locked on his tongue.

He didn't need to speak because Elena pressed on, "And I want to get my own place."

That sent agitation blustering through Silas, and he roughed a hand incessantly through his hair.

Pacing three steps in one direction then the other.

Before he stopped and looked at her.

"This is what you really want?"

"Yes."

He inhaled through his worry before he gave. "Okay. But only if you agree to let Trevan go with you."

It was just as Trevan stepped through the shop doors. His and Elena's eyes locked.

I wondered if Silas just didn't want to feel the severity that rocketed between them, and instead pressed on and said, "You're the only one I trust."

And I was pretty sure by the look on Trevan's face that he didn't trust himself.

Acknowledgments

Ahh thank you so much for reading Forged in the Fire!! What a way to kick off this new series. Silas and Brinley had me from page one and quickly became one of my favorite couples ever!

Up next we have Trevan and Elena in Carved in the Shadows! Anyone else ready for a forbidden age gap with an obsessed, overprotective hero?! These two are going to scorch!

Be sure to pre-order yours today!